It wasn't that easy for Chris. She had been still, in another woman's arms for hours. Her body felt a mixture of contentment and excitement; her mind battled the same. Now she understood the feeling of intimacy Lynn had described to her almost a week ago, a feeling that until now, she had never known. But she was lying with a woman, and this is what was troubling her. She had never thought that love between two women was wrong. But she had never, in her wildest imagination, thought that she would be one of the two women.

Visit

Bella Books

at

BellaBooks.com

or call our toll-free number

1-800-729-4992

Risky Investment

Beth Moore

Bella
BOOKS

2005

Bella Books, Inc.
P.O. Box 10543
Tallahassee, FL 32302

Printed in the United States of America on acid-free paper
First Edition

Editor: Pamela Berard
Cover designer: Sandy Knowles

ISBN 1-59493-019-8

*To those special ones in my life who took the time to edit and critique
for someone who does not take criticism well. And to Brewster, my
Labrador retriever, who sat with me until all hours of the night
while I wrote, and didn't complain once. I miss you.*

Acknowledgments

A special thanks to Pamela Berard and those at Bella Books who made this process such a pleasant experience. I have to admit, in the beginning, I was scared to death.

To all of those who love and support me continuously, I can never thank you enough.

About the Author

Beth Moore was born, raised, and continues to reside in the San Joaquin Valley in California. She splits her time between working in the business world and sharing time with her family and friends. Her passions include football, gardening, and cozy nights by the fire. Writing has also become an important part of her life and she hopes to complete many more books in the future.

Prologue

Lynn sped down the freeway, her blonde hair blowing in the wind. She darted in and out of traffic in her dark blue BMW, a car that she considered to be a shining example of her successful business career. At thirty-one, she was one of the top investment analysts in her field. She had risen quickly through the ranks and was a partner in one of the most prestigious firms in the nation. But her financial success had come with a price. Many called her a "coldhearted bitch" when it came to her business reputation, a fact with which she could not disagree. Over the past couple of years, she had let that coldness envelop her personal life, as well. She was conscious of the problem and struggled with it daily. On this warm spring day she was speeding home after hearing news that would forever change her life.

Several months ago, Lynn had made an investment in an unlikely business venture. If it hit, it would hit big, leaving her financially set for the rest of her life. That morning she learned that the investment had gone through the roof. Now, she would be able to cut down on her working hours, giving her time to work on a much-needed attitude adjustment. She traveled down the freeway to share the good news with Susan, her companion of eight years.

Lynn had met Susan at a fund-raiser for the local university. A history professor, Susan first caught Lynn's attention by speaking of little-known facts about lesbians in history. Later that same night, Susan captured Lynn's attention with her knowledge of little-known facts about erogenous zones. After only a few dates, Lynn asked Susan to move in with her. Several years later, they purchased a home together in an affluent area of Los Angeles.

The couple had their problems, like any other, but all in all Lynn thought their relationship was almost perfect. She felt a shiver when she thought of how they had made love the night before. After all of these years, Susan still made Lynn feel as if their love was brand new. Excitement rushed through her as she imagined Susan's face when she learned the news. Knowing that Susan would be finished with her classes for the day, Lynn left the office early to surprise her.

Lynn pulled into the driveway next to Susan's red Ford Mustang. She heard the music as she opened the front door. It was a familiar sound; Susan always loved to play music in the house. Lynn called out to her as she walked through the rooms but stopped in her tracks when she entered the hallway and heard sounds coming from their bedroom. Slowly sliding the door open, she froze when she saw Susan and another woman in their bed.

After realizing that she had been standing there for more than a minute, she cleared her throat. That's when she saw the look on Susan's face. It wasn't an "Oh my God, what have I done" look. It was an "Oh my God, I've been caught" look. Devastated, Lynn was able to get only one sentence out—"I'll be back for my stuff in the morning."

Somehow she was able to walk out of the house that afternoon. By the time she had gotten to the front door, Susan had pulled on a robe and was pulling at Lynn's arm to stay and talk to her. If Susan had been pleading, "Please stay. This was a mistake. This is the only time . . ." maybe Lynn would have stopped. But all Susan would say was "I can change, I promise, this is the last time." These words stunned Lynn. When had been the first time?

Lynn spent the next several hours sitting at the beach, reviewing the past months in her mind. She discovered that there had been many clues. Clues that she had chosen not to see. Lynn had called many friends that day. She used the term "friends" loosely now as they told her that they had been aware of Susan's indiscretions but hadn't wanted to hurt her. All were hoping that Susan would get tired of the flings.

Lying on the bed in a hotel room, Lynn struggled with her feelings. Was she wrong to just walk away from their life together? Hadn't Susan already left their vows of commitment behind? Lynn had always believed that if you were truly in love, you wouldn't want to be with anyone else. She knew she hadn't. The pain overwhelmed her as she questioned if Susan had ever really loved her at all.

After a sleepless night, she came to the numbing conclusion that there was nothing worth saving in Los Angeles. After all, she had no lover, no real friends, and since she was set financially, she saw no reason to continue the ridiculous hours at the firm. She felt a need to reprioritize what was important in her life. Calling a meeting of the partners in her firm, Lynn notified them that she would cut back on her workload. Reluctantly the partners agreed to her terms. She would keep a few of her most lucrative clients but would only come into the office when absolutely necessary.

Lynn pulled into the driveway of the home she had shared with the woman she loved. She breathed a sigh of relief, because Susan's car was not there. Lynn had been worried about the confrontation. Susan was probably letting things cool down, she thought to herself. Lynn was known for her bad temper, but truth be told, at this point she wasn't sure if she was more angry with Susan or herself. Angry at Susan for all of the lies and infidelities. Angry at herself for letting her career take over her life, for not giving Susan whatever it was that she needed, and most of all, for being oblivious to the situation.

Walking through the rooms of the house, she picked up a few items, then put them back in their place. She could find little that she wanted to keep. With suitcases and garment bags loaded, she set the note that she had written to Susan on the table. To prove that this was permanent, Lynn placed her set of keys next to the note. She took one last look at the house that now brought her only tears, and shut the door.

Chapter One

One year later

Lynn climbed into her '57 Chevy truck and slid behind the steering wheel. She unbuttoned her overshirt to prepare for the drive home. The truck had no air-conditioning, and only an AM radio, but for some reason she felt more comfortable in it than in the BMW. Soon after leaving her former home, she had purchased the pickup and stored her BMW in a garage in Los Angeles. Putting the truck into reverse, she flipped on the radio and hummed to the music.

Suddenly, a red Mercedes appeared out of nowhere. The driver pressed on his horn as he sped past her, spitting up dirt and gravel in his wake. Shaking her head, she felt irritated with the man. What could be so important that he would risk driving so recklessly? Catching herself in the thought, she laughed. She used to be just like him. How things had changed in the past year.

The first few weeks after leaving L.A. were a blur. Lynn drove up and down the California coast, stopping at every lesbian bar that crossed her path. Falling into a deep depression, she found many a port in her dark storm. She wasn't sure how many women she had slept with, just that almost every morning she woke up in an unfamiliar place. The remainder of the day was usually spent escaping the situation, both mentally and physically.

Lynn looked into the rearview mirror and ran her hands through her now shortly cropped hair. Running her finger down her ear, she examined the many earrings that had mysteriously appeared one dark and fuzzy morning. That same morning, she realized how out of control her life had become.

Pain turned to anger. Lynn couldn't believe that she had let the situation get the best of her. She was always a strong and self-sufficient woman. Refusing to dwell on the pain any longer, she channeled her emotions out of the bottle and into something positive. Lynn had always kept up a vigorous exercise regimen, but during the next few weeks she brought new meaning to the term "blood, sweat, and tears." The weight lifting, running, and rowing machine not only helped drive out her pain and anger but gave her body back the muscular tone that had disappeared over the past few years.

Lynn did a lot of soul searching in that time. It was during those hours that she realized she had become so focused on her career that she hadn't taken the time to enjoy life or relationships. She was tired of being pressured to maintain the standard of excellence, the standard that had been set not only by her peers but also by herself. What she really needed was to simplify her life.

Turning onto the main road, she looked back and smiled at the roadside restaurant, which she had grown to love. The shingle-sided restaurant was only open for breakfast and lunch, which meant that Lynn's workday began at five-thirty a.m. and ended at two p.m. She worked as a waitress alongside seven employees. No one was aware that she actually owned the Blue Moon Café, a fact she kept hidden to avoid the day-to-day problems of owning a business. She made all transactions through a CPA friend of hers. Lynn didn't need the money but worked basically to keep an eye on the place and to keep herself busy. She was hired, as explained to the manager, because she was a friend of the owner's.

Lynn turned onto the road that led closer to the beach line and her house. Although it was nothing in comparison to her former residence, she felt like this place was really home. The two-bedroom, two-bath house was right on the beach and Lynn loved living near the water. She shared the house with Matt, a friend she had made along the way to her new life.

Lynn thought back to when she and Matt first crossed paths. She had climbed out of the truck that had towed her BMW and wandered into the office of his repair shop. As soon as she crossed the threshold, she heard Matt on the phone. Not wanting to eavesdrop she cleared her throat to let him know that she was there, but the conversation was not going to be interrupted.

"Just like that, after all this time, you want me out?" Matt was shouting. "Peter, can't we at least talk about this? I thought you cared about me!" Turning around, his face red with anger, he saw Lynn standing there. Holding up his index finger, he motioned for her to wait one minute, and walked farther back into the parts area. Calmer now, Matt questioned, "Okay, okay. I don't understand, is there someone else? Is it Stan? Is that who you're leaving me for? What do you mean it doesn't matter? It matters to me!" His voice got louder but then panicked. "Don't hang up, no, don't hang up. Can I come by and pick up a change of clothes? Okay, I'll come by after I close the shop. Fine, you don't have to be there. Bye."

Matt walked back to the front of the shop, hung up the cordless phone, wiped his face with his hands, and looked toward Lynn. Not really looking at her, but everywhere else, he asked if there was something he could help her with.

"Yeah, I was the person who called for a tow truck, my car is right outside." Lynn paused. "Are you all right?"

"Just peachy, my whole life is falling apart, but let's go take a look under the hood," Matt replied sarcastically.

"I don't know what happened. I was driving along, and it just quit. It's done plenty of things before, but never just quit."

"Are you out of gas?" Matt quipped.

"No, I am not out of gas. I may be blonde, but I know when I'm out of gas," she snapped back. "Look, I'm sorry that my timing isn't convenient, but don't take it out on me."

Matt sighed. "Sorry, I'm really not a jerk. Obviously, you heard my telephone conversation. You know what's going on. Just give me a minute." He opened the hood of Lynn's BMW and started tugging and tightening miscellaneous hoses and bolts, looked in the radiator, checked the oil, and examined the battery. "Okay, try to turn her over."

Lynn climbed behind the wheel and turned the key, but nothing happened. Matt asked her to wait at the café next door.

Lynn offered to buy Matt lunch after her car was repaired. She listened to his sad story, and feeling connected to him somehow, told him about Susan. They talked for hours and as she was leaving she noticed that the restaurant was for sale. Deciding that she must have broken down there by fate, she made a few calls. Within days, Lynn had a new business, a new home—and since Matt desperately needed a place to stay—a new roommate.

Since that day, the two had commiserated, fought, teased, cried, and celebrated together, making them more like siblings than friends. He was the one who brought her back to reality. She was the one who helped him aim a little bit higher in life. He was the one who humbled her. She was the one who gave him a little more confidence. He was the one who scolded her from time to time for being too promiscuous. She was the one who scolded him from time to time for never going out. He was the one who egged her on the night that she drank a little too much and auditioned for the band at their favorite bar. She was the one who rubbed it in his face when she got the job.

With a sigh of relief, Lynn pulled into the driveway at the house. She was exhausted. In a moment of insanity, she had agreed to work both Saturday and Sunday for a waitress at the restaurant who wanted to go away with her boyfriend for the weekend. Lynn hadn't worked during the weekend since she had accepted the position as lead singer with the band. She now played Thursday through Saturday night along with rehearsals on Tuesday. Usually her schedule conflicted only with singing on Thursday night and waitressing Friday morning. But this week she found herself working on Friday night, and after working this morning, she was managing on only three hours of sleep. She needed to get some sleep before it started all over tonight at nine.

Lynn walked into the house and threw her keys on the table. Noticing that the sliding glass door which led out onto the deck was open, she wandered over and looked out. Matt was leaning on the railing with his head in his hands.

"Hey, are you all right?" she asked, stepping out onto the wood.

Matt turned around with a look of relief. "I'm glad you're home. I need some help with something."

"Make it quick, okay? I've got to get some sleep."

Matt nodded, motioned for her to have a seat at the patio table, and began. "My parents are coming to visit."

"Great! When are they coming?" Lynn responded excitedly. She loved Matt's parents. Then, seeing he was annoyed that she had interrupted, she signaled for him to continue.

"They may have the idea that I have a girlfriend." Matt paused, then admitted, "Okay. I gave them the impression that I have a girlfriend. Actually—a fiancée."

"What?" Lynn exclaimed. She was aware that Matt hadn't told his parents that he was gay, which Lynn didn't agree with, but she was confused by this new development.

"Lynn, I know what you're thinking, but they just keep bugging me about it!" Matt mimicked his parents' questions, " 'Are you seeing anyone special?' 'Haven't you found anyone that you want to settle down with yet?'"

Lynn shook her head. "So how are you going to get out of this one?"

Matt scooted out a chair and sat down. "This is what I need

your help with." He paused for a moment to organize his thoughts then began again. "I thought that if I could find someone to pretend that she's my fiancée, you know, just for the week that they're here . . . then when they've left, after a couple of weeks or so, I could just say that it didn't work out."

"Matt, this sounds like a bad episode of *Three's Company* or something! What are you going to do? Hire a call girl or something?" Lynn asked with irritation in her voice.

"Not exactly." Matt folded his hands on the table. "I think that I've found someone who will play the part. She came into the shop needing some repairs done. She doesn't have much money, so I asked her what she thought about the idea of trading my services for her services, so to speak."

"You just happened to run across some girl willing to do this?" Lynn asked. Upon thinking further, she asked with suspicion, "How long have you been thinking about this? When did you find out that your parents are coming?"

Matt lowered his eyes and pretended to scrape at something on the table. "I found out several days ago. I've been trying to think of a way out of the predicament, and this woman just kind of fell into my hands."

"Yeah, I bet. Who is she?" Lynn questioned.

"Her name is Chris Newman. She's a student at the university. We had lunch together. She seems really nice. She's not too crazy about the idea, but I think if we both beg her, she'll come around."

"What's this *we* business?" Lynn said. "I inch around the truth too much as it is with your parents. Now you're asking me to out-and-out lie to them?"

"Please, Lynn. I'll owe you big-time. You always say that you'll do anything for me . . ." Matt whined.

Lynn knew that it was true. She would do anything for him. But this? This was really stretching it. She slowly walked to the door.

"Let me think about it for a little bit, okay?" she asked as she turned around.

Matt nodded and watched her disappear into the house.

Lynn walked down the hall and into her bedroom. Glancing over at her computer, she saw the small envelope on the corner of the screen signifying that she had awaiting e-mail. She clicked on the envelope, which brought up the message: *Funds sent to Mercy Hospital in the amount of $5,000 as per your instructions.*

The message brought a smile to Lynn's face. She knew these funds would lighten the financial burden of a very dear man and his companion. Curling up on her bed and pulling a blanket over her weary body, Lynn felt a deep sense of contentment. She learned during the past year that her greatest happiness came from sharing her newfound wealth with those in great need, and remaining anonymous was important to her.

Several hours later, after a nap and a shower, Lynn reappeared in the living room. Leaning over the back of the couch to look Matt in the eye, she conceded to the arrangement. "When do I meet her?"

Matt sat up with a smile in his eyes. "Tomorrow at four."

Lynn nodded, grabbed her keys, and headed out the door to the long night ahead.

Arriving a half-hour ahead of the band's scheduled starting time, Lynn slid onto a bar stool and scanned the dimly lit space.

"Looking for your next conquest?"

Lynn turned to find Sam, the owner of the bar, who also doubled as her good friend.

"Anyone interesting?" Lynn asked.

"Since when did you care about interesting?" Sam kidded. "You're not exactly looking for a good conversationalist, are you?"

Lynn laughed. "You know me, as long as she can pronounce my name . . ."

Sam shook her head and leaned on the bar. "When are you going to settle down?"

Lynn's face sobered. "I tried that already, remember?" Finished with scanning the room, she turned on the bar stool, grabbed her bottle of beer, and stood. "Oh well, I need some sleep tonight anyway. Early shift tomorrow."

Sam reached for Lynn's arm as she began to walk away. "Why do you do this to yourself? You could have such an easy life."

Lynn turned back toward Sam and looked her in the eye. "Sam, remember, you're my friend, not my mother."

"Hell, I remember! I'm too young and too beautiful to be your mother!"

Lynn smiled as she made her way to the stage. "I'd have to agree with you there!"

Chapter Two

Pulling into the driveway, Lynn saw Matt's El Camino parked alongside what Lynn recognized as the loaner car from the garage. She remembered their discussion last night, and decided that this must be the woman he told her about. Taking in a deep breath, she got out of her truck and made her way to the door.

Lynn unlocked the door and stepped into the living room. Matt stood near the fireplace with a young woman. They were looking at the photographs displayed on the mantel. The woman was thin, with straight shoulder-length brown hair. Lynn guessed that she was about five feet four. She was clad in a white V-necked T-shirt, button-fly jeans, and white tennis shoes. All in all, pretty attractive. Lynn guessed Matt's parents would believe the two as a couple, a very cute couple.

"Chris, this is my roommate, Lynn," Matt said, motioning to Lynn.

The woman had a surprised look on her face. "I thought Lynn

was a man. I mean, I thought you were living with a man! Why can't she pretend to be your fiancée?"

Lynn answered quickly, "I'm a lesbian."

"So let me get this straight—no pun intended. Your parents think that you're straight and that Lynn is gay?" Chris asked.

"No, they think Matt is straight, and they *know* that I'm gay," Lynn responded before Matt could answer the question.

"And what makes you think they *know* you're gay?" Chris asked suspiciously.

Smiling, Lynn met eyes with Matt and answered, "Well, it might have something to do with finding me and Shelly half-naked on the couch one night."

"So, does your girlfriend live here too?" Chris asked curiously.

"My girlfriend?"

"Shelly."

Matt chuckled. "No, no, Shelly isn't her girlfriend. Shelly was just one of many in a line of Lynn's endless one-night stands."

Lynn acted astonished. "You make me sound like a slut! There haven't been that many."

Matt raised his eyebrows, mocking Lynn's statement.

Lynn reacted quickly. "Besides, Matt's just jealous. How long has it been since you've been laid, Matt? The truth is, Matt is just too picky!"

"They're called standards, Lynn! I'm sure you don't know the meaning of the word!" Matt snapped back.

Chris, who had been following the conversation much like a tennis match, finally broke in, "Excuse me! Are you sure that you're friends?"

"We're sorry Chris, what bad manners we have," Matt responded. "We are friends. We just seem to argue a lot."

"The bottom line is this." Lynn ran her fingers through her hair, then continued, "I know it sounds odd, but it is on the up-and-up. Chris, Matt really needs you to do this."

Chris nodded, sat down on the couch, and put her head in her hands.

"Who wants a beer?" Matt called on his way to the kitchen.

After both women responded positively, Lynn sat down next to Chris. "You would be doing us a big favor," Lynn said quietly.

"*Us?*" Chris took her hands from her face and looked Lynn in the eyes. "What's in it for you?"

Still seeing the suspicion in Chris's eyes, Lynn decided that honesty would be the best policy. "Look, I know we argue," Lynn explained. "But the fact is, Matt is my best friend, he's like family to me, and although I don't necessarily agree with what he's doing, what makes him happy, makes me happy." Lynn paused, then whispered, "And if you ever tell him I told you that, I will adamantly deny it!"

Just as Lynn finished her confession, her stomach rumbled, breaking the silence. "I'm sorry," Lynn apologized as she clutched her stomach. "I haven't eaten all day!"

Chris smiled softly as she tucked her hair behind her ear. "I've been so nervous about this whole thing, I haven't either."

"Hmm, maybe I could sway your decision . . ."

"Lynn!" Matt glared at his roommate as he came into the room without hearing the entire conversation.

Lynn glared back as she accepted the bottle he had thrust at her. "Matt, I was just going to suggest that we talk a little more over Chinese food."

"Yeah, right," Matt said suspiciously.

"Actually, Chinese food sounds great!" Chris said, not quite understanding the tension in the room.

Lynn headed toward the kitchen to retrieve the menu, with Matt on her heels. Matt waited until they were out of hearing range before cornering Lynn.

"You do realize that she's straight, Lynn?" he questioned. "I mean, you're not going to try and make a move on her are you?" Then folding his hands together in a praying position, he went on, "Please, Lynn, she's my only hope, don't mess it up."

"Matt, I never make a move on a straight woman, you should know me better than that! You're acting like I'm a letch or something!" Lynn answered, her feelings hurt.

"I'm sorry. I know you're just trying to help," Matt replied, sorry to have said what he did.

Chris wandered over to the mantle and took another look at the photographs. Upon second glance, she noticed that Lynn had been in all the pictures. She had somehow overlooked the woman before. Chris smiled at the photographs. Each had captured friends in what seemed like special, joyous moments. Everyone was laughing or smiling. The pictures showed dozens of different people, but Chris's eyes kept coming back to Lynn. There was something about her. The warmth in her eyes, the sincerity of her smile, yet, a certain sadness.

"What do you want?" Lynn had grabbed the menu, and walked out into the living room calling out to Chris.

"What do you guys usually get? I like just about everything, except anything fishy," Chris answered.

"We usually get the number ten dinner. Sweet-and-sour pork, orange chicken, egg rolls, pork fried rice . . ."

Chris interrupted Matt, "Sounds yummy! Stop talking and start dialing!"

Matt chuckled, dialed the restaurant, and ordered the food.

"Twenty minutes!" Matt said to Lynn. Lynn grabbed her keys and headed out the door.

Lynn returned an hour later and found Matt and Chris out on the deck discussing a rather intriguing subject—auto mechanics. Chris looked relieved as Lynn stepped out onto the patio.

"Gee, Matt, sounds like a real entertaining subject," Lynn said sarcastically.

"Hey, she was interested," Matt answered.

Lynn looked at Chris, who yawned, then back at Matt. "I think she was just being polite Matt."

Chris smiled and changed the subject. "You need any help there?" she asked as Lynn unloaded the cartons on the table.

"No, Matt will go get the paper china, won't you Matt?"

"Like I have a choice!" he said as he scooted his chair back, stood and headed into the house.

Plates overflowing, the three dug into the awaiting noodles, rice, and other delectables. For several minutes all anyone could hear through the still evening air was the rolling waves, the crunch of egg rolls, and the slurp of noodles.

Chris finally broke the silence. "So how often do your parents visit?"

"Too often," was Matt's response as he refilled his fork with rice.

Lynn gave a more complete answer. "Several times a year. Do you see your parents very often?"

Chris lowered her eyes as she finished chewing. "My parents died several years ago in a car accident."

"I'm sorry," Lynn apologized. "Were you close?"

Chris nodded. "Very close."

"That must be hard. So do you have any other family around here?"

"No. I have some family back east, but none out here."

"How did your family end up in California?"

"Well, my father was in the military. We moved around a lot. When I was accepted at the university, my dad decided to retire from the service, take a job in the private sector, and settle down near their only child. Unfortunately, they died soon after that." Chris paused, and wanting to get the focus off of herself turned to Matt. "So if your parents are visiting, you must not be from around here either?"

"No, actually I grew up in this area. My dad is a retired judge. Now he owns a string of car dealerships across the country. When I graduated from high school, they decided to uproot and move to a more central location, Florida. My dad expected me to attend college and go into the family business, but I had other ideas."

Chris nodded and took a drink from her bottle in order to clear her mouth for another question. "So how long have you two lived together?"

"Umm . . . about a year, I guess," Matt replied, then looked at Lynn for confirmation. Lynn nodded.

"And how did you guys meet?"

"Pretty much how you two met," Lynn answered, then smiled at Matt. "I guess your shop is a pretty big pickup place for women, huh?"

Matt laughed. "Too bad it doesn't work equally as well for men!"

"So here's the story. My car broke down and for the first time, I couldn't repair it myself." Lynn paused and then explained, "I really can do a lot of the repairs myself."

Matt rolled his eyes and Lynn slapped his arm. "I can!"

"Yeah, then why have I done all the work on it since we met?" Matt questioned.

"You don't usually give me a choice. Usually I tell you something is wrong and the next thing I know, you're out there tinkering with it!" Lynn argued.

"Could we get back to the story?" Chris interrupted.

"Sorry," Lynn apologized, and continued the tale. "So anyway, I had it towed to the closest garage, which was Matt's. I walked into the shop office having survived the worst tow truck drive ever . . ."

"Big fat guy, greasy hair?" Chris cut in.

"No. Exactly the opposite, nice looking, buff guy. He'd brought his girlfriend along," Lynn answered.

"So what was the problem?" Chris asked, confused.

Matt laughed and struck his hand on the table. "Yeah Lynn, tell her why the guy practically threw you out of the cab of his truck, go on, tell her!"

Lynn felt her face turning red. "I don't know, something about me flirting with his girlfriend . . ." Placing her hand over her heart, she continued, "I swear I wasn't flirting. I merely admired her blouse."

"And . . ." Matt prompted.

"And . . . I admired the way that she filled it out," Lynn said with a mischievous smile.

"That would do it!" Chris laughed. "Are you always that forward?"

Lynn shook her head as Matt nodded his in unison. Lynn reached over and slapped him again. Then Matt admitted, "No, she's not. She was just having a bad day."

"To get back to the story. I walked into the shop office and found Matt on the phone, shouting then pleading, then shouting again at Peter, his lover at the time. Anyway, he started telling me how Peter had done him wrong, and he said to me, 'You know how guys are' and I said to him, 'No, I really don't,' and we just hit it off."

Matt finished the story. "Then Lynn found this great place, I needed a place to stay, and here we are a year later."

Chris nodded and as the conversation lulled, heard music in the distance. "Where's that coming from?" she asked.

"Oh, on Sunday evenings they have kind of a farmers' market thing out on the pier. Wanna go?" Lynn offered.

Chris looked over at Matt, who shrugged.

Chris accepted, "Sure, sounds like fun!"

"But first, open your fortune cookies!" Lynn directed.

Matt broke open the hard shell and straightened out the small piece of paper. "'Find release from your cares, have a good time.'"

"Wow, that really fits!" Lynn remarked then turned to Chris. "Your turn."

"'You will win success in whatever you adopt,'" Chris read.

"Hopefully that means we'll be successful in our little charade," Matt mumbled.

Lynn cracked her cookie, silently read hers, smiled and handed the paper to Matt. "'If you continually give you will continually have,'" he read, then turned to Lynn. "That's eerie."

Chris didn't understand but felt uncomfortable asking what was meant by the remark. Instead, she stood and started gathering the paper goods on the table. The other two joined her, and soon everything was cleaned up and they were ready to head to the beach.

"You might need a jacket for later. Would you like to borrow one of mine?" Lynn asked as she tied a windbreaker around her waist.

"No. I'm pretty warm-blooded, I'll be fine," Chris replied.

The threesome left the house and began walking along the beach toward the pier. Lynn looked out at the horizon, where the deep blue sky sank into the dark green water. She squinted, watching the last few surfers trying to catch the now small rolling waves. There was no doubt about it: she loved this place.

"Hey! Watch out!" they heard voices screaming from behind as a football crashed into the water beside them. Lynn waited for the tide to bring in the object, then snatched it up off of the wet sand.

"Hey! Throw it here!" a voice again shouted from in back of the group. Lynn gripped the ball, drew back, and fired the ball back down the beach directly reaching the young man whose arms were waving.

"Hey! Good throw!" the voice yelled back.

Matt turned to Lynn and gave her a light shove. "Show-off!"

Lynn shrugged her shoulders and the three continued along their way.

Chris watched as Lynn picked up the ball and drew back to throw. She hadn't noticed the muscles in Lynn's arms before, her biceps flexing as she released the ball into the air. Chris reviewed Lynn's legs and found the same muscular tones. She admired the strong thigh and calf muscles as Lynn stepped into the throw. Chris stopped and looked around to make sure that no one had seen the way she was admiring the muscles within the tan, smooth skin. For a moment the feeling made her uncomfortable. Then she shook it off by telling herself that for a physical therapy student it was perfectly natural to be interested in the muscle tone of someone's body.

As they approached the pier, a familiar Neil Diamond tune floated through the air. Lynn began humming. Matt joined along with the words. Soon all three were singing at the top of their lungs.

The song ending, Lynn turned to Chris. "How would you know that song? Isn't that a little before your time?"

Chris shrugged. "My dad was a big Neil Diamond fan."

"Her dad," mumbled Matt as he elbowed Lynn, signifying that their age was showing.

As she climbed the stairs up onto the pier, Lynn felt the rhythm of the music run through her body. She began swaying her hips and moving her body to the beat as they walked into the crowd.

Matt stopped and called out, "Singing is one thing, but if you're going to do that, I'm not going to be seen with you."

Chris laughed, glad that she had controlled her urge to move with the music. Lynn however ignored Matt's sarcasm and continued on her way through the crowd. Matt shook his head, placed his hands on Chris's shoulders, and prodded her to follow the bouncing body ahead.

The threesome moved along until they came to a stand selling fresh eggplant. Matt stopped and began speaking with the man behind the table.

Lynn put her hands on her hips and turned to Chris. "Why did he want to stop here? He doesn't even like eggplant!" Then eyeing the man selling the vegetables, she nudged Chris, and smiled. "Oh, that's why. Come on, let's let him flirt awhile."

Chris followed Lynn through the booths of fresh fruits and vegetables while Lynn paused, examining the contents on each table. Finally, Lynn found some items worthy of her purchase.

"Do you like squash?" Lynn asked Chris.

Chris nodded as Lynn placed a plastic bag into her hands. "Go pick some out over there," she said. pointing to the far end of the table containing several varieties.

Chris walked to the end of the booth, selected several different types of the vegetable, and returned to Lynn's side to find her haggling with the vendor.

Chris whispered in Lynn's ear, "Let me handle this."

Lynn stepped aside, letting Chris argue with the man. After a few seconds, Chris had the price of the vegetables reduced by three dollars. Gathering up the bags, the two left the booth happy.

"Where did you learn to do that?" Lynn asked in amazement.

"I've lived in a lot of different places, even overseas. I learned to do that over in France. If you didn't learn, they'd rob you blind."

"Well, I am very impressed," Lynn responded. *This woman is full of surprises*, she thought.

Strolling over to the next booth, Lynn picked up a slice of watermelon from a sampler tray and took a bite. "Mmm . . . this is great!" Cupping a hand under Chris's chin to stop any runaway juice, Lynn offered the slice to her. "Chris, you've got to try this!" Chris took a bite; the juice ran down her chin but was stopped by Lynn's awaiting hand. Lynn gently wiped away the dripping juice on Chris's chin with her thumb. Then, realizing that this motion had a tone of a seductive nature, she turned her attention to the fruit before her.

"That is so sweet!" Chris agreed as she wiped the remaining liquid from her chin with the back of her hand.

After surveying the lot of watermelons, Lynn made her choice, pulled some cash out, paid the vendor, and slung the melon onto her shoulder.

The two continued on their way. Lynn, keeping her eye on Matt's whereabouts, smiled and asked Chris, "You think he'll have the nerve to ask for a date?"

When she received no response, she turned around to find Chris had stopped to engage in conversation with someone. Upon second glance, Lynn recognized him as a local playboy. Immediately she walked over to the two.

"Leave her alone, Dave!" Lynn called out to the man.

Dave lifted his hands in a form of surrender and backed away. "Sorry, I didn't realize she was with you, Lynn. She doesn't look like a dyke."

Lynn shook her head. "She's not a dyke, Dave. But she may decide to switch sides after she's gone out with you!"

Dave laughed nervously, turned, and walked away.

Lynn looked at Chris with an apologetic smile. "Sorry, but he's a real loser, you can do a lot better than him."

Chris nodded. Just then Matt rejoined the two.

"Was Dave hitting on her?" he asked. Turning, he put his arm around Chris. "You don't want anything to do with him, honest."

Matt looked over at Lynn, who had suddenly focused on something else. "Hey, look! Caramel apples!" Handing him the watermelon and other bags, she was drawn to the booth several yards away.

Matt moaned to Chris, "She loves caramel apples."

Chris broke into a smile and followed Lynn. "Me, too!"

Lynn was already at the booth when Chris caught up with her. "One," requested Lynn.

"Make that two," Chris added.

"With or without nuts?" the vendor asked.

Lynn looked at Chris for a response. "With," Chris replied.

"One with, one without," Lynn answered the man, then turning to Chris, explained, "I don't like nuts."

Chris laughed, wondering if there was a double meaning in that statement.

Lynn smiled as she realized what Chris had found humorous and handed the man four dollars. Looking over at Chris, who was holding out some cash, Lynn pushed away her hand. "My treat."

Matt came from behind the two. "Are you ready to go now?"

Lynn smiled. "I don't know, are you ready to stop flirting now?"

Matt blushed. "His name is Gregg."

"Well, did you get his number?"

Matt shook his head. "I couldn't get up the nerve."

Lynn laughed, motioned for Chris to go ahead of her, and followed the two out of the crowd.

The threesome climbed down the stairs back onto the sand. The sky had turned from dark blue to black. The moonlight danced across the rolling tide. A cool breeze whispered through the air. The three walked along in the dim light, the two women content with their apples.

"Boy, it does get kind of chilly down here at night." Chris said, rubbing her arms.

"I told you," Lynn said as she untied her jacket from around her waist and hung it around Chris's shoulders.

"Thanks," Chris said shyly.

Matt poked Lynn in the ribs. "Very chivalrous of you," he smirked.

Lynn answered his comment with a slap to the back of his head.

"Ouch, you've been kind of physical tonight, haven't you?" he whined, rubbing his head.

Matt opened the glass door and slid it closed behind them. The three stood in deafening silence.

"Well," Matt spoke up, "I guess it's time for the million-dollar question." Looking over at Chris, he continued, "Will you help me out? Will you play the part of my fiancée?"

Chris lowered her eyes and drew an imaginary line with her toe. She looked up, first at Matt, then at Lynn.

For a minute, Lynn was caught off guard by what she saw in the deep blue eyes staring back at her. Chris's warmth and caring nature shone through like a long-lost friend. Shaking off the feeling, Lynn gave Chris her best pleading look.

Smiling, Chris nodded. "Okay." She added, "So, give me the specifics."

"Well," Matt began, "they're arriving late Friday morning. We'll pick them up at the airport and take them to their hotel. My guess is that they'll want to rest up after the flight for awhile. Later we'll go to dinner. Saturday is the club's 'Sun and Fun' day, which is one reason that they're coming this weekend. The rest of the week will be full with whatever else I can fill their time with."

"So a week, tops, right?" Chris asked.

"Right!" Matt responded. "Okay then, I'll see you Friday around ten a.m.?"

Lynn broke in, "Wait a minute, that's it?" Glancing at Chris, she exclaimed, "Men! Definitely not big in the detail department!" Lynn went on, "Don't you think that your parents are going to want to know certain things? About Chris, about how you met, about a wedding date?"

"I agree," Chris responded. "All parents are going to want to know those things. What have you told them about me, about your 'fiancée,' so far?"

Matt shrugged. "Nothing much. Actually, nothing. I just told them that there was someone special that I wanted them to meet, and then my mom assumed that there was an engagement, and I didn't disagree."

Lynn stood and ran her fingers through her hair as she began thinking about the details. "Well, the first thing that we need to figure out is why you haven't, and won't, set the wedding date. Otherwise, they'll try and get you to set the date while they're here."

Chris began pacing. "She's right. How about that I'm still in school, and we want to wait until I graduate?"

Lynn shook her head. "No, because they'll ask you when you graduate, and they'll want to set the date right after graduation." She began again, "How about, Matt, you take your parents aside right away and tell them to please not talk about the wedding date because you're afraid that Chris will feel pressured, and you don't want her to feel any more pressure, with school and all. Maybe you two talked about it before she said yes and the only way that she agreed to marry you is that you would set the date after she got out of school?"

"Yes," Chris said with a nod. "And if they ask me when I will be through with school, I'll be really vague, saying that there is post-graduate work to be done . . . I can just be really vague."

"Does that work for you, Matt?" Both women looked at Matt, who had leaned back on the couch and was watching them in amazement.

"Yeah, sure, I can do that. Now, how did we meet?" he asked.

"You can tell the real story. About her car breaking down and all," Lynn replied.

"Okay, what else?" Matt asked.

"You guys need to tell each other about your parents, about growing up, and . . ." she added sarcastically, "all about your hopes and dreams."

"Well, I'm pretty tired, can we do it tomorrow night?" Matt asked. "Chris, do you want to grab a bite to eat?"

"How about I cook dinner? About six o'clock?" Lynn asked the couple.

"Does that mean that you're going to eat with us? And listen to all the gory details of our lives?" Matt quipped.

"Don't you think that your roommate should know some of the gory details?" Lynn snapped back.

"Do you two ever stop?" Chris asked as she threw up her arms in frustration. Then turning to Lynn she answered, "Tomorrow night sounds great."

"Okay, see you tomorrow night!" Matt began walking down the hall to his bedroom, then stopped and turned. "And Chris? Thanks."

Chris smiled and waved good night. Matt disappeared behind a door and swung it shut.

"Well, I guess I'd better be going," Chris remarked.

"Umm . . ." Lynn said, pointing out some caramel still remaining on Chris's chin.

Chris wiped away the sticky substance and smiled. "You could be a really bad influence on me!"

Lynn smiled back, then, trying to shake off the impure thoughts racing through her mind, responded, "It was just a caramel apple."

But as Chris closed the door behind her, Lynn's impure thoughts returned, and she felt it necessary to repeat to herself—*she's straight, she's straight, she's straight.*

Chris climbed into the loaner car from Matt's garage. She would be glad to get her Jeep fixed and back on the road. She could never stand the closed-in feeling of a regular automobile. She loved the feeling of the wind in her face and hair when she took the soft top off her Jeep.

Thinking back over the evening, Chris smiled. She had a really nice time. It was amazing how comfortable they all were with each other. She was surprised at how she was actually looking forward to the little charade. Turning on the stereo, she located the Neil Diamond tape in her pack of cassettes and slipped it into the tape player. She sang to the familiar tunes all the way home.

Chapter Three

The next evening, Lynn opened the door with a smile. "I hope you like two things, tri-tip and games!"

Chris chuckled. "That's kind of an odd combination. What do they have in common?"

"Well, I barbequed tri-tip for dinner, and Matt wants to play a kind of different version of Scrabble tonight," Lynn replied.

"I'm up for both. I hope we're eating first, I had to skip lunch today."

"Yeah, it's almost ready. The baked potatoes are done. I'm just waiting for the veggies to steam."

Chris entered the living room and was lifted away by the heavenly scent of the meal being prepared. She hadn't had a home-cooked meal in quite a while.

"Anything I can do?" Chris followed Lynn into the kitchen.

"You can grab whatever you want to drink from the fridge," Lynn answered. "And grab the butter and sour cream while you're in there."

Chris opened the door to the refrigerator. *Wow*, she said to herself. She hadn't seen a fridge so stocked since . . . her parents were alive. Trying to wipe the thought from her mind, she grabbed the items and asked, "Where's Matt?"

"He's in the shower. He'll be right out. He's been working like a dog in order to have some free time while his parents are here."

"Where do these go?" Chris asked regarding the condiments.

"Oh, out on the deck please."

Chris slid the glass door open and was overcome by the aroma of the barbeque, the ocean view, and the cool breeze. Placing the items on the already set table, she stood for a moment taking in her surroundings. Last night she had been so nervous that she hadn't been able to appreciate the beachfront setting. Tonight, though, she felt strangely at peace. *I could live like this*, she said to herself.

Lynn came out of the house with a basket of garlic bread. "This should calm your appetite until Matt is ready to eat," she said, offering the basket to Chris. "Beautiful evening, huh?"

Chris took a piece of bread and hungrily took a bite. "Thanks, actually my stomach thanks you. Yes, it is beautiful." Chris suddenly felt tongue-tied. Her mind went blank. *Think of something to say, stupid.*

Lynn broke the silence. "Well, I need to check on the vegetables."

Chris, finally able to open her mouth, asked, "Anything else that I can do?"

"No, just sit down, relax, and enjoy the view. Feel free to have some more bread, there's plenty more," Lynn answered as she stepped back inside.

Chris grabbed another piece of bread, took a drink from her bottle, and leaned on the railing.

"Hey, sorry I took so long," Matt apologized as he stepped out onto the deck still shaking out his wet hair.

"I hear you're starving!"

"No problem." Chris smiled as she held up a piece of bread. "I was saved."

"So, did Lynn tell you about the game that I want to play tonight?" Matt asked.

"No, this was your idea, I thought I'd let you explain it," Lynn said as she brought out the remainder of the meal.

"Well, I played a different version of Scrabble once at a party. Kind of a get to know each other kind of thing," Matt explained as he pulled out a chair and sat down. "You see, every word that you make, you have to use to tell a story about yourself."

"That sounds kind of fun!" Chris said as she loaded her plate. "Oh man, this is great!" she said as she took a bite of the meat.

"Yep, you really outdid yourself this time!" Matt said upon swallowing his first bite.

Lynn smiled. "Aw, it was nothing," she said as she took a bite, and leaned back in her chair, appreciating the food and the company.

"Okay, I'll go first," Matt said as he laid down the letter tiles to form the word FAMILY.

The meal had been cleared away and replaced with the Scrabble game board. Matt sat back and related the first story of the evening.

"Every year my family would take a summer vacation. One year, we went to Hawaii and our luggage went to someplace like Arkansas. When our luggage finally caught up with us, we opened it up and found hay mixed in with our clothes!"

"You're kidding!" Lynn chuckled.

Matt shook his head and raised his right hand. "I swear!" Turning to Chris, he said, "Okay, let's hear your story about family."

Chris looked down and fiddled with her napkin. Most of her memories made her feel so melancholy. Then she remembered something that made her smile. "Well, I told you that my family traveled around a lot due to my dad's career in the military. It got so that every house or apartment looked the same. My mom never really kept many knickknacks or anything, because she got tired of packing and unpacking them. So no place really felt like home. Until one day, my dad brought home a bouquet of daisies. For some reason, they just warmed up the place. And from then on, everywhere we moved, the first night my dad would bring home a bunch of daisies." Chris paused and shook her head. "Those simple daisies would always make wherever we were . . . home."

After a moment of silence, Lynn looked at Matt. "I liked her story better."

Matt threw his napkin at Lynn. "It's not a contest!" He motioned to Chris. "Your turn."

Chris placed her letters on the board, connecting with the "F" in FAMILY. FOOD.

"Not quite as deep as 'family' . . . but just as important!" Chris smiled and continued, "My favorite food is Mexican food. Anything Mexican—tacos, enchiladas, burritos—mmm!"

"I'd have to say, Italian food would be my choice," Matt responded. "I love all the sauces, the marinara and Alfredo sauces are my favorite."

Matt placed his letters off of the "D" in FOOD. DRINK. "What's your favorite drink?" he asked Chris.

"Alcoholic or non-alcoholic?" Chris questioned.

"Either, both. Mine are Sprite and Long Island iced tea."

"Diet Coke and Malibu rum and Coke."

Lynn listened to Chris's choices and remembered the taste of the slight hint of coconut provided by the specialty rum. The thought brought back another memory. The taste of coconut as she kissed the neck of a coconut-oiled woman in the hot sand not far from where they were currently seated. The next word on the board brought Lynn out of her daydream.

MONEY was the word Chris set down, off of the "Y" in FAMILY.

"Money is something I am constantly worrying about. And next year they are raising the tuition costs again," Chris complained.

"Well, I'm no stranger to money problems," Matt explained.

"My shop just barely makes ends meet. That's one major complaint that my dad has with me."

Lynn found herself lost in another thought. Matt was repairing Chris's car for free for her participation in this charade. Maybe Lynn could find another way to show Chris her appreciation for helping her best friend. Lynn made a mental note to herself to find out the current tuition costs at the university.

Matt placed the word ILL off of the "I" in DRINK. "When I was ten years old, I had my tonsils out. It's the only time that I've been ill enough to be in the hospital. How about you?"

"I threw my knee out when I was a senior in high school while playing volleyball. I had surgery and was on crutches for several weeks. But I've never actually been in the hospital with an illness," Chris replied.

Chris laid her letter tiles down from the "M" in MONEY to form MOVIE.

"Favorite movie?" she asked Matt.

"*Bird Cage*," Matt replied.

Chris smiled at Lynn, then looked back at Matt. "I can't tell your parents that your favorite movie is *Bird Cage*!"

"Why would you have to?"

"You never know when something like that may come up."

"Okay, okay, something more masculine, right? How about the *Lethal Weapon* series?"

Chris and Lynn nodded in agreement.

"And yours?" Matt asked Chris.

"Give me anything Doris Day. I love the old Doris Day movies!" Chris answered.

Matt looked at Lynn then back at Chris. "You're kidding, right?"

Chris shook her head. "No, why?"

"Lynn drives me crazy with those movies. She has a whole collection, you know."

"Cool!" Chris replied.

"Yeah, I've got them all. *Pillow Talk, Move Over Darling, Please Don't Eat the Daisies* . . ." Lynn rambled on.

"Yeah, yeah, you two can reminisce later. My turn." Matt laid down FUN, connecting to the "N" in MONEY. "What do you do for fun?"

"I guess I'm kind of boring. In the summer, I have some friends that I go camping or hiking with. Sometimes, I just hang out at the pool. In the winter, I like to snuggle in with a good book, or if a game is on, I love to watch football."

"I love to go camping and hiking, but you can keep the football. You'll have to get with Lynn on that. I swear that's all she does in the winter!"

Chris turned to Lynn. "Really? Who's your team?"

"Denver Broncos," announced Lynn.

Chris named her favorite, "Cowboys."

They both laughed.

"Neither of our teams has been doing very well," Lynn explained to Matt.

"Okay, okay, enough football talk," Matt said, jealous that the two had so much in common.

Chris laid the tiles SEA on top of FOOD to form SEAFOOD.

"I'm allergic to seafood. Shrimp, crab, lobster—one bite and I swell up like a balloon. If that happens, just take me to the hospital," Chris explained.

"Wow, that's good to know. Any other allergies that we need to know about? Bee stings, aspirin, penicillin?" Lynn asked.

"Nope, just seafood."

"Hey, I thought you said that you'd never been to the hospital due to an illness," Matt questioned.

"Oh, sorry, that's just an emergency room thing, I didn't think it counted," Chris explained.

"Okay. Well, I'm not allergic to anything," Matt responded.

"Speaking of penicillin," Matt said as he connected with the "S" in SEAFOOD to form DRUGS. "Any addictions that we need to know about?"

Lynn looked at Chris with an apologetic smile. "Not very tactful, huh?"

"That's okay," Chris replied and looked Matt straight in the eye. "No addictions, Mr. McKinley. Not drugs, not alcohol, nothing!"

"Well, I needed to know!" Matt answered Lynn's glare.

"Let's lighten up the mood a little," Chris said, placing the word MUSIC off of the "U" in DRUGS. "I like most kinds of music except rap. And I can only stand maybe one reggae song at a time. But my mood usually determines what music I listen to."

"Matt's a jazz freak," Lynn commented.

"What do you mean by freak?" Matt argued. "Just because I don't like all that headbanger music that you warp your mind with!"

"Matt, I really don't consider Van Halen and Def Leppard to be 'headbanger' music," Lynn said in her defense.

Then turning to Chris, Matt asked, "Do you even know who those groups are?"

"Of course I do," Chris answered. "They have some great songs!"

"Now, she's just trying to be polite to you, Lynn," Matt explained.

Lynn shook her head. "Your turn, Matt."

Matt placed his letters on the board, CRIME, connected to the "E" in MOVIE.

Chris looked at Lynn. "I guess we're not lightening up the mood." Then turning to Matt, she asked, "I suppose you want to know if I've ever been arrested for anything?"

"Matt!" Lynn glared across the table once again.

"It's okay, Lynn. He found me out," Chris said with a serious look on her face. "I've got a criminal record. I was arrested as a Russian spy!" Chris kept the serious look on her face as long as she could, but upon seeing Lynn holding in a laugh out of the corner of her eye, she broke out in laughter.

"Funny, funny. But she'd thank me if it turned out you were a murderer or something!" Matt exclaimed, pointing at Lynn.

"Yeah, like she'd really tell you if she were a murderer!" Lynn said through her laughter.

Matt's face remained solemn, so Chris took his question seriously. "No, Matt, I've never been arrested or convicted of any crime."

"Thank you," Matt mumbled.

Lynn watched as Chris set down the letters with a mischievous grin. If Matt wasn't going to lighten up, then she would give him a little bit more information than he really wanted. The word she placed was HOTEL off of the "L" in ILL.

Chris took a swig of her beer. "Okay, HOTEL. I lost my virginity in a hotel, prom night, to the captain of the football team."

"Hey! Me too!" Matt exclaimed.

"You mean on prom night?" Chris asked, surprised by his reaction.

"No, not actually on prom night, but it was the captain of the football team!" Matt replied.

Lynn, after being taken aback by Chris's openness, suddenly woke up. "Wait a minute, I haven't heard this story!"

"Nothing much to tell. I was dating his sister, but I scored with the brother," Matt explained.

"I'm sure his sister was thrilled about that!" Lynn remarked.

"Oh, she never found out. It was the summer after high school. He left for college, I never saw him again."

"And his sister?" Chris asked.

"We ended up having sex, too. But the experience with her brother was much better. That's pretty much when I figured out that I was gay."

"Well, Matt!" Lynn remarked. "I never knew that you had such a sordid past!"

"I just hope they never figure it out!" Matt joked.

They both looked over at Lynn, waiting for her story.

"Well?" Matt asked.

"Well what? I'm not part of this game!" Lynn answered.

"Oh, so now you're not part of this game. You can't just put your two cents on one subject and not another!" Matt quipped.

"So, no football captain in your past, huh?" Chris smiled.

"Uh-uh." Lynn shook her head, then smiled. "Cheerleader."

"Behind the bleachers?" Matt kidded.

"No, up at summer camp. We were both camp counselors. Funny what you can accomplish in one of those little rowboats in the middle of the lake on a hot summer night!" Lynn smiled, remembering fondly. "And oh, what a pair of pom-poms she had!"

"Ohhh!" the other two both moaned, throwing their napkins in her direction.

"Well, that's enough openness for me for one night," Lynn said as she examined her watch. She stood and stretched. "I'll clean up the dishes. You guys can keep playing."

"What time is it?" Chris inquired.

"Past ten. Early class tomorrow?" Lynn asked.

"I never schedule my classes very early. I'm not exactly a morning person," Chris replied. She scooted back from the table. "But it is getting pretty late. I'll help you with the dishes and then I'd better be on my way."

"Yeah, I'm pretty tired myself," Matt said and started cleaning up the game.

"There's really not many dishes. Don't feel like you need to stay and help," Lynn said as she gathered the various dishes around the kitchen and stacked them at the side of the sink.

"Well then, two should make it go faster, huh?" Chris replied as she turned on the water, picked up the first dish, and proceeded to rinse it. The problem was, Chris thought to herself, that she really didn't want to go home.

Lynn opened the dishwasher and slid each dish in as Chris handed them to her. Within minutes, the kitchen was clean.

"See? So much quicker with two!" Chris remarked, then realizing that it was time for her to leave, felt a loneliness overcome her. She stood there, drying her hands over and over again.

"Yeah. Usually Matt helps though. Where'd he go?" Lynn said as she walked over to the glass door. Looking out, she watched as Matt leaned against the railing, staring out into the darkness. Chris joined Lynn at the glass to see what she was observing.

Lynn put her arm around Chris's shoulder, giving Chris a shiver down her spine, and softly spoke. "I'm really worried about him. He's really taking this whole thing much too seriously. I wish that I could be there every minute his parents are here, but I can't."

"That's what he's got me for, Lynn. I know that I'm a complete stranger, but please know that I understand this isn't a game, and I'll do my best."

"I believe you will," Lynn said as she squeezed Chris's shoulder, then released her arm. "Thanks again for doing this."

Chris unlocked the door to her apartment and set her backpack on the couch. She listened to the silence. Realizing how empty it made her feel, she flipped on the television and plopped down on the couch. She had never minded being alone before. How could things change so quickly? She had only known these people for two days, really less than two days. Maybe it was just that she hadn't let anyone in for so long.

During her youth, she wasn't allowed the luxury of close friends. She always knew that in a short time her family would be transferred to yet another location. Chris had learned quickly to keep people at arm's length. This avoided any heartbreak when she would be pulled away to start over again. Now she had friends, well, not close friends, but friends that she did things with. But she couldn't think of any she wanted around all the time.

Chris stretched out on the sofa and buried her face in the pillow. She felt so comfortable with Matt and Lynn. Well, she had felt comfortable with Matt. Lynn made her feel comfortable and uneasy at the same time. She thought back to how she froze when she had been alone with Lynn before dinner, and the contentment that she felt later, when Lynn had her arm around her shoulder. Warm and content. Still feeling these sensations, Chris drifted off to sleep.

Chapter Four

Chris walked down the wine aisle in the grocery store. Matt had requested that she bring wine this evening, her donation to the meal that he was preparing. However, she had forgotten to ask what they were having, and therefore found herself staring at the wide array of selections.

"Red, I believe, goes with Italian food."

Chris turned to find Lynn next to her, with a shopping basket containing various salad items.

"I wasn't sure if he told you what he was cooking," Lynn added.

"No, he didn't," Chris answered. "How much wine do we need?"

"He's a good cook, so you don't need to be soused to eat it, if that's what you're asking." Lynn chuckled.

"Well, I was trying to be polite, but that is what I was getting at." Chris smiled.

"Don't get more than one bottle. First of all because I can't drink too much before I play tonight, and second, if Matt drinks too much you may find out more than you really need, or want, to know."

"You have to play tonight? As in, 'playing around'?" Chris asked with a mischievous smile.

"See, now Matt gave you the wrong idea about me! I'm not a nympho or anything!" Lynn explained, "I play at the Rainbow Room, it's a gay bar." Realizing this didn't sound any better, she added, "I mean I sing. Well, I play guitar and the keyboard too, but I basically sing."

"You see, I learn something new every day. I didn't even know there was a gay bar around here!"

"Yeah, well, we don't really advertise, we don't want to attract the riffraff."

"Do people just sit and listen, or is there a dance floor?"

"You ever try to keep a gay man from dancing?" Lynn chuckled.

"So . . . you must sing Broadway songs, huh?" Chris laughed.

"No, no Broadway tunes, that's how we keep most of the gay men out." Lynn laughed at the stereotype and wondered if Chris really believed it. "There are a few gay men that come in, like Matt, but it's basically known as a lesbian bar."

There was a moment of silence, Lynn guessed because she had said the word "lesbian," so she broke the uncomfortable pause. "So wine, salad, bread, and Matt's manicotti, sounds like a feast, huh?"

"Well, what are we having for the most important part of the meal?" Chris asked. Lynn looked at her quizzically.

"Dessert," Chris answered. "The most important part of the meal is dessert!"

"Oh God, a woman after my own heart. Bless you!" Lynn smiled. "Well, Matt doesn't really eat sweets, thinks they're bad for you or something." Lynn rolled her eyes and continued, "But I, on the other hand, think that they should have their own place in the food groups. How about ice cream?"

"You won't have to twist my arm! What flavor?"

"Let's go look," Lynn said. Finding the freezer aisle, they stood gazing at all of the cartons.

"What do you think?" Lynn asked. "Do you want a one-mile-run ice cream or a five-mile-run ice cream?"

"Excuse me?"

"That's how I judge what flavor to get," Lynn explained. "I love sweets, but I also know how much exercise I'll have to do to make up for eating them. It's kind of my trade-off. Call it ice cream for miles!"

"So you run? I love to run. I bet it's great living on the beach, running along the water every day."

"Yeah, I run every day after work, kind of a stress reliever. I work out at the gym too, but not every day, maybe two, three times a week."

"Every day after work, you mean you run in the middle of the night? Is that safe?" Chris asked.

"Oh, the singing thing. That's not really a job, just kind of a hobby. Monday through Friday I'm a waitress at the Blue Moon Café, the restaurant just on the other side of Matt's shop. It's only open for breakfast and lunch, so I'm out of there about two in the afternoon."

Chris nodded in understanding and looked back toward the ice cream. "So, what's your favorite?"

"Definitely pralines and cream, a lot of people go for something chocolate, but not me. And your favorite?" Lynn asked.

"I'm the person for something chocolate. Rocky Road," Chris answered.

"Well, I say we get both. I mean, Matt's parents will probably be over and want something sweet, don't you think?" Lynn tried to justify the purchases.

"Oh, definitely!" Chris agreed and reached into the case for the containers.

"Here, let me." Lynn smiled as she took the containers from Chris's hands. "I hear that you're a struggling student."

Chris let Lynn purchase the ice cream along with the salad ingredients while wondering to herself if Lynn was any better off financially working as a waitress. The two walked out into the parking lot, climbed into their respective vehicles, and drove toward the house.

Lynn rolled down the window and turned on the radio. Her stomach growling, she reached into one of the sacks, took out a carrot, and took a bite. Could Matt and Chris really pull off this escapade? She wondered if Chris was overwhelmed by the situation. She didn't seem to be, but some people put on a good front. She knew that she was going to have a hard enough time pretending for Matt's parents that he and Chris were a couple. She hoped that they wouldn't run into any of Matt's friends while he and Chris were entertaining his parents. Lynn made a mental note to ask Matt if he had clued any of his friends in on his scheme.

Chris rolled down the window and breathed in the crisp evening air. She looked over at the bottle of wine that she had purchased and wished that she could have a glass before she stepped into another question-and-answer series. What she really wanted was to drink the entire bottle, to relieve the uneasiness in her stomach. It's funny, she only felt this nervousness when she was alone with Lynn. It hadn't really bothered her to learn that Lynn was gay, or had it? Brushing off the nerves, she pulled up in front of the house. Taking another deep breath, she grabbed the wine bottle and walked to the door.

Lynn opened the door and ushered Chris in before her. "Hey, Matt! Look who I found at the grocery store."

Matt looked around the kitchen wall and rolled his eyes. "What a coincidence," he mumbled.

Lynn gave him a dirty look for what he was thinking as she brought the sacks of food through the living room. Chris followed Lynn into the kitchen and took the lid off of one of the pots to check out the contents. The creamy Alfredo sauce made her mouth water. "If you guys keep feeding me like this, I'll never want to leave."

"Tomorrow night, it's your turn to cook!" Matt joked as he stirred the pasta.

"Yeah, you'd better be joking." Chris laughed. "You two wouldn't want to eat anything I can cook!"

"You've been on your own for a while. What do you eat if you don't cook?" Lynn asked as she removed the contents of the plastic bags.

"A lot of salads, sandwiches, nothing that takes too much effort."

"It's different when you're alone too," Matt commented. "Who wants to do all this cooking for just one person, right?"

Chris nodded, salivating as Matt stirred the sauce. Lynn tore off two chunks of French bread and dunked them in the cream as Matt went over to the refrigerator. Lynn quickly popped one of the pieces into her mouth and offered the other to Chris. Smiling, the woman opened her mouth, letting Lynn place the bread on her tongue.

Matt turned at the sound of her moans of delight. "Hey! What's going on?" he exclaimed.

Lynn looked innocent as she went back to preparing her salad, leaving Chris to fend for herself. Chris could not answer as she was still savoring the bite. She simply shrugged and smiled. Matt looked at one woman and then the other, then went back to his search in the refrigerator. Lynn glanced back and gave Chris a wink. Chris felt her face turn red, and not understanding her own reaction, quickly turned away.

"Well guys, I need to get going." Lynn slid her chair back from the table and stood. "I just hope that I'll be able to sing with this full stomach. Another great meal, Matt!"

"Thanks. Have a good practice," Matt said with a wave good-bye.

Chris looked up as Lynn opened the sliding glass door and stepped into the house. "Hey, what about . . ."

"I'm sorry, I'm just too full for ice cream right now, but you can go ahead if you want to!" Lynn said apologetically.

"Wait a minute," Matt called to Lynn. "Ice cream? Oh no, have you corrupted her already?"

Lynn stuck her head back out the door with a mischievous smile. "Depends on what you mean by corrupting her!"

"Lynn . . ." Matt glared at her, remembering their conversation in the kitchen the first night.

"I'm just teasing! Can't you take a joke?" Lynn laughed, shrugged her shoulders, and glanced over at Chris.

Chris smiled. Matt mumbled something under his breath and swallowed the last drop of wine from his glass.

Lynn grabbed her keys and headed out the door. "Shoot!" she said to herself as she looked at her watch and realized it was later than she thought. For some reason she wasn't as excited as usual about going to practice. She wanted to stay home. Why? she wondered. It was just going to be another evening like last night, Matt and Chris trading details about their lives, pretty boring. Actually, Matt's life details were boring, but she was interested in learning more about Chris. And that smile. Oh brother! Lynn slapped herself on the head—*she's straight, she's straight, she's straight,* she repeated to herself. She drove into the bar parking lot and saw all the other band members' vehicles in the lot. Parking quickly, she jogged to the door.

"You're late!" Nikki called from the stage. "You're never late! What's the matter?" Nikki was the lead guitarist and the other vocalist in the band. Tall, thin, much too confident, and bisexual, Nikki did not appeal sexually to Lynn at all. Lynn could never get involved with a bisexual. The concept was totally repellent to her. She and Nikki flirted while playing on stage, but that was as far as it went, and Lynn had made that clear to Nikki the first time they played together.

"Nothing is the matter, I just lost track of time, that's all," Lynn answered as she climbed the stairs to the stage. Strapping a guitar on, she said hello to the rest of the members, and went right to work. "Okay, let's start with the usual songs, and we also have that special request that I faxed to you guys yesterday." And with that said, the practice began.

Chris and Matt stared at each other. Two hours of making small talk was wearing on them. Chris felt like she knew everything that she needed to know about Matt. She was bored, she was tired, and she wished Lynn was there. Lynn would have broken the silence with some witty comment or sarcastic remark.

"We need to get out of here." Matt stood suddenly.

"Yes, we definitely need to get out of here," Chris agreed as she pushed out her chair. "Any place in particular?"

"No—any place that you usually hang out?"

"I actually never just hang out. My life for the past four years has been eat, study, sleep, eat, study, sleep."

"Well, the place that I usually hang out is a gay bar, and I don't think that you would feel comfortable there, so . . ."

"Is that where Lynn plays?"

"Yeah, the Rainbow Room."

"Let's go there. I don't think that I'll feel too uncomfortable."

Matt tried to hide the shock he felt. Most straight people wouldn't go near a gay bar. Chris must really have an open mind. He was glad that he had found her.

"Okay, let's go!" Matt grabbed his wallet and keys and ushered Chris out the door.

Chris was a little scared. Had she actually suggested that they go to a gay bar? Was she crazy? Yesterday, she didn't even know that there was a gay bar in the area, and now tonight she was hanging out there? *Act cool*, she told herself, *you don't know what you are going to see, just act cool.*

Matt pulled his El Camino into the parking lot and parked right next to Lynn's truck. He prepared himself to leave the bar at the first sign of uneasiness from Chris. Matt swung the door of the bar open and held it for Chris. It took a while for their eyes to adjust to the dim light. There were only about a dozen people there, half of them sitting at the bar, the other half dispersed throughout the seating area.

"What do you want to drink?" Matt shouted over the music.

"A beer is fine," Chris shouted back.

"Nancy! Two beers!" Matt called to the bartender and motioned for Chris to follow him. Matt pulled out a chair at one of the tables at the back of the seating area and took a seat.

Chris sat down and looked around. It looked like a regular bar, with regular people, except for the two women kissing at a table at the far end. She tried not to stare. She glanced toward the front of the bar and was taken aback to discover that the voice she was hearing was Lynn's. Again, she tried not to stare. The music stopped, Lynn said something to the drummer, and the music started again. What did they need practice for? They sounded great!

"This band is really good. Lynn has a great voice!" she said to Matt as the bartender set the beers on the table.

Matt took a swig from the bottle and shouted, "Yeah, I know!" Just then the music stopped and there was silence. Matt stood up and yelled, "Encore! encore!" and clapped loudly. Lynn swung around to find where the voice had come from and smiled.

"You damn hecklers!" she yelled back. Grabbing her beer and a towel, she jumped down from the stage and strode across the room.

"Hey, what are you guys doing here?" Lynn asked. "Are you two sick of each other already? How is your marriage ever going to last?" She laughed, wiped her face off with the towel, and took a gulp of beer.

"You're really good!" Chris said.

"I've been told that several times," Lynn answered with a teasing smile. Then glancing at Matt, she straightened her face. "Sorry." Turning to Chris, she said, "Thank you."

"Hey, are we done or what!" someone yelled from the stage.

"No, we still need to rehearse that special request!" Lynn yelled back. Turning around, she said, "See you guys later," and strode back to the stage.

Chris felt like she was blushing. Her tongue felt tied when Lynn made those teasing comments. She definitely needed to practice her comebacks. Finishing her beer, she watched Lynn on the stage. The band was laughing and Lynn was trying to convince them to do something. Finally, they all went to their instruments and slowly began picking at a tune. A few moments later they were playing the song as if they had known it all their lives.

Chris smiled as she recognized the song "Close to You" by the Carpenters. Obviously not a regular song heard in this type of establishment. Obviously, by the smirks on the band members' faces, not a regular song of the band. She wondered what the occasion was.

She hadn't even noticed Matt was gone until he set a new bottle in front of her and sat back down.

"This place is really packed on the nights that they sing. Thursdays aren't as bad as Fridays and Saturdays."

"They play on Thursdays? Bands don't usually play on Thursdays, do they?"

"No, not usually, but for some reason a lot of people here come out on Thursdays. I guess people figure they don't get much work done on Friday anyway, so why not be tired or hungover."

Chris nodded. "But doesn't Lynn work on Friday mornings? How does she work half the night, and then go to work again so early in the morning?"

"Sometimes she just doesn't go to sleep at all. Then she crashes when she gets off work Friday afternoon, and sleeps until she plays on Friday night."

Matt and Chris sat and talked about an hour more, until Lynn was finished with her practice, then they all headed home. Once in the car, Matt asked, "So, what did you think of the bar? Was it like you imagined?"

"No, I thought it would be like a big orgy!" she answered sarcastically. Rethinking her answer she began again, "Actually, I don't know what I thought it would be like, but I didn't feel uncomfortable at all."

"That's good," Matt said as he yawned. "I didn't realize how tired I was. I hope I didn't keep you out too late."

"Well, it is a school night, but my class doesn't start until nine, so I should be okay. If I fall asleep in class, I'll just blame it on my fiancé keeping me out too late." Chris smiled.

Matt pulled in front of the house. Lynn pulled in behind him. Chris got out of his vehicle and walked toward hers.

"See you tomorrow night about five-thirty?" Matt called.

Chris nodded. She would make it an early night, because she had a test on Thursday.

"See you then!" Lynn called out as she climbed out of the truck and followed Matt to the door.

Lynn had barely locked the front door when there was a knock. Lynn looked through the peephole to find Chris standing there.

"Did you forget something?" Lynn asked as she opened the door.

"No . . . do you mind if I use the bathroom?" Chris asked shyly.

"No problem." Lynn stepped back as Chris quickly passed and disappeared behind a closed door.

Chris came back into the living room after using the facilities. "Well, I'm going to get going."

Lynn turned around from sitting on the couch and looked at Chris. "Are you okay? Don't take this the wrong way, but you look like crap!"

"Yeah, all of a sudden I'm not feeling so hot," Chris answered while rubbing her stomach.

"Are you sure you're okay to drive home? You're welcome to stay here for the night."

"No, I'll be fine. I'd kind of like to get home," Chris said as she headed to the door, stopping once to balance herself.

Lynn stood and started toward the door. "Chris, how much did you have to drink tonight?"

"Not enough to feel like this!" she replied.

"Let me take you home, Chris. You have a forty-five-minute drive ahead of you."

"No, no. I'll need my car in the morning and so will you," Chris replied.

"Okay then, I'll follow you home. Let me tell Matt and I'll just grab my keys."

"Lynn, I don't think that's necessary . . ." Then feeling her stomach cramp again, she agreed.

Lynn walked to Matt's door, called out her plans, grabbed her keys, and followed Chris out the door. Chris slid in her car seat, rolled down the window, and gave Lynn directions, just in case they got separated. Lynn climbed into her truck and pulled out in back of her.

Chris tried to focus on the road ahead instead of on the pains shooting through her stomach. Leaning toward the open window, she tried to cool her flushed face. She hadn't felt this sick in a long time. Maybe it was something she ate. She reviewed everything she consumed that evening and came to the conclusion that she hadn't eaten anything even related to seafood. And if the food had been spoiled, wouldn't Lynn and Matt be feeling this way, too? Chris ran her hand over her face, trying hard to concentrate on getting home quickly. It had been really nice of Lynn to see her home. Kind of something an older sister might do, she thought. "Thank goodness," she said out loud as she reached her apartment complex and coasted into her assigned space.

Lynn pulled into a parking space next to Chris. Walking around to Chris's vehicle, she opened the driver's-side door.

"How are you feeling?" Lynn inquired.

"Like the world is spinning. I thought I'd never make it home."

Lynn helped Chris up the stairs to her apartment, where Chris immediately excused herself and made her way to the bathroom. Lynn wandered around the living room taking in the new surroundings. She picked up a picture that she decided must have been Chris's mom and dad, then set it back down as she heard footsteps from down the hall. Chris made her way to a chair and plopped down. Her face was white as a sheet.

"Come on, you need to get to bed," Lynn said as she helped Chris out of the chair, down the hall, and into her bedroom.

"Do you have any kind of medicine for an upset stomach?" Lynn asked as she turned down the bed.

Chris shook her head. "I just don't get sick that often," she explained.

"You know, it's probably just nerves," Lynn suggested.

"Nerves?" Chris asked for clarification.

"Think about it. In the past two days you've been forced into a situation where you've had to expose yourself and many intimate details of your life. Not to mention your visit to the bar tonight."

"Maybe," Chris replied as she collapsed onto her bed.

"You get into bed, I'll be right back." Lynn walked out of the apartment and down to her truck, where she pulled a small duffel bag from behind the seat. Unzipping it, she proceeded to look through its contents while climbing back up the stairs. By the time she reached Chris' bedroom she had located what she had been searching for.

"Here we go!" Lynn said, showing the bottle of medicine to the woman now lying in bed.

"You keep that in your truck?" Chris asked suspiciously.

"Well, along with a few other things." Lynn pointed to the bag she had placed on the bed. "Many mornings, waking up who knows where, I've been pretty thankful for this bag," Lynn said, showing Chris the contents. "See? Toothbrush, mouthwash, hairbrush, deodorant . . . Well, you get the idea."

"And you felt it necessary to include this medicine?"

"Well, I hate to admit it, but sometimes the reason I wake up in those places is the result of drinking too much," Lynn said as she wandered down the hall to the kitchen.

Chris could hear drawers being opened and closed and wasn't surprised when Lynn returned with a spoon.

"I can't say that it tastes great, but it seems to do the job," Lynn said as she poured the liquid into the spoon and offered it to Chris.

Chris took the spoon and swallowed the medicine. "Yuk!"

Lynn shrugged. "Sorry."

Chris lay back on her pillow and closed her eyes. "Thanks, doc!"

"No problem. I'm going to crash on your couch just in case you need something in the middle of the night."

"You don't have to do that. You have to be at work in a few hours."

Lynn smiled and pulled out a travel alarm clock from her bag. "See? Quite a handy little bag, huh?"

Chris smiled.

Lynn switched off the light and turned to leave the room but was called back.

"Lynn?"

"Yes?"

"Oh, never mind, it's silly."

Lynn smiled, knowing exactly what she was asking. She too wanted the same exact thing when she was ill. Lynn climbed up on the bed next to her and softly stroked her hair. "It's not silly."

Lightly rubbing Chris's back, Lynn was reminded of Susan. She would always do this when Lynn had been crippled by a migraine. The memories rushed through her mind. A warm feeling overwhelmed her body. The feeling of someone holding her, loving her, trying to make the pain subside. Lynn felt a tear roll down her cheek. She feared she would never experience that again.

Chapter Five

Lynn's alarm rang, jolting her awake. It took a minute for her to remember where she was. Stretching after being curled up on the sofa for the last few hours, she stood and tiptoed down the hall to check on Chris. Finding her sound asleep, she returned to the living room, where she pulled on her shoes and tied the laces.

Wanting to leave some kind of note, Lynn reviewed the contents of the room around her for a pen and a piece of paper. She walked into the kitchen and still found nothing. Lynn eyed the backpack sitting on a living room chair. Should she dare to open it? Wouldn't that be like searching through someone's purse? She convinced herself that it would be okay as long as she only looked for the items needed.

She unzipped the main zipper: books, note cards, appointment book, notebook. She tore out a blank sheet from the notebook and proceeded with her search for a pen. Unzipping a pocket from inside the pack, she inserted her hand and pulled out a handful of objects. Lynn smiled at her catch. Mechanical pencil, eraser, gum, lipstick. Taking the cap off the container, she screwed the base exposing the color. Lynn tried to imagine Chris's lips covered with this dark, moist substance. A shiver ran down her body just thinking about it. Taking her eyes off the lipstick just for a moment, she noticed something else in the pile to snap her back to reality. Condoms. Admonishing herself for her previous thought, she crammed all of the items except the pencil back into the pocket.

Lynn left a brief note, returned the pencil to its place, and zipped the pack closed. *Serves me right for looking in someone's personal belongings*, she told herself. Grabbing her keys she walked softly to the door, turned the lock on the doorknob, and closed it behind her.

"Hey, it's me." Lynn phoned Matt on her eight o'clock break.

"Hey! I didn't hear you come home last night."

"I didn't. I stayed at Chris's place."

Lynn heard nothing but silence on the other end of the line. "She was sick, Matt. I would have felt bad for just leaving."

"Uh-huh." Matt sounded unconvinced.

"Whatever. Can I have Chris's phone number, please? I want to see how she's feeling."

"Lynn . . . aren't you getting a little too involved here?"

"Dang it, Matt! Just give me the number, would you?"

Lynn got the number and dialed.

"Hello?" the voice on the other end said sleepily.

"Hi Chris, this is Lynn. I hope I didn't wake you. I just wanted to see how you are feeling."

"I'm feeling much better. I think it was like you said, just nerves."

"Good. I'm glad to hear it. I'll see you tonight, then?"

"Five-thirty. And Lynn . . . thanks for last night."

Lynn smiled as she hung up the receiver. She had to admit that she had actually heard those words quite often over the last year, but in an entirely different context. She leaned her elbows on the counter and imagined Chris lying in her bed with just a sheet covering her body, her tousled head of hair covering the soft pillow, a soft smile on her lips . . . Suddenly Lynn's thoughts snapped back to the condoms she had discovered. *Damn, the way a mind can bring you back to reality in a matter of seconds!*

Standing straight, Lynn ran her fingers through her hair. Reaching in her pocket for the customer bills within, she tried to concentrate on the tickets before her. Which ones needed to be rung up? It was no use—her mind kept going back to her daydream. The pale green sheet rising and falling with Chris's breathing. Lynn shook her head and repeated to herself—*condoms, condoms, condoms.* Maybe Matt was right. She was getting too involved.

Chris arrived at the house at five-thirty sharp and knocked on the front door. Lynn swung the door open and reviewed the lean legs which were swallowed up in jogging shorts at one end and short socks and tennis shoes at the other. Chris was somewhat more casual in attire this evening than she had been before.

"Hi there!"

"Hi! Long time no see!" Chris chuckled as she entered.

"Matt just called and said that he was going to have to work late. I hope you don't mind just hanging out with me for a while."

"How late?" Chris exclaimed. "I was going to call it an early night so I could go home and study for my test tomorrow!"

"Oh, sorry, I didn't ask how late."

"Great. Doesn't he realize that I have another life? I mean, I can't spend all my time on this little charade of his!" Chris quipped.

Lynn stepped back, not knowing what triggered this attitude.

"I'm sorry," Chris apologized. "I'm just stressed. I am just so unprepared for this test. It's not anything that's your fault."

"Okay, how about this. Let's call in for a pizza, and while we wait for delivery, if you feel like it, we can go for a run to relieve some of that stress."

"I would like to, but I'll get sweaty, and I don't have any other clothes with me."

"No problem, I'll find something for you to wear. What kind of pizza do you want?"

"Combination is fine with me."

Lynn called in the pizza and quickly changed her clothes.

"Let's go!" Lynn walked to the sliding glass door and slid it open. "Perfect weather for running."

They went down the stairs off of the deck and began jogging out to the water's edge. The beach was empty and there was a cool breeze coming off of the water.

"So, I set my watch alarm to go off when we need to turn around, if you need to turn around before then, just tell me," Lynn said.

"You mean if I get tired before you do?" Chris smiled.

"Well, I do this every day, I'm probably more used to running on the sand than you are."

"We'll see who gets tired first!" Chris took off in a sprint down the beach.

Oh man, I had to open my big mouth! Lynn said to herself as she took off after Chris.

Lynn caught up to Chris. "Okay, so you're in great shape. Take it easy on me, I'm a lot older than you."

"How much older?" Chris asked.

"Well, I'm guessing you're about twenty-two, so about ten years older."

"Wow! That old!" Chris looked over at Lynn with wide eyes, then smiled and continued, "You guessed wrong. I'm twenty-six, it's just taken a long time for me to get through school. I've gotten student loans, but I've still had to work full time during the summers to be able to support myself throughout the school year."

"What kind of jobs have you had?"

"Usually I get a job as a trainer at a gym." Chris smiled at Lynn and took off in a quick sprint.

No wonder she was in such great shape. Lynn groaned. "You little con woman! And I was trying to be nice about the sand and all!" She laughed and took off after her again.

"Ouch!" Lynn cried out, stopped in her tracks, and leaned over to massage her leg.

"What! What's the matter?" Chris called out from down the beach.

"I think I pulled something!"

Chris jogged back to Lynn, stopped, and put her hand on Lynn's shoulder. "Are you okay?"

Suddenly Lynn stood straight up, grabbed Chris by the shoulders, and pushed her down into the water, which had come up behind her. "Now, I'm fine!" Lynn laughed.

"Oh really?" Chris reached up and pulled Lynn down beside her.

Both women were sitting in the water, laughing, when the timer on Lynn's watch went off.

Chris stood up. "Race you back to the house!" she cried, and sprinted off in the direction of the house.

Her competitive spirit is going to kill me, Lynn said to herself, as she once again raced after her. By running at full force, she reached the soft sand at the same time as Chris. Lynn would not let Chris beat her. They were neck in neck as they trod through the sand that seemed to pull at their feet. About fifteen feet from the house, all her energy gone, Chris moaned and slowed down.

Lynn, feeling her last kick of adrenaline, was able to reach the deck first. "Ha! Take that!" she cried out, then sank to her knees in the sand in exhaustion.

"You win. I admit it," Chris conceded. "You're in better shape than me!"

Lynn, not knowing if the muscles in her legs would even allow her to stand, puffed out, "I think we're about equal. If it hadn't been for that last spurt of adrenaline, it would have been a tie."

"Come on, you need to find me something to wear so I can get out of these clothes that are sticking to me." Chris offered her hand to Lynn and pulled her up out of the sand.

Indoors, Lynn pulled out an oversized T-shirt for Chris. "I don't think I have any shorts that will fit you. You can just wear this, and throw your clothes into the washer if you want. They should be dry by the time we finish eating."

Lynn took a quick shower and came out of the bathroom clad in only a towel. She bumped into Chris, already showered and wearing the XXX T-shirt. Suddenly, the words on the T-shirt "Make Love Not War" took on a whole new meaning to Lynn, and she once again found it necessary to repeat to herself—*she's straight, she's straight, she's straight.*

Lynn had let Chris use the bathroom connected to her room because she thought Chris would feel more comfortable there than showering in the guest bathroom. Chris slid on the T-shirt that Lynn loaned her and hoped it hid all the necessary parts. She was a little uncomfortable with the idea that she was totally nude underneath.

"Oh, excuse me!" she said, as she collided with Lynn as she walked out of Lynn's room. Chris felt her heart skip a beat when she saw that Lynn was covered only with a towel. Then she felt herself blush. *What was that about?* she asked herself. *It's just another woman.* She had seen plenty of women with and without towels, especially during her job at the gym.

"Sorry, I need to grab something to wear."

Trying to cover for how uncomfortable she felt, Chris asked, "Do you have a hair dryer somewhere? I'd like to dry my hair."

"Sure, in the top right-hand drawer. Help yourself," Lynn answered, and pulled out a pair of shorts and a T-shirt.

"Thanks." Chris walked back into the bathroom, pulled out the hair dryer, and proceeded to dry her hair.

Lynn walked into the living room just as Matt was opening the front door, carrying the pizza that had just been delivered.

"I guess we're having pizza for dinner?" Matt asked sarcastically. "Where's Chris?"

"She just got out of the shower. She'll be out in a minute."

Just then, Chris walked into the living room wearing only the borrowed T-shirt. Looking at Lynn, who still had wet hair, Matt asked suspiciously, "What's going on here Lynn?"

Lynn, rolling her eyes with disgust, replied, "What do you think?" Not getting an immediate answer, she crossed her arms over her chest. "We went for a run. Chris threw her clothes in the washer, and I loaned her a T-shirt. Is that okay, Matt?" She threw her arms in the air. "God, Matt! I gave you my word!" Taking the pizza from his hands, she walked into the kitchen. "Chris, your clothes are done, I'll throw them in the dryer for you."

Not really understanding the exchange that had taken place, Chris called back, "Thanks!" Then turning to Matt, she gave him a look of confusion.

"Honey, I'm home?" Matt said to Chris, trying to look innocent. "I think it's my turn to take a shower," he said as he slunk down the hall.

"Come and get your pizza!" Lynn called from the kitchen.

"What was all that about?" Chris asked in regards to the former conversation.

"Don't worry about it. You want beer, wine, or soda?" Lynn asked as she opened the refrigerator.

"Better make it soda if I'm going to get any studying done," Chris answered. "What time is it, anyway?" she asked as she looked around the kitchen for a clock.

"You've got plenty of time," Lynn replied. "What class are you studying for?"

"Kinetics. I have a whole bunch of flash cards made up, I just need to go through them over and over again."

"Can I help? I mean if you have your materials with you?" Lynn asked.

"Really? That would be great, if it's not too much trouble!" Chris cut some pizza and placed it on her plate. "I'll go out to my car and get my stuff . . ." Then, looking at her outfit, she said, "Would you mind getting it out of my car? I feel a little indecent."

Lynn picked up her plate and their drinks. "No problem, what am I looking for?"

"Just the backpack," Chris answered as she took her plate and followed Lynn into the living room. She grabbed her keys off the entry table and handed them to Lynn. "Thanks again."

For the next hour, between bites of pizza, Lynn quizzed Chris off of the flash cards. Matt finished his shower, served himself some pizza, plopped down on the couch, and proceeded to flip through channels with the remote control.

"Excuse me, can't you tell that Chris is trying to study?" Lynn quipped.

"I'm sorry, is this disturbing your concentration?" Matt questioned.

"It's okay, I probably should be going anyway . . ." Chris said as she started gathering her materials together.

"No, we're not finished with your flash cards, we can just go into the bedroom . . ." Lynn, raising her eyebrows, said sarcastically while looking at Matt.

"No! I'm turning it off, I'm turning it off!" Matt glared, then flipped the television off, threw the remote back on the table, and lay down on the couch.

Lynn couldn't believe that he didn't trust her. "Now, where were we?"

The two women continued until they heard a loud snore coming from the couch. Turning, they found Matt fast asleep. Trying not to giggle, Lynn whispered, "Are you sure you want to marry this man?"

Chris shook her head no and smiled. "I've heard much worse, believe me. One guy I dated, I swear, the walls were going to cave in!"

Lynn, taken aback at realizing that Chris had a sex life, tried to recover. "Guys aren't the only ones who snore. I thought one woman was going to suck the sheets right off the bed!"

Chris laughed nervously. She wanted the picture going through her mind to vanish. She got up from the couch and turned away. "Well, I really should be going. Thanks for all of your help."

Helping collect all of the books strewn around the couch, Lynn looked up and saw the curve of Chris's nipples through the white shirt. Feeling a burning sensation below her belly, she stood and walked briskly out of the room. "I'll get your clothes from the dryer!" she called back.

Chris was anxious to get back into her clothes. All evening, she had felt her nipples rubbing against the cotton material. She was sure that they were taut because she was a little chilly; at least she hoped that's what it was.

"Here you go, still nice and warm." Lynn was also anxious for Chris to get back into her clothes. It seemed that it was all Lynn could do to keep from looking at Chris's breasts.

Chris changed and picked up her backpack. "Well, I guess tonight was a bust, I mean for me and Matt. Apologize to him for me, will you?" Just then Matt let out a tremendous snore. Chris smiled and looked at Lynn, who was also smiling. "I guess we'll have to cram tomorrow night, since it's the last night before his parents arrive. I'll be here around five-thirty again." Chris backed away from the intense eye contact between her and Lynn. "Good night."

"Good night," Lynn said and watched as Chris climbed into her vehicle. Closing the door, Lynn walked directly to the bathroom and turned the cold water on full blast.

Chris drove home with her windows wide open. She needed the cool breeze hitting her face. She was enjoying the preparation for this charade more than she thought she would. Or was it just the company that she was enjoying? Shaking off the feeling, she pulled into her parking space and lugged her backpack up the stairs to her apartment. Once she had settled in, she opened her backpack in preparation for another hour or so of studying. She reached in to pull out her flash cards and felt something wrapped in foil. Retrieving the package, she found several pieces of leftover pizza. She smiled when she read the note affixed to the wrapping. "Just in case you need a midnight snack!" was written in Lynn's handwriting, and, "Good luck on your test, I know you'll do great!" Chris leaned back on her couch. She hadn't felt this good in a long time.

Chapter Six

"Okay, I'm ready for another game of Scrabble!" Chris said as soon as she entered the doorway the following day.

"Great! Dinner is ready, so we can play while we're eating," Matt answered, and then whispered, "Lynn made her chili verde burritos. I just wanted to warn you, before you take the first bite, sometimes they're extremely hot, spicy hot."

"Cool, I love hot and spicy food."

"Not me, it gives me heartburn. There, that's something my fiancée would know."

Lynn popped her head around the corner of the kitchen. "Hi! Grab what you want to drink and head out to the deck."

When they were all seated at the table, Matt just sat, staring at the burrito in front of him.

"Matt's a real wimp when it comes to spicy foods. I hope you're not!" Lynn said to Chris.

"I love hot things! The hotter the better!" Chris popped her first bite into her mouth.

Lynn watched as Chris chewed and swallowed. "Well?"

"Delicious! Come on Matt, dig in, they're not that hot!" Chris teased.

Matt cut a small bite and tested it with his tongue before slowly putting the food into his mouth. His face turned red. He swallowed, and immediately drank his entire glass of water. "I can see this is going to take more than water," he choked out.

Standing, he went back into the kitchen and returned with a gallon of milk. The women laughed and proceeded to dig into the burritos.

"Hey, how did your test go today?" Lynn asked Chris.

"Great. Thanks for the help. And the care package." Chris smiled at Lynn.

Recovering from his choking attack, Matt set up the game board, picked his first set of letters, and offered the remainder for Chris's choice.

"Too bad we're not playing for points!" Matt said as he lay down all seven of his letters.

FRIENDS. "I was thinking maybe you should know something about my friends. Lynn thought that I'd better tell a couple of them what was going on, in case we run into them. My best friends are Pete and Jeff—"

"Jeff's the one with the big mouth," Lynn interrupted.

Matt turned to Chris. "Obviously, Lynn doesn't get along with Jeff. He is a bit obnoxious at times, but he has a good heart. Then there's Pete, I've known him since I was in grammar school."

"Well, I don't have any friends dating back to grammar school." Chris paused. "All of my friends have come from the university and the little odd jobs I've picked up here and there. Although none of them are extremely close, a day doesn't go by that I don't get a call to go do this or go do that. I really have to limit my time due to all the studying that's required of me." Chris stopped. She was rambling. She always seemed to ramble when she was stretching the truth. However, this truth seemed much more pleasant than reality.

Chris remembered all of the photographs arranged on the mantel inside. The two people before her had no shortage of friends.

The photographs led her to lay down the next word, VACATION. "Tell me about some of the places that the pictures in your living room are from."

"Oh," Lynn answered instead of Matt. "Most of those were just taken around here. Except for the one in the snow. Several of us drove up to Yosemite for a week. We skied, we snowboarded . . . that picture in there is our attempt at making a snowperson." She finished her story through her laughter, "We couldn't quite agree on the gender!"

"But my favorite vacation . . . hmm . . . oooh . . ." Matt smiled. "That time I went to Acapulco with Doug . . . skinny-dipping in the ocean . . ."

"Hey, we don't need all of the details! And if you mention to your parents that you went with Doug, you better throw in that you picked up a couple of senoritas!" Lynn laughed.

Chris nodded in agreement. When the laughter subsided, Lynn and Matt expected her response.

"I can't really say that I've been on a true vacation. We lived so many exotic places. They all started out feeling like a vacation, but after a while they all turned into . . . just regular day-to-day life."

Chris groaned when she saw the next word that Matt put on the board. EMBARASS, off of the "R" in FRIENDS. She knew that it was misspelled, but it wasn't a real game anyway. Lynn, however, felt it her duty to call it to his attention. Matt gave her a dirty look and motioned for Chris to relate her story.

Shifting in her chair, Chris chose one of her many embarrassing moments. "I guess it would be the time I got caught sneaking into army housing after curfew."

"What was so embarrassing about that?" Matt questioned.

"It kind of turned out not to be my house," Chris admitted. "You know all of those houses looked exactly the same—especially after smoking a few joints."

Lynn laughed. Matt looked irritated. "I thought you said you don't use drugs!"

"Oh, come on! Everyone experiments during their teenage years." Then placing her hand over her heart, she promised, "I don't touch the stuff anymore."

Matt didn't look convinced but shrugged it off and relayed his story about the time that he made a pass at a straight man.

"Yeah," Lynn broke in. "That turned out to be one of my most embarrassing moments too!"

Chris looked confused. "How so?"

"It turned out the man that I thought was giving me the eye, was actually giving Lynn the eye," Matt said sheepishly.

"After the man rejected Matt's advance, while I was in the ladies' room, by the way, he came on to me," Lynn explained. "Not knowing what Matt had done, I made a big scene at how he was making a pass at me, right in front of my boyfriend."

Matt continued the story. "The man proceeded to tell Lynn about what I had said to him, and then told her that she should leave me and join him."

"Needless to say, we had to come clean. By this time, the entire restaurant had overheard the conversation. The man wasn't too happy with us." Lynn mumbled, "I still think he was the one that broke my windshield that night."

"Just another story about my unluckiness with men," Matt whined. "If they don't want to hook up with Lynn, they want to hook up with the guy next to me . . ."

"Hey, just another story of Matt's bad judge of character!" Lynn said sarcastically.

Chris felt the conversation turning into an argument and focused on her tiles before her. She smiled because earlier that day she had thought long and hard, trying to make a mental list of items to get revenge for some of the items that Matt had asked of her the other night. She laid down the letters SEX. Turning toward Matt, she asked, "How many guys have you slept with?"

"Why do you need to know how many guys I've slept with?" He looked up at Chris, expecting an answer.

"It just tells me about your character, you know, if you've been the promiscuous type, or if you've stayed at home alone, waiting for that one special person," Chris replied.

Matt shook his head again, then smiled. "You're answering this one first. How many guys have you slept with?"

Chris leaned back in her chair. "Let's just say more than I should have."

"I don't think that's a clear enough answer," Matt teased.

"Okay, more than ten and less than fifty," Chris teased back.

"Okay, that's a little less vague." He smiled and continued, "I guess I'm more inexperienced, I'll say less than ten."

Lynn laughed. "You should say less than five!"

"Okay, Miss Smarty Pants, you answer the question!" he snapped.

"I'd have to stick with the 'more than ten, less than fifty' answer," Lynn replied.

"Ha! Maybe in the last six months!" Matt exclaimed.

Lynn looked at Chris. "He's exaggerating just a little!" She explained, "He's just jealous because he doesn't get it as often as I do."

Feeling a little hot under the collar, Matt said sarcastically, "Why should I? I'm not the one trying to break Susan's record!"

Lynn glared at Matt. "You know, you can be a real bastard sometimes." Lynn felt the tears welling up in her eyes and quickly excused herself. "I believe that's my cue to leave," she said as she turned away and rushed into the house.

Chris looked at Matt. This was another conversation that she did not understand. She had seen the tears in Lynn's eyes. "What . . . ?"

Matt put his head in his hands and ran his fingers through his hair as his face reddened. "Shit!" he exclaimed. "Here's one of my flaws. I take things too far, I just don't know when to stop." He looked up at Chris, then looked through the glass door, just as they heard the front door slam. The sound made Matt wince; he stood up, walked over to the railing, and leaned on it as if for support.

"Matt, what was . . . who's Susan?" Chris asked.

"Someone that hurt Lynn really bad."

"What happened?"

"I'm sorry, I don't think that it's my place to tell you. You can ask Lynn sometime." Matt's expression softened. "All I can tell you is that a broken heart must be the worst thing to carry around with you, day after day." He sat down across the table from Chris and began, "My last serious boyfriend dumped me after a couple of months, and I thought that I was going to die at the time, but I eventually got over it." Matt shook his head and ran his fingers through his hair again before continuing, "But I don't know if Lynn will ever allow herself to really *feel* anything again." He stopped and looked into Chris's eyes. "You know, she has all of these one-night stands, just so that she can leave it behind in the morning. I mean she's honest with the women, she never leads them on. She just walks away in the morning." After a moment he asked, "Would you like to hear my diagnosis?"

"Oh, please," Chris said sarcastically, as if she had a choice.

"I think Lynn thinks that the breakup was her fault. That she couldn't keep Susan satisfied, and therefore drove her to promiscuity." Matt paused and then continued, "In some way I think that Lynn is sleeping around to make up for that."

Chris looked confused. "How so?"

"You know, trying to satisfy other women because she couldn't keep Susan satisfied."

Chris shrugged, not wanting to make a quick judgment without all the details.

Matt began again, "Or, it's like I stupidly said before, Lynn is just trying to get even with Susan by sleeping with more women." Then finally stopping, he admitted, "I don't know, I'm just a mechanic!"

They sat in silence for some time. Chris had never been hurt like that. She thought back over her relationships. She had never really cared that deeply about any of the men that she had been with. The truth was, she hadn't really cared for them at all. She had seen the tears in Lynn's eyes. Lynn's tough exterior hadn't shown any of the pain before, yet the mere mention of Susan's name had sent her spinning. What would it be like to be that devastated over someone?

Matt broke the silence. "Well, I guess we need to clean up the dishes." He stood and started collecting the plates. "Would the future Mrs. Matt McKinley like to rinse or load the dishwasher?"

"Oh, I see the honeymoon is over already!" Chris tried to lighten the mood. "I'll rinse."

Matt and Chris rinsed the dishes, loaded the dishwasher, and cleaned the counters. When all was finished, Matt looked at the time. "You know, I could really use a drink, and Lynn should be at the bar by now. Would you mind dropping by there so that I can apologize? I feel like a real jerk."

"I could really use a drink too. By tomorrow at this time I'll officially be engaged, you know."

"Did you bring a change of clothes so that you can spend the night tonight, like we discussed on the phone today? I just think it will be a lot easier than you having to get home late tonight and then having to get up early in the morning just to drive back."

"Yeah, my stuff is in my car, or rather, your car." Chris smiled.

Entering the bar, Chris could see that Matt had told the truth, a lot of people came out on Thursday nights. The music was loud, and the voices straining to rise above it were even louder.

"You might want to grab onto my hand, I wouldn't want you to get lost in this crowd," Matt shouted to Chris.

Chris agreed and latched onto his hand, which pulled her through the wall-to-wall bodies, mostly women, to the bar, where he screamed out his order. The bartender nodded and came back with two beers and shook her head when he offered her money. Matt grabbed the bottles and said something to the bartender that made her laugh.

"They never let me pay for drinks, they always get put on

Lynn's tab. I told her that I didn't know if I liked being a kept man!" Matt laughed.

He grabbed Chris's hand again and led her through to the seating area. "Luckily not too many people actually like to sit down." He motioned for her to have a seat. "I'll be right back. Don't pick up any women while I'm gone!" he kidded.

Matt headed through the dancing crowd to the front of the stage. He reached up and pulled on the bottom of Lynn's jeans. Lynn looked down and showed surprise that Matt was there. She waited until her vocal was finished, then leaned down while Matt yelled in her ear. She signaled for him to wait a minute by raising her index finger, and sang a few more lines into the microphone before ending the song. Turning, she motioned for the band to take five, jumped down from the stage, and followed Matt to the side of the stage. Chris watched as Matt held Lynn's hands in his, looked Lynn in the eyes, and apologized. She couldn't see what was said exactly, by Matt, or by Lynn who responded to his apology, but she knew when the two embraced that all was forgiven. Lynn wiped her eyes and Chris knew when Matt led her to what must have been the dressing room, off the side of the stage, that Lynn was still in pain.

Matt exited the dressing room and called one of the band members to the side of the stage. The woman listened to Matt, nodded, and instructed the band to start playing. Matt walked back toward the table as this woman, obviously the other vocalist, began singing.

"She'll be okay in a minute," he said as he pulled out a chair and sat down.

"You weren't kidding when you said this place was busy on Thursday nights. If it's this packed tonight, what does it look like on Friday and Saturday nights?" Chris asked.

"Not too much more crowded than this, there wouldn't be room! This is the only gay bar in this area. There's another bar down the highway, but it's mostly men. I don't really like it, too much of a meat market for me. I don't really like meeting men in bars."

Just then, Chris saw a nice-looking man approaching their table. He placed his hand on Matt's shoulder and said something in his ear. Matt leaned over to Chris. "Do you mind if I dance with him?"

Chris smiled. "I thought that you didn't like meeting men in bars?"

"True, but there's nothing wrong with an innocent dance, right?" Matt answered.

She nodded. "No problem, I'll be fine," then watched as the man led Matt to the dance floor.

Chris found herself looking around. It was hard to believe that all these women, very attractive women, were gay. A chair slid out and Chris turned to find a woman sitting beside her.

"Hi, you're new around here, aren't you?" she asked Chris, placing her arm around the back of Chris's chair.

"Umm . . . I'm . . ." Chris didn't know quite what to say. Just then, another woman came around the back of their chairs and scooted the occupied chair beside Chris away from the table. The woman was like an amazon, muscles rippling from every exposed area on her body.

The woman spoke to the seated woman. "Later, Trish," was all she had to say. The seated woman stood, looked at Chris, shrugged, and walked away.

"Hi, I'm Samantha. My friends call me Sam," she said as she extended her hand to Chris.

Chris shook it and replied, "Look, I'm just here with a friend . . ."

Sam smiled. "I know, Lynn told me to keep you company while Matt was away from the table. Chris, right?"

Chris looked up toward the stage at Lynn and met Lynn's eyes. Lynn saluted her with her beer bottle. Chris picked up her bottle, smiled, and saluted back. Then realizing that she had ignored the question posed to her, she responded, "Right. Nice to meet you. That was nice of Lynn."

"Yeah, she's great. You must be pretty great too, to be helping Matt out like this," Sam said, and seeing the worried look on Chris's face, continued, "Don't worry, I won't let the secret out, I'm trustworthy." Sam put her hand on her forehead as if to salute Chris, then smiled and looked at the stage.

Chris's eyes wandered back up to the stage area and watched as Lynn and the other vocalist shared a microphone. The two looked cozy, Chris thought to herself. The other vocalist turned with her back to Lynn and started playing a guitar riff. Lynn stepped behind her and molding their bodies, the two moved together, very seductively. Chris turned away. For some reason this really bothered her.

"Who's that?" Chris asked Sam, nodding with her chin toward the action taking place on the stage.

Sam smiled. "That's Nikki."

Chris tried to look unconcerned. "Do they have a thing going or something?"

Sam, still watching the stage, replied, "No way, that's just an act. They get carried away up there. Lynn won't have anything to do with her offstage. Nikki is 'bi.' Lynn won't have anything to do with that."

Chris nodded. It sure seemed real.

The song ended and Matt found his way back to the table.

"Hey, Sam. You better watch out, you're starting to look more buff than me!" Matt smiled and curled his arm to show his bicep. Laughing, he poked at his arm with his finger. "I know it's here somewhere!"

"That's okay, Matt." Sam's eyes were occupied on something over his shoulder. "I don't think it bothers that guy over there, you know, the one you were dancing with."

Matt turned around to catch the man looking his way, then swiftly turned back toward the women with embarrassment.

"What's his name?" Chris teased.

"Yeah, and did you get his phone number?" Sam joined in.

"His name is Paul," Matt gushed. "And he took *my* phone number!"

The three spent the rest of the evening talking and laughing, broken only by the band breaks when Lynn joined them. At midnight, Matt and Chris said good-bye to Sam and found their way home.

Lynn unlocked the door, trying to be quiet. She looked at her watch: two a.m. Walking into the living room, she wondered if she should try and sleep for a couple of hours, or just find a good movie to watch before leaving for the restaurant. Through the dim light, she saw a bundle on the couch. On closer look, she realized it was Chris, snuggled up in a blanket. *I can't believe that Matt is having her sleep on the couch,* she thought to herself, *he couldn't give up his bed?* Shaking her head, Lynn tiptoed down the hall, into her room, turned on the bedside lamp, and changed the sheets on her bed. "Chris needs a good night's sleep tonight of all nights," she caught herself saying out loud. She knew that tomorrow would be a very stressful day for Chris. Lynn grabbed some clothes, then went back into the living room and gently shook Chris's arm.

"Chris," she said softly. "Chris."

Chris slowly opened her eyes. "Is it morning already?" she asked.

"No, come on, you're going to sleep in my bed."

Chris looked at Lynn with a hint of confusion.

"Come on, you need a good night's sleep. I changed the sheets on my bed. I'll sleep on the couch." Lynn helped Chris up from her crumpled position and led her down the hall. Chris climbed between the sheets and rested her head on the pillow.

"Thanks," Chris whispered before closing her eyes and immediately falling back asleep.

Lynn stood there for a moment, watching Chris's steady breathing. Then for some reason, before she could catch herself, she leaned over and softly kissed Chris's forehead. Realizing what she had done, she quickly backed away. Watching to see if she had woken Chris, she felt her heart melt as Chris sighed and faintly smiled in her sleep.

For a moment, Lynn thought Chris reminded her of a young

child. But as she gazed further, down to the firm breasts barely contained in the white cloth, then to the tan legs curled up in such a way to be daring Lynn to feel the smoothness of the skin, her lower extremities reminded her that Chris was indeed a woman.

Lynn tiptoed out of the bedroom and closed the door. Coffee, she needed coffee, and another cold shower. She wandered into the kitchen and started the coffeemaker. Picking up her clothes, she quietly entered the guest bathroom and shut the door. She peeled off her sweaty clothes and turned the shower faucet on. Letting the cool water run on her head and down her body, she examined the feelings going on inside of her. What exactly was she feeling for Chris? And more importantly, how could she push it away? She pictured Chris's faint smile just moments ago. Once again, she repeated to herself—*she's straight, she's straight, she's straight.*

Lynn turned off the shower, dried off, and got dressed. Returning to the kitchen, she poured herself a mug of coffee and wandered back into the living room where she plopped down on the couch. She could still smell Chris's perfume in the air. She flipped on the television and searched through the channels. Sipping on her coffee, she settled on a *Mary Tyler Moore* marathon on TV Land. At five o'clock, and a pot of coffee later, she headed out the door to the restaurant. She was exhausted, and—after smelling Chris's perfume for the past few hours—frustrated.

Chapter Seven

"Chris, are you awake?" Matt's voice boomed through the bedroom door. "I thought maybe we could grab some breakfast before we started out on our adventure." Chris rolled over, not quite remembering how she had gotten into Lynn's bed. Focusing, she remembered being woken up on the couch, climbing in between the cool sheets, Lynn's soft voice in the dark. And then she saw them. There on the bedside table sat a vase full of daisies. Chris smiled.

Realizing that she hadn't answered Matt's question, she quickly replied, "Sure, give me a half an hour to shower and dress. I'm starving!"

A half an hour later, Chris emerged from the bedroom, wearing a pair of white shorts and a lavender sleeveless shirt.

"Do I look all right? I wasn't sure what you wanted me to wear," Chris said to Matt, who was pacing in the living room.

"You look great. Everything is going to be just fine, don't you think?" Matt asked for reassurance.

"Yes, I think everything is going to be fine. I really am going to try my best, Matt."

"I know you will. I'm just really worried about making a mistake."

Chris grabbed her purse and opened the door. "Well, maybe you'll feel better with a full stomach."

Matt followed her out the door and walked to the driver's-side door.

"Uh-hum." Chris cleared her throat. "If we're going to make this real, you'd better be opening my car door!"

Matt rushed over to the passenger-side door, unlocked it, and opened it for Chris. "See, I think we needed more time . . ."

Chris smiled and slid in so that she was seated in the middle of the seat, where a woman would sit if driving with her boyfriend. "I'll try and remind you of the little things, now get in!"

Matt walked around to his door and slid behind the wheel. He started the ignition, put the car into drive, and slowly pushed against the gas pedal. "Here we go!" he said, trying to sound calm, while his stomach did flip-flops all the way down the road.

Matt and Chris walked into the diner and sat down at a booth.

"Well, good morning!" Chris looked up from the menu to find Lynn's smile.

"Good? I don't know about good, I mean this could be the beginning of the end . . ." Matt started.

Lynn looked at Matt and then over at Chris. "I can see that he's a little nervous. Want coffee?"

"A *little* nervous? Quite an understatement!" Chris laughed. "Yes, coffee please, and definitely decaf for Matt. He's driving me crazy already!"

"I only have decaf to offer, I already drank all the heavy stuff trying to keep my eyelids open!" Lynn laughed and walked behind the counter.

"By the way, thanks for the daisies, they really calmed my nerves this morning," Chris said to Matt.

Matt looked confused. "Daisies?"

Chris examined Matt's face. "Never mind," she mumbled, realizing that he wasn't the one who had left the daisies for her. It must have been Lynn. *That was really sweet*, she thought.

Chris began examining the menu again, just to be interrupted for the second time.

"Hey, you two don't look like you're in love!" commented another waitress standing in front of their table.

"Hey, Betty. I guess Lynn clued you in on this little charade, huh?" Matt answered.

"Yeah, she was afraid that you'd come in with your parents and I'd say something inappropriate about you being with a woman and all." Betty then smiled, blew a tiny bubble with her gum, and pulled it back into her mouth. "Really though, you guys need to be sitting closer, holding hands or something, or you'll never fool your folks."

"Thanks Betty, good advice," Matt said politely.

"Yeah, it is good advice," Lynn said as she slipped in with the coffeepot and poured the two cups of coffee. "You didn't really practice any of that."

"Are you trying to make me more nervous, because you're doing a good job at it," Matt said sarcastically while placing his menu on the table.

"Sorry. What do you guys want? The regular, Matt?"

Matt nodded his head and turned to Chris. "Everything is great here. What do you want, eggs?"

Lynn shook her head. "Haven't you listened to a word she's said? She doesn't like eggs. How about some waffles?"

"That sounds good, and some bacon, well done, please," Chris answered, feeling uneasy about treating Lynn as a waitress.

Lynn returned in a few minutes with their breakfasts.

"God, I'm glad you're back. I was tired of watching Matt roll up pieces of his napkin into little balls!" Chris said.

"Just one of his little quirky habits that made you fall in love with him, huh?" Lynn chuckled. Matt rolled his eyes and took his first bite.

"You mind if I take a break with you guys?" Lynn asked as she slid in beside Matt with her cup of coffee.

"Not at all. Thanks for the bed last night, I really slept well."

Lynn turned to Matt and slapped his arm. "I can't believe that you didn't offer her your bed! I don't know if I'd marry this man!" She smiled at Chris.

"Well, we know that you wouldn't marry this man," Chris said sarcastically, "or any man for that matter!"

Matt laughed. Lynn was taken aback, and then smiled. She was glad that Chris was finally feeling comfortable enough to tease back.

"Hey, Lynn! Where's our food?" a man yelled from another table.

Lynn turned to look for the voice, then yelled, "Hold your shorts, Andy, Betty's getting your food!" After searching the diner and not finding Betty, she stood. "I'll be back in a minute."

Lynn walked over to the counter, retrieved the plates of food, and sauntered over to the men. "You boys owe me one!" she kidded. The men chuckled and Andy reached over to pinch Lynn's butt. "Yeah, I'll give you one!"

Lynn swiftly took the man's wrist and bent it backward, bringing Andy halfway off his chair. "Do I need to teach you a lesson about manners again, Andy?" she said with a serious look on her face.

"No, ma'am," Andy said, wincing with pain.

Lynn released her grip, smiled, and tousled the man's hair. "I didn't think so," she said as she walked away from the table, leaving his buddies laughing.

Chris watched in amazement, then smiled when Lynn caught her gaze. "Remind me that I don't ever want to be on your bad side!" Chris laughed.

"They just caught me on a bad day is all. I have no patience for little boys today," Lynn replied.

She slid back into the booth beside Matt. "Anything else I can get you guys?"

"Yeah, more coffee," Matt complained.

"Sorry! I wouldn't want to lose my extraordinary tip!" Lynn rolled her eyes, walked over, grabbed the coffeepot, and filled their cups. "I can't wait to fall into bed, or rather on top of the bed, since it seems like Matt, the gentleman that he is, isn't going to offer you his bed. You are going to stay at the house, aren't you?"

Matt looked at Chris. "You know, it probably wouldn't be a bad idea for you to stay the whole week, that is, if you don't mind."

Chris shrugged. "I'll have to pick up a few more things from my apartment, and you guys will have to remember that I have to study."

"Yes, dear," the two said in unison and then made motions like they were crossing their hearts.

Several customers walked in the door of the diner. "Looks like it's back to work!" Lynn stopped and looked into Matt's eyes. "You're going to do fine, I really believe that. And if you don't, and your parents disown you, which I seriously doubt, just remember, you will always be a part of my family." Then she was off to seat the customers.

Since Matt was obviously not in the mood for conversation, Chris found herself observing Lynn as she finished her breakfast. She sure was putting on a good act for being so tired, laughing and joking with the three women at the next table. Of course, they were nice-looking women, she may be flirting, Chris thought to herself. Chris's suspicions were confirmed when the women left.

Lynn rushed past Matt and Chris's table. "Hmmm, a phone number left on a napkin, what in the world could that mean?" she teased and pocketed the piece of paper.

Chris felt a twinge. Could it be jealousy? No, she was sure it was just nervousness. Earlier this week it had been stress, now it was nervousness, she convinced herself.

"You ready to go? We should probably head on over to the airport," Matt moaned as if going to face a firing squad.

Chris slid out of the booth, stepped over to Matt, and offered her hand as he slid out. "Come on, relax, this is going to be fun!"

Matt took her hand in his, waved good-bye to Lynn, and the two made their way to the door.

"Now that's more like it! Now it looks like you at least like each other!" Betty called across the restaurant, "Good luck, sweetie!"

Matt smiled at Betty, opened the door for Chris, and followed her out the door. They were on their way.

"You'd never know Lynn was tired, huh?" Chris said, trying to break the unbearable tension within the vehicle.

"Yeah, Lynn's never too tired to flirt!" Matt smiled.

"Well, it looks like it paid off. How did she even know any of those women were gay? They didn't look gay to me."

"That's why they call it 'gaydar'!" Matt laughed.

"I mean, I guess not many of the women in the bar looked gay to me either. I just can't believe how crowded it was last night!"

Matt nodded as he weaved in and out of traffic.

"So, how many of those women at the bar do you think that Lynn has been with?"

Matt chuckled again. "God only knows! I don't know if Lynn even knows!"

Matt steered the car into the parking space at the airport and pushed the gearshift into park. Then he just sat there, silent. Chris slid out and walked around to the driver's side and opened the door. Matt turned toward her, his face white with worry. As he climbed out of the car, Chris took his hand. "Matt, take a deep breath. Anytime you feel a panic attack coming on, just squeeze my hand. I'll be right here."

They walked into the airport and strolled to the arrival gate. Matt squeezed her hand. "Your hand feels strange, so tiny and soft. I'm used to feeling a strong, masculine hand in mine." He took her other hand and looked into her eyes. "I don't know if I've told you lately how much I appreciate this. Thank you." Chris smiled and kissed him on the cheek.

"Okay you two, no making out in the airport!" the loud voice called from the gate. It came from a distinguished-looking man, his arm around an elegant-looking woman. Chris, realizing that these must be Matt's parents, squeezed the hand that was shaking in hers.

"Oh, Charles, this must be her!" the woman cried as she hugged Chris tightly. Then, realizing that she had ignored her son, she gave him a hug. She stepped back to take a look at the pair.

"Son," Charles said sternly, and offered his hand for his son to shake. Turning, he offered his hand to Chris. "And you must be . . ."

"Mom, Dad, this is Chris. Chris Newman."

"Chris." Charles shook Chris's hand.

"Mr. and Mrs. McKinley, it's nice to finally meet you. I've heard so much about you."

"Honey, call us Charles and Marie," Marie warmly suggested.

Chris nodded in agreement, then turned to Matt. "Honey, why don't we go locate their luggage?"

"Marie, why don't you go with them to get our luggage. I'll pick up the rental car and meet you out front," Charles said as he walked away.

"Okay, lead the way!" Marie said as she turned to Matt. Wedging her way between the two, Marie put her arms around both, and followed their lead. "Oh honey, you don't know how long we've been waiting for this day! Matt's our only child you know! We've felt so lucky to have him!"

Chris looked over at Matt and smiled. "Well, I feel pretty lucky to have him, too!"

The three stood waiting for the luggage to come down the ramp. Matt grabbed both bags and led them out to the loading area. Charles was just arriving with the rental car, a Mercedes. He popped the trunk and Matt lifted the baggage into the compartment.

"You want to follow us over to the hotel? We can grab some lunch and then I'm afraid these old bones need a nap," Charles said as he opened the door for Marie, who slid into the passenger seat.

"Oh yes, my tummy's rumbling! Can you imagine that they only gave us a sweet roll on the plane?" Marie complained.

Matt agreed to follow them to the hotel, then put his arm around Chris and led her toward their parking area.

"God, I don't think I can eat again!" Chris remarked.

"Sorry, I guess I didn't think things through very well," Matt answered.

"Oh well, now that I've caught my man, I don't need to worry about my girlish figure!" Chris said, trying to lighten the mood. It worked: Matt smiled.

Matt followed the rental car to the hotel, where the valet parked both cars. The three wandered around the lobby while Charles checked in.

"Just send our bags up to the room, we're going to grab a bite to eat," Charles instructed the desk clerk.

The two couples were seated on the patio, overlooking the ocean. Marie, with her hand settled on her chin, stared out over the water. "I know why you can't bear to leave here, Matthew, it's just so beautiful!" Then, turning, she asked, "Have you lived here all your life, Chris?"

"Actually, I've lived many places. Before my parents died, my dad was in the military, so we moved around a lot," Chris answered.

"A military brat, huh?" Charles chuckled. "We have a lot in common, young lady. I too was the product of the military system."

"That's what Matt has told me." Chris reached for her glass of water, took a sip, and continued, "What made you decide not to follow in your father's footsteps, into the army, that is?"

Matt smiled. Chris had led his dad into a conversation that could take up the rest of the afternoon. Which it did, through their lunch, through dessert, through what seemed like the tenth cup of coffee they had had today.

At a break in the conversation, Charles looked at his watch. "Well, I think it's time for that nap. Are we going to the club for dinner?"

"You bet, I already made reservations!" Matt replied.

"Lynn's coming too, I hope. It's been ages since we've seen her!" Marie said.

"Sure, I know she'd love to join us," Matt answered as the two couples separated in the lobby. "Meet you there at seven o'clock?"

"See you then, honey. Good-bye, Chris!" Marie called back.

"I didn't know Lynn was joining us tonight," Chris said as they waited for the valet to bring around their car.

"Yeah, she doesn't either," Matt replied.

Matt and Chris arrived back at the house after stopping by Chris's apartment. When they walked in, Lynn was flipping through the television channels.

"Hey, we thought you'd be passed out by now!" Matt joked.

Lynn looked exasperated. "I'm exhausted, I have a splitting headache, and I can't seem to go to sleep!" She paused. "But enough about me, how'd it go?"

"It actually went pretty good, thanks to Chris. She started dad talking about why he didn't go into the military," Matt answered.

Chris bowed and smiled. "His parents are really nice people. Frankly, I don't know what you were so nervous about."

"By the way, Lynn, my parents requested your presence at dinner tonight," Matt said, then bit his lip, afraid of her answer.

"Matt! I would, I really would, but, were you listening about, what, one minute ago when I said 'I'm exhausted, I have a splitting headache, and I can't seem to go to sleep'? Plus, I have to play a full night in"—she looked at her watch—"six hours?"

"Seven hours, it's Friday night. Come on Lynn, please?" he whined.

"Hey, I bet you're just really tight, let me give you a massage!" Chris offered.

"A massage?" Lynn remarked. *Just what I need, your hands all over my body, like that would make me relax*, she thought.

"I bet I can help you go to sleep. You know, a big part of physical therapy is massaging. I have great hands!" Chris pleaded.

"You have great hands?" Lynn smiled, looked at Matt, and winked.

"You could at least try it." Matt ignored the suggestive wink.

Against her better judgment, Lynn agreed.

"Come on, you can lie down on the bed," Chris suggested. She started down the hall. Lynn followed her reluctantly and lay face-down on the bed.

"Okay, just relax," Chris said softly as she began rubbing Lynn's back. "You know, this isn't going to work," she said as she got up and closed the door. "You need to take your shirt off. I can't do it through this material."

Lynn cringed. *First she wants to rub all over my body, now she wants to do it with my clothes off.* She added, *I feel another cold shower coming on.* Nevertheless, Lynn pulled her top off to reveal her bare skin. She was glad that she had already taken a shower.

Chris watched as Lynn pulled off her top and felt that sharp twinge again. Ignoring the feeling, she placed her hands on Lynn's bare back. She began softly pushing her thumbs into Lynn's back muscles. Lynn let out a moan, which made her smile. Chris felt like she was getting warm as she slowly let her fingers massage the firm muscles. Climbing off the bed, she turned on the fan in the corner of the room and positioned herself to begin again. Chris watched as small goose bumps rose from Lynn's tanned skin. The fan might be cooling Lynn, but it was doing nothing to relieve the heat Chris was feeling.

Lynn felt Chris's fingers against her bare skin, pushing, massaging, kneading her skin. Chris's fingers were on her back, but she felt them through every inch of her body. She had been glad when Chris turned on the fan, but now the cool air assisted in Chris's touch, sending even stronger sensations through her. She was trying to remain calm. *Pretend it's someone else, pretend it's a man,* she tried to convince herself. Little did she know that all the heat in the room was radiating not only from her body but from Chris's body, too.

Chris didn't know how much longer she could stand it. She was feeling hot, weak, and lightheaded. She could feel herself pulsating below. She tried to recover from the feeling by massaging up and down Lynn's arms, but then found herself kneading the skin on the tan legs. She felt possessed, like someone else had taken over her hands. She massaged farther and farther up the long legs, onto Lynn's buttocks. She had to stop. She had to stop now. The feeling was so unprofessional. She had done a lot of massages, but none made her feel like this. She pulled her hands away and watched as Lynn's back raised and lowered with her steady breathing. *Great, she's asleep, and I'm—could it be—turned on? Damn!* She tiptoed into the bathroom and splashed cold water on her face. Looking in the mirror, she searched the image to see if it was still the same reflection that had always stared back at her. She ran her hands over her face, down her neck, and over her breasts. She still looked the same, so what had changed?

Lynn felt the heat of Chris's hands as they roamed over her body. This didn't feel like an ordinary massage; it seemed that Chris was putting much more into it. She probably just didn't want to go out to dinner alone with Matt and his parents tonight. Lynn tried to disguise her heavy breathing as Chris made her way up her legs and kneaded her buttocks. It did feel good, but also bad . . . oh, so bad. Lynn ended up drifting off to sleep, repeating to herself—*she's straight, she's straight, she's straight.*

Lynn opened her eyes and slowly sat up. She did feel much better. Getting up, she pulled on her shirt as she wandered down the hall. Matt was relaxing on the couch watching some sci-fi movie.

"Where's Chris?" she asked, still rubbing her eyes.

"Right after you went to sleep, she went out for a run. I haven't seen her since," Matt answered.

Lynn looked at the clock; it was five-thirty. "Wasn't that like, two hours ago? And you haven't worried about her?" she accused as she headed over to the sliding glass door leading out onto the deck.

"She's a big girl," Matt replied, not moving a muscle.

Lynn slid open the door and stuck her head outside. There was Chris, sitting on the steps of the deck.

"Never mind, she's right here!" she called to Matt as she stepped out onto the wood. Crouching down, she reached out her hand to brush the hair away from Chris's face. "Hey, you okay?"

Chris looked down, then out to the waves crashing against the shore. "Sure, it was just so nice and peaceful out here." She looked at Lynn. "How are you feeling?"

"Better," Lynn answered, then added sarcastically, "Now I guess I have to go with you guys."

"Sorry." Chris chuckled at the hint of sarcasm. "What time is it?"

"Five-thirty. You need to start getting ready?" Lynn asked.

"No, you can go ahead, it only takes me about half an hour," she replied, again looking out at the water. "I'm enjoying myself out here."

"Are you sure you're okay?" Lynn prodded. "Did Matt do something?"

"No. Honest. I'll come inside in a few minutes," Chris answered and watched as Lynn stood, slid the glass door to one side, and then closed it behind her. How could she tell her that Matt wasn't the one that she was bothered with? How could she tell her that she was having feelings that she didn't understand? Chris let out a deep sigh and watched as the seagulls pranced around the sand. How easy their lives must be. Finally, she stood, brushed the sand off of her clothes, and went inside to prepare for the evening ahead.

The three drove up to the club, Matt and Chris in one vehicle, Lynn in another. The valets took their keys. Matt and Lynn looked at each other and chuckled as they were walking through the very ornate club doors. It always amused them the way the valets reacted about having to park their cars. The valets were used to the BMWs and Mercedes, and almost acted insulted when the two drove up in their beat-up old vehicles.

Before they had left, the three had discussed separating upon arrival. The women would pretend to use the facilities as Matt went on to the table. This way, Matt could have the little discussion with his parents about downplaying the wedding plans.

Matt stopped at the entrance to the restaurant, trying to locate the table where his parents were seated. Marie stood and waved politely. Matt walked through the maze and approached their table.

"Where's Chris and Lynn?" Marie asked, looking over Matt's shoulder for their whereabouts.

"They needed to use the restroom, and I thought this would be a good time for us to discuss something." Matt pulled out a chair, sat, and began as his parents listened attentively. "Please don't mention setting a wedding date to Chris. We've discussed it and she'd like to wait to set a date until after she's through with school."

"When will that be?" Charles asked.

"Well, it's complicated. There's her bachelor's degree and then some postgraduate work that has to be completed. I'm really not too sure. The important part is that there will be a wedding. It's just that it might be a little down the road." Matt tried not to sound nervous.

"Yes, that is the important thing, but—" Marie started.

"Mom, that is the important thing. She's got a lot on her mind right now, a lot of stress with school and all. Just please don't mention anything about the wedding date, or the wedding plans, for that matter," Matt pleaded.

"Well, we hadn't said anything about the wedding since we hadn't seen an engagement ring—" Marie started again.

Matt interrupted, "Just another stress that I didn't want to put her through right now. I'm just so happy that she said that she'd marry me, the ring will come later, when she decides she's ready."

"Well, I agree with her," Charles stated. "She's a smart girl and there's plenty of time for the other things after her career falls into place. If I'd had waited a little longer before your mother and I got married—"

Now Marie interrupted. "If we had waited any longer, I would have married someone else, Charles."

That announcement brought a round of silence at the table. Marie finally broke the stillness. "We'll do whatever you want, Matty, frankly, I'm just glad to see that you found someone." Marie looked over Matt's shoulder. "And here she is now!"

The seated family rose from their chairs, the parents making their way to Chris and then Lynn.

"Hello again," Marie said to Chris as they hugged. Turning to Lynn, she remarked, "Lynn, so glad to see you again!" then hugged her.

Charles reviewed Lynn. "Lynn, you're more beautiful than the last time I saw you. Looks like life is treating you well."

Lynn smiled. "I have no complaints," she said, then paused as if she was rethinking her comment. "Well, not many anyway!"

The five of them laughed and sat down, Matt taking Chris's cue to pull her chair out for her. The waiter arrived at the table with a bottle in an ice bucket.

"I hope you don't mind, I took the liberty of ordering champagne," Charles said, motioning for the waiter to open the bottle and pour five glasses.

"So, Lynn, what do you think of our Matty's girl?" Charles asked while the waiter poured champagne all around. It was obviously a rhetorical question, as he cleared his throat, raised his glass, and announced to the table, "Here's to Matt and Chris! And to Lynn, may you find someone as special someday!"

Lynn smiled and made eye contact with Chris. "I should be so lucky," she said directly to her and then clinked her glass against all the others. Chris, caught off guard by the sincerity of the look in Lynn's eyes, clinked her glass a little too hard, spilling the liquid onto the linen tablecloth. Recovering quickly, she laughed. "I just can't seem to hold my liquor!"

Minutes later the waiter returned to their table with a tray full of appetizers. "Oh, I ordered some of those fabulous little quiches!" said Marie excitedly as she took the dish from the waiter and proceeded to pass them around.

"Those look delicious!" Chris said, taking an appetizer from the plate.

Lynn looked worriedly at Matt, who was unresponsive. Lynn leaned over and whispered into Matt's ear, "Those have crab in them!"

84

Matt looked at Lynn, totally clueless. Lynn leaned over and whispered again, "Chris is allergic to shellfish!"

Matt caught Chris's hand, just as Chris was about to take a bite of the appetizer. "Honey, I believe that contains crab in the mixture." Then looking at his parents, he explained, "She's allergic to shellfish, swells up like a balloon. Wouldn't want to spend your first night in town at the hospital, would we?" he joked.

Chris put the appetizer down immediately and gave a relieved look at Lynn. *I'm glad she remembered*, she thought. She was obviously paying more attention to details about Chris's life than Matt was. Matt was just nervous, she tried to convince herself.

The group ordered and ate leisurely, enjoying the atmosphere and the music, although somewhat corny. A full orchestra playing "Love Shack" was not Lynn's idea of music. A new song began.

"Oh, I love this song," Chris remarked. "It reminds me of my parents."

Lynn looked at Matt, whose mind was obviously somewhere else. Lynn did what she had to do—she elbowed him in the side. Matt flinched and was brought back to earth, then looked at Lynn curiously. Lynn mouthed the word "dance" and nodded to Chris. Matt took his cue.

"Honey, may I have this dance?" Matt asked Chris. Chris accepted and they made their way onto the dance floor.

"Shall we follow his lead, Marie?" Charles stood and held out his hand to his wife. Marie stood and they floated away.

Lynn sat there watching, enjoying the way that Chris was obviously trying to get Matt to lighten up. Finally, Matt broke into a smile. Then she almost fell over in her seat as Chris kissed Matt lightly on the lips. Lynn knew that it was going to happen, should happen, to look natural to his parents, but she was clearly unprepared. She gulped down the rest of her drink and tried to fix on something else. It was no use, her eyes, like magnets, kept centering on the "happy couple."

"Excuse me, are you alone? Would you like to dance?" asked a man, probably in his thirties, with slicked-back hair. Could this night get any worse, she asked herself. Just then, like a knight in shining armor, she heard Charles's voice.

"I'm sorry, young man, this enchanting young lady owes the rest of this dance to me."

Lynn smiled as she took Charles's hand and mouthed "thank you" to Marie who was seating herself. Marie smiled back and waved. Lynn and Charles finished the song out on the dance floor.

Chris tried to make Matt smile. She told the dirtiest joke she knew. That did it. Matt's face cracked into a smile and he let out a laugh. "That's what I like to see!" she said and reached up to kiss him lightly on the lips. Matt looked at her as if confused.

Chris answered his look. "Keep smiling, I'm just doing what your parents would expect, trying to look natural, you know, like two people in love?"

His smile returned. "What would I do without you?" Matt noticed that Chris was looking away, toward Lynn, and at the man who had seated himself next to her. They watched as Matt's father swooped in to save the day. Then, returning to their dance, they smiled at each other, both glad to see that Lynn had been rescued.

Chris's eyes wandered back over to the other couple. She watched as Charles guided Lynn around the dance floor. Chris had been surprised at Lynn's attire that evening. The black slacks made Lynn appear even slimmer than usual. The cobalt-colored sweater that hung just off her tan shoulders and scooped down her back made Chris break out in a sweat. Charles's hand was placed gently on Lynn's bare back. Chris remembered the soft skin under her fingertips and felt a tingle run through her body.

"Hey, Earth to Chris. Where are you?" Matt woke her from her daydream.

Not able to tell him the truth, she chose a vague response. "Nowhere really." She was saved from further questions as the music stopped and Matt led her back to the table.

"Thanks, Charles," Lynn said as Charles pulled out her chair. "I am forever in your debt."

"No, actually, I'm the one in your debt." Charles paused, then continued, "That investment advice that you gave me the last time we were here, well, let's just say it was right on the mark. In fact, it built our new swimming pool!"

"Well, I'm glad it worked out for you," Lynn replied. "I'm always happy to help out."

"If you have some time before we leave, I'd like to speak with you about another venture that I'm interested in."

"No problem. Just give me the details, and I'll take a look at it."

Chris was surprised, to say the least. Lynn the waitress, the singer, also gave investment advice? Would her talents ever end?

"Well, I hate to break up the party, but I'm on in half an hour," Lynn apologized as she grabbed her jacket from the back of her chair.

"We understand, how do they say it, 'That's showbiz'!" exclaimed Marie.

"Lynn, you are joining us for the picnic tomorrow, aren't you? I'm afraid none of us are as good at sports as you, and we don't want our family to look entirely pathetic!" Charles joked.

Lynn smiled. Happy to be included, she replied, "I wouldn't miss it!" Pausing, she placed her hands on Chris's shoulders. "But you know, Chris here is pretty athletic herself. You may actually win a trophy tomorrow!"

Chris blushed, not knowing whether it was because of the compliment, or who it came from. With that said, Lynn waved good-bye and showed herself out of the room.

The evening lingered on, longer than either Matt or Chris had anticipated. At two o'clock, the music stopped, and the night was declared over. With a sigh of relief from both, the couple slid into the El Camino and settled side by side. Aware that his parents were still watching, Chris whispered, "Put your arm around me." Matt, now used to following her cues, did just that, and pulled out from in front of the building, waving good-bye. Looking in the rearview mirror, Matt chuckled and shook his head as he watched the valet, who was clearly unhappy with the tip that he had been given.

"Boy, it was a good thing we knew all the right answers, huh?" Matt said. "All that practicing sure paid off!"

Chris agreed and slid away slightly from Matt to give each of them some space. "So, what time is the picnic tomorrow?"

"It starts about ten o'clock. Get a good night's sleep, 'cause Dad likes to enter a lot of events."

"You know, you misled me. Before, you called it a picnic, now it's a sports event!"

"Oh, stop whining. At least you're athletic, you'll laugh when you see my family try to compete!" He laughed, then turned serious. "But please don't laugh, at least not to our faces!" His face broke out into a smile, which turned into another laugh.

Matt parked the car in front of the house and opened the door for Chris.

"I'm going to get out of this monkey suit and into something comfortable," Matt said as he slid off his tie and began pulling off his shirt while walking down the hall.

"You're the first gay man I know who doesn't like dressing up!" Chris called after him.

"Oh hell, I'm probably the first gay man you've known!" He laughed. Sticking his head out of his bedroom door, he called out, "True?"

"True," she admitted. "But I've seen a lot of movies."

Chris entered the bedroom, closed the door, and began stripping off her clothes as well. She pulled on a T-shirt and a pair of flannel boxers and padded into the kitchen for a bottle of water. "You want anything from the kitchen?" she yelled to Matt.

"How about a bottle of milk of magnesia?" she heard him answer; she yelled back, "You'll have to settle for a glass of milk!"

Carrying the water and milk into the living room, she plopped down on the sofa, exhausted. Matt followed her lead and plopped down on the adjacent couch. Just then they heard keys in the front door.

"Hey, how'd the rest of the evening go?" Lynn asked as she threw her keys onto the table.

"Good, really good," Matt answered. "Thanks for that save on the shellfish."

"No, I'm the one who should thank her for that!" Chris laughed.

Matt started giving Lynn the details of the rest of the evening, but Lynn interrupted.

"Wait, I want to hear all this, but I really need to shower first. I swear they're not turning the air-conditioning on in the bar anymore!" Lynn disappeared down the hall.

When Lynn returned, she asked, "Anyone for ice cream?"

Chris's face lit up. "Count me in!"

"Come tell me how much you want!" Lynn motioned for her to follow her into the kitchen. They re-emerged with bowls overflowing with each of their favorites.

"Sure you don't want any, Matt?" they teased.

"No thanks, I don't want that stuff floating around in my belly all night!"

Matt and Chris filled Lynn in on the events of the evening. When they were through, and tired of laughing, Matt excused himself, saying that he had to rest up for the next day, which was only a few hours away.

"How about you? Are you going to poop out on me, too?" Lynn asked Chris.

"Actually, I'm wide awake," Chris replied.

They sat in silence for a few moments, both focused on their ice cream. Chris broke the silence first. "So, you know all the details of my life, but we never got around to your life."

"That's because I'm not an integral part of this charade."

"Well, to quote you, 'I think Matt's fiancée should know something about his roommate's life,' unquote. Well, I mixed up a few words, but you get the gist of it."

"Okay, so what do you want to know?" Lynn conceded.

"How about where you grew up, your parents . . ." Chris added sarcastically, "your hopes and dreams."

"I grew up in a small town in the valley, both of my parents are still alive. My dad still works as an architect. My mom, a computer programmer, is semi-retired, so she says, but she still works out of

89

their home. I have one brother, younger than me, who is a landscape designer. I see them a couple of times a year. We're not extremely close."

"And do they know that you're gay?" Chris asked.

"Yes, I knew very early on, and made them very aware of it. They're pretty accepting of my lifestyle." Then Lynn sarcastically added, "As long as they don't have to know where I sleep and whom I sleep with."

"You mean the thousands and thousands of women?" Chris teased.

"I know what Matt believes. But I don't think he really understands. I think a lot of men only sleep with women, or other men as the case may be, because they get horny, you know for the actual sex act." Lynn paused in thought and then continued, "But I don't sleep with women— and believe me, he has way over exaggerated about my sexual exploits—because I'm horny." She looked at Chris, trying to make her understand. "Once you've had true intimacy, you keep searching it out, wanting that feeling again. So sometimes, I just need to feel wanted. I need the intimacy, even if it's only for a few hours, even if it's someone I don't even know."

Lynn continued, "Tell me Chris, of all those 'ten or more' men that you've slept with, how many have you actually loved?"

Chris lowered her eyes and played with the fringe on the afghan she was holding while she spoke. "Actually . . . none of them. I don't think I've ever been in love. You know the old saying, 'The right one just hasn't come along'? Well, that's me, I'm the poster child for that saying." Chris raised her eyes to meet Lynn's. "So, you said that you've had true intimacy, that must be that you've been in love?"

Lynn felt the tears in her eyes. She admonished herself for starting along this subject. Pushing back the tears, she replied, "Yeah, I was in love, but I guess she wasn't."

"Susan?" Chris softly asked.

Lynn gave a heavy sigh, and a tear escaped down her cheek. She nodded and admitted, "Susan."

Chris heard the hurt in Lynn's voice. "I'm sorry, if you don't want to talk about it . . ."

"We were together eight years. I found her in bed with one of her students. From what my supposed friends told me, it wasn't her first affair." Lynn's voice quivered. "It's been a year, but every time I think about it, it's like it's happening all over again."

"So the saying, 'Better to have loved and lost, than never to have loved at all' . . ."

"Must have been said by a very masochistic person." Lynn smiled as another tear made its way down her face.

Wiping the tear away, Lynn looked at Chris through the dim light. "So, now that you know the reason why I've slept with so many women, tell me why you can't seem to find the right guy. Standards too high?"

"I don't know. It's just never felt right. I mean, I'm not looking to hear bells or anything, I've just never had that emotional connection with any of them." Chris paused and began again, "You don't know how many times I've said to myself, 'Maybe if you just sleep with him' . . . do you know what I mean?"

Lynn nodded and smiled. "And then you wake up, the dreaded morning after, and think, What have I done?"

"Exactly. So I guess you have the same problems—"

"Whether you like to sleep with men or with women," Lynn finished Chris's sentence.

"So tell me, what does a woman look for in another woman?" Chris asked.

"Well, I can't answer for all women, that would be like asking a man the same question. Each woman looks for something different," Lynn replied.

"Most men look for big boobs." Chris laughed. "How about you?"

Lynn laughed and shook her head no. "More than a mouthful's a waste." Lynn's eyes strayed to examine Chris's breasts. When she raised her eyes, she found that she had been caught.

Chris looked down to her chest, shook her head, and smiled.

"Just barely a mouthful." Her eyes lowered to review Lynn's breasts. "Definitely more than a mouthful there!"

Lynn felt her face turn red. Was Chris flirting with her?

Chris began again. "Okay, so what do you look for?"

"I think the first thing I look at is the eyes. The eyes tell you a lot about a person."

"Oh, and what do you see in my eyes, Madam Fortune Teller?" Chris kidded.

Lynn looked Chris straight in the eye for a moment, before giving a serious answer. "Well, the first thing I saw when I met you was a warm, caring nature." Lynn paused. "But now I would have to add that I see someone who likes to portray herself as a loner but longs for companionship."

Chris looked at Lynn, fear developing in her eyes.

"And now, I see fear, fear that you may have let me see a little bit too much into your psyche." Lynn gave Chris a half-smile. "Don't worry, I won't tell a soul."

"Do you want to know what I see in your eyes?" Chris asked.

Lynn shrugged. Chris walked over and sat next to Lynn on the couch.

Looking straight into Lynn's eyes, Chris told her, "I see that you're really not who you portray yourself to be, either."

Lynn swallowed hard. Did Chris know who she really was?

Lynn breathed a sigh of relief as Chris explained. "You portray yourself as a hard, tough woman. But actually"—Chris placed her hand on Lynn's heart—"there's a heart of gold in there."

They both smiled, and after a moment of silence, Chris sank back against the couch next to Lynn.

"So, have you ever been with a man?" Chris asked with a slight sense of uneasiness.

"No, never really wanted to," Lynn answered. "Have you ever been with a woman?"

Chris felt herself blushing. "I'd never really thought much about two women . . . until I met you."

Lynn laughed quietly. "You mean that I'm your first encounter with a lesbian?"

"No," Chris explained, "there's a couple in the group that I go camping with every once in a while."

"But you never thought about being with a woman until now?" Lynn questioned.

Chris shook her head, then looked at Lynn. "It's getting late. I think that we'd better get some sleep. Big competition in the morning, you know." She reached out and hugged Lynn. "Well, if my opinion matters at all, I think Susan blew it big-time. Definitely, her loss."

Lynn, frightened by the feeling of Chris being only inches away, broke away and smiled. "Thanks." Then trying to cover for her uneasiness, Lynn changed her smile into a mischievous one. "Now, go get some sleep so you don't have any excuses when I whip your butt at the picnic!"

Chris got up and walked down the hall. Lynn smiled when the last thing she heard from Chris before she heard the bedroom door close, was a devilish, "You wish!"

Chapter Eight

Chris felt the soft lips slowly climbing up her stomach, then the wetness of the tongue as it encircled her nipple. Teeth biting, teasing, then the soft sucking of her nipple. The sensation moved to the other nipple until she could stand it no longer. She brought the lips to hers, hungrily exploring the mouth on hers with her own tongue. The lips gently pulled away, she slowly raised her eyes from the lips that just left hers, to reveal the face of her lover . . .

Chris sat straight up. The face that was revealed was . . . Lynn's! *It was only a dream, it was only a dream,* she repeated to herself as she paced the room. If it was only a dream, then why was she so upset? Could it be the heat she felt within her body? Could it be the way her nipples were hard and sore? Could it be the moisture that she could feel between her legs? She would not have time for answers as she heard the knock on the bedroom door. She looked at the clock—it was nine a.m.

Matt's voice came from the other side of the door. "Hey, you up in there?"

Chris opened the door. "Yeah, I'll jump in the shower and be ready in fifteen."

"God, you look as bad as Lynn. What time did you guys get to bed last night?"

"Thanks a lot. I just need a little time to wake up is all," Chris replied, knowing that she dare not tell him she had only had four hours of sleep. "What's for breakfast?"

"The club has a breakfast buffet. Can you wait an hour to eat?" Matt asked, following her like a puppy into the bedroom while she grabbed some clothes.

"No problem, now get out of here!" Chris said as she pushed him from the room and closed the door behind him. The truth was that she wasn't feeling hungry at all. Her stomach was upset with confusion.

"Hey, can I come in?" Lynn knocked on the door. Receiving no reply, she guessed that Chris was still in the shower. She edged the door open. "I'm coming in!"

"Okay!" Chris yelled from the bathroom.

Lynn glanced at the direction of the bathroom, the door ajar to let the steam out. She felt flushed, knowing that on the other side of the door Chris was probably nude. Just then, Chris opened the door wider. Lynn saw that she was not nude, but clad in a towel. Walking over to the dresser, Lynn proceeded to change.

Looking in the mirror, Chris caught herself concentrating on what was going on behind her. She saw Lynn drop her towel and pull on her underwear. Then, Lynn turned and Chris could see Lynn's breasts as she pulled on her sports bra. Embarrassed for watching, Chris pushed the bathroom door closed behind her. She turned on the hair dryer to camouflage the moment she was taking to understand her confusion. Leaning on the counter, she told herself that she was under too much stress. That had to be the problem, way too much stress.

They arrived at the picnic just in time to hear the club president's annual speech. Walking through the crowd, they located Matt's parents at the sign-up table.

"Matt! It's about time you guys got here!" Charles said as he put his arm around his son. "Margaret, you remember my son, Matt," Charles said to the woman behind the table, who nodded. "And this is his fiancée, Chris, and of course our niece, Lynn."

Chris looked at Matt with confusion. Matt whispered, "She has to be a member of the family to compete."

"Isn't that cheating?" Chris whispered back.

"Not really," Matt explained, pointing first at a muscular young man to the right, and another to the left. "See him? He's supposedly a cousin. And he's supposedly an illegitimate son."

"Supposedly?" Chris asked.

Matt smiled and shrugged. "Yeah, but we know differently. My dad says 'All's fair in love and war.'"

Chris laughed and thought, *when first we practice to deceive* . . .

Lynn nudged Matt. "Hey, I need food!"

"Okay, okay. Dad, we're going to grab some breakfast."

"Don't eat too much, we're on for the three-legged race in forty-five minutes," Charles responded with excitement. "First one is the couples race, that's Matt and Chris, and you and me, Lynn."

Matt whispered in Chris's ear, "My mom doesn't participate, she gets overheated really easy."

Charles continued, "Then the second race is for men only, and the third, for women only." He paused to look at Chris and Lynn. "You're up for two in a row, right?"

The women smiled and nodded, as if they had a choice. Suddenly Chris felt that twinge again. She was going to have to run the three-legged race with Lynn. She was going to have to get over this feeling.

Lynn was having the same thought. *Great. Tied together, arms around each other, bodies moving together.* She was having hot flashes just thinking about it.

"Just juice for me," Lynn said to the buffet attendant, who handed her a glass of orange juice.

"Yeah, me too," Chris said, and she reached for the glass.

"What's wrong with you guys? I thought that you were starving?" Matt exclaimed as he reached for his third croissant.

96

Lynn shrugged, trying to come up with an explanation for her sudden change of heart.

Chris looked at her curiously, then answered, "I don't want to be running on a full stomach."

"Yeah, that's what it is." Lynn followed her lead.

The three were lounging at a table after finishing what breakfast they had when Charles approached the table.

"Come on, come on! It's time for the first race!" he called out.

The group jogged over to the event. After participating in this event last year with Matt, Lynn knew the drill and proceeded to strap her and Charles's legs together. She laughed at the other couple; they were having difficulty just getting their legs joined together. She smiled as she remembered that Matt, as athletic as he looked, was a little uncoordinated. The race began, and Charles and Lynn quickly left the other couple behind. Although they ran a good race, neither couple came in first, second, or third. The men's race was next, Charles and Matt finishing sixth out of a group of ten. The next race was to start in five minutes.

Chris paced as the women couples began buckling the straps. Lynn was feeling just as uneasy.

"Come on, girls! You're our last hope!" Charles said as he pulled the two together and began fastening the straps. Lynn, being taller, threw her arm around Chris's shoulder as Chris put her arm around Lynn's waist.

"You can do it!" Charles called as he backed away from the starting line.

Lynn looked down at Chris, who smiled up at her. "You know, we probably could win, if we really try."

The two walked a few steps, discussing their strategy, then backed up to the starting line. They prepared for the starting gun. "Pow!" The gun rang out. The two got a good start and continued down the grassy area. They were moving as one, both of their competitiveness showing on their faces. The women around them dropped like flies, except for one couple who ran neck and neck with them.

"We've got to lose them!" Chris shouted. They sped up, and passed the finish line one step ahead of the opposing team. They were so elated, they lost their footing, immediately falling on top of each other. Falling, laughing, then all of a sudden realizing how close they were, they stopped. Breathing heavily, Lynn reached out to pick out the grass that had lodged itself in Chris's hair. Chris looked up into Lynn's eyes and suddenly time seemed to stop. For a moment it was just the two of them, locked in each other's eyes.

"Hey! I knew you guys could do it!" Charles broke into their world. He leaned down and removed the straps.

"Way to go, guys!" Matt chimed in. He reached out to help Chris up. Then turning, Chris reached her hand out to Lynn, who was still sitting on the grass. Lynn accepted and leapt to her feet.

"Well, I had to carry her half the way, but we did it!" Lynn teased.

Chris pushed Lynn's shoulder. "Ha! I was dragging your butt!" she joked back. "So what's next?" Chris asked.

"Four-man volleyball!" Charles said, looking at his watch. "We have half an hour. Shall we go take a look at the competition?"

The four wandered over to the court and sat down on the grass. Chris eyed the table of water bottles across the way. "Want some water?" she asked Lynn. Lynn nodded.

Matt, tired of waiting for the same question to be posed to him, said, "Yes, I would like some too, how 'bout you, Dad?"

Charles, who was busy watching the action on the court, did not respond. Matt nodded to Chris to grab an extra bottle. The group sipped their water and sat on the sidelines until the game in play ended. The winners would play the next team, the McKinley family.

"Andersons and McKinleys," their game was announced, and the four scrambled onto the court. There was a slow start, their team members uncertain of their coverage areas. After the first few minutes, their game started clicking. The opposing team fell apart. The game ended, the score 15–6. Charles was elated and showed it by hugging each of his team members. Their next game was to start immediately.

"Is there anything that you're bad at?" Chris asked Lynn while they waited for the other team to take the court.

"I haven't had any complaints!" Lynn teased.

Matt, overhearing Chris's question, jumped in. "It's sickening, isn't it? She can't even let me look good in front of my dad!"

"Is it my fault that you arrange flowers better than you hit a volleyball?" Lynn kidded.

The team took their positions as the opposing team served. The ball was hit directly to Chris, who bumped it to Lynn. Lynn took it high and spiked it over the net, the ball hitting hard against the chest of a member of the opposing team. This style of play continued for the rest of the game. After the tenth point, the other team basically gave up. The four had prevailed again, Chris hitting the winning point.

Lynn approached her with a high five. "Now, is there anything that you're bad at?"

"I haven't had any complaints," Chris said with a teasing smile and gave Lynn a wink.

Matt caught the wink out of the corner of his eye. He was glad to see the two women in his life getting along so well.

After the third victory, Charles called the group over and admitted, "I'm sorry guys, I can't play another one. I'm just not in the shape that I used to be."

"That's okay, Charles, I'm pretty worn out, too," Lynn said as she patted him on the back.

"Come on guys, we can't quit now! I'll go see if we can play with only three players." Matt jogged over to the judges' table and came back. "They said it was okay."

Charles nodded, went over to the sideline, and sat on the grass with Marie, who had finally decided to join them.

"You know, Matt, I don't think that we should continue. It may look to your dad as if we didn't really need him," Chris suggested.

Lynn followed Chris's lead. "I agree, Matt, you could really score some points if we decided we couldn't do it without him."

Matt shook his head. "No. I want to show him that we can do it." He motioned for the opposing team to take their positions.

But Chris and Lynn had other plans, and slowly but surely, they intentionally missed enough shots to lose the game. Matt hadn't noticed their less than average play. The threesome walked to the sidelines after admitting defeat.

"I guess we just couldn't pull it off without you, Charles," Chris admitted.

Charles shrugged. "Well, it's tough without a fourth player."

Marie smiled and winked at both women, who returned the wink. It would be their little secret.

"You had some good moves out there for such a little thing!" Charles said as he put his arm around Chris, then looked over at Matt. "Matt, she's definitely a keeper!"

"I think so!" Matt agreed, happy to be in favor with his dad.

"Me, too," Lynn mumbled under her breath. Chris was just within hearing range of that comment, but chose to keep the comment all to herself.

The group sat on a blanket and proceeded to watch the next few games. At four o'clock, Lynn's stomach began to rumble. Realizing that she hadn't really eaten anything all day, she suggested that they return to the buffet area, knowing that it was still fully stocked. Charles stood and helped Marie up. Matt and Chris stood and joined hands. Lynn followed behind, feeling a sudden twinge of jealousy. She wondered what it would be like to hold Chris's soft hand in hers.

"Look at all this food!" Marie exclaimed.

"Dig in, everybody," Charles said, handing plates to Lynn, Chris, and Matt. The group went down the buffet table, each filling their plate with its offerings. Just as they were nearing the end, Matt's buddy Jeff approached. Knowing that Jeff had a big mouth, Lynn thought the charade was over. She immediately went to Matt's side for damage control.

Matt, seeing the panic in her eyes, whispered, "It's okay, Lynn, I filled Jeff in since I knew that he would be here." Then, seeing his father approaching, Matt pulled Chris to his side. "Jeff, you remember Chris, don't you?"

Jeff played along. "Of course. I was watching you guys in some of the events here today, too bad about the volleyball loss."

"Yeah, well, we were just about to sit down, would you like to join us?" Chris asked politely.

"No thank you. I've had enough food today to last me the rest of the summer!" Jeff laughed. "Maybe I'll catch up to you later." He turned and left them to their meal.

"Ohhh, I believe that I've overeaten again!" Charles exclaimed as his stood rubbing his stomach. "Why do you let me do that, Marie?"

Marie looked at the other three and said sarcastically, "Like I have anything to say about it! Chris, I hope Matt listens to you more than his father listens to me!"

Chris smiled. "He doesn't listen to a word I say." Turning, she smiled at Matt. "Like father, like son, huh?"

"Well, I'm going to go for a little stroll, try to settle my stomach a little bit. How about it, Marie?" Charles asked his wife as he slid her chair out for her. They joined hands and strolled away.

"Excuse me, I think I'll go to the little boys' room." Matt stood and went off to locate the restroom.

Chris and Lynn were left alone at the table, both still nibbling at their desserts.

"Umm . . . you have got to try this!" Chris said to Lynn, offering her a forkful of lemon-filled cake.

"I don't think so, it looks too rich for me," Lynn answered.

"Oh, come on, it's so moist and creamy . . ." Chris teased, circling her fork toward Lynn's mouth. Lynn blushed, she couldn't refuse such a description, and put her mouth over the fork. Chris, caught up in the sexual overtones, withdrew the fork and slowly licked the remains off of the utensil.

Lynn, surprised at the action but refusing to back down, took a bit of the key lime pie from her plate and offered it to Chris saying, "Then you must try a bite of this, it's so smooth and tangy . . ."

Chris took the fork with her hand and put the dessert in her mouth, slowly bringing the fork out and chewing slowly while letting out a deep moan.

"God, you're good at that, too!" Lynn was breathless with excitement.

Chris smiled, glad to have succeeded in yet another competition.

Charles and Marie resurfaced with Matt, who was carrying drinks from the bar. Lynn looked at her watch. She really needed to go home and shower before she played tonight.

"I'm sorry, it's been fun, but I'd better get going. If I go to the bar like this, I'd be laughed off the stage!"

"Oh, but you'll miss the awards ceremony, and we actually won one this year!" Marie said with disappointment in her voice.

"I know, but the other half of the winning team will be here to accept the award." She motioned to Chris, refusing to look directly in Chris's eyes. She was afraid that the heat would rise in her face again.

They said their good-byes and Lynn went on her way, disappointed for having to leave Chris but glad to be going home to yet another cold shower.

It was after midnight when Matt steered the El Camino onto the freeway. "God! I am so glad that you won an event. My dad has been wanting to win something for so long."

Chris blushed. "Well, I didn't do it alone, you know. I couldn't have done it without Lynn. She's in great shape!"

"Yeah. She keeps in shape for the ladies."

Chris turned in her seat in exasperation. "You know, you make it sound like all Lynn cares about in life is sex! She doesn't seem like that to me. She's been really nice this week, helping you out with your little charade, being there when I got sick, giving me her bed."

Matt ran his fingers through his hair. "I'm sorry, you're right.

I've been giving you the wrong picture of Lynn. She really is a great person and a great friend. She'd give you the shirt off her back if you needed it." Matt laughed. "Especially since you're a woman!"

Chris slapped Matt's arm. "You're incorrigible!"

"I'm pooped, it's straight to bed for me," Matt said.

"Yeah, me too," she agreed as she headed for the bedroom. Showering, Chris changed into her bed clothes and stretched out on the bed. She lay there on her back, in the dark, for what seemed like hours, her mind reviewing the last few days. She rolled over onto her stomach, trying to get comfortable, trying to feel comfortable with her surroundings and with herself. Frustrated, she switched on the light. Maybe if she had something to read. She hadn't brought any novels with her, because she hadn't thought that she would have the time. She pulled out Lynn's bedside drawer, looking for a book or a magazine. She analyzed its contents: an address book, an empty notebook, investment magazines (this puzzled her), and a romance novel. Pulling the novel from the drawer, she flipped it over to read the back cover: *Michelle pulled away her blouse to reveal her bare breasts. Trina brushed her hand against Michelle's hardened nipple and their lips met hungrily, their desire for each other . . .* Chris dropped the book. The book was describing two women! She never knew books like this existed. Actually, she had never thought about it. Nevertheless, Chris, feeling like she had uncovered a secret, picked up the book and guiltily stuffed it back into the drawer. Maybe there was something on television.

Lynn sat on the edge of the stage watching people file out the door, some coupling up, some leaving alone. She always got melancholy this time of the night, realizing that she would be leaving alone. There were those few occasions where she had hooked up with someone during the night, and then, she knew there would be a few hours of pleasure, just to end being alone again. Tonight she felt even more alone than usual.

"Hey, you all packed up? If you haven't noticed, the bar is closed," Sam called from the seating area as she helped wipe off the remaining dirty tables. Noticing that Lynn wasn't budging, Sam dropped her cloth on a table, sauntered up to the stage, and sat beside her.

"What's wrong? Why aren't you going home?" Sam asked softly, peeking around Lynn's face, which was tilted down.

"Chris is there," Lynn replied, not lifting her eyes.

"Yeah, so Chris is there. She seems like a really nice person. Cute, funny. So what's the problem?" Sam asked as she put her arm around Lynn's shoulder.

"That's the problem. That's exactly the problem," Lynn answered as she finally raised her eyes to Sam's.

Sam looked into Lynn's eyes and understood. "Oh Lynn, all the women that you've been with, and you fall for a straight woman?" Shaking her head, Sam squeezed Lynn's shoulder. "Honey, I feel for you, I really do, but you know the odds."

"Yeah, life's a bitch, isn't it?" Lynn smiled halfheartedly.

Sam hugged her. "I would say that you could come home with me, but . . ."

Lynn released Sam from the hug. "That's okay, I need to go home and face my demons." With that, she slid down off the edge, her feet landing on the floor, and walked arm in arm with Sam right beside her, to the door. The two embraced again. "I'd say, find some one-night stand to go home with, but as you can see, everyone's gone." She smiled softly and grabbed Lynn's chin with her fingers. "Plus you know how I feel about meaningless sex."

Lynn nodded. Her friend did not believe in one-night stands. She was a one-woman lady, and that one woman was Beth, and had been for years. As Lynn climbed in her truck she thought about what Sam was going home to. Sam had beaten the odds in more ways than one. She was going home to someone who loved her and was faithful to her, unlike Susan. She needed to think about something else, so she reached for the radio dial. Flipping it on, she heard, "Why don't you play another somebody done somebody wrong song . . ." *Great,* she thought to herself. Flipping off the noise, she began wiping away the tears that were rolling down her face.

Lynn unlocked the door to the house. The room was dark, except for the light of the television. As she adjusted her eyes to the dimness, she saw eyes peek over the edge of the couch.

"Hey," whispered Chris, who was stretched out comfortably on the cushions.

"Hey," Lynn answered. "You know that you're supposed to sleep in my room, don't you?"

"Yeah, I just couldn't sleep. Then I got hooked on this movie. Ever seen it before?"

"What is it?" Lynn strained to see the picture before her, thankful that Chris couldn't see her puffy, red eyes.

"*Some Kind of Wonderful,*" Chris replied.

"The story of a guy who didn't know what he really wanted until the girl showed how much she cared for him," Lynn remembered.

"Yeah, I guess I never thought of it that way," Chris replied. "Are you sleepy? Do you need to go to bed?"

"No," Lynn answered. "I need to wind down a little. Want some popcorn?"

"That sounds good." Chris followed Lynn into the kitchen.

Lynn flipped on the light, grabbed the popcorn, and threw it in the microwave. Turning to Chris, she asked, "And to drink, madam?"

Chris looked at Lynn. Reaching out, she touched Lynn's face. "God, your eyes are so red! Don't they hurt?"

Lynn turned away. "No. Must have been the smoke in the bar. Um, I'm going to grab a quick shower. Watch the popcorn, okay?"

"Yeah, sure," Chris mumbled as Lynn left the room. Chris was confused. The Rainbow Room was a nonsmoking bar. The popcorn stopped popping, and as Chris had previously found out, you get it out when it stops, whether the timer has rung or not. Emptying the bag into a big bowl, she grabbed a couple of sodas and napkins, and plopped back down on the couch. She was munching away when Lynn re-entered the room.

"Feel better?" Chris asked.

"Feel better. Probably smell better too." Lynn smiled as she ran her hand through her short wet hair and plopped down next to Chris. Grabbing a handful of popcorn she asked, "So where are we at?"

"They're at the museum," Chris answered.

The movie continued and the bowl of popcorn was soon empty. Lynn dozed off, and woke to the sound of gunshots. Confused, she found the noise coming from the television. She tried to reach for the remote, but her body felt heavy. Looking down, she found that Chris had fallen asleep and her head had ended up in Lynn's lap. Lynn sat there in the dim light watching Chris sleep. She slowly stroked Chris's hair, wanting so badly to brush her lips against hers. Wanting it so badly, it hurt. She looked up at the television, trying to regain her composure. When she glanced back down, Chris's eyes were slightly open. Neither woman moved for several minutes, Lynn lightly stroking Chris's hair, Chris lost in Lynn's eyes.

Finally, Chris took Lynn's hand and held it against her cheek. "I think I better go in to bed," she said softly. Releasing Lynn's hand, Chris slowly raised her body to a sitting position. She turned to Lynn, looked into her eyes, paused as if she wanted to say something, then lightly squeezed Lynn's hand.

"I had a really good day today," Chris whispered, not releasing her hold on Lynn's hand.

Lynn raised her other hand, placing her palm on Chris's cheek, then lightly smoothed her thumb across Chris's soft lips and quietly replied, "Me, too."

Chris moved Lynn's palm over to her lips and kissed it softly. "Good night," she said as she stood, then disappeared down the hall. Lynn, savoring the moment, turned off the television, reached for the blanket balled up at the end of the couch, curled up, smiled with contentment, and drifted off to sleep.

What just happened in there? Chris sleepily asked herself.

Chapter Nine

Chris woke Sunday to the sound of the alarm. She rolled over and shut off the noise, thankful that she had set it before she had originally crawled into bed last night. It was nine o'clock, why was she so tired? Then the memories came flooding over her. Lynn's fingers through her hair, on her cheek, on her lips. The feeling rushing through her body was overwhelming. But overwhelming in a pleasant way, intoxicating and warm, like the way the first sip of a liqueur feels on a cold day, slowly penetrating every inch of your body. She stretched out under the sheets, enjoying the sensation. Then suddenly, she sat up and rubbed her hands over her face. Was she actually thinking about another woman this way? What was wrong with her! She could not let herself feel this way! She shook off the sheets, jumped out of bed, and hurried into the bathroom.

Chris climbed into the shower. As she leaned against the wall, the warm water enveloped her. She closed her eyes, water running over her face, trying to clear her mind. But instead, her thoughts drifted back to the day before, the joking, the teasing, the hidden glances, and the times that Lynn had caught the glances and returned them, making her feel hopelessly lost in her eyes. *Damn*, she said to herself. Never had her heart and her mind been in such conflict.

Chris turned off the shower and grabbed the towel that she had placed on the rung just outside the tub. Drying off, she thought to herself, *What am I so worried about? It's not like we had sex or anything.* But she then realized what had taken place last night made her feel more intimate with Lynn that she had ever felt with a man. She had never felt that closeness, that connection with anyone before. The truth was, the feeling scared her to death.

The aroma of coffee filtered through the bedroom door and drew Chris into the kitchen. Grabbing a mug of the fresh brew, she stopped, leaning against the wall connecting the kitchen with the living room. She watched as the body curled up on the couch slept.

Chris sat down on the edge of the couch. "Hey," she whispered, softly caressing the bare arm that had held her last night.

Lynn slowly raised her eyelids. She could smell the scent of the vanilla shampoo on Chris's wet hair. It made her smile.

Smoothing Lynn's hair out of her face, Chris suggested, "Come and get in your bed and get some decent sleep."

"Okay," Lynn replied. Chris stood and walked back to the bedroom. Lynn lay there for several minutes, then finally forced herself to get up. She wandered sleepily down the hall and was greeted with the intoxicating smell of Chris's perfume. The fragrance led her into the bathroom, where Chris was putting on her makeup.

Leaning against the doorway, Lynn commented, "You smell really good!"

Chris felt a shiver run through her body at Lynn's seductive smile reflected in the mirror. Chris softly smiled. "You're not making it very easy for me to get ready."

"Hey Chris! Are you almost ready or what?" Matt's voice boomed as he walked down the hall toward the bedroom.

"Yes, I just need to throw my clothes on," Chris answered.

When Matt didn't move, she asked, "May I have a little bit of privacy, please?"

Matt's face turned red as he backed out of the room and closed the door.

Lynn left the doorway and crawled in between the sheets. She lay on her side, positioning her head on the pillow so that she could watch Chris in the mirror. Chris put the finishing touches on her makeup and reached down to release the belt of the robe. Suddenly looking up, she caught Lynn's eyes in the mirror and immediately caught the robe as it was falling from her shoulders. Chris smiled and shook her head as she returned Lynn's stare. Turning, she closed the door behind her. Lynn sighed and closed her eyes. Maybe her dreams would turn out better.

Chris stood outside the gallery next to Matt as they waited for his parents to arrive. Matt ran his hand through his hair as he became more and more impatient.

"Where are they? They left the club at the same time as us!"

Chris shrugged. All four had gone to the club for brunch and were to attend the gallery showing of one of Matt's friends. She had thought it a bad idea, knowing that many of Matt's friends didn't know about their little charade. But Matt had insisted, and so they waited.

"I don't know how you guys get used to this." Charles's voice boomed from down the sidewalk. "We had to park a half mile away!"

Chris took Matt's hand and squeezed it. Patience, Matt, patience, it was meant to imply. Matt squeezed back, signifying that he had received her message.

"I didn't mind the walk, Matt," Marie soothed. Her eyes sparkled. "I'm so glad that we're here! Your father never lets me go to art galleries or museums."

"I knew you'd like it, Mom. Let's go inside." Matt motioned toward the door.

The four wandered into the crowded gallery. Marie stopped at every piece, admiring the color or texture. Charles looked bored. Chris listened to Marie and responded with comments of her own. Each piece made her feel different things—calm, peaceful, sad, even angry. Then she came upon a painting that truly disturbed her. A mixture of shades of blue from pale to almost black. The lines swirled as if to show confusion, desperation, then curved as if all emotions calmed. She tried to think of what this piece reminded her of. Closing her eyes, she felt the emotions it had provoked. It came to her in a wave, enveloping her entire body. It was the feelings that she was having toward her relationship with Lynn. Opening her eyes, she felt an overwhelming need for space. She pretended to be interested in a piece across the room and wandered away.

Matt watched as Chris left his side. His eyes scanned the room and found his friend Jeff trying desperately to get his attention. Matt motioned for his friend to join him and so Jeff approached the group of three.

"Mom, Dad, you remember my friend Jeff. You met him yesterday."

Charles and Marie smiled politely, then went back to discussing the artwork before them.

"So come here for a second, I need to talk to you," Jeff said, pulling at Matt's arm.

Matt followed Jeff into the next room.

"I thought you said that your 'fiancée' is straight?" Jeff asked.

"Yeah. Because she is," Matt replied as if annoyed.

"Are you sure?"

Matt sighed. "Jeff, what are you getting at?"

"Well, I was just watching her yesterday. For a woman who's straight, she sure spent a lot of time with her eyes on Lynn."

Matt looked bored. "She and Lynn have become—"

"Close?" Jeff finished Matt's sentence.

"Yes, close, but not how you're inferring," Matt said, disgusted with his friend. Maybe Lynn was right about Jeff.

"I don't know about that. There sure were some heated looks between the two."

"Oh, first you said that Chris was looking at Lynn. Now you say that they were returned by Lynn?"

"That's exactly what I'm saying. And did you notice how often they *casually* touched each other?"

"Oh come on, Jeff."

"When you and your parents left the table yesterday, they ended up feeding their desserts to each other."

"God, how close were you watching them?" Matt said with exasperation.

"Well, I didn't actually see that. Someone else told me," Jeff explained.

Matt ran his fingers through his hair. He didn't know what to believe. "Lynn promised not to play around with Chris."

"Hey, from what I heard and saw, it wasn't all on Lynn's part, if you know what I mean."

Matt nodded in understanding.

Jeff put his hand on Matt's shoulder. "Look, I'm just telling you so that your little charade doesn't get fucked up."

"I know. Thanks, buddy," Matt said, as he gave Jeff a hug.

Matt pulled the car away from the gallery and onto the frontage road. The conversation with Jeff still fresh in his mind, he thought back to the times that he, Chris, and Lynn had been together at the same time. Had he noticed a special connection between the two of them? Had Lynn made Chris her latest victim? As he turned the car onto the highway, he concentrated on the conversations that they had all had together. Was there flirting? He and Lynn had always been so comfortable together. He hadn't really paid attention to any sexual innuendos, any hidden glances. Had they been there?

The traffic slowed. Another California traffic jam. Matt sighed. Chris turned and asked, "Is there something wrong?"

Matt looked at her. "Can I ask you a really personal question?"

"Nothing's too personal, we're engaged, remember?" Chris grinned.

Matt shook his head. "No, this is really personal, oh, forget it, it's none of my business."

"Matt, just spit it out."

Matt looked ahead at the traffic, then turned toward her. "It's just that Jeff asked me . . . well, if anyone could do it, Lynn could. I mean she's good looking and sexy. I guess . . ."

"English, Matt. Complete sentences, please!" Chris was getting confused.

Matt looked out the side window, glanced down, then began again. "Jeff asked me if you and Lynn . . . if you . . . He thinks that there may be some flirting going on and some staring. I told him you were straight, but—"

Chris interrupted, her face beginning to turn red. "What exactly are you getting at, Matt?"

Matt blurted, "Is something going on between you and Lynn?" He glanced toward Chris, then began pulling at some imaginary string on the steering wheel cover. "I mean, I have noticed the closeness that has developed. And you seem to have a lot in common. It wouldn't be the worst thing in the world, she's really a great person, it's just that—"

Chris interrupted again, looking at him, her face now hot. "Is that what you think?" She suddenly turned toward her side window, knowing that if he looked into her eyes, he might see the truth, that she was so confused about her feelings at this point, that she couldn't be sure what was happening between her and Lynn.

The traffic at a standstill, he shifted the car into park and turned toward her. "Look, I don't know what I think. I just want you to be happy. I really love Lynn. It's just that she's not real great with relationships and all, and I wouldn't want either one of you to get hurt."

Chris could not look back at him. She knew he was being sincere. She knew exactly what his face would look like, the look in his eyes. She just stared out the window and was relieved to see the car beside her begin to move forward.

"The traffic is moving," was all that she could say.

Matt took the car out of park and slowly pressed the gas pedal. "Chris, I didn't mean to upset you," he said with sincerity, glancing first at Chris and then back at the road ahead.

"Please, just drop it!" Chris said in anguish. She felt tears welling up in her eyes. Had it been so obvious to complete strangers? Had Lynn thought it obvious, too? She could not look away from the side window. She could not move.

The traffic now at a steady speed, the silence unbearable, Matt ran his fingers through his hair and reached to turn the volume up on the radio. The car passed by an area of the highway under construction. A worker holding a sign with the word "stop" stood on the side of the road. "Hey, wasn't he one of the Village People?" Matt kidded.

But Chris didn't respond. There would be no more words uttered in the car until they pulled into the driveway of the house.

Matt fumbled the keys as he withdrew them from the ignition. "You're all thumbs!" joked Chris, trying to act as if recovered from the conversation. "No wonder you haven't had a date in a while!"

Matt laughed. He was glad that she was speaking to him again. He was also glad that they had this conversation. He now knew the truth; he knew that Chris was as confused about her relationship with Lynn as he was.

Matt unlocked the door, and immediately Chris headed for the patio. She walked onto the deck, desperately in need of some fresh air.

"Thank God!" came a voice from the sand below.

Chris looked down to find Lynn sprawled out on a beach towel. Her tan body glistened in the sun from baby oil, which had been applied generously. Chris felt her body temperature rise, from the beads of moisture on the dark skin, coupled with the fact that Lynn lay there practically nude, her bathing suit top straps unfastened and falling to each side.

"Come here, please! I've got an itch in the middle of my back that I've been trying to reach for an hour!" came the voice again.

Chris climbed down the stairs and knelt next to the oily body.

"It's right between my shoulder blades!"

Chris reached out and gently scratched; the rich oil coated her fingers.

"Oooh . . . right there." The body moaned beneath her. "Thanks, Chris."

Chris felt lightheaded. She imagined rubbing her naked body against Lynn's oil-coated skin. She had to clear her head. Maybe a nice quick jog would do the trick.

"While you're there, can you fasten my straps, please? I'm going to go cool off in the water."

Chris carefully picked up and fastened the straps. On second thought, maybe a grueling run would be better.

Knowing that she was short on time, Chris rushed into the house and changed into her running clothes. Her body temperature had just returned to normal when she headed out the door to begin her run. Stepping out onto the deck she was suddenly captivated by the figure walking toward her.

The swimsuit that she had just helped fasten barely covered any of the slim, tan, toned body. Moisture beaded on the dark skin due to the layer of oil that lingered even after the saltwater wash. A glimmer of gold sparkled from Lynn's stomach. Chris focused her eyes. Lynn's belly button was pierced. The gold hoop made a shiver run down Chris's body. Stopping, Lynn looked up at the sun and used her hands to slick back her hair. The view was right out of a *Sports Illustrated* swimsuit issue.

"What's wrong?" Lynn called out to Chris.

Chris shook her head, trying to shake out the dozens of impure thoughts running through her mind. She ran down the stairs and away from Lynn, knowing that seeing that body any closer could send her over the edge.

Matt watched Chris from his seat on the couch. He saw her rush in then rush out of the house in her running clothes.

"Are you going for a run?" he asked.

"Yeah," Chris replied as she dashed past him and slid open the glass door.

"Hey! Are you sure you have time?" Matt called out to her as she slid the door shut behind her. He rose quickly and walked over to the door to catch her, calling out, "Chris!"

Approaching the glass door, Matt stopped as he watched the same scene that had Chris hypnotized. He had forgotten just how beautiful Lynn was. And if he, a gay man, had been caught off guard by the view, he could just imagine what Chris, a very confused woman, was feeling.

Matt went back to his seat after watching Chris take off in a steady run. She probably really needed to let off some steam.

Matt turned at the sound of the door sliding open, and then the voice.

"What's wrong with Chris?" Lynn asked, still toweling off.

"I think that she just needed some time alone," Matt replied. "But I hope that she doesn't lose track of time."

"She has plenty of time," Lynn answered.

Matt looked up at Lynn. "Do you think that you could wear anything a little *more* revealing?"

"Matt, this is my tanning suit. You've seen it a million times and it's never made you uncomfortable before," Lynn said as she walked toward the bedroom.

"It's not me that you're making uncomfortable," he muttered to himself.

Halfway down the hall, Lynn turned around and smiled. "You're not turning straight on me, are you?"

"Ooh, baby, I want your body!" Matt said as he grabbed a pillow from the couch and hurled it toward her.

Chris's feet pounded the hard wet sand as she ran along the water's edge. She passed by a group of guys playing football and thought to herself, *See, I still think those guys are good looking.* Next she came among some women in bikinis, sunning themselves. Stopping for a moment, she concentrated on each one, and then, realizing that she was staring, began her jog again. She smiled to herself. She had not thought one of them attractive. So what was going on between her and Lynn? Was it all in her mind? No, Matt had made that perfectly clear. She looked down at her watch and realized that she needed to quicken her pace to make it back to the house with time to shower. She reached the house with no answers to her questions. It was going to be a long night.

Lynn found herself sorting through everything in the closet. *Jeez, what am I doing?* she asked herself, thinking that she was looking not just for something suitable but something that would make her attractive to Chris. *Get ahold of yourself!* she thought, reminding herself of one fact about Chris—*she's straight, she's straight, she's straight!* Grabbing a pair of black jeans, a red silk shirt, and her black boots, she proceeded to get dressed.

Lynn stepped out onto the patio deck and leaned on the railing, taking in the red and orange sunset. She glanced at a small figure coming down the beach. As it drew near, she saw that it was Chris.

"You'd better get your butt in gear, girl, you don't have much time!" Lynn yelled out to her.

Chris sped up as she reached the deck of the house and heard Lynn's voice. "Oh God, here we go again!" she mumbled to herself as she felt her heart jump a beat seeing Lynn in the red silk shirt. Blowing in the breeze, it opened just enough to show a thin gold chain glimmering on her tan neckline.

"I'm sorry, what did you say?" Lynn asked.

"Oh, nothing, I said I lost track of time," Chris puffed as she stretched out her leg muscles before entering the house.

"Is there anything I can do to help you get ready? Iron something maybe?" Lynn offered as she followed Chris into the house.

"That would be great." Chris pulled out a short black dress. "It just needs a little touch-up."

"No problem." Lynn took the dress and headed to the ironing board. *Sure, no problem, just seeing you in this dress is going to drive me crazy all night,* she thought to herself.

And it did. Chris came into the living room, where Matt and Lynn sat waiting, with five minutes to spare. Matt glanced up at Chris. "Wow! You look great! Doesn't she look great, Lynn?"

Lynn did not want to look up. She raised her eyes slowly. *Don't blush, don't blush, don't blush,* she said to herself. Chris did look as good in the dress as she had imagined. Lynn immediately stood, turning so that Chris could not see her face just in case she was blushing. "Yes, great! Are you guys ready to go?"

They both nodded and began to file out the door.

"You know, this is nice," Marie commented. "Nice to have a quiet evening between the big party last night and the big dance tomorrow night."

"Big dance?" Chris questioned as she shot a stabbing stare at Matt. Matt winced and smiled as if he had been caught with his hand in the cookie jar.

"Didn't Matt tell you about the big annual hoedown?" Charles chuckled.

"No," Chris responded with a chuckle of her own. "A hoedown?"

"Oh, Chris! It's so much fun!" Marie said. "I just love that two-step dancing!"

Charles groaned then smiled as he patted his son on the back. "And this year Matt doesn't have an excuse not to dance."

Lynn laughed. "I would love to see Matt doing the two-step!"

"Lynn, I wish you would reconsider coming, although I understand." Marie read Lynn's eyes.

"Thanks," Lynn said. "But I think I'll stick to the holiday dance at the bar. At least I'll have someone to dance with there."

Charles interrupted by clearing his throat. "Lynn, how about we go up to our suite so that I can show you the information on the investment that I'm interested in?"

Lynn nodded and pushed back her chair.

Chris watched as the two left the room. It was very odd how Charles relied on Lynn's investment advice, considering that Lynn had no professional training.

Charles unlocked the door of the suite and ushered Lynn through the door. He walked over to the table and picked up a manila envelope.

Handing it to Lynn, he motioned for her not to open it. "Please don't feel like you need to open it right now. Just take a look at it later and see what you think."

Lynn nodded. "What kind of money are we talking about, Charles?" she asked.

"Well, it's quite a chunk. But it promises a rate of return of about twenty percent."

Lynn looked suspicious. Nothing she knew of promised that kind of return these days. "And you're going to pull some of the funds from your established portfolio?"

Charles raised his hand and scratched his chin in thought. "I'm sure that you know about the loan I made Matt to start up his shop. The note comes due next month. If he comes up with the money, I'll use that to make the investment. If not, which I highly suspect, yes, I'll have to pull some out of my existing portfolio."

Lynn had no clue about the loan Charles spoke of. Wanting more details, she pretended to have forgotten. "Wow, has it been that long already? I know he's told me, but I can't remember—how much is the balance on that loan?"

"Enough to get into this investment. Somewhere around thirty thousand," Charles answered.

Lynn nodded, but inside, she was angry. Was this what had Matt so troubled? This entire charade was due to money that he owed his dad? She could have solved this problem so easily! Then she remembered the last time that she tried to help Matt out. He adamantly refused, saying that he didn't want money to come between them because it could ruin their friendship.

Lynn's thoughts were interrupted by Charles's question. "So, you'll check this out for me then?"

"No problem, Charles. I should have something for you at the end of the week," Lynn answered.

Charles ushered her out of the suite and into the elevator to return to their group.

"So how's business going?" he asked.

"Good. Really good," Lynn replied, still preoccupied with the recent conversation.

"So the whole up-and-down thing with the stock market?"

"Oh, you know. It was bad for the short-term investors. But most of my clients are in it for the long haul."

Charles nodded. He was happy to have their investment relationship. The elevator opened and the two made their way back to the table.

Lynn sat down and put the packet beside her chair. Picking up her drink, she suddenly was shaken by Chris's knee knocking against her own. She looked over at the woman who was deep in conversation with Marie, but received no response.

For a moment Lynn was lost in a daydream. *She slid her hand onto Chris's knee and continued up her soft skin, under the black dress, onto her upper thigh, turning inward . . .*

Her daydream was interrupted by another nudge from Chris's knee. Shaking herself back into reality, she caught the gist of the topic at hand. Marie was talking about the details of a wedding she had just attended. Lynn heard the woman ramble on—the flowers, the colors—that's what Chris's nudge had been about. She needed a way out of this conversation.

Lynn waited for Marie to pause, then butted in, "So Marie, how was the gallery opening today?"

Marie turned to Lynn. "Oh Lynn, it was wonderful."

Chris rubbed her knee against Lynn's as if to say "Thanks for the save." Lynn tried to continue the conversation but had trouble concentrating because of the knee pressed against hers. Neither Chris nor Lynn moved for the rest of the evening.

Matt unlocked the door and plopped down on the couch while Chris excused herself and headed toward the bathroom. Lynn went to the refrigerator and grabbed three beers. Setting the beers down on the coffee table, Lynn asked Matt about the conversation that she had with Charles earlier.

"So, I had an interesting conversation with your dad this evening," Lynn said.

Matt reached for the beer and unscrewed the top. "Yeah? What about?"

"The money you owe him," Lynn said dryly as she opened her bottle.

Matt almost choked. "What?"

Lynn took a drink from her bottle and made a solemn face. "You heard what I said."

Matt stood and started pacing. "I can't believe he said anything to you about it!"

Lynn's face turned red with anger. "Is this what this charade is all about Matt? Money?"

Matt kept pacing, ignoring the question.

"I don't understand. Why did you think being engaged would solve your problem?" Lynn asked.

"The deal was, if I couldn't repay the loan when it came due, that I had to go to work for him. I thought that if he saw that I had a life here, a future here, that he wouldn't hold me to those terms. I thought maybe he would just give me an extension on the loan," Matt explained, still pacing. He stopped and looked at Lynn. "What did he say about the loan? Do you think that he's still going to hold me to it?"

Lynn shrugged and tried to control her temper. "Matt! This could be solved so easily!"

Raising his voice, he answered defiantly, "No! It can't Lynn!"

"But, Matt," Lynn pleaded, "let me help."

Matt's face showed his anger. "We've been through this before. I don't want your help!" With that, he stormed down the hall and slammed his door.

Chris walked into the living room. "Did I miss something?"

Lynn shook her head and handed her the remaining beer.

Chris plopped down onto the sofa. "I have a small confession and a big favor to ask."

For some reason, Lynn's heart skipped a beat, thinking of how Chris's knee had made her temperature rise earlier that evening. She listened as Chris continued.

"I don't know how to two-step," she admitted. She looked at Lynn with begging eyes. "Can you teach me?"

Lynn smiled. Another chance to hold Chris in her arms. Could her heart take it?

"Sure, no problem," her heart answered before she had time to think. She walked over to the stereo and found a country song with a good beat. Turning, she sauntered back over to Chris and offered her hand. Chris took it and stood for her lesson.

"We put our hands together here," Lynn said, placing their hands together. "And place your other hand here," she went on, placing Chris's hand on her shoulder. Lynn moved her other hand to the small of Chris's back. "And my hand goes here."

Lynn continued the instructions. "I guess you could say it's a lot like the three-legged race that we ran yesterday. Pretend your legs are strapped to mine, and we move together like this." Lynn began moving her feet to the beat. "When I first was learning, I had to count while I stepped. One, two, one, two," she explained, showing her by example. Within minutes, they were gliding around the floor.

"See, I knew you would pick it up quick!" Lynn exclaimed.

"Yeah, it's not so hard, I guess, as long as you have a good leader," Chris answered, still watching every step she made.

"Well, that could be a problem. Have you noticed that Matt has a hard time dancing?" Lynn asked.

Chris nodded, still watching her feet. "I thought the way he moved and everything, that he would be a good dancer."

"Well, that's because he's not used to leading," Lynn explained. "The guys he usually dances with, lead. So it's really hard for him to switch."

"I guess I really never thought about it." Chris finally looked up. "I guess that means that you tend to lead the women that you dance with, huh?"

"Yeah, just a natural born leader, I guess," Lynn kidded.

The song on the stereo changed to a slower beat. Chris and Lynn slowed their steps, making the dance seem more intimate. Lynn was intoxicated by Chris's perfume, floating in the air between them.

"So, how do you slow-dance western style?" Chris asked softly, as they continued to move together.

Lynn reviewed the woman in her arms. She tried desperately not to concentrate on how the neckline of the dress fell, revealing Chris's cleavage. Or how the thin straps had fallen from the shoulders and were now loosely hanging from her arms, revealing the soft, bare skin. She tried to discourage the thoughts of how her lips would feel as they made their way down from her neck, to her shoulders, to . . . Finally, she decided to come clean.

"Look, Chris, I'm going to be brutally honest with you. I'm having some thoughts about you that I shouldn't have. If I'm going to continue with this dance lesson, it would really help if you would change out of that dress."

Chris raised her eyes from Lynn's lips to her eyes. Ignoring Lynn's admission, she stepped closer to Lynn. Moving her hand from Lynn's shoulder to the back of her neck, she said seductively, "Probably not much differently than regular slow dancing, huh?"

Lynn looked back into Chris's eyes and swallowed hard. She felt her temperature rising quickly. Softly she replied, "Just basically tuck your hands in closer, like this"—Lynn pulled their intertwined fingers close to her body—"and move in closer together, like this." She demonstrated by pulling Chris's body close.

Chris broke eye contact and lay her head on Lynn's shoulder. Lynn could feel Chris's breath as Chris snuggled closer into her neck. Lynn was confused and lightheaded. What was this woman doing to her?

Their bodies were moving together when the song ended and a commercial began playing. Lynn both cursed and thanked the DJ under her breath, and began to pull away. Chris slid her hand from Lynn's neck up into her hair and moved her cheek so that it rested on Lynn's.

"Please don't stop," Chris whispered into Lynn's ear.

Lynn began to sway again. She slid her hand from Chris's lower back down onto her firm buttock and pulled Chris even closer. Chris did not object.

Just a few more inches, Lynn said to herself, just a few more inches and their lips would be touching. She could already imagine Chris's soft lips on hers. *This is really going to happen*, Lynn thought to herself.

And then something did happen. But not what Lynn had planned. Instead, Chris stopped abruptly, pulling away and staring over Lynn's shoulder. Lynn didn't want to look. She thought that she would turn to find Matt watching, and was frantically trying to think of an excuse for holding Chris like this. But instead, what she found was their reflection in the mirror hanging on the living room wall. She looked at Chris, who obviously hadn't been prepared for the image she saw—two women in a romantic embrace.

Chris looked at Lynn, released her fingers, and backed away.

"Lynn, I'm sorry . . . I can't . . . I just . . ." she mumbled as she put more distance between them. Running her fingers through her hair, Chris turned and scampered down the hall. Lynn heard the bedroom door shut. Damn that mirror! She had never liked it there. It would have to be destroyed.

Stumbling back, Lynn leaned against the back of a chair. She ran her hands across her face, then down the length of her body, down to the area where the burning remained. She could almost feel her wetness through the denim covering her heated pulse. God, what this woman did to her!

After regaining her composure, Lynn went into the kitchen and grabbed the pack of cigarettes hidden on top of the refrigerator. She quit smoking several years ago, but still felt the need when she needed to calm her nerves. Stepping out onto the deck, she lit a cigarette, leaned against the railing, and stared out into the darkness. She felt like she had been on an amusement park ride for the past week. And although she usually loved roller coasters, this one was making her ill.

Chris closed the bedroom door and collapsed against it. The image in the mirror had given her a shock. She peeled off her dress, which had stuck to her body from the heat penetrating from within. She threw back the sheets, turned off the light, and plopped down onto the bed. Her body writhed with frustration. She lay there staring up at the ceiling for what seemed like hours. Okay, she finally said to herself, she had to admit the attraction was there. It scared her senseless, but it was there. What if she had allowed it to go further tonight? What if they had kissed, what came next? What exactly do two women do? With those questions still unanswered in her mind, she drifted off to sleep, a very restless sleep.

Chapter Ten

"That table over there is asking for you, hon," Barb said to Lynn, pointing to table five. Lynn glanced over, and there sat Matt, Chris, Charles, and Marie.

"So, where are you two handsome couples going on this fine day?" Lynn asked, trying to avoid Chris's eyes.

"We're just having breakfast together," Marie announced cheerily. "Actually, Charles and I are spending the afternoon with the Mayes. Lynn, you remember the Mayes, and their daughter Kay, don't you?" Marie asked and winked at Lynn. "She's still single, you know!"

Marie turned to Chris. "Lynn went out with Kay once, you know."

Matt stopped the conversation immediately. "Mom, you know that didn't work out." Then, turning away, he chuckled and whispered to Chris, "Have Lynn tell you that story sometime."

No matter how hard Lynn had tried, she found her eyes drawn

to Chris's eyes. When their eyes met, Chris softly smiled, but Lynn could only look away. Chris saw hurt and sadness in those eyes. She could see she had caused some serious damage to whatever their relationship had become.

"And you have the big dance at the club tonight?" Lynn politely changed the subject.

"Yes, we do. We all wish that you would join us, but we understand," Marie answered. Lynn smiled, took their order, and handed it directly to the cook. She just wanted them to eat and leave so that she didn't have to look at Chris anymore.

"Put a rush on that, would you, Eddie?" Lynn said as she gave the cook their order.

The family was on their way within the hour.

Lynn walked in the door, threw her keys on the table, and let out a deep sigh.

"Tough day at the office?" Matt kidded.

"Memorial Day must be some kind of aphrodisiac. I don't think I've had to avoid so many men's hands in all the time I've worked there," Lynn replied.

Matt laughed. "I guess you didn't avoid the women's hands?"

"Wouldn't you like to know?" Lynn joked back.

"Hey." Matt sat up, turned to face Lynn, and smiled. "That reminds me. Tell Chris about Kay Maye!" Turning back to Chris, he said, "Or as we like to call her, 'Kay Will,' as in Kay *will* do anything!"

Lynn forced a smile. She really wasn't in the mood to tell the story. "You start, I'll fill in the details," she said to Matt.

"Okay." Matt started, "Picture this. My parents set up this blind date between Lynn and Kay. Lynn goes to pick her up, everything seems normal. She gets in Lynn's truck and is suddenly overcome by Lynn's perfume, or something! She starts unbuttoning her top, right there on the freeway, begging Lynn to—whatever! Lynn almost gets in an accident trying to fend her off. I mean she's in the truck like five minutes and she becomes a raving nympho!"

Lynn remembers the situation and laughs. "I'm going down the highway, trying to keep this woman from basically, sitting on my lap! I thought we were goners for sure."

Matt is laughing hysterically. "So Lynn gets off the highway, stops the pickup, and is trying to get this woman to settle down. But the woman won't stop. So Lynn has to take her home right there and then."

"I had to drive at like, 20 mph, trying to keep one hand on the wheel, and one hand *out* of her pants!" Lynn shook her head, still finding it hard to believe.

Chris broke in, "So what happened when you took her home?"

Lynn, slightly blushing, told her, "Well, I satisfied her. What a job. And let me tell you, it took forever. That woman had stamina!"

"Oh, like you didn't get a thing out of it?" Chris asked with a mischievous smile.

"Not really," Lynn answered. "Oh, unless you consider not having to pay for dinner and a movie."

Chris smiled, and shook her head in disbelief.

"What?" Lynn sat up and accused Chris, "Are you telling me that you've had an orgasm every time that you've been with a man?"

Matt covered his ears. "God, this conversation took a turn for the worse! You guys will talk about everything! Is there anything that you won't share?"

Reminded of last night, Lynn felt her stomach tighten. "Excuse me," she said. She stood and proceeded down the hall.

Matt watched Lynn leave, then turned to Chris. "Wow! Did the temperature just drop about a hundred degrees, or what?"

Chris gave Matt a half smile, crossed her arms, and looked down at her lap. Lynn re-emerged in her running clothes. She slid open the glass door and escaped to the beach.

Lynn felt her feet slam into the wet sand. Usually her emotional weight lifted with each step. This afternoon it just seemed to drain all of the energy from her body. After a mile, Lynn stopped and sank into the loose sand. Taking a handful, she let it slowly run

127

through her hand. She chuckled, "As sand through an hourglass, so are the days of our lives." What was she making such a big deal out of this for, anyway? Chris wasn't the only woman in the world. There would be plenty to choose from at the bar tonight. She rose and shook the sand from her body. Running back toward the house she had one thought on her mind: Tonight, she just needed to get laid.

Sitting on the deck, Lynn watched as the sun disappeared into the water. She had been careful to avoid Chris while she showered and dressed for the evening. Leaning back, she drew on her cigarette and felt the sensation of the smoke filling her lungs, then exhaled. She heard the sliding glass door open as she took a swig of beer and prayed that it was Matt. Her prayer went unanswered. She heard Chris's voice.

"Hey."

Lynn stood and leaned against the railing.

"Don't ignore me, Lynn, please." Chris pleaded softly.

Turning, Lynn leaned with her back on the railing.

Chris looked at the woman before her. Her eyes took her in from head to toe. The dark emerald suede shirt gently blew in the breeze. It was unbuttoned, revealing the white tank top–style undershirt underneath. Her eyes traveled down to Lynn's nipples gently pushing against the material. Chris shivered, knowing how the soft suede would feel against her bare skin. She longed to reach out, to slide her palms across Lynn's breasts, down the tight black jeans . . .

"God, you look great," Chris said, breathless.

Lynn shook her head. *Great, this is just what I needed,* she thought to herself. She tried to act cool.

"Yeah, well let's hope the women at the bar think so, too!" Lynn barely got out the words. To hide her nervousness, she drank the rest of her beer. "Well, gotta go!" Lynn said as she walked over to the door.

Chris moved out of her way. "Have a good time," she mumbled. Lynn did not respond.

Matt climbed in behind the steering wheel. "Looks like Lynn has started smoking again." He waited for a response, but when he didn't receive one, he continued, "She only smokes when she's really hot and bothered about something." Casually looking over at Chris, he asked, "You wouldn't happen to know anything about that, would you?"

Chris shrugged and turned away, gazing out her passenger window. Matt shook his head and started the vehicle.

Lynn wandered into the bar and took a seat next to Sam.

"Hey, you're looking pretty sexy tonight, girl!" Sam said.

"Thanks," Lynn said, clearly not excited by the attention.

"I can see that you're in a good mood. Still troubles at home?" Sam asked.

"You can't even imagine," Lynn said as she accepted the bottle that had been put down in front of her by one of the bartenders. She then filled Sam in on the details of the night before.

Sam shook her head. "I don't know what to tell you that I haven't already told you. You need to forget her, Lynn!"

Lynn softly smiled and shrugged.

Sam smiled and leaned over to Lynn. "Jeez! You've only been here a few minutes and you've already got an admirer." Sam looked over Lynn's shoulder. Lynn followed her point of vision to a pair of smiling dark brown eyes. The woman raised her glass as if to say hello.

Lynn raised her bottle back and turned to Sam. "Wow! She could definitely help me forget!"

Sam smiled and looked up. The woman approached their table and was scooting out a chair.

"Buy you a drink?" the woman asked. Then, feeling foolish when she saw Lynn already had a drink, she shyly laughed. "Or . . . another drink?"

Lynn nodded. Sam stood and said, "I'll see to that," as a way of excusing herself, and walked away to get the drinks.

"Hi. I'm Terri," the woman said, extending her hand.

"Lynn."

"I know who you are," Terri said.

Sam brought the drinks back to the table and left again. Terri leaned forward. "Wanna dance?"

Lynn nodded once again and stood with Terri. Terri dug in her pocket, pulled out some cash, and threw it onto the table. The two joined the crowd on the dance floor.

After a couple of fast songs, the pair sat back down. Lynn finished her beer and started on another one. The two made small talk for a few minutes, until a slow song began.

"Come on! I thought they'd never play anything slow!" Terri said. She grabbed Lynn's hand and pulled her back out onto the dance floor.

Terri put her arms around Lynn's waist, allowing Lynn to lead.

"So how do you know who I am?" Lynn asked. Terri was so close that she could feel the heat from her body.

"I've seen you sing here before. You have a great voice . . . among other things," Terri replied suggestively. "I've always wanted to get to know you a little better."

"Well, what would you like to know?" Lynn asked.

Terri slid her hands down to Lynn's buttocks and slowly massaged the muscles. "I wanted to know if your ass felt as good as it looked up there on stage."

Lynn was taken aback. "What else did you want to know?"

"Mmm . . . I wanted to know how your neck tasted." Leaning closer, she nuzzled then began kissing the smooth skin.

Lynn closed her eyes, feeling the passion climbing inside. "What else?"

Terri pulled her lips away and drew her finger across Lynn's lips. "I wanted to know if those lips that release that sexy voice were as soft as they look."

Lynn leaned over and hungrily kissed Terri's awaiting mouth. They continued the slow movement and kissing for several songs, through fast and slow, ignoring the others around them.

Lynn slowly pulled her lips away. "Anything else you want to know?"

Terri smiled seductively. "Nothing that you can show me in public."

Lynn smiled back. "So this is basically a physical thing, right?"

"Do you have a problem with that?" Terri replied.

Lynn simply answered, "We'll need to go to your place."

Terri took Lynn's hand and led her out of the building. Lynn smiled and waved at Sam as they passed through the bar. Sam just shook her head.

Lynn followed Terri back to her place. Unlocking the door, Terri flipped on the lights. Lynn stood in the living room while the woman grabbed two beers from the refrigerator.

"Nice place," Lynn commented.

Terri handed her one of the bottles, took her hand, and led her down the hall. "It's even nicer in here."

While Terri turned on a soft lamp and put on a CD, Lynn guzzled down the beer. Terri moved toward her, and taking her into an embrace, began swaying to the soft music.

"Now where were we?" Terri said with a mischievous smile.

The two began moving just as they had in the bar. Terri rested her head on Lynn's shoulder. The music changed to a familiar song and for a moment Lynn flashed back to the previous night when she had been dancing with Chris, slowly rocking to the music, lips coming up to meet hers. She took the mouth hungrily. Lynn felt hot as hands moved from her back and smoothed over her breasts. She felt the heat grow as lips moved down her neck.

"Oh, Chris . . ." she moaned. She knew what she had done as soon as the words left her mouth.

Terri pulled back. Lynn smiled in embarrassment.

"You can call me anything you want, baby," Terri said excitedly and started unbuttoning Lynn's shirt.

Lynn grabbed Terri's hands to stop her. She suddenly realized that she could not go through with this. She could not have sex with someone pretending it was Chris.

Lynn backed away. Running her fingers through her hair, she apologized, "I am so sorry. I can't do this."

"What?" Terri exclaimed.

"I swear, this has never happened to me before, but I just can't go through with this. I can't seem to get someone else out of my mind."

"Please tell me that 'Chris' is a woman."

"Yes. Unfortunately, a straight woman," Lynn admitted.

Terri shook her head. "A straight woman? Lynn . . ."

"Look, I know it sounds stupid, but I think she might be coming around, and if there's a chance . . ."

Terri moved in toward her and traced her finger down the zipper of Lynn's jeans, coming to rest on the source of Lynn's heat.

"But you have a sure thing here, baby. I can make you feel so good . . . let me soothe the heat . . ."

Lynn shook her head. "Terri, I just can't," she said as she backed out of the bedroom.

Lynn left Terri frustrated and let herself out of the apartment. Climbing into her truck she realized she was in no condition to drive. She pulled out her duffel bag and found and set her travel alarm, wishing that she was where she had been the last time she used the device. Folding up her jacket, she curled up on the seat and settled in for the night.

Matt and Chris collapsed into their chairs and groaned.

"I don't know when I've ever been so tired!" Chris complained.

Sam set two bottles of beer down on the table and pulled up a chair beside the two. "You two cowpokes look like you could use a drink!" She laughed. "How'd the dance go?"

"Let's just say that it will take a long time for my toes to heal!" Chris smirked.

Matt smiled sarcastically. "Where's Lynn?" he asked, scouring the array of bodies for his friend.

"She left already," Sam answered.

"Oh, I guess we'll just catch her at home then."

"No, I don't think you will." Sam smiled and winked at Matt.

"Oh, you mean she left with someone."

"Yeah, it was about time, too. They were all over each other,"

Sam said to Matt, watching out of the corner of her eye for Chris's reaction. What she wanted to see from Chris was that she didn't really care. What she saw was a look of disappointment, even hurt. Maybe her advice to Lynn wasn't that good after all, she thought to herself.

Chris tossed and turned under the sheets. She could not get the image from her mind of Lynn with another woman—dancing, kissing—but then what? What would Lynn be doing with this other woman tonight? Then it dawned on her. She knew where she could find out. She turned on the light, slid the bedside table drawer open, and picked up the novel she had found previously. She opened the book. Chapter one, page one.

Later on, Chris looked at the clock. After three, and Lynn still wasn't home. Looking back at the book in her hand, she found that she was about halfway through. She would've been finished except that she had closed it and set it aside several times. Twice she had even turned off the light, just to turn it back on and reopen the story she had become obsessed with. She had no trouble staying awake. The book made her aware of things, thoughts and feelings that she had never let herself imagine. Although she could now admit that she was attracted to Lynn, she would not concede that she was like the women in the book. These women hopped from bed to bed, looking for sex with every woman they met. She had never had the desire to be with a woman before. And really, she questioned herself, did she want to be with Lynn in that way? All she really wanted was to be held, in those strong arms. Oh, brother. Chris watched the clock now intensely as it clicked minute by minute. She was definitely feeling jealous, and a little hurt, although she could not figure out why. She was the one who had pushed Lynn away. What did she expect?

Chapter Eleven

Lynn woke to sunlight streaming through the window of the truck. Rubbing her eyes, she looked at her watch. Damn! What had happened to her alarm? Examining the clock, she laughed. The batteries had run out. Her little overnight bag wasn't infallible after all. She started the truck and raced toward the house.

Chris woke to hear someone rifling through drawers. "Lynn?" she whispered. Rolling over, she looked at the clock. It was five in the morning.

"Hey," Lynn answered from the darkness of the room. "I'm running really late. Gotta go."

Chris sank back into bed and thought to herself, *I guess satisfying the woman had taken all night. I wonder if she had satisfied Lynn . . .*

Lynn leaned against the railing of the deck, cooling down from the strenuous run she just completed. She realized she had only a few cigarettes left. Either she was going to have to get over her feelings for Chris, or she would have to buy a new pack. She lit the cigarette and drew in her first smoke, wishing that the nicotine didn't work so well at calming her nerves.

Matt slid the glass door open and stepped out onto the deck. "Oh, real healthy, Lynn. What did you do? Go for a run before you lit one up? Did you really think that one would counteract the other?"

Lynn kept her eyes on the waves crashing against the shore. "Is Chris here?" she asked.

"Not yet. I guess she went to the library today after class. Probably because she felt the tension here," Matt quipped. Placing his hands on his hips, he continued in a sarcastic manner, "What's going on between you two, anyway? Are things not going according to your game plan?"

Lynn turned and looked Matt straight in the eye. "It's not a game, Matt," she said. Solemnly, she turned back to the water.

Matt was taken aback. With Lynn, romance had always been a game. It was always the thrill of the hunt. This was hard for him to comprehend. "You mean . . . what you mean is . . ."

"What I mean is that I really care for her." Lynn flung her arms in the air. "There, I admit it! I've fallen for a straight woman!" she blurted out. "Pretty stupid, huh?"

Matt nodded. "Yeah, pretty stupid."

"Thanks for your support," Lynn said, saluting him with her bottle.

Matt paused for a moment. Irritated, he asked, "If you care for her so much, why did you go fucking around with that other woman last night?"

Lynn sighed. "I didn't have sex with her."

Matt mimicked like he was cleaning out his ears. "Excuse me? I think I heard you wrong," he said, never knowing Lynn to walk away from a woman primed and ready for a night of passion.

Lynn shook her head. "No, you heard right." She took a swig from the bottle. "Pretty hard to believe, huh?"

Matt nodded and walked over to join her at the railing. He couldn't believe that he hadn't seen this before. All this time he had been irritated at Lynn for lulling Chris into her trap. He thought back to the conversation that he and Chris had on Sunday. He had thought that Chris was just confused and had fallen victim to Lynn's charms. Now he had to look at the situation differently. Maybe Chris was confused over her feelings for Lynn because she was falling for Lynn, just like Lynn had fallen for her. Damn! How could he have been so blind! He was sure of it now. The questions Chris had asked him, the way she acted last night when she found out that Lynn had been with another woman . . . He had to do something.

Matt turned to Lynn. "I can't believe that I'm going to say this. But I think that if you give Chris a little more time . . ."

"Excuse me?" Lynn asked.

"I think that she just needs a little more time . . . to sort out her feelings."

"I don't know if I can take it anymore, Matt. One minute I feel like it's going to happen, the next minute she pulls away."

"Lynn, I think you've forgotten what a real relationship is like. You've gotten so used to jumping into bed with people that you've forgotten that a real relationship takes time. That's what you're talking about, right? A real relationship?"

Lynn ran her fingers through her hair. "Quite frankly, the whole idea scares the hell out of me."

"Well, I guess you just better decide if she's worth it. In my opinion, she is. She must be, she's the first woman to get you this hot and bothered since I met you." Matt backed away from the railing. "You know, you surprise me. You have so much patience in your stupid investments, then something like this comes along and you can't handle it."

"I don't make stupid investments. Risky maybe, but not stupid," Lynn snapped.

Matt looked her in the eyes. "I don't think Chris would be a stupid investment. Risky, but not stupid," he said.

Lynn smiled at his hint of sarcasm and remembered why he was her best friend. He shrugged, then strolled back into the house, trying to figure out what he could do to help.

"Yes, a very risky investment," Lynn mumbled to herself. She snubbed out the fading cigarette and reached for another.

"Hey, Lynn, keep your groupies away from the stage, would you?" Nikki called out.

Lynn stopped messing with the amplifier and turned around to see Terri standing in front of the stage. "Five minutes, okay guys?" Jumping down from the stage, she led Terri off to the side.

"Hi," Terri said shyly. "You don't look too happy to see me."

Lynn smiled. "Well, I didn't think I'd see a reminder of one of my life's most embarrassing moments so soon."

Terri reached out and touched Lynn's arm. "You shouldn't be embarrassed. I should be embarrassed."

"You?" Lynn questioned.

"Yeah," Terri replied. Then looking down, she pretended to smooth out a crease in her jeans. "I don't usually come on quite that strong."

Lynn smiled and blushed, remembering the night before. "Yeah, well . . . you don't have anything to be embarrassed about."

Fidgeting with a button on her shirt, Terri said, "Look, Lynn, I just wanted to come by and say that if things don't work out between you and that straight woman . . . well, I really would like to get to know you better, and not just physically, okay?" Terri reached into her pocket, pulled out a small piece of paper, and handed it to Lynn. Lynn took the paper and examined the phone number she had just been given. Smiling, she thought that if things didn't work out with Chris, she would definitely call this woman.

Lynn shoved the paper into her pocket. "I'm not sure I'll be much company for a while if things don't work out between me and Chris."

Terri smiled seductively and reached out to touch Lynn's arm. "I'd love to help you forget." Then covering her face, she laughed. "God, there I go again! I'd better leave while I'm ahead!"

Around that time, Matt and Chris walked in and waved to Sam, who was tending bar.

"The regular?" Sam called to Matt, who nodded and held up two fingers.

The couple strolled to the seating area and took seats at a table. Both noticed Lynn as soon as they walked in. She was speaking with an extremely attractive African-American woman. Chris watched the tall, thin woman who seemed to be very interested in Lynn as she spoke, and was frequently touching Lynn's arm.

Sam set the bottles of beer on the table, including one for herself, and sat down.

"Who's that?" Matt asked Sam, nodding to the woman talking to Lynn.

Sam looked in the direction that Matt had nodded. As she began peeling the label off of her bottle, she answered, "She's the one Lynn was with last night." Glancing up, she saw Chris's intent stare at the two women talking. Sam continued, "I don't know if I would've passed that one up."

"What do you mean?" Chris asked, suddenly interested in their conversation.

"Lynn didn't sleep with her," Matt answered, casually looking at Chris.

"She didn't?" Chris said.

"That's what I heard," Sam replied, as she continued to watch Chris.

After Chris turned her eyes back to the women, Matt and Sam smiled at each other mischievously, glad to have conspired on the telephone that afternoon.

Terri began to walk away from Lynn but then suddenly turned around and said, "What was that bartender's name last night? I think I may have shorted her on our drinks."

"Her name is Sam, but she's not just the bartender, she's the owner."

Lynn's eyes wandered to the bar looking for Sam and saw her sitting at a table with Matt and Chris. She definitely didn't want to go over there. She motioned to Terri. "She's over there."

Terri nodded, turned, and walked over to the threesome.

Climbing back onto the stage, Lynn organized the other women and started rehearsal again.

"Sam?" Terri asked as she leaned on the table.

Sam looked up to see Terri. She answered with a nod. "Can I help you with something?"

"Hi. I'm Terri." She paused, looking at the group, then continued, "I'm afraid I may have shorted you on my drinks last night, I was a little preoccupied . . ."

Sam smiled. "Yes, I noticed."

Terri blushed. "You see, when I got home I noticed that I probably gave you two ones instead of two fives." Terri handed over the two five-dollar bills.

Sam raised her hand up to show that she was not going to take her money. "Don't worry about it." Then, remembering her manners, she scooted out her chair and stood to make further introductions. "Terri, these are Lynn's friends, Matt and Chris."

Terri gave a full smile and extended her hand to Chris. "So, you're Chris! Oh, and Matt, nice to meet you, too!"

Chris shook her hand in confusion, not understanding why Terri knew her name.

"Please join us," said Matt.

"No, I really need to get going, but thanks anyway." Terri turned to Sam, again offering her the cash. "Are you sure you won't take this?"

Sam shook her head. "Nope. Just grace this place with your pretty face again sometime!"

Terri nodded and left.

"God! Was I just flirting?" Sam said in embarrassment.

Matt patted her on the back. "I believe you were!"

"Whatever you do, don't tell Beth!" Sam made Matt promise not to tell.

Matt placed his hand over his heart. "I promise. Now if you two will excuse me, I need to visit the little boys' room." Matt stood and walked toward the restrooms.

Sam turned to Chris. "As if he's a little boy!"

The two sat in silence for a moment watching the action on the stage.

Chris broke the silence. "So, I've been in here several times now and I've never seen your . . . significant other."

Sam looked down, still tearing at the label on the bottle. "Beth doesn't come in very often. It's hard for her . . . she's a recovering alcoholic." Looking up at Chris, she smiled. "Imagine that—a bartender falling in love with an alcoholic." Then looking back down at the torn paper she explained further, "Of course, that's not how we met or anything. She had gone on the wagon way before she met me. But I already owned the bar, she knows I love it, so—"

Sam stopped in mid-sentence and looked Chris straight in the eye. "It just goes to show you, you can't help who you fall in love with. Sometimes your heart just has a mind of its own."

Chris nodded, then contemplating if Sam had an ulterior motive with the statement, cocked her head to the side and re-examined the look on Sam's face. Sam just smiled and went back to work on her label.

Later that night, Lynn arrived home and threw her keys on the table. It took a minute for her eyes to adjust to the dim light of the television, but she could see Chris sitting by herself on the couch. Lynn placed her jacket across the back of the couch, signifying to Chris that she was not going to stay at home. Chris muted the sound on the television set.

"You going out again?" Chris asked.

"Yeah, I'm going over to Terri's place," Lynn replied, not meeting Chris's eyes.

There was silence for a minute while Lynn emptied her pockets on the table.

"You didn't sleep with her," Chris stated quietly.

Lynn, pretending to review the piece of paper that she had found in her pocket, replied, "Matt has a big mouth."

"Why?" Chris asked.

"Excuse me?" Lynn asked back.

Chris rephrased her question. "I mean, why didn't you sleep with her?"

Lynn looked up and found Chris's eyes waiting for an answer. "I'll answer that if you answer a question for me."

Chris shrugged and motioned for Lynn to continue.

Lynn paused, trying to figure out exactly how to pose the question. "Why do you want to know?"

Chris was clearly taken aback by the question. "What?"

"Why do you want to know?" Lynn's voice took on a frustrated tone. "I mean if you don't know by now!" Lynn started pacing, then stopped. "I think it's obvious, Chris! I think it's pretty damn clear just exactly why I couldn't have sex with her!" Exasperated, Lynn raised her hands and strode over to the hallway.

Trying to calm her temper, she stopped and looked back. "Let's just say that it was tempting but it wasn't who I really wanted . . ." Lynn paused, then continued, "And if there was a chance, well, I decided that it was worth the wait." Looking Chris straight in the eye, she asked, "What do you think?"

She leaned forward to hear Chris's quivering whisper. "I'm sorry. I don't know what to say. I just know that I . . ." Chris was trying to organize her thoughts and, looking at Lynn, finally was able to spit out, "want you here with me." She looked at Lynn and tried to blink away the tears in her eyes.

Lynn didn't know quite what to do. She broke away from Chris's gaze, walked to the bathroom, and shut the door quietly. She turned on the light and leaned against the counter. Lynn's wall, that she had worked so hard building all day, was crumbling. Her memory kept repeating what Matt had said, "Just give her a little more time." She opened the door a crack and saw Chris still struggling with her tears. Running her hands through her hair, Lynn called out, "If I stay, do I get some popcorn?" She saw the smile emerge on Chris's lips, and the nod that followed. Lynn closed the door, looked in the mirror, and said to herself, *Yes, I'd like to buy another ride on the roller coaster, please.*

Lynn grabbed the popcorn bowl, set it between them, and plopped down on the end of the couch.

"Don't you need to make a call?" Chris asked Lynn. Lynn looked confused.

"To Terri, to tell her that you're not coming over?"

Lynn smiled and shook her head. "I wasn't really going over to Terri's."

"Where were you going?"

Lynn shrugged. She really didn't know. She just hadn't wanted to stay there.

After a moment, Chris asked, "Are you going to sit way over there?"

"I'm afraid so," Lynn replied. "I believe it's probably safer that way."

"Safer for whom?" Chris teased.

Lynn smiled. "Probably for both of us." She stuffed a handful of popcorn in her mouth. Swallowing, she asked, "What are we watching tonight?"

"*Ghost* is on the movie channel," Chris said after scanning the *TV Guide*.

Lynn, remembering the scene in the movie at the pottery wheel, vetoed that selection. "I don't think so."

"*Aliens* is on another channel," Chris said sarcastically, then looked at Lynn.

"Yeah, that's safe," Lynn replied.

Chris shook her head and switched the channel to *Ghost* anyway. Looking over at Lynn, she smiled mischievously. "I believe whoever has possession of the remote control, gets to decide!"

"Is that right? Well, we'll see about that!" Lynn said as she lunged toward the remote. Chris drew it into her body, protecting the device. As the two began wrestling, they fell off the couch and the popcorn spilled onto the floor.

"Hold on." Lynn motioned for Chris to be quiet. "Was that just a knock on the door?"

The two listened for a moment. Then came another knock.

Lynn tiptoed over to the door and looked into the peephole.

"It's Charles and Marie!" Lynn whispered. "What kind of people drop by at eleven o'clock at night? Go get Matt!"

"Just a minute!" Lynn called to the couple at the front door, then turned back to Chris, who hadn't budged.

Chris shook her head. "I guess I neglected to mention that he's not home. He left with some guy named Paul."

Lynn ran her fingers through her hair. "What are we going to do? Both of your cars are out there! Isn't that going to look kind of funny?" she asked Chris, who looked like she had just had a brainstorm.

Chris jumped up and hurried down the hall. "Go ahead and let them in!"

"What?" Lynn said, panicking.

Chris stuck her head around the corner. "Trust me! Go ahead and let them in!" Then Lynn heard a door shut.

Lynn swung the door open. "I'm sorry it took me so long! I spilled my popcorn," she explained as she pointed to the mess on the floor.

"No problem, dear." Marie's eyes searched the living room. "Where's the kids? We saw Chris's car still out front and thought we'd stop by for ice cream." Marie held out a bag from a local creamery.

"Umm . . ." Lynn searched for something to say, then as if on cue, she heard a door open and Chris's voice from down the hall.

"What do you want, babe?" Chris said loud enough for her voice to carry. Then pretending to answer Matt's question, she laughed. "God, Matt, let me have a break! I need sustenance!" Lynn heard the door close lightly and footsteps coming down the hall. Just then, Chris emerged.

Clad in just one of Matt's button-down oxford shirts, Chris emerged from the hall, looked over at the couple still standing at the door, and pretended to stop dead in her tracks.

"Mr. and Mrs. McKinley!" Chris exclaimed. Acting embarrassed, she pulled the shirt, which had only a few buttons buttoned, unevenly at that.

Charles turned away and remarked to his wife, "See, I told you that eleven o'clock was too late!" Then turning back to Chris, trying to hold in a smile of pride for his son, said, "I'm sorry, please forgive us. We'll see you all tomorrow!"

Marie, obviously embarrassed, rushed to Chris and handed over the bag of ice cream. "Here, it's his favorite," she said. She turned and was escorted out the door by her husband.

Lynn closed the door and gave a sigh of relief.

"This worked out great!" Chris laughed, holding out the bag of ice cream. "Makes up for the spilled popcorn!" She opened the bag, pulled out a carton of orange sherbet, and shrugged. "Figures!"

Lynn rolled her eyes. Chris was getting too good at acting.

Chris leaned over to pick up the receipt that had fallen out of the bag. "Come on! Let's dig in!"

Lynn unconsciously watched as the shirt fell away from Chris's skin to reveal just enough of Chris's breasts to make her quiver.

"Umm . . . not until you put some more clothes on," Lynn said to Chris, who shrugged, handed Lynn the ice cream, and pattered back down the hall. Lynn thought there was nothing sexier than a woman wearing only a button-down shirt.

Lynn picked up the remote and changed the channel to *Aliens*. Setting the remote back onto the table, she walked into the kitchen and grabbed a couple of spoons. Chris had added a pair of shorts to her wardrobe and was changing the channel back to the previous movie.

"Chris!" Lynn whined as she motioned toward the picture on the tube.

Chris took the remote and slid it under the band of her shorts. "Sorry. If you want it, you'll have to come and get it!"

"Okay, then you can't have any ice cream!" Lynn teased, plopping down with the carton and the spoons on the far end of the couch.

"Fine!" Chris replied, plopping down in the other corner.

Lynn took the lid off of the ice cream and dug a spoon in the center of the mixture. She could tease just as well as Chris. Besides, it would do Chris good to receive some of her own medicine. She put a spoonful in her mouth and slowly withdrew the utensil. "Ummm . . ." she moaned as she let the ice cream linger in her mouth.

"Sure you don't want some?" Lynn smiled as she dipped the spoon into the ice cream again. This time drawing out only a tiny bit of the substance, she waved the spoon in Chris's direction and coaxed Chris out of her corner. Chris crawled across the couch on her hands and knees and reached for the spoon with her mouth. Lynn brought the spoon close to Chris's mouth, then pulled it away; brought it close, then pulled it away; and finally let the spoon rest on Chris's awaiting tongue.

Another spoonful was dipped, this time more than overflowing with the mixture. Lynn offered it to Chris, who took it all into her mouth. A drop escaped from her lips, and made its way down her chin. Lynn leaned forward, so close that Chris thought Lynn was going to capture the liquid with her tongue. Chris swallowed hard, feeling her heartbeat grow faster. Chris wiped the cream from her chin with her index finger and offered it to Lynn. Lynn took Chris's finger in her mouth and sucked off the orange juice.

This teasing is getting pretty serious, Lynn thought to herself, as her body began to overheat. She took the next spoonful and playfully licked it off the utensil, savoring every last drop. Then dipping in again, Lynn took the spoonful, and leaning forward, traced the full spoon up Chris's bare skin, from the first fastened shirt button all the way up Chris's neck to her chin, and finally, to her mouth.

Chris felt the liquid dripping down her warm skin, then felt the excitement of Lynn's tongue as she licked the melting dessert from her skin. "Oh my God!" Chris let escape under her breath.

After removing the creamy treat from Chris's skin, Lynn brought her face up to Chris's face. "Excuse me? Did you say something?" Lynn whispered, her lips only a breath away.

Chris looked into Lynn's eyes, then paused, trying to regain her composure. Her heart was racing, her skin hot, not to mention the burning below. She scooted back and away from Lynn's hot body. She watched as Lynn's eyes traveled from her eyes, down her neck, to her breasts and then watched as Lynn's mouth slowly formed a smile.

Chris looked down to find her nipples taut, pushing their way through the cloth. She crossed her arms, trying to hide her arousal. "You know, I'm suddenly feeling exhausted!" she said as she stood, ready to make her escape.

"No more ice cream?" Lynn teased.

"No, I think I'll just head off to bed," Chris replied, feeling her face hot with desire. She turned and staggered down the hall, stopping as she heard Lynn's voice.

"Hey, aren't you forgetting something?" Lynn called.

Chris paused and turned around. *Forgetting something? Like wanting to tear off this shirt, right here and now, to expose my nipples for you to lick and bite and suck until I come in your arms?* she thought to herself, suddenly recalling passages from the book she had read the previous night.

Lynn watched her and smiled. "The remote, please?"

Chris felt her face turn even redder, if that was possible. She padded back down the hall, withdrew the remote control from the band of her shorts, and handed it to Lynn.

Lynn reached, lingering on Chris's fingers still grasping the device. Chris, feeling an inner spark run through her body, immediately released it.

"Good night," Chris whispered. She turned and backed her way down the hall.

"'Night!" Lynn called after her in satisfaction.

Chapter Twelve

Chris slid into the booth at the café and caught Lynn's eye across the room. Lynn finished with her customer and made her way over to the booth.

"Hey, I thought you had some kind of lab class this afternoon." Lynn looked at her watch. "It's only one-thirty."

Chris smiled. "My lab was canceled this afternoon. Can you get away early? I thought maybe we could go catch a movie."

Lynn looked around the restaurant. It wasn't that busy. Then she caught herself. Sitting close to Chris, in a dark place . . . maybe she shouldn't. She was still horny from last night.

"What? Come on, it's not that busy in here!" Chris whined.

Lynn smiled, and against her better judgment, agreed to leave in fifteen minutes. Grabbing a paper from the counter, she placed it in front of Chris so that she could review the movie times while she asked another waitress to cover for her.

"My truck or your car?" Lynn asked as they walked out into the warm sun.

"Look at my car. Do you really want to go anywhere in that car?" Chris joked.

The two slid into the truck and headed to the movie theater.

"So what are we seeing?" Lynn asked.

"If I tell you, you'll probably turn around and go back to work, so let's just let it be a surprise." Chris smiled mischievously.

"Great. Some romantic flick, right? Look, I like a good romantic movie as well as the next guy—er—woman, but I just don't think it's a good idea," Lynn explained.

"Shut up and drive, woman!"

Lynn parked the truck in the parking garage next to the theater and opened Chris's door for her.

"Man, I hardly ever get a man to open my door for me!" Chris exclaimed.

"Well, maybe you've just been dating the wrong gender, ma'am," Lynn kidded.

Chris slid out and they walked to the ticket booth. Lynn grabbed Chris's hand from her wallet, pulled out the money from her own pocket, and paid for the tickets.

"Struggling student, remember?" Lynn looked at Chris and smiled.

The women entered into the lobby where they were met with the heavenly aroma of freshly popped corn and warm butter.

"Popcorn?" Lynn asked, already knowing the answer.

Chris smiled and nodded. "I'll go to the bathroom while you get it, okay?"

Lynn purchased the popcorn and soda and was leaving the line when she answered a tap on her shoulder. Thinking it was Chris, she swung around with a smile. The smile quickly faded when she turned to find . . . Susan.

"Hello, stranger," Susan said seductively.

Lynn felt the blood draining from her face and her knees beginning to buckle. Susan reached up to trace the line of hoops in Lynn's ear.

"You look great, Lynn. I hardly recognized you with your hair so short. I love the earrings, they make you look so sexy."

Lynn promptly removed her hand and backed away.

"Is that any way to greet me? After all we had together?" Susan questioned, moving again toward Lynn.

"Oh, yes, I'm sorry, forgive my manners. We parted on such good terms, didn't we?"

"You never let me explain, Lynn. You disappeared without letting me explain," Susan said in her bedroom voice. Placing her hand on Lynn's cheek, she continued, "Let's go somewhere and talk."

Just then, Chris walked up and cleared her throat. Lynn pushed Susan's hand away from her face.

Lynn quickly made introductions. "Chris, Susan. Susan, Chris."

"Susan?" Chris said as she felt her heart drop.

Susan swung around to find Chris staring at her. "Is this who you're fucking now, Lynn? A little young, isn't she?"

Chris looked at Lynn, and seeing the shock and hurt in her eyes, decided to answer the question herself.

"The answer would be yes. Of course we don't really like to call it 'fucking,' Susan, we prefer 'making love.'" Chris paused as if remembering something, then looking at Lynn she smiled mischievously and began again. "Well, I guess we could call that time under the pier 'fucking' and that time in the restroom in that Mexican restaurant, that was definitely 'fucking.' God, this whole subject is making me quite hot . . ." Chris fanned herself with her hand.

"So has she lived up to her reputation? You know, the best at everything she does?" Susan asked sarcastically.

"Well, I don't know about her reputation, but it's the best sex I've ever had," Chris answered with a straight face.

"Yes, she is good. But then again you haven't had me," Susan snapped back.

Lynn felt her blood flowing again and took her turn. "She

wouldn't have you, Susan. She's a much better judge of character than I obviously was."

Susan acted shocked. "Lynn Gregory, are you actually admitting you made an error in judgment? Wow! Miss Perfect made a mistake!"

Lynn raised her voice and felt her face turn red. "If you remember my temper at all, I suggest you leave before you see it again."

Susan raised her hands in surrender and looked at Chris while backing away. "If you ever want to try a real woman, I believe Lynn has my number," she said.

Lynn was livid. How dare she say those things! And to say that Chris was too young? After all, most of her affairs had been with her own students, college students. And right in front of her, to make a pass at her date . . . Lynn stopped. Chris was not her date.

Chris stepped toward Lynn and put her hand on her arm. "Are you okay?"

"Yeah, thanks for stepping in like that," Lynn replied

Chris took the snacks from Lynn and motioned for her to lead the way to the theater. The two walked into the darkness and took their seats. Lynn chose seats at the back, to the side.

"So, you have a temper, huh?" Chris smirked.

"Yeah, not something I'm real proud of," Lynn admitted and lowered her eyes.

Chris smiled, remembering what Lynn did to the man in the café the other day. "Well, I saw what you did to that guy in the café. If you have a temper to go with that . . ."

"Don't worry. I've really been working on it. I'm as cool as a cucumber these days!" Lynn assured her.

The lights went dim, signaling the start of the movie trailers. A couple wandered in and took seats just down the row. Lynn watched as they seated themselves.

"Oh, great!" Lynn exclaimed. Chris turned to see what was going on just as Susan gave them a little wave.

"Just ignore her and enjoy the movie. I'm here to protect you," Chris soothed her.

The movie trailers over, the main feature began. Lynn tried to calm her racing heart, though she wasn't sure if it was due to Susan, or because Chris's knee was resting against hers. Lynn talked herself into concentrating on the movie, and was enjoying the plot until she felt a hand on her knee.

Chris leaned over and whispered into Lynn's ear, "Susan's watching. You can take my hand if you want to continue our 'charade.'"

Lynn's racing heart came to a stop. She felt short of breath. Why did this woman do this to her? Ignoring the question in her mind, she slowly took Chris's hand into her own. Chris intertwined their fingers and snuggled her body closer. Lynn didn't care that Susan was there anymore, she just wanted this movie to last forever.

The picture continued, right into the scene where the two main characters made love for the first time. Lynn was embarrassed as she felt her hands getting sweaty.

Chris must have noticed, too, as she released her hand and leaned over to whisper to Lynn again. "Why don't you put your arm around me?" she suggested.

Lynn hesitated but remembered that they were seated in a safe area. No one could really see the activity in the back by the wall. Lynn always sat there just for that reason.

Lynn slowly raised her arm and slid it around Chris's shoulder. She absentmindedly caressed the skin on Chris's upper arm. Chris moved even closer. Now Lynn was praying for the movie to end. Here she was watching two people having sex on the screen, and with the excitement of Chris's body so close, she thought she might explode.

Luckily, Lynn made it to the end of the movie. She hoped Chris wouldn't want to discuss the plot on the way home. She hadn't really paid attention to anything since she had placed her arm around Chris's shoulder. The movie credits rolled onto the screen and Lynn reluctantly removed her arm from its position. Chris rested her hand on Lynn's arm and remained seated tightly next to Lynn. They sat in this position until the lights were raised and the people began shuffling out.

"Good movie, huh?" Susan said to the couple as she stood, completely ignoring the woman she was with.

Lynn simply looked up and said, "Good-bye, Susan."

Susan huffed and ushered her date down the aisle, leaving Chris and Lynn alone.

"Well, I think that went quite well, don't you?" Chris asked softly as she looked straight ahead.

"Uh-huh," was all Lynn could get out of her mouth. She decided that she'd rather concentrate on cooling down the heat between her legs than make conversation at that moment.

Chris wasn't in a hurry to move either. She looked down to her nipples hoping that they weren't showing her arousal. Unfortunately, they were. Chris crossed her arms, hiding the protruding lumps. She didn't understand. She had never been that aroused simply by having a man's arm around her. But yet here she was. She had been turned on just by Lynn's hand in hers. Finally, feeling her chest returning to normal, she stood.

"Ready?" Chris asked.

Lynn nodded, stood, and made her way down the aisle followed closely by Chris. The two exited the auditorium and made their way through the lobby.

Upon their approach, an employee swung the exit door open and asked, "Was the movie good?" He looked confused as the women walked out the door and both muttered under their breath, "What movie?"

The two walked to the truck in silence. Lynn opened the door for Chris and then proceeded to open her door and slide in behind the wheel, all in silence. It wasn't until they had pulled onto the city street that Chris dared to ask the question that was on her mind.

"So, this is the first time that you've seen her?"

Lynn sighed heavily. "Yeah."

Turning toward Lynn, Chris continued, "Was she always so—"

"Brash?" Lynn finished her sentence.

Chris chuckled. "Yeah, brash, that's a good description."

"I guess so," Lynn answered. "I hadn't really seen it that way before."

"Can I ask what you saw?"

"I think I just admired her self-confidence."

Chris shook her head slowly. "I just can't imagine you with her."

Lynn laughed. "I'm glad. I guess that I've changed a lot in the past year."

Several minutes passed as Lynn replayed in her mind everything that Susan had said. Had Susan really believed that Lynn thought of herself as perfect? Had that been the problem?

"If it matters at all, I don't think you're perfect."

Lynn snapped her head toward the direction of the statement. "How did you know . . ."

Chris softly smiled and shrugged. "I just knew that it would bother you."

"Well, your opinion matters a great deal. But do I act like I think that I'm perfect?"

"Sometimes." Then laughing, Chris continued, "But I never take you seriously!"

Lynn joined in Chris's laughter. "You and Matt, you're really good for me."

Chris turned forward and pretended to dust off the dashboard. "So . . . you wouldn't mind keeping in touch with me after this little charade is over?"

Lynn's heart burst with happiness. She tried to calm her voice before answering. Unfortunately, her brain and tongue did not cooperate. "I'd love to touch . . ." Lynn's face turned red. "What I meant was . . ."

Chris smiled softly and her eyes warmed Lynn's heart. "I'll take that as a yes."

"Whose car is that?" Lynn asked as they climbed out of her truck in front of the house.

Chris shrugged. "Are you sure it isn't another one of your old girlfriends? They seem to be coming out of the woodwork today."

Lynn unlocked the door and pretended to strangle Chris as they walked into the living room.

"Are you killing my fiancée?" Matt asked from the couch. Sitting next to him was a very attractive man.

Lynn laughed. "And you're next if you don't introduce us to your friend within the next ten seconds."

Paul stood. "Hi, I'm Paul. You must be the best friend and enemy." And then turning to Chris, he remarked, "And you must be my competition."

That got a chuckle out of Chris. "Well, I don't think that I have the necessary parts to be any kind of competition."

Lynn had to put her two cents in after that comment. "Oh, I think you have great parts!"

Matt groaned. Paul clapped his hands together. "Girl, you and I are going to get along just fine!"

The four sat around the living room sharing stories and laughter over drinks. Suddenly, Lynn looked at Chris. "Did you happen to tell Matt what happened last night?"

Chris shook her head and turned to Matt. "We had sex last night."

"Well, I'm gone for one night and I miss all the fun!" Matt chuckled and looked over at Paul.

Lynn, feeling like the statement needed some clarification, looked over at Matt. "No, she means *you* had sex last night," she said, motioning to Matt and Chris. She looked at Chris, who had lowered her head and was blushing at the misunderstanding.

"Well! I guess I really did miss something! Was I good?" Matt kidded.

"You were terrific!" Chris responded and then filled him in on the details of what had happened the night before.

"You should've seen the looks on your parents' faces!" Lynn laughed.

Matt's face looked panicked as he quickly glanced at his watch. "Speaking of my parents, we're meeting them in an hour."

"Uh-oh," Chris remarked. "I'd better go get in the shower. Lynn, do you . . ."

"Want to join you?" Lynn finished her sentence with a straight face.

Chris smiled. "In your dreams!" she answered as she made her way down the hall.

Lynn looked at the men and shrugged. "Can't blame a girl for trying!"

An hour later, the three joined Charles and Marie, who were waiting in front of the restaurant. Charles immediately approached and put his arm around Matt. "Hey son, hope we weren't too much of an interruption last night!" Laughing, he pulled his arm tight around his son as if to show Matt that he was proud of him.

Marie blushed and turned to Chris. "We really are sorry about barging in last night."

Chris, pretending to be embarrassed, laughed softly.

The next hour dragged on, partly because of the slow service, but mostly because the conversation lulled. Lynn attributed it to Marie, who kept her fingers at her temples most of the evening.

When Marie excused herself from the table, Matt seemed to jump at the opportunity to call it an early evening.

A short time later, the three walked out of the restaurant and into the lobby. Matt turned to Chris and asked, "Would you mind if Lynn took you home? Since it's so early, I thought that I might drop in on Paul."

"Weren't you with him all afternoon? Matt, is this serious?" Lynn kidded. "But I promised to stop by Sam and Beth's place."

Matt rolled his eyes and looked at Chris for her answer.

"I don't mind, if Lynn doesn't mind me tagging along," Chris said.

"No problem," Lynn responded.

Lynn turned onto the highway and headed toward their next destination.

"Sam told me about Beth being an alcoholic," Chris remarked. "That has to be hard, her owning the bar and all."

"Yeah, it is. But they must be doing something right, they've lasted longer than most couples I know."

"How long is that?" Chris asked.

"They're having their ten-year anniversary in September."

"Wow, that's great!" Chris said, thinking that even some of her straight friends didn't last that long. "What do you think their secret is?"

"Compromise, definitely compromise," Lynn stated, then upon further analysis continued, "and respect, honesty, and faithfulness."

"Sounds like things that should belong in any relationship."

"Yeah, sometimes people just forget what is really important," Lynn answered, feeling a little guilty about her lack of honesty with Chris.

Lynn drove into the condominium complex and parked. Walking around to the passenger side, she again opened the door for Chris. Chris had come to expect it and was waiting patiently.

"Nice place," Chris commented as they walked down a pathway to arrive in the doorway of their hosts.

Lynn rang the doorbell, which was immediately answered by Sam.

Swinging the door open, Sam tried to hide the surprised look on her face upon seeing Chris. "Well, look who we have here, honey."

Chris stepped into the house followed by Lynn. She was approached by a tall, slender woman with long blonde hair, which was pulled back in a thick braid. Chris was taken aback by the woman's beauty. She hadn't really had a clear picture in her mind of what Beth would look like, but this definitely wasn't close to anything she would have imagined.

"You must be Chris! Lynn didn't tell us you were coming with her!" Beth exclaimed.

"Kind of a last-minute thing, I hope you don't mind," Chris explained.

"Not at all. I've been dying to meet the woman who has"— Beth thought quickly; she was going to say, "who has smitten Lynn," but instead, she finished—"graciously saved Matt's butt."

Chris smiled. "I was just telling Lynn how beautiful your place is."

"Yes, we got it for a steal!" Sam exclaimed. Turning to Lynn,

156

she said, "Lynn helped . . ." Quickly noticing the look in Lynn's eyes, Sam who was about to say, "Lynn helped us out with some investment advice," stopped cold. "Lynn helped us move," she corrected herself.

Beth, catching Lynn's glance, offered Chris a tour of the house while Lynn and Sam stayed to discuss matters.

As soon as the two women left the room, Sam questioned Lynn. "You mean you haven't told her yet?"

Lynn, acting as if she was examining a picture on the wall, replied, "Told her what?"

"Don't act dumb with me!" Sam exclaimed. "I saw the look on your face when I was about to tell Chris how you helped us get this place!"

Lynn turned to look Sam straight in the eye. "No, I haven't told her yet. I don't know, there just never seems to be the right time."

"You're just asking for trouble, Lynn. How do you know that she won't get mad when you finally tell her? She'll probably feel like you've been lying to her!"

"Isn't this coming from the person who told me that I was asking for trouble just falling for a straight woman?" Lynn argued. Then lowering her eyes, she mumbled, "Besides, what will it matter? The feeling isn't mutual."

Sam sighed and finally admitted to Lynn, "I may have been wrong about all that."

"Why do you say that?" Lynn asked, confused.

Sam shrugged. "Just a feeling I have."

Lynn smiled. "Really?"

"Yeah, really," Sam said as she picked up the packet meant for Lynn, threw it to her, and walked from the room.

"I hope that I'm not imposing," Chris said to Beth.

"Don't be silly. There's plenty to go around!" Beth assured her as she pulled a pan of hot brownies from the oven.

"Can I help with anything?" Chris asked as Beth ran a knife through the chocolate, cutting the brownies into squares.

"Well . . ." Beth began to answer as she pulled some bowls out of the cupboard.

"No. Why don't you go relax in the living room, you've had a tough week," Sam said, entering the room and the conversation all in one sweep. Sam grabbed ice cream from the refrigerator.

Chris shrugged and turned to leave when she saw Beth place a brownie into one of the bowls.

"Umm . . . you may want to leave the brownie out of Lynn's dish. She doesn't like nuts," Chris suggested as she left the room.

Beth looked over at Sam in amazement. "How long have we known Lynn and I never knew that she didn't like nuts. Did you?"

Sam shook her head. "Maybe it's just a coincidence."

Beth smiled as she scooped the ice cream into the dishes. "Yeah, just a coincidence that this woman has gotten to know Lynn better in two weeks than we have in over a year. I don't think so."

Chris strolled into the living room to find Lynn focused on the paperwork in her hands.

"Hey, what's that?"

"Oh, nothing, just something Sam wanted me to look at," Lynn replied, shoving the papers back into the envelope.

Chris nodded. A picture album sitting on the coffee table caught her attention. Sitting down on the couch, she leaned forward and opened the book.

"Are these their wedding pictures?" she asked, looking up at Lynn.

"Yes, among other things," Lynn replied. She walked over and sat down on the floor in front of Chris. Chris placed her hands on the shoulders in front of her as Lynn flipped through the pages.

"Okay! Dessert time!" Sam said as she entered the room carrying the tray of bowls. Beth followed her with a pitcher of tea.

Beth nudged Sam and whispered into her ear, "How cozy they look. She can't even keep her hands off Lynn!"

Sam shrugged and continued on her way toward her awaiting guests.

"What are you guys looking at?" Sam asked.

"Pictures of you when you were younger," Lynn answered sarcastically.

Sam set down the tray and handed out the bowls, while Beth handed out the glasses of tea.

Lynn looked into her bowl, then into Chris's bowl. "Hey, how come I didn't get a brownie?" she exclaimed.

"Nuts," Chris answered nonchalantly. Lynn nodded in understanding.

Sam sat down on the couch and Beth settled down in front of her, adjusting the album so that all could see.

"Yeah, ten years sure adds the wrinkles!" Beth commented.

"Honey, you're more beautiful now than you've ever been," Sam replied. Beth just rolled her eyes. "Hey, there are a few pictures of you in here, too, Lynn!" Beth said, flipping ahead a few pages.

"I want to see!" exclaimed Chris, leaning over for a better view.

Beth looked through the photographs, then found the one she was looking for. Picking up the album, Beth handed it to Chris.

"Where were you guys?" Chris asked, focusing on the picture in front of her.

"I think that was the time we went down to Tijuana, thus the sombrero," Beth answered.

Sam took the book from Chris to examine the picture. "Yep, that was a wild time!" Then, looking at the opposite page, she said, "Look, here's another one of Lynn and one of her conquests of the week."

Sam handed the book back to Chris, pointing at the photograph in question.

"Conquests of the week?" Chris questioned.

"Yeah, you know, seducing women is kind of a game for Lynn." Sam chuckled. Realizing what she had said as soon as the words left her mouth, she backpedaled. "Well, not all the time . . ."

Beth reached up and slapped Sam's leg and turned to Chris. "Please excuse my wife, sometimes she doesn't think before she speaks."

Chris laughed and ran her fingers through Lynn's hair. Looking down, she teased, "Is that right Lynn? Always a game, huh?"

Lynn's face turned red. Beth watched as Chris's fingers stroked Lynn's hair, then nudged Lynn and made her face turn even redder.

"I think we've seen enough pictures for one evening!" Lynn exclaimed as she reached up and snatched the book out of Chris's hands. Then trying to change the subject, she complimented the chef. "Really good dessert, Beth!"

"Well, ours was really good. Yours wasn't much without the brownie. I'm sorry that I wasn't privy to your likes and dislikes," Beth said sarcastically.

"Oh well, more for me!" Sam teased. "I hope we didn't use all of that fudge sauce. Lots of things that I can think of to do with that fudge sauce!" she said seductively to Beth.

Chris tried to erase the mental picture that this brought to mind. Unfortunately, it only reminded her of the feeling of Lynn's tongue on her skin the night before.

"Well, I see that ten years of marriage hasn't slowed down your sex drive, Sam," Lynn said, trying to embarrass Sam the way she had embarrassed Lynn earlier.

Sam didn't even turn red before she struck back. "And I don't think anything could slow down your sex drive, Lynn!"

Lynn felt her face heat up once more. She should know better than to trade quips with Sam.

Lynn stood. "Well, I think I'd better get out of here while some of my integrity is still intact!"

"No, Lynn, don't let her run you out of here!" Beth pleaded.

"I think you'd better leave, Lynn. I think my wife might just like your company better than mine!" Sam teased.

Lynn laughed, offered her hand to Chris, and pulled her up off the couch. "No, we really need to get going, but thanks for the ice cream and the intriguing conversation," Lynn said as the four walked to the door.

"Yes, thanks for everything!" Chris exclaimed. With that, the two left.

Beth leaned against the door after the two had departed and

looked at Sam. "I think she's a goner!" she exclaimed, referring to Chris.

Sam nodded. "I think Lynn's a goner, too. I just hope she knows what she's doing."

Beth waltzed over to Sam and took her hand. "Well, I don't know if she knows what she's doing, but I know what I want to be doing."

Sam read her mind. "I'll go get the fudge sauce!"

Back at Lynn's place, Chris plopped down on the far side of the couch.

"You going to sit way over there?" Lynn said, mimicking Chris's question of the night before.

Chris mimicked back, "I believe that it's probably safer that way."

Continuing the game, Lynn replied, "Safer for whom?"

Chris laughed and finished, "Probably for both of us!"

They both smiled, knowing that the statement was true.

Chris threw Lynn the remote. "Here, I know what happens when you don't have control."

Lynn chuckled, getting the hidden meaning in that statement. Turning on the television, she began clicking through the channels. She stopped on a rerun of "The Dick Van Dyke Show" and looked over at Chris for approval. Chris nodded as she rubbed her neck. "I have a little bit of a headache."

"Do you want a massage?" Lynn offered. "Hmm . . . someone gave me one the other day . . . who was that . . . Jill, or Lisa . . . hmmm," Lynn said teasingly.

Chris threw a pillow at Lynn. "I knew it. I knew you'd forget my name as soon as my hands left your body."

Lynn shivered with the thought of those hands on her body, then looked Chris straight in the eye. "No, my dear. You, I will never forget."

They both paused, and breaking eye contact, pretended to

161

watch a commercial on the television. Lynn glanced back over at Chris, who was now massaging her temples.

"Come on." Lynn motioned for Chris to sit in front of her on the couch. Then seeing the apprehension in Chris's eyes, Lynn raised her hand over her heart. "I promise—my hands will be on their best behavior."

Chris, remembering how Lynn's tongue felt on her skin the night before, replied, "It's not just your hands that I'm worried about!" Moving across the couch, she settled in front of Lynn. Lynn slowly placed her hands on Chris's shoulders and began to gently rub. Her hands kneaded the tight muscles, starting on the shoulders and moving down Chris's arms to her hands. Lynn's fingers massaged through Chris's hair, stopped at her temples and continued down her neck. After half an hour, Lynn pulled away.

"How was that?" Lynn asked.

"Almost . . . orgasmic!" Chris replied, surprising Lynn with her choice of adjectives.

"Just another satisfied woman," Lynn joked.

Chris smiled, thinking Lynn didn't know how close she came to the truth. She leaned back against Lynn and brought the strong arms around her. Both were overcome with contentment.

"I need to stretch out a little," Lynn said, finally deciding that she was too cramped in her position.

"Go ahead and lie down," Chris replied as she let Lynn's arms loose.

Lynn stretched out on the couch. To her surprise, Chris stretched out right beside her, settling her head on Lynn's shoulder. Lynn brushed a strand of hair from Chris's eyes. "So, what's 'Chris' short for?"

Chris smiled. "Christine," she said with a sheepish grin.

"What's that smirk for?" Lynn questioned.

"Nothing, never mind . . . you'll laugh."

Lynn acted hurt. "I've never laughed at anything you've said!"

"Okay, okay." Chris paused. "Christine is my middle name. My first name is Edith. It's a family name."

Lynn tried to hold back her laughter, but was unable. "Sorry." She chuckled. "You just don't look like an Edith!"

"Thus the name Chris!" Chris pushed away from Lynn and nearly tumbled off the side of the couch. Lynn caught her just as she was going off the edge. Chris grabbed onto Lynn. The swift movement caused Chris to land tightly against the other woman. Lynn immediately loosened her hold, but Chris did not pull away.

The twinkle in Chris's eyes made Lynn feel a little uncomfortable.

"So . . . don't you have a middle name?"

Lynn grinned. "Ashley. It's just so prissy sounding. I hate to be prissy."

"Oh! Like that really surprises me!" Chris said sarcastically.

"I have a feeling that not much surprises you," Lynn commented.

"I don't know." Chris shrugged, then looked into Lynn's eyes. "This past week has been full of surprises."

"Really?" Lynn asked. "Like what?"

For a moment it seemed as if time stood still. Lynn watched the light flicker in the eyes that were fixed on hers. She felt the light touch of Chris's fingers trace the outline of her lips, then the soft whisper that followed.

"Like you, Lynn Ashley Gregory, you have been the biggest surprise."

Chris felt herself inching forward. She could not control the action, as if a magnet was pulling her closer and closer. Just a breath away from Lynn's lips, she paused, letting her fingers glide over the lips that were beckoning her.

Lynn did not move. She gathered all of her self-control as she waited. She ached in anticipation. In all her past experiences, she had been the one prolonging the moment, making the other woman squirm. Now Lynn knew how those women had felt— watching, waiting, the longing inside. She vowed never to put someone through that again.

Chris lay there, the heat within her body almost unbearable. She felt lightheaded as she traced Lynn's lips with her fingers. She knew after pulling away the other night that Lynn would not make the first move. Chris inched her lips closer.

The two were so close now that they breathed the same air. Seconds turned into minutes as both lay still, lost in each other's eyes. Chris had moved so that the soft skin of their lips was just a whisper away. The next move would be considered a kiss. Lynn could hear her heart beating, or was it Chris's? Either way, she could not hold out for much longer.

Suddenly, the lock on the door clicked. Matt tiptoed in the door and closed it softly behind him. By the dim light of the television, he could see two bodies intertwined on the couch. He smiled, hoping that they were as content in each other's arms as he had been in Paul's. Quietly stepping down the hall, he reached his room and settled in for the remainder of the night.

The two women opened their eyes. Each had pretended to be asleep. Chris had moved her head farther back onto Lynn's shoulder. The mood was broken.

Chris looked up into Lynn's eyes and softly smiled. "Good night." She then raised herself and disappeared down the hall. Lynn squeezed her eyes shut in frustration as she willed the tingling sensation in her body to stop. Impeccable timing Matt, impeccable timing.

Chris climbed into bed and pulled the covers tightly around her. Concentrating on the darkness of the room, she tried to let it cool her body down. But the burning within would not calm. Her mind kept picturing the lips that she had almost touched with her own. She had almost stepped over the imaginary line in her brain, the line between being straight and being a lesbian. She didn't want to be a "lesbian," but she knew what she did want, she wanted Lynn.

Chapter Thirteen

Lynn's internal alarm clock woke her at five the next morning. She struggled to rise, but every time she tried to move, her body protested. Every muscle in her body ached. She had to admit, she was getting a little too old for the schedule that she was keeping. The lack of sleep was taking its toll. Finally, taking a deep breath she swung her feet to the cold hardwood floor and stood. Ignoring the moaning muscles in her legs, she made her way to the shower that she hoped would relieve her spirit. A half an hour later Lynn climbed behind the wheel of her truck, took another gulp of the extra strong coffee she had prepared, and prayed for a slow morning at the café.

Two o'clock came quickly. Lynn had prayed for a slow day, but the busy crowd had actually helped her keep awake. For that she was thankful. She would have loved to go home and take a nap, but she knew that she had a lot of work that had piled up and needed attending to. Wednesday was usually Lynn's day to put on her

Investment Analyst cap. She had always used that time to do research and contact clients. Unfortunately, her little day trip with Chris yesterday had thrown her off schedule.

Matt caught Lynn in the parking lot just as she was retreating from the restaurant.

"Hey, my mom and dad canceled on us this evening. I guess my mom still isn't feeling well. How about if the four of us go out instead?"

"You mean, you and Paul, and me and Chris?"

"Yeah, kind of like a double date thing."

Lynn shook her head. "I wouldn't call it that in front of Chris."

Matt looked confused. "What do you mean? I saw you two on the couch last night."

"Yeah, I meant to thank you for your great timing," Lynn said sarcastically.

"I'm sorry. Did I interrupt something?" Matt questioned.

"I don't know if I'll ever know."

Matt smiled. "Things still going a little slow for you?"

"I'm living with frustration twenty-four hours a day, Matt."

Putting his arm around his friend, Matt soothed, "Well, take a couple of those hours and kick back and relax a little."

Lynn shook her head. "I've got mounds of work to catch up on. Having Chris there, I can't even make any business calls."

"You could if you told her . . ."

Lynn raised her hand to stop Matt in mid-sentence. "I haven't found the right time yet!"

A car horn blasted from the direction of Matt's shop to interrupt their conversation. Turning quickly to attend to his customer, he called out, "So what about tonight? That Mexican place okay? About six o'clock? I'll pick up Paul and we'll meet you there?"

Lynn sighed. "Yes, yes, yes, and yes. See you later!"

Lynn towel-dried her hair as she set her briefcase on her desk, and then flipped on her computer. She drew the towel around her neck, pulled several files out, and lay them on the desk before shutting the case and setting it back on the floor. As she waited for her computer program to open, she finished her hair, and then sank down in the desk chair to pore over her latest research. Sometime later her concentration was interrupted by the slamming of the front door. Shocked to see that it was after five o'clock, Lynn hurriedly shoved the files in her briefcase and had just begun closing her program when Chris entered the room. Lynn struggled to cover her tracks by telling her friend that she had been bored and was surfing the Internet. She took a deep breath as Chris accepted her explanation and the dinner invitation proposed.

At five-thirty, the two women walked into Los Amigos and put their names on the waiting list.

"I need to go to the bathroom," Chris whispered.

"Go on," Lynn instructed. "I'll go get us a drink."

Lynn wandered into the bar and climbed up on a bar stool. The conversation between the two men to her right immediately caught her attention.

"Hey, look at her!" commented the man with a little too much gel in his hair.

"I know her," answered the other as he loosened his tie. "That's Chris Newman, she's really hot!"

"Yeah, she is. Did you go out with her, Rick?"

He chuckled, then answered, "We did a lot more than go out!"

"You nailed her?" the other man asked with jealousy.

"Yeah. She was really good, too. She kept me going all night long!" Rick elbowed his drinking companion.

"Did she . . ."

"Oh yeah! Everything you can imagine . . ."

As he started to give details, Lynn decided that she had had enough. She did not want to hear any more. She decided to end the conversation right then and there. Leaning over, she said to the men, "You're right, she is good!"

The men both turned and looked at Lynn. The former lover looked confused. "Excuse me?" he asked.

"Oh, I was just agreeing with you," Lynn answered with a smile. "She is really good!"

Rick still looked confused.

Just then, Chris walked into the bar and toward Lynn.

"Hey babe," Lynn said, holding out her hand to the woman.

Chris looked a little confused, but by now she had learned to go with the flow and grabbed Lynn's hand.

"Hi, sweetie!" she responded.

Lynn took Chris's hand and pulled her in close. Putting both arms around her, Lynn smiled. "Honey, I think Dick would like to say hello."

"Uh, it's Rick . . ." he said, correcting Lynn.

Chris turned and finally understood what was going on.

"Hi," she said without a trace of excitement.

"Hey Chris," he responded with a half-smile.

"Honey, Rick was just saying how well he knew you!" Lynn said with a sarcastic smile.

"Really?" Chris asked as she tried to hide her amusement. Then with a serious look in her eyes, she reached out and touched Lynn's cheek. "That was the night we had that big fight, babe."

Then, leaning into Lynn's ear, she whispered, "He couldn't even get it up!"

Lynn chuckled as Chris pulled back with a smile.

"What?" Rick asked, his face turning red. He feared Chris remembered exactly what had happened that night.

"Sorry," Chris apologized to Rick. "I was just reminding her how we made up after that fight."

Chris smiled as Rick and his friend tried to keep their jaws from dropping.

The restaurant beeper sounded, and Chris led Lynn away from the men. As the waitress gathered their menus, Lynn whispered to Chris, "I hope you never wanted to go out with him again. You should've heard what he was saying about you!"

Chris shook her head and smiled. "I'm probably glad that I didn't hear!"

"Well, I was just returning yesterday's favor," Lynn remarked.

Chris laughed. "He's probably thinking that he couldn't get it up because I'm a lesbian!"

All of a sudden, Chris's face went white as she realized the words that had just left her mouth: "I'm a lesbian."

Lynn thought Chris was going to faint. She had watched the color leave her face and felt disappointment as she realized how much the word "lesbian" still bothered her friend. Maybe this relationship really wasn't going to go anywhere. For the first time Lynn felt uncomfortable as the two women sat alone. She was extremely relieved when the two men joined them a short time later.

"Hey, Lynn, do you know that woman over there?" Matt said without looking up from his menu.

Lynn raised her eyes and looked around the restaurant. Catching the eyes of a woman seated at a nearby table, she smiled politely and then lowered her eyes back to her menu.

"Nope. Never seen her before."

"Well, she keeps staring at you," Matt commented.

"Maybe she's staring at you!" Lynn laughed.

"Uh, I don't think so." Paul smiled as he looked in the woman's direction.

Lynn looked up again. They were right.

"She's cute, I guess," Chris mumbled. "But she's not your type."

Lynn turned and smiled at Chris, relieved to finally hear her voice again. "Really? And what exactly is my type?"

Chris shrugged and smiled back. "I don't know. Just not her."

Chris's smile made Lynn feel warm all over. Matt elbowed Paul and tried hard not to smile at the flirting going on.

The waitress stepped up to the table and took their orders. Matt and Chris went to the salad bar. Lynn watched as they left, unable to keep her eyes off of Chris's butt. She remembered how her hand felt the firm surface during their dance on Sunday night. The memory made her blush.

"Get your mind out of the gutter, girl!" Paul chuckled.

Lynn looked over at him, her face turning even redder. "I know, I know," she said, shaking her head. She downed the rest of her drink, then looked back at Paul and smiled. "It's just so damn hard!"

"Lynn, you just need to give her some time."

"You think?" Lynn asked.

Paul nodded, then looking toward the salad bar, mumbled, "Uh-oh."

Lynn looked over and saw Chris standing at the salad bar speaking with the woman who had been staring from the other table. Lynn watched as the two women separated and Chris continued building her salad.

Meanwhile, Matt approached the table with his plate piled high. Leaning over, he whispered in Lynn's ear, "After what she said to that woman making eyes at you, I think she's coming around."

Lynn turned. "What'd she say?" she asked curiously.

Matt smiled. "She told her 'If you don't stop making eyes at my girlfriend, I'll make sure that you don't see anything through those eyes for quite some time.'"

"She said that?" Lynn said, softly laughing. Just when you think the market is crashing, you're surprised to see that one lone stock slowly on the rise. She spent the remainder of the dinner enjoying her latest investment.

Chris looked up from her book as Lynn walked in the door and set her keys on the table.

"God, you look exhausted!" Chris exclaimed.

"I am," Lynn replied, then looking at her watch added, "and I have to be at work in four hours."

"I'm sorry, you probably didn't sleep very well last night," Chris teased.

Lynn softly smiled. Chris knew that she had left her frustrated the previous night.

"I'm going to take a quick shower," she said as she headed to the bathroom.

While Lynn was in the shower, Chris made a decision. When Lynn was towel-drying her hair, Chris leaned against the doorway.

"You need some decent sleep. Come sleep in your bed tonight," Chris suggested.

Lynn shook her head. "No, if you sleep on the couch, I'll wake you when I get up."

"I'm not going to sleep on the couch," Chris answered.

Lynn met Chris's eyes in the mirror. She was too exhausted to do anything tonight. Please don't let this be the night.

Chris blushed, realizing what Lynn had thought. "We're both adults. We can sleep in the same bed, right?"

Lynn nodded and lowered her eyes. She could lie in the same bed with Chris, but she didn't know if she would get any sleep.

Lynn wandered into the bedroom and turned down the bed as Chris shut off the lights in the living room. She climbed between the soft sheets, which smelled of Chris's perfume. Trying to calm her feelings of arousal, she rested on her side and shut her eyes. She had almost drifted off to sleep by the time Chris slid into bed.

Chris walked into the bedroom and shut the door. Turning, she saw the outline of the body in the moonlight streaming through the window. As she approached the bed, she saw the slow rise and fall of Lynn's chest as she drifted off to sleep. She felt the heat growing in her body as she slid into bed next to Lynn and noticed the tank top stretched tight, Lynn's nipples protruding against the material. Chris crawled into bed and spooned her backside into the silent body.

Lynn felt Chris's body mold into hers. She gently placed her arm around Chris's stomach and held back a moan as she felt the smooth skin under her hand. Try as she might, she could not resist the temptation to caress the softness under her fingertips. Chris responded by intertwining her legs with Lynn's. Hesitantly, Lynn moved her hand over Chris's hip, sliding across the flannel of Chris's shorts and down onto the firmness of the woman's thigh. The sensation made her own thighs tingle. Receiving no negative reaction, Lynn brought her hand back up, this time slightly lingering on Chris's buttock before smoothing back over the bare skin on her stomach. Lynn smiled as she ran her fingertips gently over Chris's belly button. Feeling the heat between them, Lynn led her palm down the same path again, over the hip onto her thigh, then back up again. This time, feeling a little more daring, Lynn slid her fingers just slightly under the bottom of Chris's shirt, almost as if by accident. Running her fingertips lightly over the indentation of the belly button then up again, this time Lynn circled farther under the shirt material. Her journey was stopped by Chris's arm, which had taken a somewhat protective stance, but Lynn was not discouraged. She reveled in the softness as she made her way down the familiar path of Chris's body several more times. Deciding to make one last attempt, she brought her fingertips under Chris's shirt, this time finding no barrier. Chris had repositioned her arm to give way to Lynn's further exploration. Lynn took her time, feeling the heat of excitement in further discovery, first letting her fingers smooth over the softness of the skin just beneath the await-ing mounds. On her next trip upward, Lynn let her fingertips glide over the area just below Chris's nipple.

Lynn's body ached as she longed for the next step of this adven-ture. She slowly made her way down the length of Chris's body, then back up again; from the softness of her thigh she moved her hands over the tightness of her buttock. She savored the sensation of her fingers ducking under the material to the focus of her desire. Gently, she caressed the soft mounds with her fingertips and let her thumb just slightly graze Chris's now taut nipple. Stifling a moan, Lynn heard a slight gasp from Chris, who was now so close to her that she could feel even the slightest movement. As she smoothed her way back to Chris's stomach, she felt fingers inter-twine with hers. Chris moved Lynn's hand under her chin and pulled Lynn's arms tightly around her. Lynn knew there would be no further exploration tonight.

To Lynn's surprise, she was completely content. This was the intimacy that she had longed for. She wanted to tell Chris, tell her that she loved her, wanted her, needed her.

"Chris—" Lynn began through the stillness. But her confession would not be heard tonight. Chris stopped her before she could utter another word.

"Sshh . . ." Chris whispered without turning her head. "I thought you were tired. Go to sleep."

Maybe Chris was right. It was probably not the right time to discuss this. Lynn snuggled her face into the sweetly scented hair and immediately began to drift into sleep.

It wasn't that easy for Chris. She had been still, in another woman's arms for hours. Her body felt a mixture of contentment and excitement; her mind battled the same. Now she understood the feeling of intimacy Lynn had described to her almost a week ago, a feeling that until now, she had never known. But she was lying with a woman, and this is what was troubling her. She had never thought that love between two women was wrong. But she had never, in her wildest imagination, thought that she would be one of the two women. Her mind experienced terror at the very concept. She could not be a lesbian . . . She finally drifted off to sleep.

Chapter Fourteen

Lynn jerked awake and slapped furiously at the button on the alarm clock to stop the shrill buzzing sound. She tried to focus her eyes. Could it really be five o'clock already? She sensed the body behind her shift and felt the arm flung around her waist pull her body closer. Oh, how she wished that she didn't have to go to work. Unfortunately, one of the waitresses was out due to a death in her family. Lynn had no choice.

She slowly slipped from the bed and turned the alarm clock off. Sighing, she tucked the covers around the sleeping woman and backed away. Quietly, she pulled clothes from the drawers and tiptoed to the door. Before leaving the room, she turned to gaze once more upon the warm body now snuggling with Lynn's abandoned pillow. Tonight she would tell Chris the truth, she decided. Lynn softly shut the door and dressed as she made her way down the hall. Running a brush through her hair, she took one last look in the mirror, and headed out to work.

Chris felt Lynn climb out of bed and clutched at the warm pillow beside her. For a moment she wanted desperately to beg Lynn to stay, but then fell back into a deep sleep. She dreamt of the softness of Lynn's hands on her skin and awoke to find her own hands caressing her body just as Lynn had done the night before.

Several hours later, after a refreshing shower and a couple of cups of coffee, Chris called her answering machine and listened to her messages. There was an urgent call from Debbie, her friend at the college administration office.

Chris dialed the number. "Yes, is Debbie available?" She was quickly transferred to Debbie's desk.

"Hello, this is Debbie."

"Hi Debbie, this is Chris. What's up?"

"Hey, I just wanted to know how you got the biggest investment firm in Los Angeles to pay for your next semester's tuition!"

"Excuse me?"

"We just received your next semester's tuition in full on a check made payable from Peabody, Smith, Hadley, and Gregory. You did know about it, didn't you?"

Chris was stunned. "No, there must be some mistake."

"No mistake. It came with a letter stating exactly what the check represented, and for whom."

"My entire semester's tuition?"

"Yeah."

"I didn't, don't know anything about it." Chris was extremely confused. "It came with a letter? On letterhead?"

"Yeah, you want a copy?"

"I would. Can I come down now and get it?"

"No problem."

"I'll be right there." Chris hung up the phone in a daze. An investment firm? She grabbed her keys and sped down to the college office.

"Yes, I'm here to see Debbie," Chris said to the person at the counter. She waited only a few moments before Debbie appeared.

"Hi, Chris," Debbie said as she ushered her into the

hallway, and handed her a piece of paper. "Here's a copy of the letter. How strange that you didn't know anything about it. You don't have any kind of trust fund or anything, huh?"

Chris took the letter from Debbie. "No, no trust fund."

Chris read the letter to herself, "This represents payment in full for the fall semester for Chris Newman." What was going on? She reviewed the letterhead, "Peabody, Smith, Hadley, and Gregory, Investment Analysts." Wait a minute, "Gregory?" She scanned the left side of the letterhead, which contained the names of the Partners and the Associates. She couldn't believe what she saw: "Lynn A. Gregory, Partner."

Debbie must have read the shock in Chris's eyes. "What? Did you figure it out?"

Chris nodded and raised her eyes from the paper. "I've been kind of hanging out with Lynn Gregory. But I had no idea that she was a partner."

"Wait a minute," Debbie interrupted. "You've been 'hanging out' with Lynn Gregory?"

"Yeah," Chris answered. "Why?"

Debbie looked at her for a moment before responding. "You do know that she's a lesbian, right? I mean, what are you doing hanging out with a dyke?"

"How do you know so much about Lynn Gregory?" Chris asked suspiciously.

"I tried to get an internship with that firm last year. I wanted to find out everything that I could about the company. The three men partners are married with children and Ms. Gregory is openly gay," Debbie explained, then asked again, "You know that she's gay, right?"

"Of course I know that," Chris answered with irritation. "Why are you acting like it's such a big deal?"

Debbie brushed at her skirt and tried to sound nonchalant when asking her next question. "So . . . are you fooling around with her?"

Chris felt all of the air leave her lungs. "What?"

"Well, you know . . . you two are friends, she paid your tuition . . . it just kind of looks like . . ."

Chris cut her friend off in midsentence. "Looks like what, Debbie?" She felt her voice rising in anger, or was it in embarrassment? "What? Payment for services?"

Debbie signaled for Chris to lower her voice. "No . . . but maybe trying to coax you to . . . you know, show your gratitude?"

Chris looked at Debbie while she pondered the question herself. Then, folding the letter, she shook her head in disbelief. She quickly turned and jogged back down the hall, and, ignoring Debbie's voice, ran out to the parking lot.

Chris climbed in her car and slammed the door shut. Then she just sat there. The questions entered her mind so quickly that she couldn't even concentrate. Why would Lynn lie to her? Why would she portray herself as she had, a struggling waitress? It was almost as if Lynn had been an actress playing a part. And how did Matt really figure into all of this? She tried to make sense of it all. Then she remembered something Sam said, something that had nagged at the back of her mind, "seducing women is kind of a game for Lynn." Could it be true? Had this been a game for Lynn? Had it taken too long, leading Lynn to play her last card . . . money? Chris knew that there was only one person who would tell her the truth. She started her car and headed back down the highway.

Chris drove like a wild woman to Matt's garage. She jogged into the building, where Matt smiled at her from behind the counter as he helped a customer. She tapped her fingers impatiently on the counter. The customer tore out the check in payment for repairs, thanked Matt, and hurried out the door.

"What's wrong with you?" Matt asked.

"This is what's wrong with me," Chris answered as she slid the letter across the counter for his perusal.

Matt picked up the letter, quickly scanning it, then ran his fingers through his hair and placed the paper back on the counter.

"Well?" Chris remarked.

"She's going to be really angry about this," Matt replied.

"So, you knew about this? You knew about her?" Chris backed away, running her fingers through her hair this time.

"Look, she doesn't like anyone to know," Matt said, trying to explain.

"She doesn't like anyone to know what, Matt?" Chris was irritated.

"That she has money and—"

Chris interrupted, "That she's working in some dive as a waitress?"

Matt smiled. "Don't let her hear you say that. She owns that dive."

Chris couldn't believe it. You could have knocked her over with a feather. "So, everything about her has been a lie?" Chris asked, feeling betrayed.

Matt shook his head. "Nothing has been a lie. She never said that she wasn't rich. She never said that she didn't own the restaurant, which by the way, her employees don't know. She never told you anything that was untrue."

"So, why did she do it?" Chris asked. "Why did she pay for my tuition, Matt?"

Matt shrugged. "I don't know, just trying to do something nice, I guess."

"Something nice? Are you sure? Or was she trying to buy me?"

"Buy you? What do you mean?" Matt answered, cleaning the oil off his hands with a towel.

"You know, her little game wasn't working. I wasn't responding to her sexual overtures, so . . ."

Matt's face turned red with anger. "Don't even go there! I can't believe that you would even think Lynn would do something like that!"

"How would I know?" Chris said sarcastically. "I don't even know the real Lynn Gregory!" She picked up the letter, folded it, and left the building.

Matt jogged to catch up with her. "Chris, this doesn't change anything! She's still the same person," Matt tried to explain.

Chris opened her car door, not muttering a word.

"You see? This is why she doesn't tell anyone. People treat her differently when they find out who she is." Matt acted disgusted and turned to walk away.

"I wouldn't have thought any different of her if I had known!" Chris called after him.

Matt turned around. "Are you sure about that? You saw her as your equal before. Now how do you see her?"

Chris paused. Matt shook his head, flipped the rag in his hand motioning her to leave, turned, and walked away. Chris sped out of the parking lot. Matt watched her drive away and thought, *This confusion about her sexuality is going to drive her crazy.*

Lynn towel-dried her hair and ran gel through it. Humming to the music that was blaring, she buttoned her shirt, and tucked it into her favorite jeans. Looking in the mirror, she checked her hair and unbuttoned one button to reveal just a bit of cleavage. She wanted to look her best, maybe even a little sexy for Chris. Looking at her watch, she felt the excitement growing inside as she hoped Chris would be home soon. She had been disappointed that Chris hadn't been there when she had gotten off of work. Knowing that Chris didn't have class on Fridays, Lynn wondered where Chris had gone.

Chris sped down the freeway, thoughts racing in her mind. *Why didn't she tell me who she really was?* After all the discussions that they had, Chris thought they didn't have any secrets from each other. She was so confused. People don't just give money away. Especially investment analysts, knowing that there was no tax benefit. And if it was supposed to be anonymous, why send it on letterhead? She screeched to a stop in front of the house and stormed to the door.

Chris walked in, confusion and betrayal filling her head.

"Hi there!" Lynn smiled as she turned down the volume of the music.

Chris began pacing back and forth in front of Lynn.

179

"Hey, calm down, what's wrong?" Lynn said, placing her hand on the woman's shoulder.

Chris pushed Lynn's hand off of her arm and shoved the letter in front of Lynn's face. Lynn took the letter and sat down on the couch. She scanned the piece of paper, placed it on the table, and turned to Chris, who was still pacing.

"I don't know what to say. You weren't ever supposed to see this," Lynn explained.

"I wasn't supposed to see it? You mean I wasn't ever supposed to know it was you?" Chris said, irritation filling her voice. "If I wasn't supposed to know, why send the money on a company check, with letterhead?"

"Those weren't my instructions," Lynn said calmly.

"Are you sure? Are you sure that maybe you didn't do it on purpose, knowing that I would find out?"

"Why would I do that?" Lynn asked, still trying to remain the calmer of the two.

"You know, just part of your little game you play with your women. Maybe you thought a little money would make it easier for me to sleep with you?" Chris shouted.

Lynn felt like a knife had just entered her heart. How could Chris even think such a thing? Standing, Lynn lashed back.

"Look, if this was just a game, I would've taken you already! I could've had you any night this week if I had wanted!"

"Taken me? Did you really use those words, 'taken me'? Why didn't you just use the word 'fuck,' Lynn? You could've fucked me already?" Chris was pacing now, words spurting out of her mouth. "That's all I am to you, isn't it? Just another person to add to your list. I didn't even have a choice in the matter, did I? The mighty Lynn Gregory set her sights on seducing me. And I was falling straight into your little trap. But I wasn't responding quickly enough, was that what it was? So you threw a little money my way." Suddenly she stopped. "God, I just figured it out. I bet you lied to me about Susan, too! I bet that you're the one that screwed around on her! That's why Susan used that term, isn't it? That's why she asked if you were fucking me now!"

Chris watched as the tears that had been forming in Lynn's eyes stopped, as if being withdrawn back into their tear ducts. She saw the hurt in Lynn's brown eyes turn into a cold, hard blackness. She felt fear as Lynn breathed out as if to release all of the compassion inside and breathe back ice to fill her veins. Chris knew she had gone too far. Whatever Lynn did was not deserving of her last statement.

Lynn felt the sting of Chris's words. Anger rose within her, overtaking her entire body. She felt the roller coaster sliding off the tracks and crashing into darkness. Lynn just stood there, frozen, unable to speak.

Chris, getting no response from Lynn, quickly walked to the bedroom and slammed the door. She again paced across the floor. She needed a response. She needed it now. She opened the bedroom door and started down the hall when she heard Lynn on the phone.

"Yes, Peter Hadley, please . . . Lynn Gregory." Lynn was speaking quietly. "Peter, Lynn. I just had a visit from Chris Newman . . . the tuition I paid out . . . yes. Peter, how did those funds get sent on a company check accompanied by instructions on letterhead?" Lynn paused and lit a cigarette, listening for a moment before raising her voice, "Always a cashier's check, Peter, always a cashier's check, and my God, Peter, letterhead?" She paused again, listening, and continued, "If she's screwing up my account, she's got to be screwing up other clients' accounts. Fire her, Peter. I mean it, fire her ass, before we lose a really big account over it."

Listening again, she replied, "I'm really happy to know that you can still see that I can be a coldhearted bitch. See what this business does to me?"

Lynn ran her fingers through her hair, then covered her face and started again calmly. "Look, what's done is done. Before I forget, that check for Miguel's hospital bills just wasn't enough. Send another five thousand, would you? And Peter—no company check!" Lynn slammed down the phone and turned to find Chris standing there.

"I thought that Matt didn't like you to smoke in the house," Chris remarked.

"It's my house, I'll do what I want," Lynn said, the ice crystals forming on every syllable. Then, seeing the look on Chris's face, she clarified her statement. "Yes, this is my house. I own it, and the café."

It had never occurred to Chris that Lynn might own the house. "And Matt?" she inquired.

"He needed a place to stay. I liked the company, so he moved in," Lynn explained coldly.

Chris nodded in bewilderment. She was having a hard time processing all these new revelations.

Lynn looked Chris straight in the eye. "Look, I'm sorry that you could even consider that this was a game for me, or that I would try and buy you like that." Lynn broke eye contact and lowered her gaze to the ground. "I'm sorry if you ever felt pressured to . . ." She paused for a second, and continued, "I'm sorry if I've made unwelcome advances. I thought something was happening between us."

Chris crossed her arms against her chest. "I'm not a lesbian, Lynn!" she stated loudly.

Lynn felt the blade turn in her heart. "I really apologize. Your little charade is almost over. I'll just stay out of your way until you leave." With that, Lynn took her keys from the table and walked out, closing the door, and their relationship, softly behind her.

Chris changed into her running gear and began jogging through the soft sand toward the harder surface. She started out slowly, letting the cool breeze blow through her hair, watching the people taking advantage of the longer days. She saw the families, with their blankets stretched out, their children building castles from the sand. She watched as young men played a game of football. She stared as she passed a couple of women, arms interlocked. She quickened her pace, and before long she was at a full run. She ran at full speed until she doubled over with pain in her side. Her knees collapsing into the sand, she felt the tears running down her face. It didn't matter how fast she had run, she could not run away from her feelings for Lynn. She sat down on the gritty surface and covered her face with her hands. What had she done? Did she really mean those things that had spouted from her own mouth? She had pushed Lynn away so hard. Now she was gone.

Chris sat in the sand, watching the sun as it shone a brilliant red, then began disappearing into the sea. She felt like the setting of the sun closely correlated with the last week. She had seen the brilliant red—then saw it disappear before her eyes. Standing, she began jogging back, not really caring that it was probably past the time they were supposed to meet Matt's parents.

Lynn wandered into Matt's shop and leaned against the hood of the car that he was repairing. Matt looked up to find eyes full of pain.

"Hey, are you all right?" he asked, already knowing the answer.

"It's over between me and Chris."

"I tried to warn you. You didn't answer the phone."

"I guess I didn't hear it. So she came here first?"

Matt nodded. "I tried to explain. She just wouldn't listen."

Lynn shrugged. "Yeah, she wouldn't listen to me either."

"What did you say to her?" Matt asked.

"It doesn't matter. She had a right to be angry. I should have told her," Lynn mumbled as she stared off into space.

"Just let her cool off, then you two can talk it out."

Lynn shook her head. "No, too many things were said. It's time for me to bow out."

"Bow out? You mean you're giving up?" Matt asked in disbelief.

Lynn nodded, then turned to Matt. "I'm through messing with her life, Matt. She's frustrated, I'm frustrated. I can't deal with it anymore."

"Wow. Stupid me, I thought you were actually in love with her." Matt acted disgusted as he cleaned off his hands.

Lynn felt the tears well up in her eyes. "I do love her. That's why I have to walk away."

"Lynn." Matt took Lynn's face in his hands and looked into her eyes. "She's in love with you, too, she's just fighting it."

Lynn backed away from her friend. "No more fighting, no more hurting, no more . . . love."

Reaching the edge of the building, Lynn stopped and ran her fingers through her hair. "I won't be around for a while, but if you need me, you know where you can find me."

Chris slowed her pace to a walk as she approached the house. Matt was dressed for the evening and was leaning against the railing watching her approach.

"She's gone," Chris said, not raising her eyes as she climbed the stairs.

"I know. Isn't that what you wanted?" Matt asked softly, still staring into the fading light.

"I don't know what I wanted," Chris replied.

Matt nodded, took a swig from his bottle, and looked back toward the water.

"Is that all you're going to say?" Chris asked, wanting some kind of reassurance that everything would be okay.

Matt turned around, leaned back onto the railing, and shrugged. "What would you like me to say?" Matt paused, shook his head, and slid open the door, stopping only to say, "I called to tell my parents that we were running late. They're expecting us at seven."

Matt turned over the ignition as Chris slid into the car next to him. She reached over and pulled the door shut and remembered fondly how Lynn had always opened the door for her. She had tried to push the day's events back in her mind during her shower. Unfortunately, just having this one memory made her eyes fill with tears.

"Oh God, Chris, please tell me that you're not going to be like this all night!" Matt groaned.

Chris sighed. "Don't worry. I'll be fine. I'm sure the concert will take my mind off of it."

Matt laughed. "You do remember that we're going to a classical music concert, right?"

"Yeah. I like classical music. I just hope it's mostly upbeat." Chris paused, then began again, "Matt . . . about Lynn . . ."

184

Matt cut her off sharply. "Chris, I don't want to hear one more word about it, not tonight, maybe ever. Okay?"

Chris nodded and dried her eyes.

Although Chris found it unbelievably difficult, she was able to make small talk all through dinner. At least the dinner conversation kept her mind occupied; the concert did not. During the first hour, no matter how hard she tried, Chris could not keep her mind from wandering. She relived the past two weeks, then the events of that day. By intermission, Chris was sitting on the edge of her seat. As the lights were turned up, she immediately excused herself to use the bathroom.

Chris rushed to the pay phone, tore open the phone directory, and searched frantically for the number for the bar. Locating it, she dialed . . . one ring . . . two rings . . . three rings . . . come on, come on.

Someone answered, "Rainbow Room," the voice yelled over the music in the background.

"Sam?" Chris asked.

"Yes, this is Sam."

"Sam, this is Chris. Is there any way that you can get Lynn to the phone, I'll wait if I have to," Chris said, sounding panicky.

"Chris, Lynn didn't come in tonight. Said she wasn't feeling well." Sam paused. After no response on the other end of the line, Sam asked, "Isn't she at home?"

"Umm . . . never mind," Chris said into the phone before slowly placing the receiver back on the base. She fed another set of coins into the device and dialed the number at the house. The phone rang on the other end—one, two, three, four, five times. *Come on, pick up, Lynn,* she said to herself. Chris heard the machine click on and waited for the beep. "Lynn, if you're there, pick up, please!" Chris waited for an answer and felt a surge of disappointment as she hung up. What was she going to do?

The two couples sat in a booth reviewing the menus. Chris had tried to give Matt "the look" when his parents had offered to buy dessert after the concert, but as usual, Matt didn't catch on. It didn't even seem to faze him when she declined on ice cream. He should've known that she was close to the breaking point from that gesture alone. Chris was having trouble keeping her mind on the conversation at hand, but the next sentence out of Marie's mouth brought her screeching back to reality.

"Matty, I hope that you can put up with us for a little longer!" Marie smiled and placed her hand on her husband's. "John and Barbara Murdock, you know, the couple that we ran into tonight? Well, it seems that they were going on a cruise with another couple next week, and the other couple had to cancel. They asked us if we'd like to take the couple's place!"

Matt gulped as he looked first at his mom, then at his dad.

"It's actually one of those three-day cruises down to Mexico and back. It doesn't actually start until Tuesday, and we get back late Friday," Charles explained.

"Yes," Marie smiled. "That means we have at least four more days to spend with you! Tomorrow, Sunday, Monday, and then next Saturday . . ."

"Maybe we'll just stay until next Sunday, that way we'll have the whole next weekend with you," Charles suggested.

Matt looked at Chris and nervously smiled. "Great! Right, Chris?"

Chris tried her best to return the smile. Another week of this charade? Could this day get any worse?

Matt pulled up in front of the house and put the car into park. He could see the disappointment on Chris's face when Lynn's truck wasn't in the driveway. They walked into the house and Chris headed to the couch.

"So . . . Chris," Matt stuttered, trying to find a way to ask how she felt about playing his fiancée for another week. "About my parents staying for another week . . . I had no way of knowing. I couldn't tell them not to—"

"Matt," Chris softly interrupted. "It's okay. I know you couldn't do anything about it. What's another week?" she said resignedly.

Matt hugged her. He knew she was in pain, and this just added to her misery. Chris pulled away and plopped down on the couch.

"Aren't you going to bed?" Matt asked. "It's late."

"No, I'm just going to hang out here for a while," Chris replied, turning on the television.

Matt sat down on the coffee table in front of Chris. "She won't be home tonight, Chris."

Chris avoided his eyes. "I'm not waiting for her. I'll go in to bed soon, I promise."

Matt sighed, stood, and walked down the hall. He hated to see the most important women in his life in such pain.

Lynn lay on the leather couch in her hotel room and stared out the door at the city lights. She had kept the room in the city as a permanent second residence so that she had a place to stay when she was working. It was easier than a regular apartment as it was always kept clean, and due to room service, she never had to cook.

Getting up from the couch she wandered over and opened the doors out onto the patio. She leaned on the railing and looked down at the cars and the people below. Nothing had changed. Her life had stopped, but everything else had continued. She tried to take a breath of fresh air but breathed in only smog. She longed for the cool, clean ocean breeze.

Back at Lynn and Matt's place, Chris flipped through the channels unable to find anything that she wanted to watch. Maybe it was because she couldn't think of anything else but Lynn. Her mind was reeling with all of the new information she had uncovered today. Lynn Gregory an investment analyst? That explained the investment magazine in her bedside drawer. Chris walked to the bedroom, changed her clothes, and grabbed the magazine she had previously found.

With a full dish of ice cream in hand, Chris plopped back down on the couch and opened the magazine. She put the first spoonful in her mouth. It immediately brought back the memories of the other night and the feeling of Lynn's tongue on her bare skin. Shivering, she shook the feeling aside and flipped through the pages. What a boring magazine, she thought, until she came upon a very interesting picture, a picture of Lynn. At least the face looked like Lynn's. She read the caption under the photograph, "Lynn Gregory at the top of her game." No wonder Lynn had kept it.

Chris settled in to read the two-page article on Lynn. When she had finished, she sat in shock, for the second time that day. The article said Lynn finished college at nineteen, made full partner in her investment firm at twenty-three and, as they said in the article, was "on top of her game" at thirty. Lynn said she was thirty-two. This woman had it all. What had happened to the woman in the last two years to make her completely change her life?

The bowl of ice cream empty, Chris closed the magazine and thought about the Lynn Gregory that she had come to know. She wasn't anything like the headstrong genius she had read about. She wasn't even sure that she would have liked Lynn if she had been like the person in the article. Maybe Matt was right. Maybe she wouldn't have felt the connection with Lynn if she had known who she was in the beginning. Chris stretched out on the couch and drifted off to sleep pondering the question.

Back at the hotel, Lynn finished a drink. Turning down the comforter, she thought back to where she was just the night before. At home in her own bed, with the woman she loved lying in her arms. She climbed into the sheets, turned off the light, and lay there feeling entirely alone. She felt the first tear roll down her cheek. Rolling over, she softly cried herself to sleep.

Chapter Fifteen

Chris awoke to someone gently rubbing her arm. She smiled and sleepily opened her eyes. "Lynn?" But as she focused she saw not Lynn sitting beside her, but Matt.

Matt shook his head. "I told you that she wouldn't come home last night. I don't know why you waited out here for her."

Chris stretched out after being cramped on the couch all night. Seeing the magazine on the table, she felt the pain of yesterday's events overwhelm her again.

Matt followed her eyes to the magazine on the table. Picking it up he said, "Where did you find this?" Without waiting for an answer he chuckled and threw it back on the table, commenting, "Totally different person now, huh?"

Chris nodded in agreement. "What happened to her?"

"I guess she just got tired of all the crap. When her personal life fell apart, she made a choice to stop and smell the roses."

"She just gave it all up?" Chris questioned.

"Yeah, well sort of. She still works once in a while. She still has a few clients and she still looks into investments for my dad. She has to do certain things to keep up her status as partner," Matt explained.

"Well, I gotta go," he said as he stood and walked to the door, holding a cup of coffee. "See you tonight."

Chris reached over and again examined the picture of Lynn in the article. Then she let her eyes scan the photographs on the mantel. The exterior differences were obvious—her hair was shorter now; she had ear piercings; her body was much more toned and muscular. But the real difference was in her eyes. Lynn had been so right: you could tell a lot about a person through the eyes. The eyes of the woman in the picture were cold and shallow. She remembered the eyes she had looked into not more than two days ago—warm, sensitive, caring. Then, the eyes grew full of anger and hurt as Chris's memory from their encounter on Friday resurfaced in her mind.

Suddenly, Chris found herself rolled into a ball, occupying only a fraction of the large stuffed sofa. She curled her knees in even closer and softly cried herself to sleep.

The shrill ring of the phone abruptly woke Chris from her dreams. Rubbing her face, she tried to wipe away the remnants of the tears that had dried on her cheeks. She rushed to the device, somehow hoping that it was Lynn. Chris tried not to show her disappointment as she heard Matt's voice on the other end.

"What'd you do, fall back asleep?" Matt laughed.

"Uh . . . yeah, I guess so," Chris answered, still rubbing her eyes.

"Well, get off your butt and bring me something to eat, woman!"

"Excuse me?" Chris smiled at Matt's attempt to sound tough.

"Oh come on, I'm starving and I can't get away," Matt pleaded. "Please!"

"You're pitiful!" She chuckled. "You'll have to wait until I shower!"

Chris hung up the phone and ran her fingers through her hair. She shuffled down the hall to the shower, thankful to have a reason to climb out of the pit that she had fallen into this morning.

Chris watched Matt pick at his food. "You're sure not eating much for being starved!"

Matt swirled a french fry in the mound of ketchup as he looked up at Chris. "Yeah, well, the truth is, I had to get you out of the house. Lynn realized this morning that she needed a few things, her briefcase, laptop . . . I guess she left in such a hurry yesterday . . ."

Chris lowered her eyes, remembering Lynn's exit all too well. "Matt—" Chris began.

Matt put his hand up to stop her from continuing. "Stop. Don't want to hear it."

"I just wanted to say that I didn't mean all the things—"

Matt put his hand up again. "She didn't tell me what was said. My guess is that she didn't want me holding it against you."

Chris sat back in her chair. "I don't have to stay at the house, Matt."

Running his fingers through his hair, Matt sighed. "That's not what she wants, Chris."

Chris nodded. "So, where's she staying? With one of her girl-friends?"

Swallowing his bite, Matt chuckled at the underlying jealousy in the question. "No." He shook his head. "She's got a place in the city. Believe me, it's more than comfortable."

Chris sat back in silence, still trying to process all of the new information that had been revealed. Matt began gathering the trash from their lunch.

"So, what are you going to do with your free evening tonight?" Matt asked.

Chris shrugged. "Study, I guess. I've gotten behind, I need to catch up."

"Exciting Saturday night, girl! You're welcome to come out with me and Paul," Matt politely offered.

"Oh yeah, let's see, going out with you on your date, or staying home studying. What a choice," Chris grumbled. A few days ago she would have loved a free evening, just to be with Lynn.

"But it's a choice," Matt suggested as he threw the trash into the can. "Well, I've got to get back to work. Paul's picking me up at six, if you're interested."

Chris rose from her chair and walked toward the door. "See you later."

Chris tried not to race back to the house. She set her expectations low, knowing that Lynn would have rushed in and rushed out. There would be no way Lynn would still be there. She was right. Lynn's truck was nowhere in sight. Upon searching the house, she could find no signs that Lynn had been there, except that the computer and the briefcase were gone. No note saying that everything would be okay. No card saying that they would still be friends. Just an empty house. Chris grabbed her backpack and pulled out a book. She would focus her energies on studying. Sinking down on the couch, she opened her book to Chapter Thirteen. She would need to get through Chapter Sixteen to catch up. She began reading, and then drifted off to sleep.

The slamming of the door woke Chris from a deep sleep. She glanced at the clock: it was almost six.

Matt looked over the edge of the couch. "I can see that you got a lot of studying done!" he chuckled. "Paul will be here anytime. Tell him that I'm running late. I'll try to make it quick!"

Chris rubbed her eyes and sat up. Damn, what a wasted afternoon.

The knock on the door startled her. Paul was early. Running her fingers through her hair, she walked groggily across the room and swung the door open.

"I take it Matt's not ready." Paul smiled.

"No," Chris replied as she motioned for him to come in. "He just got home. He said he'd hurry."

Paul entered the room and followed her lead in plopping down on the couch. He sat in silence, wringing his hands nervously. Chris watched the man, wondering if there was something wrong. Finally, she broke the tension.

"Is there something wrong, Paul?"

"Can I ask you a question? I mean, you don't have to answer if it makes you feel uncomfortable," Paul said with a bit of hesitation.

"What is it?" Chris asked.

Paul paused; looking down, he nervously asked, "Is Matt seeing anyone else? I just want to know. You see I'm kind of new at this dating thing. I wanted to ask him . . . but I didn't know if it was too soon . . ."

Chris sat down across from him. "What do you mean, new to the dating thing?"

"Well, I was with someone for a long time. He died in a car accident about a year ago. It's taken me a while to get over him. I've just started going out again."

"I'm sorry. How long were you together?" Chris softly asked.

"Seven years this month," he replied, and, running his hand over his face, began to apologize. "Sorry, I still keep counting as if he were still alive. I guess it's hard to get over your first love." He looked up at Chris and slightly smiled.

"He was your first love?"

"Yeah, believe it or not, I had never even been attracted to a man before. But he was really special. He had this look in his eye that just made me melt, and his laugh . . ." Paul answered as if getting lost in his memories.

"Sounds like you have some great memories," Chris said sympathetically. Then, deciding to ask the burning question in her mind, she asked, "So if you had never been attracted to a man before, what made you decide that all of a sudden you were gay?"

Paul paused to gather his thoughts, then replied, "You know, everyone has so many labels . . . the plain truth is that you can't help who you fall in love with. I just happened to fall in love with a man, there was no 'decision' to make."

Chris was taken aback with his thoughts. It seemed so clear to him. She wanted to continue the conversation, so she asked, "Okay, so you fell in love with a man. Is it so clear to you now that you want to be with another man?"

Paul thought this question over carefully, and answered, "I've come to realize that there are certain qualities that I admire in the male sex." Then, shaking his head, he reconsidered his answer. "No, I don't want to use that word 'sex,' that's the wrong word. It's not just a physical thing. I'm sorry, you know, I don't know how to describe it. I guess it's just a connection that I feel." Paul looked up and chuckled. "Does that make any sense? God, I must sound like a complete idiot!"

Chris found it hard to reply. It was as if he had read her mind.

Paul reached over and touched her knee. "Hey, are you okay? Did I say something wrong?"

"No, no, I'm sorry," Chris forced out.

Paul smiled, knowing that he had planted a seed. "Well, did I pass the interview?"

"The interview?" Chris asked, a little confused.

"Well, I figured you were checking me out before you answered my question about Matt."

Chris smiled; did he really think she was that stupid? She answered, "No, Matt isn't seeing anyone else."

"Did I hear my name?" Matt called from down the hall.

Chris laughed out loud. "I was just asking if Paul's intentions were honorable!"

Matt stuck his head around the corner. "I hope not!" He smiled.

Paul's face turned red. Chris looked at Matt. "Oh yeah, and you wanted me to come with you guys tonight? I think that's where the saying 'three's a crowd' comes into play!"

There was laughter down the hall and then the sound of the blow-dryer.

"You really are welcome to come with us," Paul offered.

"Thanks, but I slept all afternoon instead of studying. I'd better stay here," Chris explained.

Chris watched Paul's eyes light up and she turned as he stood to meet Matt as he entered the room. She smiled, seeing Matt's eyes glow in return. Remembering similar exchanges between her and Lynn, she lowered her eyes.

Matt saw the smile fade from Chris's face and felt her pain. He walked over and knelt in front of the woman.

"Are you sure that you won't reconsider?"

Chris reached out and stroked his cheek. "Go, have a good time. I won't wait up," she said with a wink.

Matt smiled and nodded; he took Paul's hand, and the two walked out the door.

Chapter Sixteen

Chris ran into the house and grabbed a bottle of water. She listened to the silence and realized Matt must still be in bed. Wiping the sweat from her face on her T-shirt, she tiptoed down the hall, quietly opened Matt's door, and then flung herself on his bed. "Now look who's sleeping the day away!"

Matt groaned and pulled the pillow over his head. "Leave me alone, I got in really late last night!" came his muffled voice from beneath the material.

"Come on." Chris tugged at the pillow. "I want details!"

Matt clung to the pillow. "Get your own love life!" As soon as the words left his mouth he knew what he had done. He pushed the pillow aside to see Chris's solemn face. "I'm sorry . . . there I go again saying the wrong thing."

Propping herself up on one elbow, she sighed. "I've never had a love life. Lust, yes. Sex, a lot. But I've never been in love."

Matt propped himself up on his elbow to meet her face. "Really? You could've fooled me!"

Chris just stared at him, then lowered her eyes, pushed herself up, and crawled off of the bed. "I'm going to take a shower," she mumbled as she left the room.

The four walked into the stadium and looked overhead at the section numbers painted on the concrete. Hand in hand, the two couples made their way through the crowd and down the steps to their seats. Chris sat down and gazed at the view of the baseball diamond—the bright green grass offset by the darkness of the dirt and the stark white lines, contrasted with the clear blue sky—she was amazed at how beautiful it all was. Her thoughts were interrupted by Marie, who had leaned over her son to speak.

"It's just a shame that Lynn got these box seats and isn't here to enjoy them with us!"

Chris nodded in agreement, knowing it was her fault that Lynn had canceled. Matt jumped into the conversation. "You know Lynn when she gets her mind set on something!"

Charles shook his head. "I just hope she isn't getting too involved with work again. I hope that she remembers that work isn't everything."

"She does, Dad. I can guarantee that she won't fall into that trap again." Matt replied. "I won't let that happen."

Marie looked over at Chris. "I'm sure you'll help, too, right Chris?"

Chris smiled nervously and was relieved when all attention shifted to the players on the field.

Matt and Chris sat in the living room after what seemed like an extremely long day. The game had gone into extra innings and there had been a traffic jam on the way out. Afterward, they had gone to a restaurant that was short on help. The two sat in silence while Matt clicked through the channels.

"Want some popcorn?" Chris asked. Matt shook his head no.

197

"Ice cream?" Chris offered. Matt shook his head again.

Matt threw down the remote. "There's nothing on." In actuality, Matt would've liked to go to bed, but he knew that Chris was a night owl and he didn't want her to feel alone. "Hey, why don't you look in the cabinet and pick out a movie to watch. Just nothing Doris Day!"

Chris smiled sarcastically and went over to the cabinet. She looked at the selection and pulled out a tape without a label. "What's on this?"

Matt shrugged. "Put it in and we'll see."

Chris pushed the tape into the VCR, pushed Play, and stood back. The picture that appeared looked like a home movie. Matt sat up immediately. "Oh, you don't want to watch that . . ." Just as he spoke, the picture scanned a scene in front of a campsite. Chris had been introduced to a couple of the people in the video, and then she saw a sight that captivated her. Lynn walked across the screen in tight jeans carrying a pile of wood. Dropping the wood, she dusted the dirt from her shirt and laughed as another woman's hands helped in the dusting.

Backing up until she reached the edge of the couch, Chris sat down without taking her eyes off of the television. She didn't even hear Matt's voice until he raised it.

"Chris!"

Turning toward him, she questioned, "When was this taken?"

"About six months ago . . . maybe longer," he answered. "I'm going to turn it off, Chris."

"No!" She kept her eyes glued to the screen in front of her, where day had turned to night, and the camera scanned the group around a campfire. They were laughing, drinking, and roasting marshmallows. The next shot was a closeup of a marshmallow being fed to Lynn, then Lynn sucking the fingers that fed her, and then lips meeting hers in a passionate kiss.

Chris lowered her eyes; the pain was almost unbearable.

"Now can I turn it off?" Matt's voice came across the room.

Chris shook her head. "No, I'd really like to watch it."

Matt sighed, stood, and handed her the remote. He could not sit here and watch her self-inflicted misery. Running his fingers through her hair, he leaned over and kissed the top of her head.

"If it matters, I can't even remember the woman's name," he said as he left the room. "I never saw her again after that weekend."

Chris lay down on the couch and watched the tape in the darkness. When it was through, she rewound it and watched it again. Then she watched only the scenes of Lynn. God, she missed her. Watching her on the screen was the next best thing to having her there. *This is just pathetic*, she finally realized. Turning off the television, she wandered into the bedroom and felt even more alone than the two previous nights. If she could just see Lynn and talk to her . . . and tell her what? Chris's mind and body still couldn't seem to agree on what kind of relationship she wanted with her. She still didn't believe that she was a lesbian, even though her body ached for Lynn. And she still didn't believe that what she felt was love, even though she missed her every minute of every day. She fell asleep as she struggled with the all-consuming conflict.

Chapter Seventeen

Chris climbed out of bed and stumbled to the kitchen. She grabbed a mug from the shelf and poured some coffee. Rubbing her face to wake up, she carried her cup into the living room and stared at the phone. Lynn would be at the diner. Should she call her? No, she shouldn't be bugging her. It was over. Lynn had said so, now Chris just had to get it through her mind . . . and heart.

"Dammit!" Chris cursed under her breath. If she could just speak to Lynn, apologize profusely, maybe, just maybe . . . Chris picked up the phone and dialed information for the number of the diner. It took several minutes for Chris to get up the nerve to dial the number that she had written down. She picked up the receiver and began dialing.

The call was picked up after the first ring. "Blue Moon Café, this is Betty speaking."

"Hi. I'd like to speak with Lynn," Chris said.

"You and all the other ladies!" joked Betty. "Sorry, hon, she's not here today, had an appointment or something. Actually, now that I think about it, she'll be gone all week."

"Thanks anyway," Chris said as she hung up the receiver.

Chris finished the last of her coffee and walked into the kitchen for a refill. As she passed by the refrigerator, she saw the same note clipped to a magnet that had been there all week, but this time it meant something. The note read: "Don't forget meeting—June 4, 9 a.m." Chris walked back to the phone, this time dialing the number that she had found on the letterhead of Lynn's investment firm.

"Good morning, Peabody, Smith, Hadley, and Gregory. How may I direct your call?"

"Is Lynn Gregory available?" Chris asked shyly.

"I'm sorry, Ms. Gregory is in a partners' meeting until noon. Can someone else help you?"

"No, thanks," Chris replied. She hung up the phone. Noon. She could get ready and make it to the office by noon. *Then she would have to talk to me.* Chris ran to the bathroom and turned on the shower. Maybe it wouldn't be such a bad day after all.

Chris stood outside the tenth-floor office of Peabody, Smith, Hadley, and Gregory. She was on time even after getting lost within the city streets several times. She swung open the glass door and was instantly impressed by the interior of the office. Marble floors, leather couches, the smooth, sleek teak finish on the half-moon-shaped receptionist counter. She approached the receptionist, who held up one finger to signal that she was on the phone and would be with her in one minute.

Finally, the receptionist acknowledged her. "May I help you?"

"Yes, I'd like to see Lynn Gregory," Chris stated.

"Do you have an appointment with Ms. Gregory?"

"No, but I believe that she'll see me."

"I'm sorry, Ms. Gregory is in a meeting at the moment. If you'd like to wait . . ."

"Yes, thank you, I'll wait," Chris said. She walked over to one of the couches and sank down into the cushions. She reviewed her magazine selections and chose the one containing the article "Muscles and Your Body. How They Work for You." She stared at the pages but could only concentrate on what she would say to Lynn. Unfortunately, she still didn't know exactly what she was going to say. She played out several different scenarios in her mind, but nothing sounded quite right.

Chris looked at her watch—one o'clock. She had been nervously waiting for an hour. She had flipped through a half a dozen articles when she heard the voice. She looked up, trying to find the sound. Suddenly, she saw Lynn. At least Chris thought it was Lynn. But this was clearly not the Lynn that was familiar to her, this was a different Lynn Gregory.

This Lynn Gregory was clad in a short navy blue suit offset by a white silk blouse, and was perfectly balanced on navy blue pumps. Her hair was slicked back, to control its usual unruliness, and her face was complemented with perfect makeup, hidden only by the pair of half-glasses balanced on her nose. Walking down the hall toward the receptionist area, Lynn was reviewing paperwork and discussing the same with a man who was clearly trying to keep up with her.

Chris sat up on the edge of the couch to get a better look. She couldn't quite decide if Lynn was more beautiful now, or as she was accustomed to seeing her.

Chris observed Lynn as she got closer. She watched as Lynn's eyes raised from the paperwork in her hands, pulled her glasses down to meet Chris's gaze, then raised them back to focus again on the documents. Not missing a step, Lynn turned and walked into an office not far down the hall from the receptionist desk.

Chris wasn't sure what to do. She was pretty sure that Lynn had seen her. She watched as the man left the office that they had just entered, and then approached the receptionist desk.

"Excuse me, is Ms. Gregory available to see me now?"

The receptionist punched in an extension number. "Ms. Gregory, there's someone here to see you." The woman listened to a response on her headset, then looked at Chris. "I'm sorry, Ms. Gregory isn't available to see anyone today."

Chris was taken aback. Maybe Lynn hadn't seen her.

"Can you call her again? I'm actually a friend of hers."

The receptionist rang the extension again. "I'm sorry, Ms. Gregory, but she says she's a friend of yours. A—"

"Chris Newman."

"A Chris Newman is here to see you." The receptionist nodded and asked Chris to take a seat.

After a few moments, a man approached and sat down next to Chris.

"Ms. Newman, I'm sorry, Ms. Gregory isn't available for anyone today. She asked me to tell you that your type of investment is just a little too risky at the present time."

The man shook her hand, stood, and proceeded down the hall.

Chris sat there, unable to move. She couldn't decide what to do. Should she run down the hall screaming her apology? No, they might call security. She weighed her options in her mind. Lynn's truck must be in the parking garage below. Maybe she could just leave a note.

Rifling through her car trying to locate something decent to write on, Chris kicked herself for leaving her backpack at the house. *Well, this will have to do,* she said to herself, finding a leaflet that had once been placed on her windshield at school. "Lose fat while you sleep," proclaimed the advertisement. Turning the piece of paper over to find an empty space, she began to write.

But she wasn't prepared to put her feelings onto paper. After she wrote that she was sorry for many of the things that she said, all she could say was that she missed her. She reread the note. It sounded so . . . juvenile. For a college student, she should be able to organize her thoughts a little better. However, she couldn't quite put her pain on paper. The ache in her stomach wouldn't translate into words. The note would have to do.

Chris drove into the parking garage and scanned the area for Lynn's beat-up old truck. No such luck. She passed through the vehicles. She saw names on the parking spaces and figured they must be assigned spaces. And where would the partners' assigned spaces be, but close to the elevator. She drove down the rows of cars toward the elevator. Bingo! Smith . . . Hadley . . . and finally, Gregory. But this couldn't be right. There was a dark blue BMW parked in this space. Maybe Lynn didn't have a space anymore, since she wasn't there on a full-time basis.

Chris pulled in behind the BMW to check out the situation. She walked down the length of the car, peering in the darkened windows. There was a pack of cigarettes on the passenger seat, the brand that Lynn had been smoking. But that didn't prove anything. Wait, the same medallion hung from the rearview mirror as did from the rearview mirror of Lynn's truck. She remembered because she had asked Lynn about it once. It was a half of a heart hung on a gold chain. Lynn said that it was a symbol to remind her how easily hearts can be broken. Quickly pulling the note that she had written from her pocket, she placed it under the windshield wiper, hoping not to set off any kind of alarm. That done, she jumped back into her vehicle and pulled away, just in time to evade the security guard leaving the elevator.

Chris looked in her rearview mirror as she heard the sound of several car alarms being unarmed. There were others who had exited the elevator behind the security guard. She watched as two men and a woman strolled to their respective vehicles.

Lynn approached the BMW, stopping to slide the piece of paper from her windshield. Glancing at it, she crushed it into a ball and threw it on the ground. She then tossed her briefcase into the car and proceeded to back out of the space.

"Dammit!" Chris said to herself as she pulled away. She didn't even unfold the piece of paper. Pulling out of the parking garage, she waited for the BMW to pass. Maybe she could follow Lynn to her destination. *Oh my God*, she thought to herself, *I've become a stalker*. Pushing that aside, she followed the BMW onto the busy street. After several minutes, Chris lost the car and her chance of reconciliation.

Matt and Chris slid into his car. Matt turned the key in the ignition.

"I went to Lynn's office today," Chris said quietly.

Putting the car in reverse, Matt replied, "I know."

"She wouldn't see me."

"I know," he said as he began tugging at the imaginary string on his steering wheel cover.

"I left a note on her car. Nice BMW."

Matt turned toward her. "That, I didn't know."

"About her BMW?"

"No, about the note."

"Yeah, well, she doesn't either."

"She doesn't?"

"No, I had to write it on the back of an advertisement. She didn't even see the note, she just crushed it and threw it away. Kind of like our relationship."

"Excuse me?" Matt asked, trying not to get angry.

"I'm sorry. I know, I'm all screwed up."

Matt threw the car into park and turned to Chris. "You know, I really didn't want to get in the middle of this, but I guess I'm going to be anyway, so just let me ask one question, Chris." Matt paused, trying to get his thoughts in order, then continued, "Why is it exactly that you want to see Lynn? Is it because you want to apologize for that ridiculous accusation you made? Because if that's the only reason, just write a note and leave it for her on Sunday."

"I can't explain it, I just really need to talk to her. Matt, just tell me where she is. Or give me her phone number," Chris pleaded.

Matt shook his head. "I can't do that."

Chris crossed her arms. "Can't, or won't?"

Matt sighed, trying to make eye contact with Chris, but she would not meet his eyes. "Look, whatever happened between you two has made it so Lynn can't just be friends with you anymore. She wants to be more than your friend, Chris, and unless you feel the same for her, you just need to apologize and walk away."

Matt took a deep breath before asking the next question. "How do you feel about Lynn?"

Chris, still not making eye contact, replied, "I'm not sure. I just know that I miss her."

"Well, maybe I can help. What exactly do you miss about her?"

"That's what I'm not sure about."

The two sat in silence for a moment, then Matt sighed with frustration. "Then I guess I can't help."

Matt put the car into reverse and backed up. Calming down, he switched the gear into drive. He placed his hand on Chris's and said soothingly, "Sometimes you just have to follow your heart."

The evening over, Chris flopped onto the couch as Matt shuffled through the day's mail.

"Matt," Chris began with hesitation, "please answer just one more question for me. Then, I promise, I won't mention it again."

Matt briefly raised his eyes from the piece of paper in his hand, then nodded.

"I just don't understand why she won't even talk to me."

Matt stood and dropped several unopened envelopes on the table. "I don't know, Chris." Running his fingers through his hair, he continued, "I guess in her business she's learned it's better to just cut your losses and move on."

As he began his way down the hall, he realized how cold his last statement had sounded. Turning back, he leaned over the back of the couch. "That didn't come out quite the way—"

Chris lowered her eyes and raised her hand to stop him. With a tearful voice she choked out, "I got the point, Matt."

Hearing Matt's bedroom door close, Chris wiped the tears from her eyes. She was glad that it was so easy for Lynn, she thought sarcastically, *Just cut your losses and move on.* Well, maybe she had overestimated Lynn's feelings for her. Maybe Lynn didn't call it a game, but a rose by any other name is still a rose. Chris vowed to begin the next day with a new attitude. After all, if Lynn could do it, so could she.

Chapter Eighteen

Chris threw off the covers and reached to turn off the alarm. Today she would not roll over and dwell on her misery, she had promised herself the night before. She was a strong, self-sufficient person. She just had to keep reminding herself.

She pulled on a pair of shorts and a T-shirt and rushed to the kitchen. Opening the refrigerator, she grabbed eggs, bacon, and milk, and began preparing one of the only things she knew how to cook—an omelette.

"A great breakfast to begin a great day," she said out loud to herself.

"Who are you, and what have you done with Chris?" Matt chuckled as he entered the room and observed her activity.

"Good morning!" Chris sang out cheerfully. "Would you like some breakfast?"

Matt looked at her with confusion. "Sure . . ."

"What's the matter?" Chris questioned as she added more ingredients to the bowl before her.

"Nothing. Just glad to see a smile on your face."

"Well, it's time that I stop moping around and move on," Chris said with a hint of sarcasm.

Matt nodded in understanding. This must be another of her defense mechanisms. He wasn't going to complain. At least he got food instead of tears out of this one.

He did, however, place a call to Sam as soon as he arrived at the shop.

"Hey, Sam, this is Matt. Do you have a minute?" Matt headed to the phone before he had even put the Open sign on the door.

"Sure. What's up?" answered Sam.

"Chris is driving me crazy, Sam. She's miserable, Lynn's miserable, between the two of them, I might end up in the looney bin."

Sam sighed. "I know, Matt. I've heard all about it on my end, too. But what can we do?"

"Well, I promised Lynn that I wouldn't do anything. But you haven't, have you?"

Sam chuckled. "No. What do you have in mind?"

Chris went through her day with a purpose—to forget about Lynn, to get on with her life, to move on. She tried desperately to concentrate in class, met with some friends for lunch, dropped by her apartment to pick up her mail, and by the time she got back to the house she was fairly pleased with her progress.

As she walked through the house after changing into her running clothes, the light on the answering machine caught her attention. Chris listened to the recorded voices as she retied her sneakers. The first message was Matt; he was spending the evening with Paul. The second message was from Sam inviting Chris to dinner the following night. She immediately dialed the number and left another message, accepting the invitation. Upon hanging up the phone, Chris strode outside ready for a nice long run.

Chris slowed her pace to wind down her run. She stretched several times on the sand and had just begun opening the glass door when she heard it. Lynn's voice rang through the space inside.

Chris's heart dropped as she hurried inside only to discover the voice was coming from the answering machine: "Leave your name and number and we'll get back to you." All of Chris's hard work on her attitude went down the drain in a matter of seconds. Her heart began aching all over again. She winced when she heard the message that was left.

"Lynn, goddammit! You're not showing for rehearsal either! We understood about Friday and Saturday night, everyone has conflicts, but this has got to end. We're going to have to discuss this as a band. We got along fine without you before, and we'll do it again if you don't stop screwing with us!" The recording echoed from the sound of the receiver being slammed down.

Chris's anger flared. She knew why Lynn wouldn't be at rehearsal. Lynn wouldn't want to be at the bar if Chris showed up. But Lynn wasn't considering the other band members' feelings. How selfish could someone get? Did she abandon her responsibilities every time she had lost at her little game? Or had this been the first time that Lynn had lost? Great, Chris thought to herself, now her heart was an aching, angry mess. She grabbed a beer and headed toward the shower.

Lynn wasn't doing any better. Finishing off the beer in her hand, she set it down on the table already filled with empty bottles. She had made it a point to go to the office again today, anything to take her mind off Chris. But now that she was back at her makeshift apartment, she felt the loneliness overwhelm her again. She was glad that Sam and Beth had invited her over for dinner the next night; they had always been there for her. Hearing the knock on the door, Lynn arose to retrieve dinner from the awaiting delivery person.

Back at Lynn and Matt's house, Matt shut the door and walked quietly over to the couch. Gently removing the book from Chris's hands, he set it on the table and turned off the television. He watched the woman curled up on the couch. If he had been stronger, he would have carried her to bed. Unfortunately he never had been the weight-lifting type. Slipping the afghan over her body, he wondered if she wasn't more comfortable out here on the sofa anyway—closer to her memories of Lynn. If Matt's plan was a success, everything would be worked out between the two of them the next night at Sam and Beth's place. Otherwise, he might just have to get tough.

Chapter Nineteen

"I really appreciate the invite," Chris said as she sat down on the couch in Sam and Beth's place. "It's pretty lonely at the house, especially when Matt's gone. I could use the time to study but I just can't seem to concentrate lately."

Beth sat down beside her. "Because of your argument with Lynn?"

Chris nodded. "I should've known that you would know about it."

"I told her that she should've told you sooner," Sam said.

"I feel like there's a whole part of her that I don't even know."

"You should be thankful," Beth commented.

Chris looked at her with confusion. "What?"

Beth clarified her statement. "You don't really want to know that side of her." Still seeing confusion in Chris's eyes, she explained further. "Lynn Gregory, 'Investment Analyst,' is a cold, manipulative bitch!"

"Beth!" Sam admonished.

"I'm sorry. I'm just telling her like it is!" Beth continued, "We've seen her in action. She's a completely different person than the Lynn Gregory that we've come to know."

Sam nodded in agreement. "She's a totally different person. That's why she had to walk away from it. She didn't like who she had become."

Beth continued, "When she's in that business mode, I just back away."

All three heads turned to the sound of a knock on the door. Taking a deep breath, Sam looked at Beth, rose, and walked to the entryway. Sam swung open the door and stepped aside to let Lynn pass by. Lynn stopped dead in her tracks as she saw Chris sitting on the couch. "What's she doing here?"

"Me? What are you doing here?" Chris exclaimed.

Sam looked at Lynn, then at Chris. "I think you two need to talk this thing out."

"Hey, I wanted to talk," Chris said sarcastically. "But obviously all she wanted to do is get in my pants!"

Lynn gave Sam a look that could kill. "Fuck you Sam!"

"Oh, I guess she wants to fuck you now, too!" Chris snapped.

"I didn't want to fuck you, Chris. I wanted to make love to you. I know it's a new concept for me, but for the first time in over a year, I felt like I wanted to make love to someone!" Lynn shouted.

"See"—Sam put her hand on Lynn's shoulder—"at least she helped you to feel again, Lynn."

"Oh yes, and it did wonders!" Lynn flung her arms in the air. "It made me leave my home, my restaurant, and now my friends. Wow, doesn't that sound familiar. You would think I would've learned the first time!" Lynn turned to leave.

Chris was irritated. "Oh, now it's my fault. This never would've happened if you wouldn't have played your little game—"

"Game?" Lynn interrupted. "The only thing that I did was to let you get to know the good side of me. I was honest with you otherwise. I told you that I had feelings for you and what did you do?

You snuggled a little bit closer, you whispered in my ear . . . talk about a game! Who played who here?"

"Chris, talk to her." Beth nudged her.

"Yes, Chris, talk to me." Lynn took a step toward her. "What do you have to say? That you've decided that you're a lesbian? That you want to be my lover?" Lynn said sarcastically.

Chris just lowered her eyes, not knowing how to respond.

"Yeah, that's what I thought. I didn't think that you had made that decision." Lynn turned around and headed toward the door. "I'm out of here!"

Sam stepped in front of the door, blocking Lynn's way.

"Sam, don't mess with me," Lynn said sternly.

Sam stood strong. "There's nothing you can do or say that's going to make me move."

"Really?" Lynn looked Sam straight in the eye. "I hold the mortgage on your house."

Sam's face turned white. Lynn bumped the woman's shoulder with her own as she walked past and out the door. Sam didn't try to stop her.

Sam heard the door slam behind her. Lynn could be a real bitch sometimes, but she had never seen her act out as she just had.

She turned to meet Beth's eyes. "Did you have any idea?"

Beth shook her head. "I knew that she was having a hard time getting financing for us, but . . ."

Sam walked over and slowly lowered herself onto the couch. Beth joined her and put her arm around her partner's shoulder.

"So, now that the shoe is on the other foot, you might understand what I'm going through," Chris stated.

Just then the phone rang. Neither Sam nor Beth budged. The answering machine clicked on; the voice on the other end of the line was familiar.

"God, you guys, I am so sorry!" Lynn apologized. "I really embarrassed myself back there. I'm afraid that this whole situation has taken a real toll on me. I know that's no reason to take it out on you, I'm really sorry. Please forgive me." After a moment of

213

silence, the voice continued shakily, "And Chris, honey, if you're listening, I don't want to end our relationship with angry words between us. Look, what I should have said is that I love you. I'm head over heels for you. I thought you felt the same way and your words really hurt me. You've got to understand that I can't just be friends with you now. It just hurts too much. I really just need to stay away from you. God, please don't hate me . . . bye."

Beth softly smiled at Sam. "Really, she was just trying to help us out."

Sam shrugged, stood, and wandered out of the room. Beth moved over to sit beside Chris.

"You believe her, don't you? You don't really think this was a game to her?"

Chris stared out into space. "I don't know what I think anymore." Pausing, she lowered her eyes. "Why did this have to happen? I was content with the way things were."

"Were you, really? You didn't want any more out of your relationship with her?"

"Beth, I'm not a lesbian," Chris stated, although she was unsure that was true.

Beth softly smiled. "Hmm . . . I just thought I saw something between you two when you came over last week. I must have been wrong." Then, tilting her head trying to see into Chris's eyes, she asked, "Was I wrong?"

Chris's face turned red. She was not ready to discuss this topic. She was certainly not ready to admit anything.

Getting no response, Beth continued along the line of questioning. "So, I guess I don't understand, are you upset because you think that she lied to you, or because of her feelings for you, or because she thought you had feelings for her?"

Chris shrugged in response.

"Okay, let's take one thing at a time. Do you think that she's a different person than she led you to believe?"

"Well, not really a different person . . ."

"Tell me what you know about her, and I'll tell you if she's different than she led you to believe."

Chris thought a minute. "No, you tell me about what she's really like, then I'll know that you're not just agreeing with me."

"Okay," Beth nodded. "She has her good points, she's kind, caring, always willing to help someone out, sensitive to people's needs."

Chris nodded in agreement.

Beth continued, "But she has her bad points, she's stubborn and headstrong, she has a bad temper . . . which we all saw tonight. She's extremely intelligent, athletic, she has a really great ass . . ."

Chris looked at her in confusion. "That's a bad thing?"

Beth blushed. "It is when you're already married!" she said, elbowing Chris in the side. "Have you ever noticed how defined her thigh muscles are? Sometimes, I ask her to get me something just so I can watch her walk across the room!" Beth exclaimed.

"Yeah, and her arms are so strong, when they're around you, you feel so safe and warm . . . and then she looks at you, and you just get lost in her eyes . . ." Chris stopped, realizing what she had said.

Beth softly smiled and continued the conversation, "And those lips, I bet they're soft, huh?"

"I don't know, I never could . . ." Chris answered, lost in thought.

"But you wanted to?" Beth questioned in a soft voice.

Chris lowered her eyes, slowly shook her head, and whispered so only Beth could hear, "That would make me a lesbian."

Beth put her arm around Chris's shoulder and pulled her close. "Well, it sounds to me like you have feelings for Lynn. I think that's what you need to concentrate on, not on the fact that you have feelings for a woman."

Chris smiled through her tears. As she pulled out of the embrace she looked Beth straight in the eye. "You don't really have a thing for Lynn, do you?"

Beth smiled and shook her head. "Sam's the only woman for me." Then she added teasingly, "But if anything ever happened to Sam, Lynn just might be my second choice."

ৎ৽৹

The three sat down to enjoy the dinner Beth had prepared.

"I'm glad you decided to stay. I made enough enchiladas for an army!" Beth said.

"I can never pass up Mexican food," Chris explained as she helped herself to a heaping portion.

Sam was still in her own thoughts as she quietly helped herself. Beth had tried to get her to lighten up earlier but was unsuccessful. The three ate in silence.

Chris was going over the conversation she had had with Beth in her mind. She couldn't help but concentrate on the fact that she had feelings for a woman, and she still wasn't sure it was love.

"So, were you lesbians when you met each other?" she asked her dining companions.

Sam almost choked when posed the question. "Didn't Lynn tell you how we met?"

Chris shook her head as she took another bite.

Beth spoke first. "Sam is my former sister-in-law."

It was Chris's turn to choke. "Really? This sounds like a good story!"

Sam smiled as she began. "Well, my brother and I never quite got along. He could never accept the fact that his sister was a dyke, so he basically pretended I didn't exist."

"She wasn't even invited to the wedding!" Beth added.

Sam nodded and continued, "My parents were furious with him. As a gesture of good faith, he accepted an invitation to Christmas dinner, even though he knew I would be there."

"So the first time you met was at Christmas? How long had it been since the wedding?" Chris asked curiously.

"Almost a year," Sam answered and proceeded with the story. "So here it was Christmas—"

"Wait, wait, you have to fill her in on what had happened that year," Beth interrupted and then explained, "During that time, I had a miscarriage. Robert, her brother, was really upset. Blamed the whole incident on me. Said I had worked too much during the pregnancy. Anyway, I'm ashamed to admit it but the whole situation drove me to drink. I had just started going to AA meetings when Christmas rolled around." Turning to Sam she said, "Okay, honey, go on . . ."

"So here it was Christmas," Sam continued the story, "Beth and Robert arrived, we were introduced, and then he pulls out this bottle of wine and proceeds to uncork it. Well, I had heard about Beth being a recovering alcoholic, and told him that I thought it was really insensitive of him to drink in front of her. That didn't go over too well with him, but I guess it made quite an impression on Beth."

"It was like we instantly connected. We spent the rest of the day laughing and joking. This made Robert really angry, but I didn't really care. We were having serious problems at the time, so I basically ignored him," Beth explained.

"So anyway, six months go by and I don't hear a word. Then all of a sudden one day, I get this phone call," Sam exclaimed.

Beth continued the story, "I had gone by to tell Sam's parents that I had filed for divorce. I thought that it was going to be a really awful situation, but they weren't really surprised at all. In fact, when I told them that I was moving out the next day, they suggested that I call Sam for help. Can you believe it? Her parents actually pushing us together like that?"

Sam smiled and reached for Beth's hand. "So she calls me and asks if I can come help her move some of her things. We spent the day moving her stuff to an apartment and then she asks me if I would go out and help her celebrate. Not just the divorce, but six months of sobriety."

Beth laughed. "Then she had to tell me that she owned a bar. That went over real big with me, but we worked it out. Three months later, I broke my lease and moved in with Sam."

Chris shook her head in disbelief. "So your family is cool with the whole thing?"

Sam looked at Beth and they both laughed. "My parents are fine with it. But boy is Robert pissed!"

"Yeah, especially since I kept his last name. Now Sam and I are like a real married couple. The same last name and everything!"

Sam got up from the table to get another soda. Chris leaned over and quietly asked, "So if you weren't a lesbian when you met Sam, how did you make the decision to become one?"

Beth put her fork down, looked into space, and smiled. "I fell in love." Turning to Chris she added, "I had never really been in love before I met Sam. Whatever I felt for Robert, at the time I thought it was love, but it wasn't. I made a connection with Sam . . . I still can't explain it . . . I just felt it."

"Yes, I inspired her," Sam admitted as she walked back into the room.

"Inspired her?" Chris asked, not understanding what she had meant.

"Didn't you know? Beth is an artist. And she says that I'm her inspiration." Sam smiled.

"An artist? You didn't do the painting hanging in Lynn's living room, did you?" Chris asked in amazement.

Beth blushed and nodded. "That's always been one of my favorites."

"That painting makes me feel so peaceful. I love it," Chris remarked, then sighed. "I'm really going to miss it when I leave."

Beth looked at Sam and shrugged. They had given it their best try. But this was something that took time; it was no good to rush Chris into anything as life-changing as this. Beth understood, Sam understood, and through it all, they knew that Lynn understood it, too.

Chapter Twenty

Chris pulled up in front of a local pub and climbed out of her car. After swearing she would not spend another night alone in the house, she planned to meet some friends. She had been there once, maybe twice, but still had trouble finding the place. As she walked in, she scanned the area for the group. Finally, Erica stood and waved to her. The rest of the women followed suit. Chris had known several of the women for a couple of years, the others only months.

"Well, long time no see, stranger!" Robyn shouted above the noise.

Chris pulled out a chair and sat down. "Oh, you know me, my head's always in the books!" She hadn't told any of them about the charade that she was participating in; she wasn't close enough to any of them to consider it their business.

"If you want a drink, you'll have to go to the bar. We waited forever for someone to take our order and finally gave up," Linda commented.

Chris nodded and stood. "Anyone else want anything while I'm there?" After taking orders, she weaved through the crowded room and shouted out her request.

"Hey, haven't I seen you at the Rainbow Room?" asked the woman behind the bar as she wiped the counter.

Chris's face turned red as she looked over at her friends at the table to make sure they weren't watching.

The woman apologized, "I'm sorry. Playing it straight tonight?" Chris fumbled with the money in her hands. Not receiving a response, the woman continued, "Yeah, I have to play it straight here, too, otherwise I wouldn't get the big tips."

Chris nodded nervously, then reached for the drinks that had been placed on the counter.

"Well, here you go." The bartender handed her the last bottle. "Oh, and tell your friend Erica that I said hello."

Chris looked at her curiously and made her way back to the table with their drinks. Setting the glasses on the table, Chris looked over to Erica. "The bartender says hello."

Erica turned around, caught the eyes of the woman, smiled shyly, and then quickly turned back to her friends.

"How do you know her?" Kelli questioned.

Lowering her eyes, Erica ran a finger around the rim of her glass, then shrugged.

"What?" Kelli insisted, "What's the big secret?"

Erica leaned in close. "Believe it or not, I slept with her once."

Chris tried to hide the shock she was feeling.

Almost in unison, the women asked, "Really?"

"God, guys! Don't act so shocked!" Erica exclaimed. "It was one time!"

"So . . . why . . . how did it happen?" Robyn asked. Her question was closely followed by Linda's, "And how was it?"

"I don't know how it happened . . . right place at the wrong time . . . wrong place at the right time . . ." Erica softly smiled and leaned in closer. "But it was incredible."

"I can't believe it," Amy said in disgust as she collapsed back into her chair. "With a woman?"

Linda rolled her eyes. "Oh, come on, Amy, it's 2005! Anything goes!"

"Yeah," Robyn agreed. "We haven't had much luck with men." The women all nodded and laughed.

"I have only one question," Kelli said, intrigued by the subject. "If it was so incredible, why did it only happen once?"

Erica looked at her friends, then traced the condensation on the glass before her. Suddenly she stood. "You know what? You're right!" Erica put her hand on Chris's shoulder. "Thanks, guys."

Just as Erica began to walk toward the bar, Kelli shouted, "Ask if she has a friend!" The group laughed and Erica stuck out her tongue.

Chris watched Erica as she took a seat at the bar, whispered in the bartender's ear, and seductively touched the woman's hand. She was surprised at how her friends reacted. Question after question ran through Chris's mind. Was this some kind of sign? Why had it been so easy for Erica? And why couldn't it be that easy for Chris? Maybe because Chris knew that if she slept with Lynn, it would have to be the beginning of a relationship. She couldn't sleep with Lynn unless she knew for sure that she was in love with her. It would break Lynn's heart if it turned out to be just a one-night stand. Who was she kidding? It would hurt them both.

Chris sat quietly and listened to the group of women chatter. None of the topics, mostly gossip, interested her. But suddenly— she caught a glimpse of something familiar. The back of a woman, the same posture, the same hairline as Lynn. Could it be? She watched intently for several minutes, hoping the woman would come closer, would turn. But Chris's heart dropped when she realized it wasn't Lynn.

The whole situation put a damper on her mood. Chris stood and began to excuse herself. "I'm going to go—"

"Oh come on, Chris! Don't be a party pooper!" Kelli interjected.

"I know, I know," Chris said.

"What could possibly compete with the good time we're having here?" Robyn questioned. "Or should I say who?"

Chris smiled sarcastically. The question reminded her of Lynn and their time together. And all the other questions about their relationship that seemed to consume her energy. She did the only thing she could do, she blamed her leaving on her studies.

"All work and no play—" Linda began.

Chris held up her hand to stop her in mid-sentence. "I play plenty, girls, you're just not privy to the details!" she quipped.

"Ohhh!" the women chorused, then said their good-byes.

Chris returned to a quiet house. The silence almost deafening, she flipped on the television and settled on the couch. If she tried really hard she could still smell Lynn's scent on the afghan that she pulled over her. The week was quickly coming to a close, along with Matt's charade. The thought both saddened and scared her. If she didn't make a decision about her feelings toward Lynn in the next two days, she was afraid she'd never see her again.

She needed to talk to someone. Someone who really knew her, understood her. Chris's first thought was Scott. He was not only an occasional lover but also a good friend. They had known each other for years. Both had grown up as military brats. He—as well as her parents—had always thought that they would marry. But Chris, no matter how hard she tried, could not love him the way he deserved to be loved. And so, they remained friends, and sometimes more. Making the decision to call Scott in the morning, she closed her eyes and let the comforting dialogue of the "I Love Lucy" show lull her to sleep.

Chapter Twenty-one

Chris dialed the number at the military base and after being put through several departments, finally heard his voice.

"Chris? My God! Where have you been?" Scott questioned. "Did you move again or something?"

"No . . . I've just been really busy," Chris answered. "I'm sorry that I haven't called you in a while, but it's really important that I talk to you about something."

"Okay," he said hesitantly. "What about?"

"Can I come over today after you get off work? I'd really like to talk to you in person."

"Are you all right?" Scott asked.

"Yes, yes, I just need to talk to you. You're still the best friend that I have, Scott. I'll even bring a six-pack of your favorite."

"Hmmm . . . nice words, alcohol . . ." Scott chuckled. "You're buttering me up for something. But I'm a sucker for a cute girl, so tonight it is."

Chris smiled as she hung up the phone. She knew she could depend on him. He was always honest without being judgmental. It was the quality she appreciated most in him. Hopefully, he wouldn't disappoint her tonight.

Meanwhile, Lynn was at her hotel and received a call from Todd, her office assistant.

"Ms. Gregory, some flowers were just delivered for you. New girlfriend, perhaps?"

She smiled at Todd's question. "Not that I'm aware of."

"Would you like me to read the card?" he offered.

"No," she replied as she let out a laugh, knowing that he just loved any juicy tidbit that she'd share with him. "Will you have the courier deliver them over to the hotel, please?" Lynn asked. She hung up the phone. Flowers. Who would send her flowers?

The courier arrived an hour later and Lynn opened the door to find a vase full of daisies. Her heart dropped. She thanked the courier and set the flowers on the table. Pulling out the card, she hesitated. Would this be good news or bad news? Slowly, she read the writing:

Even daisies can't make this place feel like home without you. I miss you. Chris.

Feelings flooded over her. Chris was missing her. Did this mean anything? Lynn called her regular florist and ordered flowers for Chris, throwing in an extra twenty dollars for guaranteed delivery within the hour. She dictated the message for the card:

I can come home right now, all you have to do is ask. But please understand, I won't be coming home as a friend. The decision is yours. I love you. Lynn.

Lynn also included her voice mail number. She didn't want Chris to know where she was, and she didn't want to talk to her. She was uneasy about what the answer would be.

When the florist delivered the flowers to Chris, she answered the door and almost had a panic attack. On the spur of the moment, Chris had sent flowers to Lynn's office with a note saying that she missed her. She wasn't really sure what it would accomplish but just wanted Lynn to know that she was still thinking of her. Now, she feared Lynn had refused the flowers and the young man was there to return her money. Chris was startled when he turned back toward the truck.

"I just wanted to make sure someone was home before I lugged the flowers up here!" came his voice from down the steps. Chris watched as he returned with a dozen yellow roses.

"Delivery for Chris Newman."

"I'm Chris."

"You must be some special lady! Ms. Gregory never sends roses. She says roses mean commitment . . . or something like that."

Chris thanked the delivery person, shut the door, and placed the bouquet on the coffee table. Her hand shook as she pulled out the card and examined the words. She slowly sank to the couch. "Ask . . . won't be as a friend . . . decision is yours . . . love" the words rang in her head. Closing her eyes, she put her head in her hands. It really was time for a decision.

Arriving on time, Chris knocked on Scott's door. As he swung it open, Chris was taken aback—she still admired a man in a military uniform. Scott pulled off his tie as he took the six-pack from her hands.

"You still love the uniform, don't you?" He laughed. She sighed. He knew her almost better than she knew herself. It was one of the things that she loved—and hated—about him the most.

"So what's the big discussion?" Scott asked as he twisted off the cap from a bottle. Then his face froze. "You're not pregnant, are you?"

"Bite your tongue!" Chris exclaimed.

"Thank God!" he breathed out. "Now, don't beat around the bush, because I've had a really hectic day."

Chris pulled Scott down on the couch next to her. "I've been having some strong feelings for someone, and I need your opinion on the situation."

"Wow! Are you really asking for my opinion . . . or my approval?" Scott questioned. "Because I don't think that you have ever asked for my approval on a relationship!" Scott's eyes narrowed suspiciously. "So what's really going on here?"

Chris lowered her eyes and twisted her hands as she tried desperately to formulate her next sentence. Scott leaned forward, cupped Chris's chin, and raised her face. "You know you can tell me anything, right?"

Nodding, she tried to explain. "This person . . . the one that I think I have feelings for . . ."—she looked directly into his eyes—"is a woman."

Chris examined Scott's face but couldn't read his reaction. His hands grasped hers and he lowered his eyes as he caressed her soft skin.

"Tell me what you're thinking," Chris begged him. "Are you totally disgusted?"

Scott looked confused. "Disgusted?"

"You know, that I may be . . . a lesbian?" Chris whispered.

Scott searched her eyes. "All I've ever wanted is for you to be happy. If this, if she makes you happy . . . then it makes me happy."

Chris's eyes welled with tears. "Lynn makes me happy." She smiled, then shrugged. "But Scott . . ."

"It's the whole lesbian thing, right?" Scott snickered as he held her hands tighter. "You just don't want to believe that you could be gay?"

"You're finding this whole situation a little too funny!" Chris pulled her hands away. "Why is that?"

"I'm sorry," Scott apologized as he reached for her hands again. "You just have to be so damned logical about everything. Do you have to overanalyze everything?"

"And what do you suggest I do, Mister Smarty Pants!" Chris said sarcastically. "Just sleep around with everyone without thinking?"

"Isn't that what you've been doing?" Scott laughed out loud.

"Ha! That's what you think! I haven't slept with Lynn yet!"

Scott's face crinkled with confusion. "Then why—"

"Why do I think that I'm a lesbian?" Chris interjected. Her face, now solemn, showed her pain. "I don't know how to explain it, Scott. I think about her all the time. Her face, her smile"—she looked into his eyes again—"her body."

"So why don't you just sleep with her and get it over with?" Scott questioned.

"Oh, as if it's just that easy!" Chris flung her arms up in the air. "Just sleep with a woman! Why didn't I think of that?" she cried out sarcastically.

"Oh, don't act so innocent!" Scott answered with his own sarcasm. "You just told me that you think about her body. You can't tell me that you haven't thought about having sex. What's the problem?" Scott continued, answering his own question, "Oh, that would make you a lesbian. No, Chris, that would make you curious. If it doesn't work out, it doesn't work out."

Chris looked at her friend curiously. "You've sure become a lot more liberal. Anyway, I won't sleep with her unless I'm sure that I'm in love with her. She's been hurt before, I wouldn't want to hurt her again."

Scott lowered his eyes but not before Chris saw the hurt that her last statement had caused.

"I'm sorry, Scott. I never meant to hurt you. At the time, I thought that I loved you."

Scott put his hand up to stop her apology. "We've had this discussion before. We both know that we make better friends than lovers." Softly smiling, he continued, "I think that right there shows exactly how much you care for her, Chris."

"Maybe." Chris shrugged. "This would be so much easier if she were a man."

"Would it?" Scott posed yet another question. "How many men have you slept with, Chris?" Then smiling, he held up his hand again, and said, "Don't answer that, I don't really want to know. My point being, maybe you weren't supposed to end up with a man. Maybe you're attracted to qualities she has that you don't find in a man."

"But how can I be sure that I won't find them in a man?"

Scott sighed. "I really never thought that I'd discuss this with you, but here goes. And I have to explain it in the only terms that I can, okay?"

Chris nodded.

"When you and I have had sex . . . I felt like I was flying so fast that I could break the sound barrier."

Chris smiled at his flying references. He always wanted to be a pilot and had succeeded.

Scott continued, "But I always felt, and tell me if I'm wrong, that you were always . . . just kind of hovering, waiting for a signal to land." Taking a breath, he asked, "Has it been like that with every man? I mean, I know you enjoy sex, but, for me, it was like every time you touched me, my arm, my face, it felt like a direct connection to my soul."

Chris watched as Scott blushed, then thought about her sexual experiences. "I've never felt anything like that."

"Maybe, if I had been a woman . . ." Scott smiled, then tousled Chris's hair.

"Ha! Ha! Such a funny man for a heterosexual!" Chris said sarcastically.

"I get my sense of humor from my dearest *lesbian* friend!" Scott hugged her. "I love you no matter what you are."

Chris sat in silence. Would she, could she ever get used to that word—"lesbian"? Scott again interpreted her thoughts.

"Would you just forget about the whole lesbian thing?" He slapped her knee. "You just need to figure out if you love her, right?"

Chris nodded. It looked to Scott like he was going to have to pry it out of her. "You think about her all the time," he mimicked. "What else?"

Chris ran her fingers through her hair in frustration. "I don't know, Scott . . . I can't describe it . . . it's just an overwhelming feeling in the pit of my stomach . . . in my heart . . ." She turned to him for understanding, this time finding tears in his eyes.

"The feeling consumes your entire soul . . . Chris, there's nothing to analyze here . . . when you're together, you're happy. When you're apart, all you want to do is be with her. When she looks at you, it's like nothing else in the world exists . . ." Scott's voice crackled with emotion.

"Scott . . ." Chris placed her hand on his leg. Scott covered it with his own. "I'm sorry, it's just hard for me to come to the realization that you've finally found someone . . . don't let her slip away, Chris. I just hope that I'm as lucky someday."

"You will be, Scott." Chris put her head against his chest. "You will be."

The two were startled when a knock sounded on the door. Scott jumped up and smoothed out his clothes.

"Who could that be?" Chris asked.

"Uh . . . that would be my date," Scott admitted.

"Your date?" Chris exclaimed. "Why didn't you tell me that you had a date tonight?"

Scott shrugged as he walked to the door. "I'm sorry, I wanted to talk to you and I couldn't get in touch with her to cancel." With his hand on the knob, he looked at Chris. "I'm going to tell her something came up."

"No!" Chris exclaimed. "I'm not going to ruin your plans for the evening!"

Scott smiled. "I *was* kind of hoping to get laid tonight."

Chris shook her head and chuckled as Scott opened the door. He made introductions as he stood nervously before the two women.

"I'm sorry, am I interrupting something?" the woman asked nervously.

"No," Chris replied. "We're just old friends having a chat. I was just leaving."

Running his fingers through his hair, Scott excused himself to change into more appropriate clothes. Turning to hug Chris, he said a little too loudly, "Can I trust you not to hit on my date before you leave?" Letting go of her, he winked and laughed, then hurried into the next room.

Chris chuckled and noticed the woman's confusion.

"Are you a lesbian?" she asked Chris.

Chris smiled as she walked over to the door and opened it. Stepping through the doorway, she answered the woman's question with her own, "Are you sure that you're not?" She left the question unanswered as she closed the door softly behind her.

Chris jumped into her Jeep, which Matt had brought home today, good as new. She felt refreshed as the wind blew in her face. Scott had not disappointed her. He had been forthcoming and painfully honest, just as she had hoped. The conversation lifted some of the weight from her shoulders. She now knew that being a lesbian wouldn't hinder her relationship with her closest and dearest friend. "Lesbian, lesbian, lesbian"—unfortunately the word hadn't gotten any easier.

Finding that she had driven around in circles for the better part of an hour, she decided to drive past the bar. Lynn's truck was not there, neither was the BMW. She stopped and parked anyway, realizing that she didn't know how many cars Lynn owned.

Chris walked into the bar and made her way over to the end of the counter. She leaned in, right next to a woman nursing a mug of beer. The woman could've been a model, Chris thought as she looked at the woman's reflection in the mirror attached to the wall behind the bar.

"What'll it be?" Sam asked. Realizing it was Chris, she shouted to the woman on the stool in front of her, "Jeez, Shel! Where's your manners? Offer this very attractive woman your seat, would you?"

The woman stood, motioned for Chris to take a seat, and leaned against the counter beside her, ready with her smoothest pickup line.

"Now scram, Shelly!" Sam shouted, motioning for the woman to leave. "There's plenty of women over there who haven't heard your bullshit!" The woman grabbed her drink and left.

"Shelly?" Chris asked curiously.

"Shelly," Sam said, nodding to confirm it was Lynn's ex.

Well, Lynn sure knows how to pick them, Chris thought to herself.

"She's not here, hon," Sam said as she wiped down the area in front of Chris.

Chris nodded in disappointment. "How about a shot of tequila, Sam?"

Sam looked surprised, then set a shot glass down in front of Chris and filled it to the brim.

Chris caught Sam's arm as she pulled the bottle of tequila away. "Leave it here, Sam, it's going to be a long night."

Sam leaned on the bar, watching as Chris threw back the first shot without a flinch. Sam poured her another.

Chris looked up into Sam's eyes. "I guess I have a decision to make."

Sam smiled, grabbed another shot glass, and proceeded to fill them both.

"The way I see it, hon, your decision has already been made," Sam said, pushing Chris's full glass toward her.

Chris picked up the drink. "What do you mean?"

"Girl, look around you. You're sitting in a gay bar. All you can think about is locating a woman you can't get out of your mind, and you're proceeding to get shit-faced because you think that you may never see her again." Sam smiled and offered up a toast with her glass. "Seems to me that your decision has already been made!" That said, she slammed back the shot, dropped the glass to the counter, and walked away.

Chris had consumed half a bottle of tequila by the time Sam came around again.

"Chris, give me your car keys, hon."

Chris looked at Sam, her face beginning to look a little fuzzy, and handed over her keys.

"Lynn would never forgive herself, or me for that matter, if I let you drive in this condition," Sam said as she stuffed the keys in her pocket.

Chris took another look around the bar. She examined every face. Was she like all these other women? She motioned for Sam to join her.

"Sam, I just don't think that I'm like these other women. I mean, I haven't been attracted to any woman until Lynn. One woman, Sam . . ." Chris tried to explain.

"Sweetie." Sam paused and put her hand over Chris's hand. "Don't you understand? That's how it was for Beth. That's how it

231

started for almost all of these women. One day each of them felt attracted to 'one' woman. Each of them had to make a decision, just like the one you're fighting with right now."

Chris's eyes teared up. Suddenly, she felt a connection with every woman there. She threw back another shot, praying that the liquid would numb the pain.

Lynn sat on the couch in the hotel room surrounded by paperwork. She had gotten more and more angry that afternoon after she sent the flowers and received no response. She felt like she had been sucked in and spit out once again. Why did she keep falling for it? Trying to immerse her mind into something else, she opted to catch up on paperwork.

She worked nine hours straight when she received the phone call. Recognizing the phone number as that of the Rainbow Room, she picked up immediately.

"Lynn Gregory," she said into the receiver.

"Hey, it's Sam."

"Hi, Sam. How are things at the bar tonight?" Looking over to find the time had slipped away from her, Lynn asked, "It's just about closing time, isn't it?"

"Yeah, that's what I'm calling about," Sam replied.

Lynn was confused. "I don't understand."

"I have someone here who needs a ride home," Sam said, looking over at the body still sitting at the bar.

"Sam, I'm a little far away for that—" Lynn began to explain.

Sam interrupted, "Look, Chris is here and she is way beyond wasted."

"Sam, please don't let her attempt to drive that way," Lynn said softly.

"Drive? She'll be lucky if she can walk! She drank almost an entire bottle of tequila," Sam explained. "Lynn, come take her home, please. She needs you. All she kept mumbling was something about making a decision. I'm sure you know what that was about."

Lynn tried to explain, "Sam, you don't understand. Even if I wanted to, which I don't, it would take me over an hour to get there! And that's if traffic is good!"

"You're over an hour away? Where are you?" Sam asked, then said sarcastically, "Or should I ask who are you with?"

Lynn resented the question. "Sam. I am alone. I am in the city. I cannot come to get her." Then changing her tone, she asked, "Please promise me that she will get home safely, will you?"

Sam sighed as she looked over to the woman in misery. "I promise."

Lynn hung up the phone and pictured the scene at the bar. The music stopped, most of the crowd would have left by now. She thought of Chris sitting alone at the bar with an empty bottle in front of her. Part of her was happy to learn Chris was in such misery. Part of her wanted to hold her close and comfort her. She put her paperwork away and shut down her laptop computer. She lay down on the bed, exhausted after having experienced so many emotions that day. Happiness and hopefulness over the flowers, irritation with herself for having hope, anger over not receiving a response, and finally guilt for the pain that Chris was feeling. It would all be over soon, she convinced herself as she drifted off to sleep.

Chris watched as Sam argued with someone on the other end of the phone line. Hanging up the receiver, Sam approached Chris.

"That's it, Chris, closing time. Time to go home."

Chris moaned and tried to stand. Sam rushed around the corner of the bar and pulled Chris's arm around her shoulder, balancing the woman.

"Come on, I promised Lynn that you'd get home safely," Sam said as she helped Chris out the door.

All Chris remembered later was Matt answering the door and helping her to bed. She rolled over and wept as the numbness wore off and the pain overwhelmed her body once again.

Chapter Twenty-two

Lynn slowly pushed open the bedroom door to watch as the body, snuggled under the sheets, slept. A million thoughts were rushing through her mind—memories of the past week, Chris's laugh, her smiles, her tears. She wondered if she would ever see her again. Matt walked up and stood behind her, placing his arms around Lynn.

"Penny for your thoughts," Matt said softly.

Lynn shook her head and continued staring at the slow rise and fall of the sheet. Matt left her to her thoughts. After a few minutes, Lynn walked down the hall, picked up her keys, and said to Matt, "Call me when she's gone."

Matt nodded and headed into the kitchen to make his "hangover special."

He stirred the ingredients together vigorously, then leaned on the counter as the liquid spun around and around. He couldn't help but be disappointed in the outcome of the situation. Oh, he wasn't disappointed in Lynn. He knew that she couldn't force

Chris to succumb to her feelings. And Chris wasn't to blame, either. Admitting that you're in love with someone of the same sex isn't an easy thing to do. He thought she just needed a gentle nudge, but he had done all the nudging that he could do.

Lynn slid onto the leather seat of her BMW. Her day wasn't going to get any better. After changing into her business attire, she was heading to a meeting that she dreaded. The investment that Charles had been so excited about, turned out to be nothing to be excited about. Turning the key in the ignition, she ran over several scenarios in her mind. She sighed as she turned onto the freeway. There was just no easy way to tell him. Maybe she should tell him that her most recent investment hadn't been successful either.

Matt sat down on the edge of the bed and shook Chris's arm lightly.

"Hey, sleepyhead," he said softly.

Chris, having trouble opening her eyes, rolled over and lay on her back. "What time is it?"

"Time for you to get up," Matt replied. "How's your head?"

Chris made an attempt to sit up, then fell back on her pillow in pain. "Ohhh," she moaned.

"That's what I thought." He picked up the glass of his special hangover elixir from the bed table and handed it to Chris. "Here, this should help."

Chris looked at the red concoction and gave out another moan. "What is that?"

"Don't worry about it. This little concoction will have you feeling better in no time," Matt answered.

Chris raised herself on one elbow and took a sip of the liquid. Not bad.

"I have to go in to work for a while but we're meeting my parents at five o'clock, okay?" Matt said as he headed out the bedroom door.

"Matt?" Chris called out, making Matt turn around. "Was it just my imagination, or was Lynn standing right there a little while ago?" Matt nodded. "Not your imagination, she was here. She just wanted to make sure you were okay."

"But she's gone again?" Chris hesitantly asked.

Matt looked at her, nodded, and sighed. "She's gone again."

Chris stumbled to the shower after drinking the entire glass of Matt's mixture. She stepped in and let the cool water rush over her face, hoping it would relieve her pounding head. She turned her back to the water, crossed her arms, and leaned her head on the shower wall. Tomorrow her life could return to normal. She could go back to her apartment, her studying, her freedom. Funny, it didn't really sound all that appealing.

Toweling off, she looked around the room. This had become her home. In just a little over a week her life had been turned upside down. And now, she wasn't at all sure that she wanted it to change back. She sat on the bed massaging her temples. She wished Lynn were here now to rub away the tension. She wished Lynn were here now, period.

Charles rose from the table as Lynn approached.

"Well, don't you look all business!" Charles exclaimed as he pulled out a chair to seat her. It wasn't often that he saw her in anything but casual attire. Now she stood before him in a business suit and heels.

"There's a reason for that, I'm afraid," Lynn answered. Not exactly sure how to approach the matter, Lynn placed her elbows on the table, folded her hands, and looked Charles straight in the eye.

"Charles, you haven't actually handed over any funds for this investment yet, have you?' Lynn asked delicately.

Charles shook his head and smiled. "Well, there was a small deposit that I had to make just to hold my position open. But I never hand over the big money until I run it by my very knowledgeable investment advisor."

"How much of a deposit?"

"A thousand bucks, why?" he asked curiously.

"I'm afraid you've been a victim of fraud," Lynn answered softly. She watched as the blood drained from the face of the man across the table.

"What? But the men seemed so professional. You saw the prospectus, all the brochures . . ." Charles stuttered.

"Yes, it all looked good on paper, but once I started checking around—" Lynn began to explain.

Charles interrupted, still in disbelief, "And you're sure about this?"

"Positive." Lynn nodded. "Charles, I hope you don't mind, but I called a friend of mine over in the Fraud Division of the FBI. He'll be joining us in a few minutes to discuss the matter."

Charles lowered his eyes and began fidgeting with his napkin. "No, of course I don't mind." Then raising his eyes to hers, he explained his nervousness. "I know I'm only out a thousand bucks on this, but I have friends . . . let's just say that they won't be as lucky."

Lynn sighed. "I hate to say it, but this kind of thing happens all the time. I'm just glad that you came to me."

"You and me both." Charles smiled halfheartedly. He hurt inside for his friends who could face financial ruin.

"Good afternoon," said the man who had approached the table during their private conversation.

Lynn looked up and stood. "Bill, thanks for coming." Then turning, she made introductions, "Bill Woods, Charles McKinley."

The men shook hands and they all took their seats. Lynn informed Bill that she had explained the situation to Charles. The two men talked about how much money was involved. Bill opened his briefcase and pulled out a folder.

Opening the folder, he scooted it across the table in front of Charles. "Are these the men?"

Charles picked up several photographs and nodded. "They sure look legit, don't they? I mean, having been on the bench and all, as a judge, you would think that I could be a better judge of character, wouldn't you?"

Bill took the folder, shoved it back into his briefcase, and shook his head. "Please don't be hard on yourself. These men are professionals. They've run this racket all over the world."

"Well, is there anything that I can do to help you get these guys behind bars?" Charles asked.

Bill nodded. "Lynn furnished me with all the material that you gave her. Their office address is listed on the prospectus. We'll start there. Anything else you can tell us will be appreciated."

Charles spent the next hour telling Bill about how he and his friends were approached and all of the details that followed. Bill interrupted occasionally with questions, making notes as the discussion continued.

Just as they were concluding, a cell phone rang. Bill checked his phone, then turned to Lynn. "Nope, must be yours."

Lynn picked up her phone and excused herself from the table to take the call. Bill leaned over to Charles.

"So, Lynn said that you were the father of a friend. Would that be her boyfriend?" he asked with a smile. "I've been trying to get a date with her since I met her. She just keeps saying that she likes to keep her personal life separate from her business life."

Charles smiled, not knowing exactly how to answer. Lynn must have her reasons for keeping this young man in the dark. If Bill was truly interested, he was sure that someone in the FBI could have found out about Lynn's lifestyle. He decided on the plain and simple truth. "Lynn lives with my son."

Bill nodded and stood as Lynn rejoined the men. "Well, I think that I have all that I need now." Reaching in his pocket, he pulled out a business card and handed it to Charles. "I'll be contacting you for a list of investors involved."

Shaking Charles's hand and then Lynn's, he said, "Nice to have met you Charles, and Lynn, always a pleasure."

When Bill left, Charles focused on the business card still in his hand. "Lynn, looks like I owe you another one."

Lynn placed her hand over Charles's hand. "You know I'd do anything for you and Marie. And of course for Matt." She felt a twinge of guilt over the current charade.

Charles smiled at the mention of Matt's name. "By the way, I may have led Bill to believe that you were involved with my son."

Lynn laughed. "I leave the table for one minute. How did that come about?"

"He asked if I happened to be your boyfriend's father. I merely said that you and he lived together. It wasn't a lie. Is there some reason why he doesn't know about your lifestyle? I thought you were pretty open about the whole thing."

"Sometimes you can just tell who is accepting of it and who isn't. I just have this feeling about him. Maybe he wouldn't be as cooperative with me if he knew," Lynn explained. "Word gets around. I'm sure that he'll eventually uncover the truth." Then smiling, she added, "So if you get a call in the middle of the night that I've been falsely imprisoned for something, you'll know what happened."

Charles chuckled and looked at his watch. "It's four o'clock. Matt and Chris are meeting us here for dinner around five. You are staying to dine with us, aren't you?"

Lynn shook her head. "No. I need to get going." She hadn't expected this to take so long. She tried desperately to think of an excuse.

"We haven't seen you in over a week. Marie thinks that there's something wrong," Charles stated.

"Oh, you know, I get busy," Lynn said as she fumbled with her briefcase.

"You know what they say about all business and no play, Lynn," Charles kidded her. "I thought that's what you've been trying to escape from!" Then his face turned solemn. "Really, Lynn, this is our last night here, surely you can make time for dinner with us."

Lynn sighed. She could not tell them the truth. She could not tell them that she had fallen in love with their son's fiancée and that it just hurt too much to see her. But she didn't want to hurt their feelings either.

Reluctantly, she agreed. "Okay. I have a change of clothes in the car. Do you mind if I use your room to change?"

Charles smiled broadly. "Not at all. It will make Marie happy to see that you're okay. Thanks for reconsidering."

Lynn walked to her car and grabbed her change of clothes. She wished that she had scheduled their meeting earlier. She was mad at herself for agreeing to this. She wasn't only afraid of the hurt and anger that she still felt, but also of Chris's reaction. Chris had clearly made her choice. She had not received a phone call to the contrary.

She made her way up to Charles and Marie's room. She knocked on the door and received a warm welcome.

"Lynn, I'm so glad you're here! I was afraid that we'd leave without seeing you again!" Marie said while hugging her.

Lynn felt warm inside. Sometimes this couple made her feel more a part of the family than her own family did.

"We'll leave you alone to change. Meet you down in the restaurant, okay?" Charles smiled as he ushered his wife out the door.

Lynn nodded and locked the door behind them. She was anxious to change out of her clothes. They did not fit her anymore. The size was fine. The persona was not. She pulled on her black jeans and boots and tucked in her shirt. She placed each earring in its proper hole and tousled her hair. Looking in the mirror, she smiled. "Welcome back," she said to her reflection.

"How are you feeling?" Matt smirked as he tucked his shirt into his blue slacks.

Chris smiled as she put the finishing touches on her makeup. "Much better, thank you. What exactly is in that hangover special?"

Matt gestured as if locking his lips. "I'll never tell."

"Well anyway, thanks," Chris said as she dabbed perfume behind her ears. "It made my head stop aching." Then, placing the lid back on the perfume bottle, she leaned back on the counter and looked at Matt. "Have you got anything to stop the ache in my heart?"

Matt saw the pain in Chris's eyes and felt his own heart twinge. "Sorry, that's something that only you can cure."

"There's the Lynn Gregory we know and love!" Charles said as she approached the table.

Marie smiled. "The kids should be here soon. It will be nice to have the whole family here for our farewell dinner."

Lynn smiled and answered instantly as a waiter approached and asked if he could take their drink order.

"Definitely need a drink," Lynn answered. "Scotch on the rocks, make it a double."

Chapter Twenty-three

"Well, this is it!" Matt gave a sigh of relief as they walked through the lobby and toward the restaurant. "Tonight's dinner, good-byes at the airport tomorrow, and it'll all be over!"

Chris also sighed, but hers was not in relief. Hers was a nervous sigh. She wasn't quite sure how to return to her old life, now that a new part of her had been awakened.

Walking around the corner into the restaurant, Chris froze in place. Her heart jumped, and her eyes glued to the most beautiful sight she had ever seen—Lynn. Her face turned red and her body hot, as the sexiest thing she had ever laid her eyes on caught her stare, softly smiled, then turned back to the conversation at hand.

Suddenly it all seemed so clear. Not even a small doubt remained in her mind. She felt as if a huge weight had been lifted. Chris turned around to face Matt, who was waiting behind her.

"I didn't know she was going to be here," he explained, then he asked impatiently, "What's the matter?"

"Suddenly it's all so clear, Matt," Chris said, almost in a trance from her sudden realization.

Matt looked confused. "What's clear?"

Chris looked up with tears of joy in her eyes, grabbed the front of his shirt, and pulled him out of his parents' sight. "Everybody has been telling me that you can't help who you fall in love with." Chris, still aware that Matt had no idea what she was talking about, continued, "It's true, Matt, I can't fight it anymore. I am utterly, irreversibly, in love with Lynn."

Matt looked into her eyes, knowing that she had finally uncovered her truth. "That's great, Chris, really great." Then, realizing his parents were waiting, he said, "You know, you could have picked a better time to come to this realization."

"Thanks for your overwhelming support, Matt," Chris said, lightly slapping his chest. Then looking back into his eyes, she said with a serious tone, "I need to talk to her."

"Okay, you can talk to her after dinner," Matt suggested.

Chris shook her head. "No, I really need to talk to her now."

"Chris . . ." Matt whined.

"Matt . . ." Chris whined back.

Matt sighed, and knowing that he was not going to win this fight, conceded, "Okay, I'll have her meet you in the ladies' room."

Chris nodded and squeezed his hand before he walked back into the restaurant. "Thank you."

Matt strolled over to the table, where the group was deep in conversation.

Marie looked up. "Matt, honey, where's Chris?"

Matt gave the answer that he had prepared on the way over to the table. "We had a little argument." Then looking at Lynn, he asked, "Lynn, could you go into the ladies' room and see what you can do?"

Lynn looked at him suspiciously.

Matt persisted. "Please, Lynn . . . she'll listen to you."

Lynn gave him a dirty look, rose and excused herself.

Matt looked at his parents, shrugged, and pulled out a chair.

"What was the argument about, dear?" Marie asked.

Matt sat down and scooted toward the table. "Mom . . ." he replied with an annoyed tone.

"Now, Marie, maybe it's none of our business," Charles said, placing his hand over his wife's. Then he looked at Matt. "Well, son, I thought you would have brought the subject up by now, but you haven't. Since we're alone for a minute, let's discuss the loan business. It's been five years, Matt. Now I know you've made a few payments, but are you able to pay off the remainder? You do remember our deal?"

Matt nodded and fiddled with his napkin. "Yes, Dad. I was meaning to talk to you about that."

"Go on," Charles replied.

"Well, you know, I'm not exactly in the position to pay off the loan, not right now. And I was thinking since I'm going to be getting married, and Chris has a life and career connections out here, well, I was thinking about an extension," Matt said, unsure how his father was going to react.

Charles chuckled. "You know, I had a feeling about this, Matt." Taking his napkin from his lap, he laid it on the table and began twisting the material. "We had a deal, Matt. I understand about Chris and all, but a deal is a deal." Pausing, he looked at his wife.

"Excuse me," Marie said as she stood. "I don't want to get into the middle of all this." Placing her napkin on the table, she walked out of the room.

Matt shrank back in his chair as his dad began plotting out his future.

"What will it take, about a month to close up your business here?" Charles asked. Getting no response from his son, he continued, "We'll get all your loose ends tied up here, then we'll move you back with us, where you can learn the ropes. We'll even fly you home every weekend to be with Chris. After she's through with school, she'll move out with us. I'm sure she won't find it hard to find a position, wherever she ends up."

Matt ran his fingers through his hair in exasperation. "Dad, nothing personal, but I don't want to be in the family business. I'm happy with what I'm doing now."

"Of course you're happy. I'd be happy too if I could ride on someone else's money, not really having to worry about making ends meet."

Charles was through with the conversation and signified it by placing his napkin back on his lap. The two sat in dead silence.

Lynn stood outside the door of the restroom, trying to gather up enough nerve to face Chris. Slowly, she pushed the door open and stepped in. Chris was at the mirror wiping away the tear lines on her face.

Seeing Lynn's reflection in the mirror made Chris's heart leap again. "Hi." She smiled shyly.

Lynn, trying to ignore the twinkle in Chris's eyes, said stoically, "You okay? Did you and Matt really have a fight? Or was this just a trick?"

"I really need to talk to you, Lynn . . ." Chris slowly approached and, reaching out her hand, placed it on Lynn's arm.

Lynn remained in control. "So it was just a trick?" Turning, she started toward the door. Chris rushed over and blocked the way. Standing just inches away, their eyes locked. Chris struggled to think of a way to make Lynn stay and listen. This time she let her heart lead the way. Chris reached up and placed her palms on Lynn's checks.

Looking deep into her eyes, Chris whispered, "I love you, Lynn. I didn't realize it until I saw you just now, but I love you." Her heart racing, she slowly brought her lips up to Lynn's. But just before their lips connected, the door eased open.

"Oh my . . . excuse me," came the woman's voice.

The two glanced over in the direction of the voice, then saw the woman back out of the room, and out the door.

The two looked at each other in shock. Then, at the same time they exclaimed, "Oh my God, Marie!"

They stood frozen, but only for a moment. They had some damage control to do.

"What are we going to do?" Chris asked nervously.

"I don't know, I don't know," Lynn replied. Grabbing Chris's hand, she pulled her out the door of the bathroom. "I'll think of something, just follow my lead."

Practically running, the two made it back to the table, but not before Marie.

Marie quickly approached the table, her face white with shock.

"Marie, are you all right?" Charles asked worriedly.

"Matt, Charles, we have a problem," she said holding her hand to her forehead. Then turning to Matt, she said, "Matty, I don't know how to tell you this, but I think Lynn just made a pass at your fiancée!"

"Marie, what are you talking about?" Charles said sternly.

Marie, trying to say this gently, replied, "Charles, I went to the ladies' room, thinking that maybe I could help . . . then I saw them. I saw them . . . in a romantic embrace."

"Marie, are you sure you're not over exaggerating?" Charles questioned.

"Charles, they were, they were, they were kissing!" Marie finally spit out.

"I'm afraid she's right Charles," Lynn admitted as she walked up to the table.

"Lynn, you made a pass at Matt's fiancée?" Charles asked in disbelief.

"Yes, I . . ." Lynn looked at Matt and, willing to take the brunt of it, started to explain.

"No!" Matt said as he stood and placed his hands on the back of his chair. The charade was over. He was not getting his extension on the loan. There was no use continuing. He looked at Lynn, then Chris, then Marie. Then, finally, looking his dad straight in his eye, admitted, "Lynn didn't make a pass at my fiancée, because . . . Chris isn't my fiancée."

"What?" the parents questioned in unison.

"Mom, Dad, Chris isn't really my fiancée. The fact is . . ." Matt paused, swallowed hard, then blurted out, "the fact is, I'm gay."

The reaction from his parents wasn't as he had expected. Marie walked over and placed her hands on Charles's shoulders. Charles looked up at his wife, then they both softly smiled.

"Well, this certainly explains a few things." Marie sighed.

Matt didn't understand. "Mom? Dad?" he said, wanting an explanation.

"Please, let's all just sit down and discuss this." Charles calmly motioned for all to take their seats.

All seated, Charles took his wife's hand and squeezed it. "Matt, we've known about your lifestyle for quite some time now. Word gets around, you know."

Marie joined in the conversation. "When you told us about Chris, we just thought that maybe you had become, oh, what do they call it, *bisexual*."

Matt couldn't believe what he was hearing. All of these years spent in hiding, for what?

"So, Chris, are you actually Lynn's girlfriend?" Marie asked.

Matt answered before Chris could reply, "Well, not in the beginning, it just kind of ended up that way."

Chris looked at Lynn. Then placing her hand over Lynn's, she said, "I think the verdict is still out on that. What do you think, Lynn?"

Lynn brought her hand up from her lap and placed it over Chris's. "I think that we still have quite a bit of talking to do . . ."

"Talking about what?" Marie asked.

Charles rolled his eyes. His wife was always putting her nose where it didn't belong. "Marie, I think that's between her and Chris, honey."

"That's okay, Charles," Lynn replied. Then addressing the woman who had asked the question, she added, "Well, Marie, I would say the major thing is . . . Chris isn't a lesbian."

"Oh." Marie was confused. "You could've fooled me. I've seen the way she looks at you. I had even discussed it with Charles, haven't I, dear?"

Charles nodded. "You mean, Chris wasn't a lesbian when she

met you? Lynn, you must have other talents besides giving good investment advice!" he joked, and then winked at Lynn.

Lynn blushed and put an end to the discussion. "Maybe this should be between the two of us."

"So you're not going to tell me how disappointed you are in me?" Matt asked, still in shock.

"The truth is, it did take some getting used to," Charles admitted. "But, over time, we've accepted it. So no, son, we're not disappointed in you because of your lifestyle. However, I am a little disappointed in you in regard to this little charade that's been going on. What did you think this would accomplish?"

"I'm sorry, Dad, Mom . . . I just thought that if you saw that I had a life here . . . that you wouldn't hold me to our little deal." Matt rolled his eyes and looked over at Lynn. "I'm not getting the loan extension."

"My offer is still open," Lynn suggested.

"A business loan, pure and simple. Monthly payments, late fees, the works?" Matt stated his conditions.

"Whatever you want," Lynn agreed.

"Well then, Dad, I guess you will be getting that payment in full," Matt said.

Charles nodded and smiled. "I know Lynn wouldn't make a bad investment decision." Then, looking at Lynn, he continued, "I guess that you played along with this little scheme because Matt asked you to. I'd be mad at you if you hadn't just saved me thousands of dollars. Let's just say that one cancels out the other, shall we?"

Lynn nervously smiled. She was glad that the charade was over but uneasy about the way the rest of the evening was going to play out.

In the parking lot, Chris took Lynn's arm and asked, "So, you are coming home tonight, right?"

Lynn, still feeling unsure, paused. "My stuff is still at the hotel."

"Well, if you don't mind, I'll ride with you to the hotel to pick it up. Then we can head on home," Chris suggested.

Lynn looked at Matt for help. She was suspicious. She was confused. She was tired of it all. Matt returned her glance and shrugged. He was no help at all.

"I hope you don't mind the BMW. I haven't had a chance to pick up the truck," Lynn said as she opened the door for her passenger. On her way around to the driver's side of the car, she pulled out her phone and made a call. She wanted to be prepared for anything.

Lynn pulled out onto the highway. "I've been staying in the city, so it will take a few minutes to get there."

Chris nodded and stared out her window. Now that they were alone, she was finding it hard to decide what to say. She was saved by the sound of Lynn's cell phone ringing. Lynn looked down at the number and sighed.

"I have to take this," she explained as she pressed the button turning on the speaker box.

"This is Lynn Gregory," she said out loud. Chris was a little nervous to hear both sides of the conversation.

"Ms. Gregory, this is Carlos Tauton."

"Yes, Carlos, what can I do for you?"

"Ms. Gregory, have you been watching the market? My stock has fallen significantly!"

"Carlos," Lynn answered in a soft but affirmative voice, "don't you trust me?"

"Of course, but—"

"Carlos, I'll make you the same offer I always do. If you want to sell that stock, I'll send over a cashier's check Monday morning for the exact amount you originally paid for it. But don't come to me Tuesday crying when the stock goes through the roof, because I'll own it then."

There was silence on the other end of the line. Then, Carlos, making the decision to ride it out, replied, "No, no, you've made a lot of money for me, I guess I'll trust your instincts."

"That's what you pay me for, Carlos. I've never steered you wrong, have I?"

"No . . . sorry to have bothered you. Have a nice evening, Ms. Gregory."

Lynn reached down to turn the speaker off, then reached up and ran her fingers through her hair. "See what crap I have to deal with?" she said, looking at the road ahead.

Chris looked over at her. "Then why do you deal with it?"

"Because that man alone brings in ten thousand dollars a month for me," Lynn replied, glancing over at her passenger.

"Ten thousand a month for the firm?" Chris asked innocently.

Lynn chuckled and shook her head. "No, ten thousand dollars for me."

Chris was shocked. "You make ten thousand dollars a month?"

Lynn sighed and admitted, "No, I make a lot more than that. You can't even comprehend how much money I bring in."

Chris sat back and stared at the road ahead. She was right. She had read the article. She saw the office. She saw the fabulous BMW that she was now riding in. But she never put it all together. In a way, the whole thing overwhelmed her. The rest of the drive was spent in silence.

Lynn drove up to the hotel and pulled into the valet strip. A young man came out from the building and immediately opened Chris's door. By the time Chris had been helped out of the car and her door shut, Lynn was by her side and had tossed the keys to the valet. Lynn ushered Chris through the enormous glass door. Chris stopped right inside the entrance. Her eyes scanned the lobby—glass pillars, marble tiled floor, and so many green plants, it could have been a jungle. She wouldn't be surprised if the decorative metal, used as chair railing around the walls, was real gold.

"Any messages, John?" Lynn asked at the counter.

The desk clerk handed her a few slips of paper and a package. "Oh, and Ms. Gregory, the taxi you requested is waiting outside."

"Thank you, John," Lynn commented while reviewing her messages, then looking up at Chris, she offered, "Here's your chance, Chris. There's a taxi outside just waiting for you."

Chris crossed her arms over her chest in defiance. "I'm not going anywhere."

Lynn turned back to the desk clerk and took five one-hundred-dollar bills out from her wallet. "John, please ask the driver to wait here all night." Then, handing him four of the bills, she continued, "Give him half now, and half in the morning, about nine, or sooner if this woman requests a ride home." Handing him the last bill, she softly said, "And this is for you."

The man took the cash and nodded. "Thank you."

Lynn started walking away, then turned around. "By the way, how is Miguel?"

"He's doing okay. Can you believe another organization just paid five thousand more of the hospital bills?" he replied.

"That's great, John. Keep me informed, okay?" Lynn requested. John nodded and headed out to the awaiting taxi driver.

Lynn ushered Chris into the elevator. "Miguel is John's lover. He has cancer." After pausing, Lynn turned to Chris. "See, some people appreciate my money."

"Well, sometimes you don't waste it on stupid things," Chris snapped back sarcastically.

"I don't consider your tuition a stupid thing," Lynn said, slightly annoyed.

"I wasn't talking about my tuition. I was talking about that wad you just dropped for that taxi," Chris quipped back.

Lynn stepped off the elevator at the tenth floor and held the door for Chris. She led the way down the long hall to a pair of double doors that she proceeded to unlock and open. Then, motioning for Chris to come in, she dropped her keys on the table, walked over to the French doors, and pushed them open. A soft breeze entered the room and Chris walked over to enjoy the view. Turning back toward the room, she examined her surroundings. Plush white carpet, burgundy leather couch, hand painted pictures—the room was beautiful. She watched as Lynn put on her glasses and proceeded to open the package she had just received.

Lynn sat down on the couch examining the contents. Looking over her glasses, she asked coldly, "Are you having a panic attack yet?"

251

Chris looked at her as if she had missed something. "Do you even remember that I told you that I loved you?"

Lynn adjusted her glasses and continued looking at the papers in front of her. "I remember. I just don't know if I really believe you."

Chris was hurt. "What do you mean?"

Lynn, still not meeting Chris's eyes, stood, walked over to the open doors, and answered, "Well, I thought that maybe you'd have reconsidered your decision by now. We both know how you run scared when it comes to our relationship."

"Wow. You really can be a coldhearted bitch." Chris backed away. "Is this really you? Because this isn't the woman that I fell in love with." Then stopping, she strode over to Lynn, grabbed her chin, and forced Lynn to look into her eyes. "Where is that sweet, compassionate woman?"

Lynn stared at her with a cold expression. She would not give in, she would not give in, she would not give in. Snapping her head away, Lynn walked out onto the balcony and leaned on the ledge.

Chris stood there for a moment, then leaning against the door-jamb, asked, "Do you really want me to leave?"

Not receiving a response, she said calmly, "Well, I'm not running away! Not this time."

Chris turned and surveyed the room: there had to be a minibar in here somewhere, and she needed a drink badly. Finally, after looking through several cabinets, she came upon the bottles. She paused, knowing how expensive these things were in hotels. Oh well, if she's rich, she can afford it, she thought to herself.

Chris poured two glasses and strolled back out to the balcony. She set one drink on the ledge in front of Lynn, gulped down the other, and began. "You said we had a lot of talking to do, so I'll start," she said to the frozen figure.

"Lynn, all my life I've felt like I didn't really belong. I passed it off to all of the traveling that my family did. I never had any serious boyfriends. Yes, I've slept with a lot of men. But I never felt that emotional attachment. I guess the truth was that I was just never that interested." Chris paused, again trying to calm the beat of her heart. "But that first night I met you, I felt a connection, a connection that I never felt with anyone before. And it felt good—really good."

Chris drew a breath and continued, "And then that connection started turning into something else, something . . . sexual. And that Saturday night, when we were alone, looking into your eyes . . . I'd never felt anything like that before. That closeness, that heat, it just never existed in my life until you. And that scared me to death. So I pushed you away along with my feelings for you. But my feelings kept pulling me back in. You probably thought that I was a big tease, but I couldn't help it."

Chris stopped. Lynn was not responding at all. Feeling the tears forming in her eyes, she struggled to continue. "Lynn, I didn't really think you were trying to buy me, or that it was just a game for you, it was just another way for me to try and convince myself to pull away. And now, I believe that I've pushed so hard . . . that I've lost you." Tears were flowing freely now. Chris could not fight them back anymore. "Please, Lynn, please tell me everything is okay. Tell me that you still care for me, because I'm crazy about you."

Lynn felt her wall crumbling inside. It was just another ploy. *I'll get close and she'll back away again. Don't fall for it, don't fall for it, don't fall for it.*

"I can't do it, Chris!" she shouted. "I can't deal with this anymore!"

"Is this your bad temper showing? Because I don't like it," Chris stated.

"Yeah, well this is how I deal with things, so you'd better get used to it if we're going to have a relationship!"

"So, we're going to have a relationship?" Chris said with frustration.

"Yes! No! It just hurts too much!" Lynn shouted. Then trying to calm down, she explained, "Don't you understand? I want you so much it hurts. Chris, I can't take you pulling away again."

"I won't pull away, Lynn. Give me another chance, please!"

Don't look at her, don't look at her, don't look at her, Lynn repeated to herself. But she turned when Chris sniffled. Oh shit. Lynn slowly moved toward Chris and wiped the tears from her cheeks. Cupping her face in her palms, she gently brought her lips to those before her. Lynn brushed her lips softly, then pulled back, giving Chris a chance to back out of the situation.

"I'm still here, Lynn." Chris placed her hand behind Lynn's neck. "I'm not going anywhere," she said as she pulled Lynn's lips to hers.

Lynn tried to remain calm, but when she felt Chris's tongue slip into her mouth and stroke hers, she lost all control. She slid her hands to the small of Chris's back and tightened their embrace. Lynn felt Chris's hands grasp her belt loops on the side of her jeans, pulling them closer still, then Chris's fingers as they slid up her back and into her hair. Lynn's hands crept down to clutch the woman's buttocks. The movement reminded her of the night that they had danced . . . and to the reflection in the mirror that had caused Chris's withdrawal.

Chris had never felt like this before, a burning growing in several areas of her body that had only smoldered before. She had been turned on before, but this was an overwhelming need, a need that she believed she could not control. Lynn's body next to her was only making the burning spread. She wanted to be closer. She pulled Lynn tighter toward her. When their tongues met, it was like a spark on a match. Suddenly she felt her hands moving up and down Lynn's back and her fingers grasping Lynn's tight muscles.

Suddenly Lynn separated from the kiss, grabbed Chris's hand, and pulled her inside. Stopping in front of the large decorative mirror on the wall, she turned Chris to face their reflection. Lynn put her arms around Chris.

"This sight scared the hell out of you before. What do you think now?"

Chris smiled and pulled Lynn's arms tight around her body. "I think we make an extremely cute couple."

Lynn's heart skipped a beat at the word "couple." She turned Chris back to face her and looked into her eyes. "Are you sure this is what you really want?"

Chris placed Lynn's palm against her cheek and closed her eyes, reveling in the sensation of Lynn's touch. Slowly she opened her eyes and met those watching so intensely.

"What I want is to feel your body next to mine, to feel your caress, your breath on my skin . . . Lynn, I want to make love with you."

Lynn could not resist. All gentility gone, Chris hungrily opened her mouth, taking in Lynn's tongue with urgency. Then Lynn's lips touched Chris's chin, her cheeks, her eyelids, and made their way down the soft skin on her neck. Chris shivered from the sensation.

Lynn slowly began unbuttoning Chris's shirt as her lips followed each unbuttoned cloth. Their lips met and tongues danced as Lynn tugged at Chris's shirt until it was off and thrown to the side. As their eyes met, Lynn caressed Chris's skin from her neck all the way down to the line of her bra. She softly ran her fingers across the nipples that were now pushing against the material.

Chris gasped under her breath; a man's touch had never felt like this. She pulled Lynn's lips to hers urgently as Lynn reached behind Chris's back and fumbled with the fasteners. The fasteners released and Lynn gently pulled the straps, removed the garment, and brought her fingers down lightly over the soft mounds and ran her thumbs over the hard nipples. Lynn felt like she was in a slow-motion movie, like time had stopped and only they existed. She looked up into Chris's eyes, searching to see what her lover was feeling. What she saw was fire, passion and longing. What she saw fueled her flames within.

Chris felt Lynn's smooth palms on her skin, she felt Lynn's eyes on hers, she felt her fire down below. She felt dizzy with passion. Wanting to feel Lynn's bare skin against her own, she tugged at her shirt to lift it over her head. She felt their skin meet, and dared to reach out and run her fingertips over Lynn's exposed breasts. Feeling the heat rise between her legs, burning hotter and hotter, and wanting it soothed, she pulled Lynn's hand down to stroke the fire. Lynn kneaded the already wet material between Chris's thighs and heard the moan escape from her lips. She could feel the need waiting there, she could feel her own need and tried desperately to remain in control of herself as she knew that this was not something to rush.

Leading Chris over to the bed, Lynn lowered her body onto the soft comforter. She unzipped Chris's slacks and pulling gently, twisted the pants and underwear from the body writhing beneath her. She reviewed the body before her, this body that she had fantasized about and found it to be even more beautiful than she had ever imagined.

Oh my God, what is she looking at? Chris thought, *she's been with so many women, is she disappointed?* She received her answer so fast that she wondered if she had said it out loud.

"You are so beautiful!" Lynn whispered as she brought her lips down to the exposed tummy and gently kissed the bare area. Chris watched as Lynn's lips and tongue traced their way down to the burning fire. She gasped as Lynn's fingertips felt her wetness for the first time. Should she be embarrassed that this moisture seemed to be flowing out of her? She couldn't ever remember being this wet before. Lynn didn't seem to think it was anything unusual as she felt the fingers gently stroking her burning flesh. Chris felt herself floating, rising higher and higher, the rush of excitement in her body getting hotter and hotter, almost unbearable.

Lynn caressed Chris's wet, hot folds of skin with her fingers, slowly at first, then gently circling faster and faster. Her lips and tongue moved from Chris's inner thighs up to her breasts, tugging, sucking, teasing. Lynn felt the heat between her own legs rising. She tried to soothe it by rubbing gently against Chris's thigh. Just as Lynn was about to faint from passion, Chris cried out, her body convulsing with pleasure. Sending Lynn over the edge, she came with the same intensity as her partner.

Chris felt her body moving uncontrollably, she felt her voice moaning with extreme pleasure. She felt like she had never felt before. And then even more as she felt Lynn's fingers enter her, easing in and out, back and forth, up and down. She felt herself rising again. Truly her body had never reacted like this with a man. She pulled Lynn down to her and grasped onto her back; for a moment they rocked together, Chris holding on tighter and tighter, until a rush of excitement flowed over her, and she came again.

Lynn rocked her fingers in and out of Chris. When Chris pulled her down on top of her, Lynn thought maybe that she was hurting her, but when she felt herself being held tighter and tighter, she knew that wasn't true. She felt Chris loosen her grasp, and then the wave of the rush as it enveloped Chris's entire body. Lynn gently removed her fingers and slid them over Chris's now tight folds of flesh, smoothly stroking again, bringing her to ecstasy once more.

Chris cried out again and again, rising to new heights each time. Finally, her body weak, she brought Lynn's lips to hers. Pulling away, Chris whispered, "I want to touch you." She moved her hand down to Lynn's moist jeans, rubbing where Lynn's heat was radiating through the cloth. Feeling to where the first button was fastened, she tugged lightly, unfastening all the buttons with one pull.

Lynn smiled. "I see that you're a pro with that."

"Men wear button-fly jeans, too," Chris kidded and helped Lynn wriggle out of her jeans, and then her panties.

Chris flipped Lynn over onto her back, slid on top, and let her passion take control. Remembering what Lynn had done, and also some of the details from the book tucked away in Lynn's bedside table, she brought Lynn to the same ecstasy that she herself had experienced.

"You sure that you've never been with a woman before?" Lynn asked, cradling Chris in her arms.

"What?" Chris said.

"You sure seemed like you knew what you were doing." Lynn chuckled.

Chris smiled and admitted, "I had some help from that book in your bedside table."

"Did you read the whole thing?" Lynn laughed.

"Yeah . . ." Chris blushed. "The night that you licked the ice cream from my skin . . . I think I freaked out so much because it reminded me of that scene in the cabin . . . you know, in the loft?"

Lynn smiled. "I think I remember the one . . ." Lynn said as she made her way down Chris's body with her tongue. Chris lay back and felt the heat rise once again. She gasped as Lynn's tongue flicked across her center of fire then dipped into her wetness.

"Oh my God!" Chris cried out as she was brought to a new height. The sensation was as close to heaven as she could imagine. Tears filled Chris's eyes as her body crashed over the edge.

Lynn kissed her way back up the body beneath her, but paused when she saw the tears wetting Chris's face.

"Why are you crying?" Lynn asked softly as she kissed away the tears.

Chris smiled and held Lynn close. "I broke the sound barrier."

Lynn was confused.

"It was just something that a friend of mine said to me. He compared the sensation he felt with breaking the sound barrier."

"He?" Lynn asked with jealousy.

"Don't worry, honey," Chris said as she ran her fingers through Lynn's hair. "After the experience I just had, I'm certain that you're the only one that I want."

Both satiated for the moment, they lay with their legs and arms intertwined.

Chris traced circles on Lynn's stomach and hesitantly asked, "So, will you go back to the house tomorrow?"

Lynn, extremely relaxed, answered with her eyes closed. "Don't you mean *we*? Will *we* go back to the house tomorrow?"

Lynn felt Chris's head nod and her lips smile against her skin. "Yes, we can go back to the house tomorrow."

"So what time do we need to check out?" Chris sighed.

"Well . . . I don't ever really check out," Lynn replied, still with her eyes closed.

Chris raised her head to look at Lynn. "Don't tell me that you own this hotel, too!"

Lynn smiled. "No, but I have an arrangement with the owner."

The two lay in silence for a moment. Chris still had questions.

"So is this where you came Monday night when you didn't sleep with Terri?"

Lynn opened her eyes, remembering that terrible night, and replied, "No, I was really in no condition to drive that night. I actually slept in my truck."

"Drink a little too much, did ya?" Chris teased.

"That, and the fact that I was just a little too frustrated to be on the road." Lynn paused and then decided to explain further. "Terri was a beautiful woman, and she did everything she could to get me to stay with her . . . but the only person that I wanted was you." Then, with a little chuckle she added, "She even told me that I could call her by your name!"

"So that's why she knew who I was at the bar that night," Chris mumbled.

Chris raised her body so that she could look into Lynn's eyes. Then, stroking Lynn's hair, she said seductively, "Well, you're here with me now. Do you still want me?"

Lynn pushed Chris onto her back and made sure that she knew the answer.

Chapter Twenty-four

Lynn woke to sun streaming into the room. Rolling over, she looked out toward the patio and smiled, seeing the drink that had been prepared for her still sitting on the ledge. Then she realized that she was alone.

Rubbing her fingers through her hair and then down her face, she stopped, smelling Chris's aroma still on her hands. She closed her eyes and told herself that she knew last night was too good to be true. Disappointment flooded her veins. Well, if that had been the only return on her investment, she guessed it had been worth it anyway.

Suddenly she was startled by a noise. Opening her eyes, she saw Chris in the doorway.

"I tried to find some coffee . . ." Chris began to explain.

Lynn smiled, trying to hide the tears of happiness in her eyes. "I just usually call room service."

Chris leaned against the door clad only in Lynn's black silk robe, and surveyed the bare body in front of her.

"I hope you don't mind, I borrowed your robe," Chris said. Then her lips forming into a mischievous grin, she moved toward the bed and continued, "but, if you'd like me to take it off . . ."

Lynn nodded and reached to untie the bow. Chris slid onto the bed and let the robe fall from her shoulders. Lynn pulled her close and whispered, "I was afraid that you were gone."

Chris softly smiled and shrugged. "I couldn't leave, the taxi left ten minutes ago."

Lynn looked over at the clock. Ten after nine. Then turning back, she brought Chris's lips to hers. Suddenly, their embrace was jolted by the ring of the telephone.

Lynn reached for the receiver but was stopped by Chris's hand. "Do you have to?"

Lynn smiled and explained, "The only calls they put through are from Matt."

Chris let go of the hand and laid her head on Lynn's chest, running her fingers over her hardened nipples.

"This better be good!" Lynn said sarcastically into the phone.

Matt laughed on the other end. "I guess we both got lucky last night, huh?"

Lynn smiled and answered, "Even still, Matt, if you know what I mean."

Matt apologized, "Oh, sorry, I'll let you go . . ."

"Matt, was there a reason you called?"

"Yeah, my parents wanted to make sure that you knew you were welcome at brunch today. It may be quite interesting, I'm going to bring Paul."

Lynn chuckled, put her hand over the mouthpiece, and asked Chris, "Matt is taking Paul to brunch today with his parents. Wanna go?"

Chris smiled and responded, "I wouldn't miss it for the world!"

Lynn agreed that they would meet the group at eleven o'clock.

"So, how much time do we have?" Chris said as she continued to run her thumb over Lynn's hardened nipple. Slowly lowering her mouth she began circling it with her tongue.

261

Lynn lay back on her pillow and moaned with pleasure, "We've got plenty of time!"

Chris let her tongue glide all the way down to the aching in between Lynn's legs. Slowly she teased as she sucked, then circled, taking her time, bringing Lynn to the top of the coaster ride.

"Oh God, please, Chris!" Lynn pleaded. Finally, Chris took her over the edge. Lynn stiffened then relaxed, overwhelmed by the sensation below. Chris made her way back up the limp body. Chris looked into her eyes and whispered, "You're amazing."

Lynn touched Chris's moisture as soon as it was within reach. She knew by instinct that Chris would be in need. Thinking about what Chris had just said, Lynn pulled away just as Chris started soaring.

"Oh sure, today I'm amazing. Last night, I believe I was a 'cold-hearted bitch'!"

Chris opened her eyes in frustration. "You surely are a cold-hearted bitch if you keep me waiting much longer!"

Lynn smiled and continued what she had started, bringing Chris to ecstasy once again.

Matt pulled into the parking lot right behind Lynn and Chris. Jumping out of his car, he opened Chris's door and ducked his head inside. He smiled at her. "I guess she gave you a positive response last night, huh?"

Chris leaned forward and picked up the cigarettes from Lynn's dashboard. Pitching them into the backseat, she smiled and replied, "Let's just say that she won't be needing these anymore!"

Paul strolled over to join the group as they walked to the restaurant. Chris put her arm through his and pulled him behind.

"It looks like it worked out for both of us!" she said with a smile. "By the way, thanks for the advice."

Paul looked at her as if he didn't have a clue what she was speaking of.

"Please, Paul. Did you really think that I fell for your little act?" Chris laughed.

Paul's face broke out into a smile, then he put his hand over hers. "I didn't say a thing that wasn't the truth."

The four walked in and located Charles and Marie. As they approached the table, Marie looked confused.

"Okay, I'm confused. Who is with whom?" she asked in frustration.

Chris laughed, not realizing that she still had her arm hooked to Paul's. She released his arm and grabbed Lynn's hand to signify that she was indeed with Lynn.

Charles chuckled. "Well now, I guess the verdict came in last night, huh Lynn?"

Lynn blushed and smiled. "Believe me, Judge McKinley, she had a very convincing closing argument!"

Charles then approached his son's companion and offered his hand. "You must be Paul."

Marie, less formal than her husband, hugged the man and winked at Matt. "I'm so glad to meet Matt's real love interest!"

"Would anyone like something to drink?" the waiter offered over the three couples' chatter. Almost in unison, the six chimed, "Yes!"

The two women said their good-byes to Charles and Marie and agreed to meet the men later for dinner.

"I'm just going to swing by Sam and Beth's place and then we'll go home, okay?" Lynn said as she slid into the driver's seat.

"I don't know if I can wait that long." Chris smiled mischievously.

"Wait for what?" Lynn asked as she started the car.

Chris leaned over, grasped the back of Lynn's neck with her hand, and hungrily kissed her. Breaking away from the kiss, Chris leaned back in her seat and looked at Lynn for a response.

"We'll make it a quick stop!" Lynn exclaimed, almost choking on the words.

Chris nodded in agreement. "So, what are we stopping by for anyway?"

Lynn backed the car out of the parking space and put the car into drive. "I found another way to finance their mortgage."

Chris looked at her partner suspiciously. "Another way?"

"Yeah," Lynn answered, purposely not looking into Chris's eyes. "I found another company that would finance them."

Chris was still suspicious. "So, you're telling me that you tried for months and months to find financing, and all of a sudden within two days you found someone?"

Lynn was silent. She was trying desperately to find another way to stretch the truth without actually lying.

"You know, if we're going to continue this relationship, you need to stop telling me half truths." Chris crossed her arms and looked out the window.

"Look, no one wants to finance an artist and her gay bar owner lover," Lynn stated.

"And . . . ?" Chris prodded for further information.

Lynn sighed and reluctantly revealed the truth. "So, I transferred ownership of the deed to one of my holding companies."

"And this is going to help how?" Chris asked.

Lynn looked at Chris and tried to explain. "I'll have them sign new paperwork. They'll think that I don't hold their mortgage anymore and that will make them feel better." Running her fingers through her hair, Lynn paused, then stared straight ahead as she continued, "You know, I don't think I've ever been as ashamed of myself as I was Wednesday night. I guess making them feel better will help me feel better, too. I just hope that I haven't ruined our friendship."

Chris nodded in understanding, then kidded, "So I guess I'm an accomplice now, huh?"

Thankful that she understood, Lynn smiled. "Partners in crime?"

Chris chuckled as she reached for Lynn's hand. "Among other things."

Lynn dialed the couple's telephone number as they drew near their neighborhood.

"Hello?" Sam answered on the second ring.

"Hey, I'm about five minutes away," Lynn responded.

"So are you going to tell me what you're coming over for?" Sam asked.

"It's a surprise," Lynn answered, then added, "Oh, and I hope you don't mind, I have someone with me."

"Someone with you?" Sam asked with irritation in her voice. "Take me off that damn speakerphone!"

Lynn picked up the receiver and smiled at Chris, who could hear the shrill of the voice on the other end. Chris gestured to Lynn to give her the phone, but Lynn shook her head and kept the receiver to her ear.

Finally, Lynn said, "Sam, we're driving into the complex now. See you in a minute."

Lynn hung up the phone and parked the car. Walking to the door, she turned to Chris. "Boy, did I just get an earful about how I must not have cared for you at all!"

Reaching the door, Chris rang the doorbell and pulled Lynn's arms around her. "Show me how much you care."

Lynn brought her lips down to Chris's just as the door opened. Neither noticed the couple standing in the doorway.

Sam cleared her throat once, then again. Finally the two broke their embrace and smiled at their friends.

"When did this happen?" Beth exclaimed with a smile.

"Well it's about damn time!" Sam added as she ushered the two in the door. "And you let me go on and on over the phone about what a jerk you are!"

Lynn laughed. "Like I could get a word in edgewise!"

Beth looked into Chris's eyes. "So tell me, what happened?"

Chris smiled. "You know, you just can't help who you fall in love with."

"So this was a good surprise!" Beth said as the four sat in the living room sipping iced tea.

"Oh, this wasn't the surprise," Lynn said to the couple. Standing, she walked over, grabbed her briefcase, and opened it on the coffee table.

"This is the surprise," she said as she handed a packet to Sam.

"What's this?" Sam asked.

"Hopefully a peace offering," Lynn stated, then continued with the explanation, "I felt really bad about the other night. After some searching, I was able to find financing for your mortgage."

Sam looked at Beth then examined the paperwork. Beth spoke up first. "Lynn, we know that you were upset the other night and we know that deep down in your own way, you were just trying to help us out."

Lynn listened to Beth, and then turned to Sam. "I know that you will feel better this way. It's at the same interest rate and the same term. All you have to do is sign where I've indicated."

"You've looked these over already?" Sam asked.

Lynn nodded and handed Sam a pen. Sam gave the pen to Beth, who signed first, then signed herself and handed the paperwork back.

"Thanks," Sam said, softly meeting Lynn's eyes.

"Friends?" Lynn asked Sam.

Sam smiled and nodded. "Friends."

Lynn put the documents back into her briefcase and smiled at Chris. "Now, if you two don't mind, we'd like to head on home."

"Are you sure you don't want to stay and watch a movie or something?" Sam asked.

Chris took Lynn's hand. "No, we have other plans."

Lynn blushed and caught Beth's eyes.

Beth chuckled. "Gee, Lynn, why are you blushing?"

Both couples stood and walked to the door.

"If you guys are free tonight, we're meeting Matt and Paul for dinner at seven. We'd love it if you could join us," Lynn said as she opened the door.

"That sounds like fun," Beth responded, then added with a smile, "Are you sure you guys can pull yourselves away from . . . you know."

Lynn smiled back. "We'll give it a try. Bye, guys!"

At home, Lynn swung open the door to her house, when the next thing she knew she had been pulled up against Chris's body and against the wall. Chris pulled her lips in for a fiery kiss.

Pulling her lips away, Chris looked into Lynn's eyes. "Take me."

Lynn looked at Chris somewhat amused. "Interesting words you've chosen, my dear."

"I merely used the words to imply urgency!" Chris said.

Lynn smiled teasingly. "So, right here, right now?"

Chris teased back, "At least I waited until we were out of the car!"

"I think I've created a monster," Lynn said, smirking.

"I'm glad you're having fun with this." Chris grabbed the collar of Lynn's shirt and brought their faces together. "I want you so bad right now I'm about to explode."

"Well, let's see what I can do about that." Lynn kissed Chris hungrily while letting her hands roam down over Chris's neck, her breasts, her hips. Bringing her hand inward, she brushed Chris's burning fire with her fingertips. Chris moaned with desire. Lynn brought her hands back up and then slowly let them run back down her body, this time following with her hot breath until she got to the waistband of the slacks. She unbuttoned and unzipped the fasteners with one motion and pulled the slacks and her underwear down, leaving her hot breath teasing the coarse hair that covered Chris's heat. Down on her knees Lynn brought her tongue to the source of the wetness. Chris stepped out of the tangled clothes and opened her legs wider for her lover. Lynn felt Chris's fingers entangled in her hair, forcing her tongue to push harder and harder until the body next to her released its pent-up frustration.

Lynn stood, pinned Chris against the wall, and pushed her fingers into her. Chris cried out with pleasure as she felt the thrust. She wanted . . . no, she needed to touch Lynn, too. With one motion, she pulled open the buttons on her partner's jeans and slipped her hand inside. The wetness she found made it easy for Chris to enter. The two pressed against the wall, moving together, slowly enjoying each other's presence. Then, the movement quickened and each cried out with the pleasure they felt inside. Slowly, they both sank to the ground and continued the dance.

◈

The three couples sat around an alcohol-free table laughing and teasing about the way Matt's charade had played out.

Sam was particularly amused at the way Marie had caught the two women in the bathroom. It seemed to trigger another memory. "Do you remember the time that you—" Lynn's glare stopped her in mid-sentence.

Chris caught on right away and turned to her new lover. "You can't stop her from telling every story, Lynn!"

"No, but I don't want you to hear about every woman I've been with, just like I don't want to hear about every *man* that you've been with!" Lynn said as she looked into Chris's eyes. She had to concentrate on her eyes, as every time her eyes wandered down to the rest of her body, she lost all control. Chris, at Lynn's request, had on the short black dress that had driven Lynn crazy many nights before.

Losing concentration for a moment, Lynn let her eyes stray. She found her mind drawn to a fantasy from a couple of weeks ago. Lynn drew her hand under the table and placed it upon Chris's bare knee. Inching her hand up Chris's thigh, she smoothed under the black material. Turning her hand inward, her fingertips reached the silk which covered the area that she had tasted just hours ago.

"Lynn," Sam interrupted Lynn's movement. Lynn looked over at her innocently. Sam continued, "If you would be so kind as to leave both of your hands above the table. Your girlfriend is about ready to have a heart attack."

Lynn looked like her hand had been caught in the cookie jar, which indeed it had. She looked over at Chris, whose face was bright red. Slowly she brought her hand above the table, placed it over Chris's and gave it a squeeze.

"Gee, Beth, how do you live with this old married woman?" Lynn asked, nodding in Sam's direction.

Beth smiled and also squeezed the hand of her lover. "I have no complaints, Lynn."

Sam smiled proudly, knowing that she had won the fight again.

"I don't think there's anyone at the table with complaints," Paul remarked.

"It's true!" Chris said. Then raising her water glass to toast, she winked at Matt. "Here's to breaking your rule about meeting men in bars!"

Matt smiled and raised his glass to Lynn. "And here's to breaking your rule about making a pass at a straight woman!" His toast was also accompanied by a wink.

Following suit, Lynn then offered up her glass with one last toast, a toast that she knew only Matt would fully understand. "And here's to the patience it takes for the especially risky investments, for they often yield a very satisfying return." Matt laughed and smiled at his best friend. Then they all clinked glasses in celebration of their futures together.

UNDER THE SOUTHERN CROSS by Claire McNab. 200 pp. Lee, an American travel agent, goes down under and meets Australian Alex, and the sparks fly under the Southern Cross.   ISBN 1-59493-029-5 $12.95

SUGAR by Karin Kallmaker. 240 pp. Three women want sugar from Sugar, who can't make up her mind.   ISBN 1-59493-001-5 $12.95

FALL GUY by Claire McNab. 200 pp. 16th Detective Inspector Carol Ashton Mystery.
                                         ISBN 1-59493-000-7 $12.95

ONE SUMMER NIGHT by Gerri Hill. 232 pp. Johanna swore to never fall in love again— but then she met the charming Kelly . . .   ISBN 1-59493-007-4 $12.95

TALK OF THE TOWN TOO by Saxon Bennett. 181 pp. Second in the series about wild and fun loving friends.   ISBN 1-931513-77-5 $12.95

LOVE SPEAKS HER NAME by Laura DeHart Young. 170 pp. Love and friendship, desire and intrigue, spark this exciting sequel to *Forever and the Night*.
                                         ISBN 1-59493-002-3 $12.95

TO HAVE AND TO HOLD by Peggy J. Herring. 184 pp. By finally letting down her defenses, will Dorian be opening herself to a devastating betrayal?
                                         ISBN 1-59493-005-8 $12.95

WILD THINGS by Karin Kallmaker. 228 pp. Dutiful daughter Faith has met the perfect man. There's just one problem: she's in love with his sister.   ISBN 1-931513-64-3 $12.95

SHARED WINDS by Kenna White. 216 pp. Can Emma rebuild more than just Lanny's marina?   ISBN 1-59493-006-6 $12.95

THE UNKNOWN MILE by Jaime Clevenger. 253 pp. Kelly's world is getting more and more complicated every moment.   ISBN 1-931513-57-0 $12.95

TREASURED PAST by Linda Hill. 189 pp. A shared passion for antiques leads to love.
                                         ISBN 1-59493-003-1 $12.95

SIERRA CITY by Gerri Hill. 284 pp. Chris and Jesse cannot deny their growing attraction . . .   ISBN 1-931513-98-8 $12.95

ALL THE WRONG PLACES by Karin Kallmaker. 174 pp. Sex and the single girl—Brandy is looking for love and usually she finds it. Karin Kallmaker's first *After Dark* erotic novel.
                                         ISBN 1-931513-76-7 $12.95

WHEN THE CORPSE LIES A Motor City Thriller by Therese Szymanski. 328 pp. Butch bad-girl Brett Higgins is used to waking up next to beautiful women she hardly knows. Problem is, this one's dead.   ISBN 1-931513-74-0 $12.95

GUARDED HEARTS by Hannah Rickard. 240 pp. Someone's reminding Alyssa about her secret past, and then she becomes the suspect in a series of burglaries.
                                         ISBN 1-931513-99-6 $12.95

ONCE MORE WITH FEELING by Peggy J. Herring. 184 pp. Lighthearted, loving, romantic adventure.   ISBN 1-931513-60-0 $12.95

TANGLED AND DARK A Brenda Strange Mystery by Patty G. Henderson. 240 pp. When investigating a local death, Brenda finds two possible killers—one diagnosed with Multiple Personality Disorder.   ISBN 1-931513-75-9 $12.95

WHITE LACE AND PROMISES by Peggy J. Herring. 240 pp. Maxine and Betina realize sex may not be the most important thing in their lives.   ISBN 1-931513-73-2 $12.95

UNFORGETTABLE by Karin Kallmaker. 288 pp. Can Rett find love with the cheerleader who broke her heart so many years ago? ISBN 1-931513-63-5 $12.95

HIGHER GROUND by Saxon Bennett. 280 pp. A delightfully complex reflection of the successful, high society lives of a small group of women. ISBN 1-931513-69-4 $12.95

LAST CALL A Detective Franco Mystery by Baxter Clare. 240 pp. Frank overlooks all else to try to solve a cold case of two murdered children . . . ISBN 1-931513-70-8 $12.95

ONCE UPON A DYKE: NEW EXPLOITS OF FAIRY-TALE LESBIANS by Karin Kallmaker, Julia Watts, Barbara Johnson & Therese Szymanski. 320 pp. You've never read fairy tales like these before! From Bella After Dark. ISBN 1-931513-71-6 $14.95

FINEST KIND OF LOVE by Diana Tremain Braund. 224 pp. Can Molly and Carolyn stop clashing long enough to see beyond their differences? ISBN 1-931513-68-6 $12.95

DREAM LOVER by Lyn Denison. 188 pp. A soft, sensuous, romantic fantasy. ISBN 1-931513-96-1 $12.95

NEVER SAY NEVER by Linda Hill. 224 pp. A classic love story . . . where rules aren't the only things broken. ISBN 1-931513-67-8 $12.95

PAINTED MOON by Karin Kallmaker. 214 pp. Stranded together in a snowbound cabin, Jackie and Leah's lives will never be the same. ISBN 1-931513-53-8 $12.95

WIZARD OF ISIS by Jean Stewart. 240 pp. Fifth in the exciting Isis series. ISBN 1-931513-71-4 $12.95

WOMAN IN THE MIRROR by Jackie Calhoun. 216 pp. Josey learns to love again, while her niece is learning to love women for the first time. ISBN 1-931513-78-3 $12.95

SUBSTITUTE FOR LOVE by Karin Kallmaker. 200 pp. When Holly and Reyna meet the combination adds up to pure passion. But what about tomorrow? ISBN 1-931513-62-7 $12.95

GULF BREEZE by Gerri Hill. 288 pp. Could Carly really be the woman Pat has always been searching for? ISBN 1-931513-97-X $12.95

THE TOMSTOWN INCIDENT by Penny Hayes. 184 pp. Caught between two worlds, Eloise must make a decision that will change her life forever. ISBN 1-931513-56-2 $12.95

MAKING UP FOR LOST TIME by Karin Kallmaker. 240 pp. Discover delicious recipes for romance by the undisputed mistress. ISBN 1-931513-61-9 $12.95

THE WAY LIFE SHOULD BE by Diana Tremain Braund. 173 pp. With which woman will Jennifer find the true meaning of love? ISBN 1-931513-66-X $12.95

BACK TO BASICS: A BUTCH/FEMME ANTHOLOGY edited by Therese Szymanski—from Bella After Dark. 324 pp. ISBN 1-931513-35-X $14.95

SURVIVAL OF LOVE by Frankie J. Jones. 236 pp. What will Jody do when she falls in love with her best friend's daughter? ISBN 1-931513-55-4 $12.95

LESSONS IN MURDER by Claire McNab. 184 pp. 1st Detective Inspector Carol Ashton Mystery. ISBN 1-931513-65-1 $12.95

DEATH BY DEATH by Claire McNab. 167 pp. 5th Denise Cleever Thriller. ISBN 1-931513-34-1 $12.95

CAUGHT IN THE NET by Jessica Thomas. 188 pp. A wickedly observant story of mystery, danger, and love in Provincetown. ISBN 1-931513-54-6 $12.95

DREAMS FOUND by Lyn Denison. Australian Riley embarks on a journey to meet her birth mother . . . and gains not just a family, but the love of her life. ISBN 1-931513-58-9 $12.95

A MOMENT'S INDISCRETION by Peggy J. Herring. 154 pp. Jackie is torn between her better judgment and the overwhelming attraction she feels for Valerie.
ISBN 1-931513-59-7 $12.95

IN EVERY PORT by Karin Kallmaker. 224 pp. Jessica has a woman in every port. Will meeting Cat change all that?
ISBN 1-931513-36-8 $12.95

TOUCHWOOD by Karin Kallmaker. 240 pp. Rayann loves Louisa. Louisa loves Rayann. Can the decades between their ages keep them apart?
ISBN 1-931513-37-6 $12.95

WATERMARK by Karin Kallmaker. 248 pp. Teresa wants a future with a woman whose heart has been frozen by loss. Sequel to *Touchwood*.
ISBN 1-931513-38-4 $12.95

EMBRACE IN MOTION by Karin Kallmaker. 240 pp. Has Sarah found lust or love?
ISBN 1-931513-39-2 $12.95

ONE DEGREE OF SEPARATION by Karin Kallmaker. 232 pp. Sizzling small town romance between Marian, the town librarian, and the new girl from the big city.
ISBN 1-931513-30-9 $12.95

CRY HAVOC A Detective Franco Mystery by Baxter Clare. 240 pp. A dead hustler with a headless rooster in his lap sends Lt. L.A. Franco headfirst against Mother Love.
ISBN 1-931513931-7 $12.95

DISTANT THUNDER by Peggy J. Herring. 294 pp. Bankrobbing drifter Cordy awakens strange new feelings in Leo in this romantic tale set in the Old West.
ISBN 1-931513-28-7 $12.95

COP OUT by Claire McNab. 216 pp. 4th Detective Inspector Carol Ashton Mystery.
ISBN 1-931513-29-5 $12.95

BLOOD LINK by Claire McNab. 159 pp. 15th Detective Inspector Carol Ashton Mystery. Is Carol unwittingly playing into a deadly plan?
ISBN 1-931513-27-9 $12.95

TALK OF THE TOWN by Saxon Bennett. 239 pp. With enough beer, barbecue and B.S., anything is possible!
ISBN 1-931513-18-X $12.95

MAYBE NEXT TIME by Karin Kallmaker. 256 pp. Sabrina has everything she ever wanted—except Jorie.
ISBN 1-931513-26-0 $12.95

WHEN GOOD GIRLS GO BAD: A Motor City Thriller by Therese Szymanski. 230 pp. Brett, Randi, and Allie join forces to stop a serial killer.
ISBN 1-931513-11-2 $12.95

A DAY TOO LONG: A Helen Black Mystery by Pat Welch. 328 pp. This time Helen's fate is in her own hands.
ISBN 1-931513-22-8 $12.95

THE RED LINE OF YARMALD by Diana Rivers. 256 pp. The Hadra's only hope lies in a magical red line . . . climactic sequel to *Clouds of War*.
ISBN 1-931513-23-6 $12.95

OUTSIDE THE FLOCK by Jackie Calhoun. 224 pp. Jo embraces her new love and life.
ISBN 1-931513-13-9 $12.95

LEGACY OF LOVE by Marianne K. Martin. 224 pp. Read the whole Sage Bristo story.
ISBN 1-931513-15-5 $12.95

STREET RULES: A Detective Franco Mystery by Baxter Clare. 304 pp. Gritty, fast-paced mystery with compelling Detective L.A. Franco.
ISBN 1-931513-14-7 $12.95

RECOGNITION FACTOR: 4th Denise Cleever Thriller by Claire McNab. 176 pp. Denise Cleever tracks a notorious terrorist to America.
ISBN 1-931513-24-4 $12.95

NORA AND LIZ by Nancy Garden. 296 pp. Lesbian romance by the author of *Annie on My Mind*.
ISBN 1931513-20-1 $12.95

MIDAS TOUCH by Frankie J. Jones. 208 pp. Sandra had everything but love.
ISBN 1-931513-21-X $12.95

BEYOND ALL REASON by Peggy J. Herring. 240 pp. A romance hotter than Texas.
ISBN 1-9513-25-2 $12.95

ACCIDENTAL MURDER: 14th Detective Inspector Carol Ashton Mystery by Claire McNab. 208 pp. Carol Ashton tracks an elusive killer.   ISBN 1-931513-16-3 $12.95

SEEDS OF FIRE: Tunnel of Light Trilogy, Book 2 by Karin Kallmaker writing as Laura Adams. 274 pp. In Autumn's dreams no one is who they seem. ISBN 1-931513-19-8 $12.95

DRIFTING AT THE BOTTOM OF THE WORLD by Auden Bailey. 288 pp. Beautifully written first novel set in Antarctica.   ISBN 1-931513-17-1 $12.95

CLOUDS OF WAR by Diana Rivers. 288 pp. Women unite to defend Zelindar!
ISBN 1-931513-12-0 $12.95

DEATHS OF JOCASTA: 2nd Micky Knight Mystery by J.M. Redmann. 408 pp. Sexy and intriguing Lambda Literary Award–nominated mystery.   ISBN 1-931513-10-4 $12.95

LOVE IN THE BALANCE by Marianne K. Martin. 256 pp. The classic lesbian love story, back in print!   ISBN 1-931513-08-2 $12.95

THE COMFORT OF STRANGERS by Peggy J. Herring. 272 pp. Lela's work was her passion . . . until now.   ISBN 1-931513-09-0 $12.95

WHEN EVIL CHANGES FACE: A Motor City Thriller by Therese Szymanski. 240 pp. Brett Higgins is back in another heart-pounding thriller.   ISBN 0-9677753-3-7 $11.95

CHICKEN by Paula Martinac. 208 pp. Lynn finds that the only thing harder than being in a lesbian relationship is ending one.   ISBN 1-931513-07-4 · $11.95

TAMARACK CREEK by Jackie Calhoun. 208 pp. An intriguing story of love and danger.
ISBN 1-931513-06-6 $11.95

DEATH BY THE RIVERSIDE: 1st Micky Knight Mystery by J.M. Redmann. 320 pp. Finally back in print, the book that launched the Lambda Literary Award–winning Micky Knight mystery series.   ISBN 1-931513-05-8 $11.95

EIGHTH DAY: A Cassidy James Mystery by Kate Calloway. 272 pp. In the eighth installment of the Cassidy James mystery series, Cassidy goes undercover at a camp for troubled teens.   ISBN 1-931513-04-X $11.95

MIRRORS by Marianne K. Martin. 208 pp. Jean Carson and Shayna Bradley fight for a future together.   ISBN 1-931513-02-3 $11.95

THE ULTIMATE EXIT STRATEGY: A Virginia Kelly Mystery by Nikki Baker. 240 pp. The long-awaited return of the wickedly observant Virginia Kelly.
ISBN 1-931513-03-1 $11.95

FOREVER AND THE NIGHT by Laura DeHart Young. 224 pp. Desire and passion ignite the frozen Arctic in this exciting sequel to the classic romantic adventure *Love on the Line*.
ISBN 0-931513-00-7 $11.95

WINGED ISIS by Jean Stewart. 240 pp. The long-awaited sequel to *Warriors of Isis* and the fourth in the exciting Isis series.   ISBN 1-931513-01-5 $11.95

ROOM FOR LOVE by Frankie J. Jones. 192 pp. Jo and Beth must overcome the past in order to have a future together.   ISBN 0-9677753-9-6 $11.95